Burroway, Janet

Cutting stone

$21.45

Cutting
Stone

Books by Janet Burroway

FICTION

Descend Again

The Dancer from the Dance

Eyes

The Buzzards

Raw Silk

Opening Nights

Cutting Stone

POETRY

But to the Season

Material Goods

FOR CHILDREN

The Truck on the Track

The Giant Jam Sandwich

NONFICTION

*Writing Fiction:
A Guide to Narrative Craft*

Janet
Burroway

◆

Cutting
Stone

HOUGHTON MIFFLIN COMPANY

Boston • New York • London

1992

For information about permission to reproduce selections
from this book, write to Permissions, Houghton Mifflin Company,
215 Park Avenue South, New York, New York 10003.

Library of Congress Cataloging-in-Publication Data
Burroway, Janet.
Cutting stone / Janet Burroway.
p.   cm.
ISBN 0-395-59300-X
I. Title.
PS3552.U76C88   1992   91-41852
813'.54 — dc20   CIP

Book design by Robert Overholtzer

Printed in the United States of America

HAD 10 9 8 7 6 5 4 3 2 1

For Tim and Alex,
who pursue their histories
in different worlds

The relative severity of what any society deems to be proper behavior bears no relation whatever to the rigor with which the members of that society uphold it; and it is not to be supposed that the idle rich are any more industrious about their prejudices than the indolent poor.

—JUVENAL

In August 1914, the United States government gave permission for Pancho Villa, Álvaro Obregón, and a limited number of troops to travel over American territory, by Southern Pacific rail from El Paso to Nogales, to settle a border incident. Venustiano Carranza and the Constitutionalists had recently entered Mexico City, Europe was newly at war, and Woodrow Wilson was anxious to maintain the precarious stability of the Mexican Revolution so he wouldn't have to face conflict on two fronts. It was arranged that General Pershing would entertain Villa and Obregón at Fort Bliss in the morning, and that in the evening they and their troops would be fed at the staid little railroad junction of Bowie, Arizona.

My mother, Alma May Milner (later Burroway), and her parents, Maude Pierce and Dana Tobin Milner, were present at this incident of historical marginalia, and they are present in this book; though I cannot, and they would not have been able to, tell you exactly where. I have stuck roughly to the historical facts, but the sort of truth I have attempted is not necessarily historical, and where accuracy seemed less urgent than my story, I have rearranged or invented freely.

J. B.

PART I

❖

Mine

1

OUTSIDE THE CLUB CAR window, flat desert nothing as far as the eye could see; endless stubble in level light. They were still two days short of Arizona. Eleanor sipped an early aperitif, perspiring jagged rings on the armholes of her pongee suit. Laurel was skimming a *Commerce Chronicle,* occasionally coughing a discreet dry cough. He had taken off his jacket, self-deprecating, murmuring, "When in Rome . . . ," and in pin-striped vest and four-in-hand he looked crisp, compact.

Under the rhythmic chug of the train ran a thinner sound, a continuous screech of metal on metal that put Eleanor in mind of rending silk. She felt this image through her abdomen as if the track were a single tear all the way back to Maryland. A copy of *House Beautiful* lay in her lap, and she read, "No nation has studied homebuilding so persistently and long as the English, and consequently none has arrived at anything like such general excellence."

This sentence had nothing to do with her and could not logically be met with grief. But the raw lot of her unbuilt house rose in her mind, overgrown with lush creeper, a stand of oak. She had spent the better part of a year imagining, then sketching, a facade in that little Baltimore wilderness, and a layout she knew so well that she could walk it out on the ground.

She was losing everything. Everything in memory and all that never was to be; and things the more poignant because she hadn't noticed that she cared for them. The wood planes in Daddy's warehouse, her hand patting along the shelf as she told over their names by heart: *plow, bull nose, dado, beading, rabbet, slitting.* Who ever would have thought she'd grieve for the planes?

"Imagine this," said Laurel. "Apparently Villa was outnumbered at Chihuahua, so he left a token force there, captured a train, and rode in to take Juárez City."

"Imagine."

"Right on the border across from El Paso. It says he pretended to be the engineer, and telegraphed to the government agent in Juárez that the desert was crawling with *villistas* and what should he do? The agent told him to come on home and welcomed him with open arms."

"At El Paso? Will he invade Texas?" She did not much care. Texas blurred by the window, no argument for its own salvation. The page that faced her showed a cartoon of President Huerta as Gulliver, bound by the lassoes of tiny Villa and Obregón. She understood well enough that Huerta was a tyrant and that Villa and Obregón were fighting for the poor, but she didn't think the cartoonist conveyed much contrast. All three Mexicans wore costume hats and brutal leers.

"No, sweetheart, don't worry. They have plenty of land if they can get a government that will divide it up. All the peons want is to stay home and have a home to stay at." He grinned up at her, patted her knee with a soft palm. The unbuilt house appeared in the curve of his spectacles: a home to stay home at. Stupefied by his cruelty, she looked away, out at weathered fences, withered grass, while the last scenes of any meaning in her life receded down the track.

It had taken 112 bottles of champagne to see the young Poindexters off to Arizona. Eleanor circulated through the Emerson ballroom, enticing Catholics into clumps of Presbyterians, infiltrating the bankers and builders with Annapolis men. Laurel entertained some medical people with variations on a financial theme ("The Bible doesn't say that money is the root of all evil, it says the *love* of money is . . ."), the two mothers stood by the ice bucket urging crab *à la creole*, the fathers stirred political discussion here and there.

Eleanor's shoulders rose opulent out of cobalt blue moiré. Her ungovernable near-black hair was piled heavy on her head. She had danced, she had held court, she had clinked glasses with two admirals, a celebrated architect, and Henry Mencken.

Then midevening she had crossed behind Mrs. Barhyte (wife of the famous Johns Hopkins nose and throat man) and heard her remark to Amy Whitney (youngest daughter of Vital Organs), "At least the Poindexters will have *dry* heat out west, and not this gawmy humi-diddy we've endured in Baltimore the past few weeks."

Amy Whitney, breathless against her stays and covertly watching the rise and fall of her décolletage, replied, "I can't imagine why Laurel Poindexter would want to open a bank in that godforsaken desert." Amy was seventeen. She wore a filigree chain with a garnet that winked into her cleavage. Eleanor stopped not three paces in front of her, but Amy had her eyes on her own flesh.

Mrs. Barhyte leaned toward Amy with her lorgnette against her mouth rather than her eyes; this generally presaged gossip. "*Ah, well* —" she said, but hesitated while a giant colored by the name of Innis Washington offered her a silver tray of Veuve Clicquot, which she refused. Then, lorgnette against her mouth, she finished, "they say it is a question of . . . consumption."

Innis Washington passed on among the Protestants, offering champagne to members of the Temperance Union. Amy brushed at her skirt with her fan. "Any rate, he's dying dapper."

Eleanor had a reputation for sass and dash — the tallest in her convent class, the one to smuggle the marmoset onto the sleeping porch, the first to pluck her eyebrows or drive a motorcar. Now she swept around Mrs. Barhyte to enfold Amy in her arms, crying, "Oh, Amy! How I'll miss you!" And almost immediately, as if being rewarded for her cheek (she was usually rewarded for her cheek), a junior lieutenant in epaulettes and yellow hair offered her his hand and whirled her in among the dancers.

Eleanor assured herself the incident had not affected her mood at all. She didn't see the point in Laurel's being so secretive about his illness anyway. She danced until she was out of breath. She joined her father quarreling with Admiral Dinsmore — Daddy in a terrible mood because he was drunk, and because Admiral Dinsmore knew more about Mexico than he did — and she turned the quarrel around by saying, "That's a ragtag army. They won't get past Chihuahua," so that it made them laugh to hear a woman voice a military opinion. She shared a crab cracker with a Maryland Supreme Court judge who lectured her on the legal peccadilloes of the Baby State.

No, she did not care in the least what Amy Whitney said, a bratling with the mental facility of a scuppernong. Only somehow, shortly after the crab cracker, she decided that she wouldn't go. She was standing under a Tiffany globe supported by griffins and armored angels. Across the room Laurel had settled into a Chippendale with the *Baltimore Sun* — a man who could read a newspaper at his own party. She was into her fourth glass of champagne, flushed and something else: wound too tight, like a hot clock. She had just assured the circle around her — mostly male, mostly Annapolis — that Bowie, Arizona, was a major dining stop on the Southern Pacific and that it was impossible to get to California without passing through.

"We'll come and visit you," said the officer who had whisked her onto the dance floor.

"You shall find me in a wrapper, shooing chickens off the porch with a broom!" She laughed.

They all laughed.

Eleanor sighted past the handsome seaman's epaulet, taking in on the one hand her husband's dark head buried in his newspaper, and on the other Mrs. Stuart Barhyte with her lorgnette against her mouth. Even at this distance you could see she was saying something malicious to Mrs. Ross Hawthorne, who was deaf on that side and wouldn't hear it anyway. The young officer — what was his name? what did he say his rank was? — was very tall and very blond, his forelock falling with the weight and drape of a gold fringe.

"The whole Eastern Seaboard will come to see you shooing chickens," he said, inclining himself with a conscious gesture of flattery. Conscious, but he meant it. He was slightly short of breath. Eleanor noticed this, but she did not notice the whole Eastern Seaboard because she had just heard what she'd said. She imagined herself on a weathered stoop, shapeless in calico, her skin red and leathered. She saw the broom — twigs bound with string like the brooms in her old copy of *Grimm's Fairy Tales* — and the chickens molting in the dirt. She crushed a handful of silk in a fist and felt one hard heartbeat in her throat. Behind the broom and the chickens all the shine of home was passing: the pastels on the dance floor, the burnish of the paneling behind lit tapers, the glow of the angels; beyond that all the granite facades and marble pediments of Fayette Street, the crescent borders of the parks, the harbor, the tidewater of the Patapsco, the Monumental City. She was swept by a wave of unhappiness so profound that the effort of smiling made her sweat, and when it passed she was beaded the length of her arched neck. She held the eye of — Lieutenant Vance Jackson, that was it — and the breathtaking simplicity of her salvation settled on her. She wouldn't go.

"Oh, well," she scolded, "people always claim they'll visit, but they don't. My cousin Peg gets up from Washington once a year, and it's no more than forty miles on the B&O." She plunged on, saying anything. The simplicity was staggering. She wouldn't go. She'd tell her mother she was afraid of Indians, tell Daddy she couldn't bear to leave him. She'd tell Father Manot she'd made a mistake to bind herself to an unbeliever, and the father would arrange an annulment (after four years and several hundred consummations it would be problematic, but there had to be a loophole somewhere). If she went to Mount Royal station early enough in the morning she could prevent all her luggage and furniture from being put on the train. Then she'd live as simply as a widow, asking nothing but to stay home. She'd do charitable works and watercolors. And even if there was no annulment, eventually she'd *be* a widow. She glanced again at Laurel, who looked over his paper and gave her a smile of almost conspiratorial tenderness. That Laurel was the central issue (that Laurel's tenderness, even, was the central issue) entered her consciousness for the first time. Guilt, the rich familiar of a convent schooling, followed at once. Lieutenant Jackson's lower teeth sat against his champagne glass as if he were about to bite it.

"My cousin thinks Washington is a more powerful city than Baltimore," she chattered on, "but in my opinion, the government is a poor excuse for power."

The lieutenant laughed again and allowed as how Baltimore had the intellect and the industry.

"And the navy, of course," said Eleanor gallantly. She would live at home again. She would occupy her time at the piano, learning the whole of Bach.

But when she waked in the half light, her nightgown tangled in Laurel's feet, the air was close and cloying, and the death of summer hung in the black leaves. Out on the veranda she leaned against the pillar where, when she couldn't sleep, it had been her habit to watch the progress of the dark. She thought: *Over time a landscape takes its shape, and then over time it takes its shape in you. I'm the shape of this place.* And even as she thought this, while dawn crossed down the ivied trunks of the old iron oaks, shaking light on the matted grass, she had known that she would be, today, where today she was, on the dusty plush of a Cotton Belt club car ten miles out of Commerce, Texas. Because Laurel was ill. Because Laurel was going to Arizona for his health. Because that is the meaning of "in sickness and in health." Because a woman must follow her husband.

Laurel set the *Commerce Chronicle* aside. Eleanor checked the light again. It was early still. It would not be dark for hours yet, and he might tire. Sometimes he tired.

"An aperitif?" she said. As far as Tennessee she had maintained a fantasy that young Vance Jackson would come barreling after her along the track, galloping into the lower corner of the window frame. By Memphis the dream had faded.

Laurel rang for the porter. "And another for you," he said amicably. She had always liked Laurel, his willingness to listen to a woman, his nimble rhetoric, his liberality. To marry a likable atheist had seemed at once her first chance for major rebellion and her first declaration of serious intent. Her mother said, "You will be sorely tested," but her mother had no more spirit than a bowl of brown Betty.

She tried not to think about being sorely tested. It is a self-defeating exercise, trying not to think, and the raw light of a Texas late afternoon is particularly ill suited to the attempt. A verse began running in her head that they used to chant jumping rope in the

courtyard of St. Agnes's, white silk stockings above kid buttontops
that thrummed on the cobbles:

> Not last night but the night before
> A lemon and a pickle came a-knocking at my door.
> I went downstairs to let them in,
> And they hit me over the head with a rolling pin.
> Oh, lady, oh, lady, turn around, round,
> Oh, lady, oh, lady, touch the ground, ground.

It was no different than always, but why had something in her
hoped, even after the loneliness of leaving home had struck her,
that different is what it would be? His skin was underlit with blue
like skimmed milk, fleshy on top of a barrel chest almost like
breasts. She wouldn't think.

Once when she was seven or eight, hiding under the stone steps
down to the cloister, she had overheard Father Berthold speaking
to the sister in a coldly instructive voice: "A woman only need
appear naked before a man at birth, at death, and in surgery —
and the surgeon holds a knife between them." She remembered
thinking that when she was grown up she would understand this.
The surgeon's knife, in particular, confused her.

Her mother had admonished: *endurance* and *a duty*. But Cousin
Peg, sly-eyed looking sideways, laughing out of that side of her
mouth, too, said: *Don't you believe it, Eleanor, we belong to a different
generation. Just give yourself up to it, let go.* She had tried.

> *Oh, lady, oh, lady, turn around, round.*

At least he no longer kissed her on the mouth; he would not risk
infecting her. Lately Mama had changed her tune, said that it was
dangerous breathing his air, and urged Eleanor not just to boil and
scour but also to insist on separate bedrooms. This was precisely
the sort of interference that brought out her streak of rebellious
piety *(in sickness and in health)*. She might shy from his mouth and
tongue, but she disdained to recoil from his microbes.

Laurel took the glasses from the porter's white-gloved hand.
"Shall I go on with the Van Dyke, Eleanor?"

"Yes, do." Anything you like. Whatever *you* like. Sometimes just
on her arm — merely affectionate, she knew that — he would

rub up and down in the same place till the flesh was raw and crying out. It was meant to be loving, she knew that, but the skin of her teeth would squeal. Then she would shrink from his touch, and she would remember his fingers like a nutmeg grater on her nipples.

"Yes, here it is." He had set down the paper and taken up a linenbound book the color of the dirt outside. *The Desert*, by John C. Van Dyke.

> *"The desert mountains remind you of a clenched hand with the knuckles turned skyward."*

Laurel read well, his voice in the middle range but with resonance in his perfect Princetonian enunciation. She sipped her sherry. The warmth in her throat was soothing, whereas the warmth that traveled in the same direction down her spine made her feel glued, through camisole and blouse and lining and pongee seam, to the carriage seat.

> *"Rising as they do from flat sands they give the impression of being deep-based, veritable islands of porphyry bent upward from a yellow sea."*

Out the window, endless stubble. His stubble grating on her neck. Part of the trouble was the heat, but it had been 105° in Baltimore for all of August and half of September, and you could bear it because of the verandas and the dark paneling in the bedroom and the wide white sheets. Here the sky stayed milky at midnight, the roll-up shade in their compartment shut nothing out, the ball fringe of the velvet curtain didn't meet. If you left your window open there was soot, and if you closed it the air was suffocating. They had to mince around each other to undress. She couldn't get her stays off in the miniature commode. She had to stand looking at her naked thighs for the lack of anywhere to look, the flesh at his belly when he bent . . . she wouldn't think.

> *"The more abrupt ranges, that appear younger because of their saw-toothed ridges and broken peaks, are lifted like cathedral spires; they shine like brazen spearpoints against the sky."*

Out the window, barren ground. *Oh, lady, oh, lady, touch the ground, ground.* He touching her, bending her any way he pleased, his fingers poking and prodding.

> *"The edge of the wind is always against the stone. The rockface falls and breaks against itself. Nature has built these mountains for a purpose and now She is cutting them down for another purpose. If She has not water to work with, wind and sand will answer quite as well. The stone itself will answer."*

Not a breath of air. The train tore past a hollow in the earth with mud cracked into drab mosaic, a few bones bleaching. The grind of bone on bone. A handful of her stomach flesh squeezed in his hand as if to burst all the capillaries of it, and that voice not his voice, gone ragged and husky, all the grace gone out of it, the disgusting words just before he opened her . . .

> *A lemon and a pickle came a-knocking at my door.*

She flushed at the revolting comparison that had just occurred to her — she had no way of knowing that it had ever occurred to a human soul before — and bent to the window just in time to see flash by before her own a pair of eyes, a child's eyes under a tangle of tar-black hair, upturned to the passing train and exuding the crusty liquefaction of some disease. For some geographically inexplicable reason the train began to bend in against itself across the infinite zero.

> *"It is the kingdom of sun fire! For every color in the scale is attuned to the key of flame, every sunbeam falls as a shaft of flame. There is no question who is sovereign in these dominions!"*

A very large insect splatted across her pane and spread like spit in the wind.

2

LLOYD WHEELER'S EYES bolted open onto the dark. There's no dark this side of the stars like the dark of a dogleg mine tunnel in Mexico in the middle of the night. Blindness has to be pallid by comparison. But like living blind, living in a mine sharpens your other senses. You can smell the difference between warm leather and cool, wet wool and dry. You can hear the difference between the tooth end of a rat and the claw. What Lloyd smelled now was human sweat with a strong whiff of horse in it — a hundred miles or more of riding with no river in between. What he heard was a damp match end struck on a rock but failing to light.

It might be that Sam had waked and was trying to light the lantern, but so far as he knew his matches and Sam's were dry, and there was no point calling out because if it was Sam there was no problem, and if it wasn't Sam, why give his position away? In any case, Sam wouldn't smell of horse, and it didn't smell of Sam. There was onion in it, and he and Sam had run out of onions weeks ago. The damp match scratched again.

Lloyd tried to think if his rifle was under the blanket roll under his head, but the truth was he hadn't seen his gun for about six days, since the last time he potted at a jackrabbit and missed. He was a good shot, but the rabbits were as skittish as they were scarce, and he was out of practice. And now he couldn't think where he'd put the gun. The damp match scratched. A trickle of sweat went down into the neck of his long johns. He was thirsty. Hungry. He began to notice his body because he was trying not to move. A chunk of ore under the left shoulder blade, a tickle in the groin, a dull singing in the molar he should've gone into Los Papalotes to see about yesterday — and if he had, he wouldn't be here knowing that any minute his stomach was going to growl, and almost wishing the damn match would take.

Which suddenly it did, with a spluttering flare that went straight to his gut and cut off his hunger. All it showed was a loose, long-fingered fist that turned slowly to let the fire climb up the sliver of wood. Lloyd slit his eyes — pretending sleep, mostly, though it wasn't clear what that would get him.

Once the flame was healthy it began to travel around, catching on a thick, well-trimmed mustache and a prominent cheekbone, then on the hacked rock wall of the tunnel, and then on the glass belly of the lantern that hung from the beam. There was a little expulsion of breath. The globe was lifted, the match applied to the wick. The light grew with a dreamy slowness. On the other side of it was a savagely elegant face under a buff hat whose crown disappeared behind the beam, although the man must have been squatting on his haunches. The man was looking directly at Lloyd as if he had seen him all the time in the dark.

Eyes still slit, Lloyd looked left to the humped jumble of blankets where Sam was either asleep or playing at it. Sam always curled his knees up to his chin, and there wasn't a boot heel or a black hair showing out the edges of the blanket. Lloyd gave up pretending sleep himself and inched cautiously up to a sitting position.

"Get the chief," the man said in Spanish, and Lloyd became aware of a second figure in dirty white, hunched behind the first. The figure turned and left with the bent-kneed, clumsy walk Lloyd knew so well, though he had only ever seen Sam in that position. The sweat let go now, and he thought on purpose: *I'm going to die, I'm going to die, I'm going to die*; but it didn't seem to have any meaning to it.

"*Buenas nochas*," he said, his voice reedier than he would have liked, and then wondered whether it was night or morning, and whether "*nochas*" didn't imply a dismissal, whereas "*buenos días*" would have said that he was a man willing to open up a negotiation. Lloyd's Spanish was good, like his aim, but just as rusty, and he spoke with a slow twang that sometimes got him giggled at in the villages. Sam couldn't use a dozen words of it after a year, didn't care to.

The wonderful brutal face remained impassive. The lantern swung idly to reveal the litter of picks, rope, empty cans, the Bunsen burner kicked over on its side, the rubble of split ore — which suddenly flashed Lloyd's old room into his head, and Mama, just before she died, saying, "Lloyd Wheeler, you may be willing to live in a pigsty, but I'm not!"

Now there was something happening at the crook of the tunnel, the white peon pajamas coming crabwise, followed by a hunched heavier and darker shape. The handsome man hung the lantern back on the beam, turned the wick up, and dragged into the light — with three fingers and no evidence of any effort at all — a pine box that had once held dynamite but now contained the whole of Lloyd and Sam's kitchen. The white-dressed one stepped aside and the new one adjusted the box so that when he sat his back lodged in a corner of the rock. He said, "*Gracias, Rudolfo*," and nodded to Lloyd in a pleasantly good-mannered way.

This one also wore a campaign hat, darker and a bit sweaty around the band, a three-piece tweed suit with a gold fob looped across the vest, and a heavy cartridge belt on the hip — and flapping out of his breast pocket a yellow handkerchief that matched his tie. The tweed was expensive stuff, English or Irish, probably, but scooped out at the knees and elbows, dusty, crumpled at the armpits. He had a mustache like the other two, but no cheekbones; a coarse brown dough lump of a face — except for those two brilliant brown human eyes. It was a face you could catch in a few bold penstrokes in a newspaper cartoon; and as the slack mouth opened to say good morning ("*Buenos días*" was the right thing after all) Lloyd had the amazing experience of realizing that Pancho Villa was sitting on his frying pan.

"*Buenos días*," Lloyd said back in a burst. The light was pretty good now, as good as it ever got in the tunnel. Lloyd tried believing he was mistaken, that this was some Chihuahua *rural* masquerading as the boss bandit of the North. But he was not mistaken. He tried to keep his eyes from sliding to Sam's pile of blankets, and saw that Villa was holding, peering at it at arm's length between his knees, the piece of crate board that Sam had lettered in charcoal and nailed over the entrance to the mine.

"I think this is the 'Gringo Chink' mine," Villa said mildly, drawing out the slang as if it were a parody of Spanish. *Green-go Cheenk.* Lloyd nodded. "That's very clever. A joke, I think?"

Lloyd nodded again. It erupted in his mind, a cross between a belch and a prayer, that if he got out of this alive he would go straight back to Bowie to tell everyone about it. At least it'd be some story his brother Frank couldn't go one better.

"We all know what a *gringo* is. But what is a *chink*?"

Villa gestured to the handsome man, who, still hunkered, produced from somewhere (oh, my God, oh, my God, it was Rudolfo Fierro, The Butcher himself) a blunt-handled but beautifully long and well-honed knife, with which he lifted a corner of the blanket heap and flipped it back. Sam Hum, a Chinese boy of nineteen, lay coiled rigid on the floor with his hands folded at his mouth. The *dorado* (that is, the peon in the white pajamas, whose status Lloyd had rapidly revised) leaned forward and caught Sam by the ear. He flung Sam up onto his knees and forward so that the bone-thin boy fell on the palms of his hands, the whorl of his ear still firmly grasped and the lobe stretched perpendicular to his head.

Villa sighed. "I think," he said to Lloyd, "that you forgot to pay your taxes."

"We haven't found anything!" Lloyd blurted. "Nothing! We thought we had a copper vein, but we've been following chicken scratch all the way back here."

It was true. They had nothing to show. It was just a year and a bit since Lloyd had left Bowie and come down to Mexico. At home he'd been half owner, with his brother Frank, of a marble quarry up a grudging twist of mountain road; and he was worn out with trying to wrestle the rock out of there, with Frank's acting boss and their father's making sour predictions. It had seemed, then, a good idea to sell his half of the business to his brother and come find some kind of rock you could carry to a bank. It had seemed even better ten months ago, when he and Sam had come upon the long, flattened crystals in the sandstone outcrop that promised malleable copper. They had whooped with triumph when the chipped-out crystals turned the Bunsen flame green. But since then they had picked, blasted, and shoveled fifty bent yards back into the hillside, following the vein without its widening or turning up any more than the same tantalizing scatter of oxidized specks.

"All foreign-owned mines in Chihuahua owe a forty percent share of their profits to the Constitutionalist cause."

"We haven't made any profits. I swear. We haven't struck a thing." In ten months of bleeding knuckles, lice, and bean mush that looked and smelled like your own shit, Lloyd had never wished so hard that he and Sam had struck it rich.

"They haven't struck a thing," Villa said thoughtfully, and turned to Fierro. "You hear that, Rudolfo?" Fierro slowly nodded and showed his teeth. "You hear that, Señor Chink?"

Sam closed his eyes. The lantern shimmered on his cap of close black hair. His fine-boned face was not a yard from Lloyd's, and Lloyd could see the quiver in his Adam's apple. Villa leaned around to watch it, too. "Are you listening?" Then, matter-of-factly, as if to reassure Fierro, "The yellow shitpile is listening."

Lloyd felt sick. He reminded himself that Sam didn't understand a word. He remembered hearing somewhere that Villa despised the Chinese. He remembered hearing in Los Papalotes the rumor that Rudolfo Fierro had personally shot three hundred *federal* prisoners, ten at a time, pausing only to rest his trigger finger. He said, "He doesn't understand Spanish, sir."

Villa ignored this. "You know, most people think the trouble with Chinamen is their eyes." Fierro reached to trace the curve of Sam's flickering lids with the bladetip of his knife. "But it's not. It's their ears. Don't you think so?" Fierro touched the point to Sam's ear canal. Lloyd was going to be sick. In spite of himself he hugged his hands to his shoulders and rocked forward, whining, "*Don't* kill him. I own the mine. Kill me and let him go. Please . . . my general."

There was a second's silence. The knife went down, and Fierro laughed. Villa said, "What's that?"

"*Please* let him go, General Villa."

"See how famous I am, Rudolfo!" Villa struck a pose, hands under his tweed jacket on his cartridge belt, one elbow forward like a flamenco dancer. "What do you say to that? My — General —

Villa!" He dropped the pose, put his elbows on his knees, and leaned forward to Lloyd, sighing. "You don't know anything about politics, boy," he said.

Sam's eyes closed again and his ear was still wrenched in the fingers of the *dorado,* but it looked like the tension had let up in the muscles that held him in his crouch. Sam couldn't have known what was said, but he must have heard that Lloyd was standing up for him. Lloyd's nausea subsided somewhat.

"At Torreón," Villa said, "I killed four hundred and fifty yellow China dogs, and all I got was a piece of paper from Agent Carothers. In Juárez I killed one Englishman and I don't think I'll ever hear the last of it. I'm telling you the truth, I'll never hear the last of it. I think even my very good friend General Carranza would like to embarrass me about it. You know my good friend General Carranza? 'First Chief'?"

Fierro barked another laugh. "I've heard of him," said Lloyd.

He'd heard of Carranza, all right, the highbrow leader of the bandit rebels — what did they call themselves? — the republicans, confederates? Constitutionalists, that was it. Carranza was supposed to be an inkhorn and a prude, who sat at a fancy desk in Hermosillo and sent out the orders to these Constitutionalists, Zapata in the South, Villa and Obregón in the North. Lloyd had heard something about Villa killing an Englishman, too — something, rolled him in a rug, maybe — but he'd never heard of any Agent Carothers. Probably no reason he should. He remembered his father saying that the "fool go'ment uses any Dick or Harry to deal with those thugs," because the "Constitutionalist" generals had no kind of official status.

"There are some little troubles between us, frankly," Villa said. Lloyd couldn't figure out what he meant. He thought the rebels were trying to put Carranza in power, make him the new president, whereas here was Villa edging himself closer on the crate and lowering his voice confidingly, as if General Carranza might have agents among the pick handles.

"But for the moment we must ignore our differences and unite against the great enemy of the people Victoriano Huerta. You understand?"

A line of sweat went down Lloyd's chest, and the thought followed it cold inside, that what Villa was saying was not the kind of thing you say to a stranger and let him live. *The trouble is their ears.* But Villa's face was right in the lantern light now, and there was no threat in it. He looked like a man who was tough and tired. He looked as if he was paying 100 percent attention to making Lloyd understand. Lloyd remembered something else, all of a sudden: The men who joined up with Villa said there was no bullshit in him. No mercy and no bullshit.

"So I need my army prepared, you understand. I need horses, money. I need arms."

"We haven't *struck* anything," Lloyd pleaded. But he understood that Villa understood that the Gringo Chink Mine was not a likely source of weaponry, or any better mount than the suck-ribbed nameless burro tied outside. He was after something else. Anything, Lloyd promised himself, and Sam, and God, and Villa. Anything.

"No, well, perhaps we can work something out. The truth is, I have a job to do, and I need a gringo for it. How about this: You do a job for me, and I let 'Señor Chink' go."

Lloyd opened his mouth to agree, but Sam said, "Hum."

Villa wheeled. "What's that?"

"Mr. Hum. Mr. Sam Hum," Sam said. He had not opened his eyes, and his ear was red, and his Adam's apple lurched. But he'd made a fist of one of the hands that supported him on the ground. Villa's eyes flashed furious but he otherwise sat relaxed, turned back to Lloyd, and returned his elbows to his knees.

"Yes, so that's settled. Is it? You won't mind doing a little job for me so your friend can go free?"

Lloyd mumbled his assent. Villa slapped his knees and gave Fierro a tight half smile. "Good. Excellent. Let him go, Guytan."

The *dorado* remained motionless, as if he hadn't heard. Or as if, his copper eyes giving back the lantern light, he had other things to think about. The crazy thought flashed through Lloyd's mind that the *dorado* didn't speak any Spanish either.

"Guytan," said Villa, "I've made a bargain with the gringo. Let the yellow shitpile go." The *dorado* crouched obdurate. Villa frowned at Fierro and shook his head at Lloyd. "Military disobedience is a terrible problem," he complained. "Now I'm going to have to find a way to make *my* friend let go of *your* friend. Rudolfo, what do you think?"

Fierro considered the problem a moment, his handsome head cocked thoughtfully. Then he reached to the right and with quick accuracy sliced off Sam's ear.

3

AFTER SCHOOL JESSIE WHEELER drowned five of the new kittens in a bucket in the henhouse. Ma was indoors topping strawberries, and Jessie made Jasper watch. She balled the kittens up in an end of old flour sack and held them under with both hands.

"Ma can't do it so we have to," she told Jasper. "It's like Pa does the chickens." There was no thermometer at the Wheelers' ranch, but when it was this hot Jessie thought of it as *hundred weather,* the air so unsteady that the sun bounced on the point of the Chiricahuas just before it went down. Jasper smudged the sweat under his nose with the back of his hand. He was nine and didn't have much man about him yet.

"You eat chickens," he said.

The corner of the sack blew up and lifted out of the water like all five kittens had breathed out at the same time, but Jessie took hold of that part in her fist. The bubbles made a squeezed sound spreading around the surface of the bucket, there was a shudder under her hand like when a steer shakes the flies off its haunch, and then the sack sank.

"They'd grow up and have kittens, and then those kittens would have kittens, and those kittens would have kittens. Do you see?"

She took the sack outside and lowered it into the coal oil drum they used for an incinerator, folding it into the ashes with a hoe.

Jasper said, "You don't eat cats."

Ma didn't notice there were only three kittens left, or anyway she didn't say so, and after supper Jessie was allowed to sit on the sofa and do her sums while Ma finished off the jam. Jasper and Deborah were already tucked in, and Pa was doing sums, too, at the supper table; his were called "estimates." The problems Miss Timkin had set were so easy that even Seth Vandercamp would get them right; the hard part was to sit still enough that the light would fade out of the kitchen window before Ma thought to tell her to go to bed.

Jessie laid her pencil on her nose and frowned like she was ciphering in her head. The jam pot bubbled clear red lumps that Ma dipped a wooden spoon in, and then she held the spoon sideways, counting the drops before the red slime parted in the middle and hung two separate clots on the side of the bowl.

"It's done," Ma said. "Near as makes no difference."

There were no strawberries in Arizona, but every summer Pa had three pecks shipped by rail from the Napa Valley, which cost a whole small beef cow and proved he loved Ma to the whole county at a rodeo picnic or a Sunday social even if he praised the jam instead of her. Now he just said "Mmm," leaning his forehead on one big hand while he clamped the other around the pencil stub, digging the point in the soft pad.

Ma swiveled the small pan in its boiling bath where the paraffin was melting. There were two dozen mason jars draining on the wood sink, and Tabatha was curled on the windowsill, no more bothered than Ma that five of her babies had disappeared. Ma stepped across and peeked in on Deborah through the half-open door, careful not to brush against it because the old hinges squeaked a way no amount of oil would hush. Jessie sat tight still in case looking at the baby made Ma think of bed, but Ma was in a brown study anyway tonight, not just about the jam. "Brown study" was what Grampa Wheeler said, as if you had lessons on dirt and rocks.

Ma went back to the wood stove and dipped the spoon again. The jam dripped fast off the bowl and then slower, and then not, and Jessie knew from other jam makings how that last drop would scab over and hold there.

"Do you want to taste?" Ma said, and carried the spoon across to Pa.

Ma was dimpled and freckled. She had hair like untwisted hemp rope, and pouty flesh under her chin and at her bosoms. She waited until Pa toted up a column of figures, then she set the spoon in front of his face, and he stuck out his tongue. It was still hot, because he drew back and blew, and blew. Then he took the whole bowl into his mouth with a sucking slurp. Jessie could remember the sweet stickiness; she smashed her tongue against the roof of her mouth. Ma pulled out the spoon.

"Mmm, mmm!" Pa reared back on the chair's hind legs, which usually made Ma complain how all four ladderbacks had gone wobbly and would have to be reglued, but she didn't pick that bone with him just now.

"That is some jam, ma'am." Pa took his little rimless glasses off, which changed him completely. With the glasses on, the way they magnified his pale eyes and pinched them closer together at the same time, he looked like a hump-shouldered clerk or a store-keeper. When he took them off and stretched his arms out, all of a sudden he was loose and long, the cowpunching muscles filled out over his bones. He could make Ma draw in her breath even after a dozen years of mending and feeding him. Under the table Shirley and Mercy, two half-grown kittens from the last batch, untangled themselves and got out of the way of his boots.

"I hope they like strawberry jam," Ma said.

Pa slipped a hand under the edge of her apron. "Everybody likes strawberry jam."

"Everybody we know." Ma twisted from him and took the spoon back to the pot, skimming the foamy pink from around the edge and flinging it into the enamel basin. "But we don't know anybody from back East. Maybe they like fish eggs."

"Why would they eat fish eggs?"

"People do, back there."

Jessie had never seen a fish except sardines in a can, but if people would stick that salt oil stink in their mouths she believed they would eat fish eggs, too. She remembered the flat eyes of the sardines and wondered would the kittens in the sack under the ashes have those eyes. Pa said, "Pssh." He put the glasses back on and bent over his sums. Jessie bent over her own.

"I shaved a little off the pumping estimate," Pa said. "I reckoned the steam engine to work for six months without an overhaul, which I don't know if it would or not. But whatever way I figure, it never comes out to much under seven thousand."

The square of the kitchen window was only pale and greenish, meaning there was sunset in back of Jessie's head. But now was when Ma would send her to bed, because Ma did not let her and Jasper hear talk about money, even though at the same time Ma said they were too little to understand. Jessie understood all about it. It was about the marble quarry up Old Camp Road, which Grampa Wheeler had made a present of to Pa and Uncle Lloyd when Pa came to be eighteen and Uncle Lloyd was littler than Jessie was now. She had heard often enough how, ever after that, Pa couldn't think of anything but getting the marble down. He wanted it so bad that he talked Grampa and Uncle Lloyd into the quarry business, and Grampa said near lost all their shirts. Then last year there was a fight — did Ma think Jessie couldn't tell when Grampa clamped his mouth and stalked away? Grampa said he wouldn't sink another dime in, and Uncle Lloyd said he had enough, and Pa said he would do it on his own then and gave Uncle Lloyd seven hundred dollars for his half.

Jessie made herself heavy down between the sofa cushion and the arm, waiting for Ma to send her to bed. But Ma just slid the pot off the fire and frowned at it, stubborn, keeping on about the fish eggs.

"Alma Timkin says they do," she said. "Fish roe."

"I keep figuring the Mexicans will work for a nickel a day less, and then a nickel a day less than that. Well, maybe they will. There's sixty men out of work in shantytown since we closed down. Maybe they'll work for four dollars a week."

"And sweetbreads," Ma said with a purse of her mouth. "I thought that was some kind of cake, but Alma says it's part of the stomach lining."

Pa looked up. "Stomach lining!"

"Of a cow."

"Alma reads too much," said Pa.

Saying something against Miss Timkin would make them remember her. Sure enough, Ma said, "Jessie, are you near done?" and Jessie said, "Last problem, Ma," which was true inasmuch as she had her pencil on the sum, tracing it over.

Ma began ladling the jam into the jars and wiping the spills with a damp cheesecloth. Tabatha came to wind around her ankles, and Ma shoved against the fur with the side of her foot. "I wish these cats would eat the scum. It's a pity to waste good sugar."

This did not make sense because the cats didn't like sweet things. Maybe the chickens or the cattle would eat it. A goat would, but the Wheelers didn't keep a goat. If old Rosaria still came to help with the baby, she'd have taken it straight out to the back stoop and smacked her lips, but the new girl, Maria Iglesias, had snooty ways. You could never tell what would strike her wrong. If you gave Maria strawberry scum she might treat it like garbage and fling it out right in front of you.

"It's all very well," Ma said. She didn't say what she meant. Across the sink from the drainboard she had laid a thick pad of newsprint to keep the hot bottoms of the jars from cracking against the cool because on that side of the sink — although the chairs were wobbly, the potbelly stove was rusted, and the floorboards were bare — for all that, on the left side of the sink was a rich slab of polished marble. It was nearly an inch thick, white as the white of a cow's eye, veined in light blue-gray swirls. Ma spooned the liquid on the jelling berries.

"Alma says Mrs. Poindexter is a *Catholic*."

"My pa's going to take care of that," Pa said. He lowered the glasses again, and the storekeeper stretched back up into the rancher. Once Jessie heard Mrs. Newsome in town say that Wally Wheeler's sons had each got half of him, Frank the brawn and Lloyd the elegance. Except they didn't talk about Uncle Lloyd anymore. There was no news. After the gossip settled they got embarrassed toward Grampa, that his younger son had run off with a Chinaman God knows where.

"When I went to get the rump roast from your pa, he asked me were you nervous about Mr. Poindexter coming."

"Nervous!" Pa scoffed.

"I said, 'Well, the banker may not lend us the money, but if he don't, there's sure nobody else going to lend it.'"

"What did he say to that?"

"He didn't come up with any offers I could notice. He just said I had no need to worry, Mrs. Poindexter would turn out to be hooknose and gimpy-legged."

Pa had stiffened up and didn't laugh. Ma turned to him with the ladle in her hand, and now she lowered her voice like she both knew Jessie was in the room and thought she wasn't. The square of sky was gray and paling. "Alma says there's ninety-nine chances out of a hundred these Poindexters *drink*. I mean it, Frank."

"Well, maybe. That's their business." But he pinched the skin on his nose.

"Frank, they'll *be* here day after tomorrow. We have to be able to sup with them. It's important."

Pa let the pencil stub topple, stuck a thumb and finger in his eyes, and rubbed. "He probably likes a good cigar," he mused. "Maybe he smokes a pipe. A pipe is all right. It's more dignified."

"Whiskey and gin I don't know," Ma said. "But I suppose wine is pretty much a part of their, well, habits. I shouldn't wonder they gamble."

"Mary *Doreen*."

Ma had said this low, but now she set the last jar down hard enough you could hear it whack against the marble through the newsprint. "Well, we don't know, do we? We don't *know* anything about Baltimore!"

Pa went to her then. He rubbed the palms of his hands on the shoulders of her sprigged blouse. He rubbed up and down, awkward, shushing the fabric.

"I want Mr. Poindexter to give you the money because of my strawberry jam," Ma said. She let the ladle slide sideways into the sink. "I want my strawberry jam to be whol-ly responsible for you getting the money."

"It won't harm if I've got the estimates in order." Pa smoothed his hands, just one direction now, down from her shoulder to her elbows, smoothing down.

Tabatha had come over on the couch and rolled belly up, nudging her chin under Jessie's elbow. The hair around Tabatha's nipples was matted down from nursing the three kittens she had left, which reminded Jessie of Ida Pack's ringworm that made her have to shave off patches of hair and paint her scalp purple.

"Where do you suppose the word *mine* came from?" Ma asked. "Is it because of claims?"

"Hmm?"

"I mean, 'This is mine,' do you suppose?"

Pa slid his hand from Ma's elbows down her arms. "I never supposed one way or other."

"This is my mine? This mine is mine?"

Pa said what he always said to Ma: "It's not a mine, it's a quarry."

She relaxed back against him. "It seems peculiar you need a human hand for the final polish. It's just rock, but you have to give it something, out of your body."

Mercy, which was a female and would have to be got rid of some way or other, jumped up and tried to nurse on Tabatha, but Tabatha shoved her away with claws half out. Too old to be nursing. Jessie thought tomorrow she would ask Miss Timkin about where *mine* came from. Then she thought that when she knew the answer she would keep it to herself.

"This mine is mine," Pa said against Ma's hair, and Ma pressed her fingertips on the marble.

Ma said, "I have to get the paraffin on before it cools."

She said, "It's light yet, Frank."

She said, "Jessie, go to bed now."

4

FROM THE SAND-SCUMMED window of the compartment Eleanor had seen not one living creature in the whole distance from New Mexico. Laurel had gone to the club car and left her alone to dress, kissing her on her damp neck as he left. "Don't look *too* gorgeous; they won't be able to bear it." It was meant as friendly, meant as loving; she knew that.

She sat on the bunk and undid the buttons of her bodice, twisting one in her fingers and staring at it, mother-of-pearl in the shape of a new moon. Mother, pearl, moon. These ideas seemed alien and fraught with pain. She dropped the bit of cloth in her lap and sat listless until she was startled by a rap on the door. She rebuttoned some of the moons and took the scant two steps across the compartment.

"Mr. Laurel says would you care for a port wine."

The porter was so tall and so black that for just a second she believed she was facing Innis Washington; and even as she thanked him, closed the door, took the little tray, and slid it onto the seat beside her, she was back in Baltimore, back at the Emerson that night, that lost last chance, late in the evening when the supply of clean glasses had dwindled to a scatter and the tapers in the sconces had burned down a second time. Then she had seen Innis catch three empty bottles off the sideboard between the fingers of one hand; and it had struck her powerfully that because the Kennys always celebrated at the Emerson, he had been present at every major turning point of her life.

She followed him back through the broom-hung vestibule toward the kitchen, where a cook sat at the massive table sucking the last bits from a pile of crab legs. The kitchen was ill lit, and hot, and needed a coat of paint. Innis said, "They be one big headache in Baltimore tomorrow." The cook swept the pile off the marble slab and into a bucket, and he turned around.

"Innis. I've come to thank you and say goodbye." She remembered it as a strange and dislocated moment, because at that point she still half believed she would not go to Arizona. The woman scratched under her stubby hair and looked coolly at Eleanor, who half turned away in a confusion that apparently communicated itself to Innis, because he not only dumped the bottles in the bucket but also picked up the bucket and held it with both white-gloved hands between them, as if he were presenting her with the garbage.

He said solemnly, "We going to miss you, Miss Eleanor. Take care with them *dorados*."

There was an awkward pause into which the cook said, "They trash on the back steps to throw out, too."

Innis inflated his chest against the silk frogs of his uniform. "What trash?"

"White trash."

"Oh."

He turned and flung open the iron door onto the alley, where half a dozen pale street scum six to eight years old were jostling each other on an overturned bin. Evidently they'd already eaten, because the alley was littered with picked-clean fish bones and pear cores gnawed to string.

"You there!" Innis thundered. "Get on outta here!" They scattered. The smallest one, filthy in a tattered cap, his knees poking through outsize knickers, slipped in lettuce mush and kept yelping all the way down to the back street. Innis upended the bucket into the nearest bin and stood facing the corncobs, cores, and rinds. The cook must have found another crab claw, from which she sucked, a liquid sound.

Now Eleanor shed her morning dress and sat for a moment in her corset, staring out at the empty stretch of dirt and sky while slow waves of panic washed through her stomach, lifted, crested, shattered, and dispersed. In New Mexico they had come through cool mountains, but since Lordsburg they had been back in the stifling flat, with only, here and there, a point of rock thrown up in the distance, like a dead ship. The desert itself could have been an Atlantic of some desiccated fantasy: undulations of choking sand, fathoms deep and to the edge of immensity.

She rose suddenly, to be doing something, to fight the panic, and poured a small port from the decanter. Turning, she struck her elbow resoundingly on the door to the commode. Funny bone, funny bone. That pain washed up her arm and into her stomach, too, churned there, fear and funny bone. "My God," she said aloud, meaning self-irony, but the mimicry of despair was too dangerous. The port had spilled over her hand and spread in a red oval on her corset stays. She hung by her good arm on to the door while the tickling pain in her elbow subsided, staring at the blurred ground willfully close, till her eyes hurt and the bile swirled and she saw herself in her mind's eye hurtling headfirst out of the window to the track.

She put on a dress in soft ivory charmeuse with a peg-top skirt and a standaway collar edged in soutache over a pale green jabot. Her pumps had crossed button straps and spindle heels. Her rich hair she piled under an emerald straw toque, from which took flight both entire wings of a macaw. She assumed, reasonably, that none of these things was usual in Bowie, Arizona.

The town of Bowie sat dead center in the San Simon (pronounced Sansa-Moan) Valley, a valley only in that it lay low among mountains; in reality a vast flat plain, sand and silt for most of the year, otherwise occasionally and briefly mud. The plain was sliced east to west by a main line of the Southern Pacific, and Bowie hugged itself around the track for no reason apparent or actual, except that it was a distance of so-and-so many miles on either side to the next such hugging of a town around the track.

There were a couple of hundred buildings if you counted the adobe shacks on the far side of the line; they wandered beyond the pump house, with its stacks and derricks, down a single street toward the mud spire of the Mexican church. The houses this side were gable and hip, laid out in neat squares like a game board or, as the women were more likely to say, a quilt, the pattern altered here and there by the station hotel, the boardwalk strip of Main Street, and the clapboard tower of Bowie Methodist. Fenced ranch-lands at the outskirts formed a border.

Sunday picnickers on Dos Cabezas or the northern peaks of the Chiricahuas had a view of Bowie that was essentially, though it was not yet called, aerial. In the arid clarity of that air it made a delight-ful view. Rectangles of lawn scratched out of the desert shone emerald in the sun, which would have killed them had the inhabi-tants not made every pail of washwater do double duty. The roofs peaked righteously. The rails of the SP glittered, polished a dozen times a day by the passage of goods and people. That straight shaft of iron and the rectilinear layout of the near side of town bespoke human will, a force of order in the random hugeness of the desert. People did come to the mountains to picnic on Sundays, in spite of its being a long haul and a hard climb. They came to taste the moss-flavored air and to see their town symmetrically shine and peak like a product of human design.

Because down here, below sea level, you came to Bowie by way of greasewood and true grit. The last fifty miles of the approach were unremitting brown flat and blue bowl. Wherever the mud had settled and dried after the last downpour, it left patches of hardpan deeply tessellated, like acres of turtleback. Out of this the town stuck up abrupt and insignificant.

The porter was blocking the opening between the cars. A ma-hogany column of neck stood directly in front of Eleanor's eyes, and for this respite she was glad, although she strained to see out the twin chunks of space on either side. Laurel had a hand on her kidney. Her breath was short and her mouth felt as if it had been washed out with glycerin soap and dried with a towel. She couldn't remember if she'd drunk another glass of port.

"Hold tight, now," Laurel said, always solicitous to the point where he made her seem inept, a woman who didn't know enough to brace for the stopping of a train. She grasped the vertical rod beside the porter's back and let herself hang toward the forward car. A body in motion tends to remain in motion. Her father had told her that, not meaning education by it but to tease her for always running. And yes, it *would* be her tendency — in motion with this railcar all the way to California, and beyond by steamer, too, to the Orient; then back-paddling the bays of the Far and Near East, the loved waterways of Venice, canals of Brugge, the chalky reaches of the Channel, the stately chop of the Thames below its bridges, the long lift and swell of the Atlantic, and so back to the Patapsco, home. She'd go that route if she were let. She felt the dryness of the air as something shriveling.

In the space of her world tour the train had slowed, squealed, jerked. Now the porter was vaulting the little distance to the ground, placing the step for her with a flourish, emptying the doorway for her first sight of her new home.

There was a crowd. Had a crowd of that size turned out to greet her in Baltimore, she had been gratified! The folk stood fore-grounded against the splintery rawness of the station, gawky in their stance and their stiff plaids and ruffles, the eyes rapacious and the mouths a little slack in jaws too square. It was both shocking and expected, the way a woman might know exactly what a new-born looks like and yet be shocked at her expectation made manifest. She saw directly below her an Adam's apple with a lump of turquoise riding it, and her dread of Arizona took a form.

The porter reached his big hand up to her with a gracious gesture. She lifted her skirt and put her left hand in that hand, but then she paused a moment, one foot in the air. There was a sort of numbness at her center and an animal-aliveness at the edges. She was aware of the huge palm in which her gloved hand sat, she could feel its papery dryness through her glove, as large and dry as her father's palm, so that she had a wave of longing for Erin Kenny even while she avoided the face of the black man whose hand she held. The pointless wandering of her will had left her a way to bear it. For after all, in Europe she had known discomforts, the bone-weariness of travel, misplaced luggage, even once a carriage that had lost a wheel on a deserted road in the cold night of Pembroke-shire. And none of that had made her despair, because it was temporary; all of it came under the heading of *Experience*. That is how she would think of this time in Arizona, would think nothing of it but that it was a garnered smidgen of experience, a scrapbook page. After all, it is always possible to go back to where one came from, as a way of going forward.

She lowered herself to the step, smiled, and greeted the nearest face, repeating a name that registered not in the slightest on her charged and wayward consciousness. For the moment what she most felt was the relinquishing of the black stranger's hand. With that freed hand she accepted some tissuebound gift while she shook some other hand with her right, heard her laugh tinkle prettily and her palate, tongue, teeth form words that sounded exactly appropriate.

She briefly scanned the faces — one rough, two round; teeth, nostrils, scar — headgear in quaint dated shapes from poke bonnet to cartwheel, and on the men ten-gallon Stetsons; they really wore them, then. The supports of the station overhang were rough-cut as railway ties, and yet they were stained and varnished, as if in some childlike attempt at decor. They were hung with tricolored bunting like on a patriotic holiday, and it occurred to her that this would be a way of honoring a new banker, a new bank. Up the track in the direction they had been headed a mountain poked the sky, unfinished as the male face to which she now returned her glance, and all the time of its own accord her mouth kept saying the things she had been taught all her life to say in social pleasantry: *So kind of you to come and meet us. My, yes, a very dry heat. I expect it will take time.*

Along the boardwalk to her left a saloon had spilled a few of its customers outdoors, who stood curious, in boots and vests, with glasses in their hands. Half a dozen Mexican children were slapping their bare feet in the dust, and behind them but ignoring them a girl of arrogant beauty hugged herself into a yellow shawl. Farther down the track a little army had been mobilized to unload their goods; the piano was easing down a ramp after the Pierce-Arrow. In the circle around her there were pin tucks and lace collars, wool serge in this temperature, as if Easter Sunday had bloomed in the station yard. A towhaired toddler thrust at her a bouquet of zinnias and some white-flowered weed.

" 'Low me to introduce," said the tall man with the turquoise goiter. "I'm Walter Wheeler, been in this town since about driving of the first spike. And this is my son Frank and my daughter-in-law Mary Doreen. Mary Do is the best cook in the county and the prettiest woman over sixteen." The damp-faced blonde with a baby on her hip shot him an irritated glance. "And this is our school-teacher, Alma Timkin, sings alto in the choir, but she can run a trail herd if there's a need."

Alma Timkin was not irritated, apparently. She trilled a laugh. "I'm just as thrilled as can be to welcome you to Bowie, Mrs. Poindexter." She was a big-boned, rawhide woman with a fluty voice and wings of auburn hair. "I mean us to be *good* friends."

Eleanor took her large hand. "I'm positive we will."

She felt the shriveling heat as dismay, and dismay as the fulfillment of a prophecy. She kept intending to turn to Laurel and say: *You can't mean it. You can't mean me to live here.* But Laurel was repeating the same things as she, their phrases counterpointed as if rehearsed. This air was what they had come for, precisely this: air a disease couldn't live in.

The closeness of the crowd made her take a gasping lungful, and as if she had caused it with her effort of breath, there was a flurry and rearrangement in front of her. The adults scrambled back, making room for a pair of children, a gape-mouthed, rodent-faced boy and a girl with a square, flat jaw, frizzed hair haloed from the angle of the sun and from some iron-red magnetism of its own. This chunky, lumpish girl — eyes very bright, however — lofted a basket between them and opened it.

Suddenly closer, the girl had a face like one of Bosch's suffering bugs, the flesh overripe and in spite of its rich color translucent, the veins too near the surface, as if the skin might split. The girl opened the basket and raised between them a gray something that in the second before she identified it made Eleanor's lungs catch with fear, believing she was about to be pelted with a severe demonstration of unwelcome — a rotten head of lettuce, a dead gopher — so that when the half-flung thing came into her focus as a rather handsome little gray cat, she turned her recoil into a reach, and took hold of it in a paroxysm of relief.

"Welcome to Bowie, Mizz Pondecker!"

"How sweet," her lips, tongue, teeth said.

The woman with the baby said, "Jessie!"

Eleanor curled the kitten to her neck. Relief, the oddity of fur in this stifling air, brought tears to her eyes, and the one who had been introduced as the preacher's wife said, and kept saying, "Aw. Aw, aw, aw, aw, aw."

5

THE THING THAT SUSTAINED Sam Hum, like a root protruding from a cliff where he hung, was that Lloyd had saved his life.

Sam's view of the scene had never been whole or clear. First he was curled into his knees and all he saw, as he listened to the threatening, gibberish-resonating voices, was a splay of five left toes in frayed cowhide sandal straps. Then he was grabbed by the ear, and the wrench of pain shot down his nape to lodge in his right wing blade. He was held facing the hewn rock, Lloyd's feet, a wrinkle of dingy white cloth at the left periphery; and then the amazing knife as it toured his face, a metal that caught the light where there was no light to catch. He had one glance of the fat face and its incandescent eyes. He understood the humorless laugh of the knife-wielder, the unctuous politeness of the higher-pitched one, the mock-stupid mutter of the one in white who held him — but he could not remember, and had not at the time understood, any words but the name of the mine, Gringo Chink, which had been his own invention, and the designation "Señor Chink," by which he knew his manhood required a gesture even if he died for it.

For some days after Lloyd and the Mexicans left, he had stayed crouched in the mine. He didn't know how many days it was because — although once the kerosene burned out the darkness did differ a little day and night — he spent most of the time curled under the blanket, his one clean pair of long johns clamped against his wound, in a monotonous blur of fear. The muscles of the hand that held the cloth cramped and went rigid. The cloth went rigid with dried blood. Awake he was paralyzed, unable to force himself out of the tunnel toward daylight, yet knowing that the danger he shunned had found him in this very cul-de-sac. He hunched back against the wall, at bay against phantoms, until exhaustion sent him to sleep. In his sleep he ceased to fear for himself and invented terrors for Lloyd. He saw Lloyd suspended upside down from the cottonwood tree by the railroad tracks at home, his face shrouded eerily in caterpillar cocoons. He saw the knife used in every configuration and on every part of Lloyd's body — no, not the ears. But the toes, carved, slit, and sliced; the nose, fingers, the flesh of the thigh, the balls lifted in the long, alien hand, the erect cock severed like a sausage. When Sam was exhausted by this he woke back to his fears for himself.

Yet through all of the tedium of terror there was the undercurrent of astonished grace: Lloyd had saved his life. For half a dozen years, since the first convolution of dominance and affection, Sam had expected Lloyd to abandon him. Now when Lloyd left, it had been against his will and with the parting gesture of ultimate loyalty. Who would have expected it? Who would have thought it?

In those first days Sam scarcely registered the more immediate miracle: The wound was not festering. Guytan Farga had honed the blade to sterility; this was his habit, as it was Fierro's requirement. It was no part of either Fierro's or Farga's intention that such a perfect edge would make a clean cut, but that was the effect of it. The veins were sliced and shocked. There was minimal tissue damage. The wound bled itself clean. When Sam finally knew he was alone and dared reach for something to stanch the blood, he instinctively reached for the one thing he had washed for the next trip to Los Papalotes. Then he stayed still for a matter of days. He might have died of starvation or dehydration, but by the time he unwound himself stiffly from under the blanket, there was a whorl of incipient scar around the hole of his ear canal, and he was past the danger of infection.

Now he knew that he could not stay in the mine, and that though nothing offered much point or purpose, the only thing that made any sense at all was to go home, where, if he could, Lloyd would eventually go, too.

Sam washed himself at the stingy well (the blood so crusted it might have been a body cast, and as he shed it he felt some little mobility come back to him). He ate what was left of the cans; he rolled jerky, beans, coffee, and a filled canteen in his blanket. He added the identity card that proved he was a born American and would get him back across the border. He sliced a section of one leg from the long johns where the blood had not reached, fashioning it into a band around his head. Over that he wound a blue bandanna, the knot hanging in the place of the missing ear. The effect in Lloyd's shaving mirror was comical and jaunty. Immediately thereafter he found his ear, by stepping on it on the tunnel floor where it had fallen. It was wizened and leathery and stank a little, sweetly. He stuck it in the bedroll with his food.

The burro had gone. At first Sam thought Lloyd and the Mexicans had taken it, but when he realized that the rope had been chewed through he wasted another day tracking and calling in the surrounding outcrop. Finally he took off as near due west as he could, moving north only when this was not possible, because he had so much farther west than north to go and because his mind had locked on to a notion of retracing his steps and Lloyd's to Bowie. This would not ordinarily have been wise — if he had thought to go straight north he could have entered Ciudad Juárez and crossed into American territory at El Paso within a week — but as it happens he would have entered Ciudad Juárez under the jurisdiction of Pancho Villa, so his confusion served him better than cunning. In any case he went mainly west.

Sam knew how to travel in the desert, but knowing how does not alter the elements or the geography. The days were very hot, and in the higher elevations the nights were very cold. Water was difficult to find and tricky to predict. He had lost a great deal of blood, and the food to rebuild his strength was hard to come by. The sun seared his eyes just at the point in the day that his energy inevitably flagged. Yet he dared not travel at night because the sun was the only compass he trusted. People he trusted none. He was strangely lonely, so lonely that more than once, hiding on the edge of a village waiting for sundown so he might steal a few eggs, he learned without understanding them the rhymes of the children playing in the streets.

¿Periquito, Mandurico,
Quien te dio tan largo pico?

He tried to keep within sight of a road or a railway track while at the same time keeping out of sight of those who might be using roads and railways, and at this unlikely endeavor he was remarkably successful. He had the gifts of both agility and stillness. He had at one time been called "Lizard" by his classmates, and by his mother "Hummingbird." Once when he was only eight he had sat for an hour with a somnolent scorpion on his ankle just out of reach, and when his father found him and killed the scorpion there had been such a jubilation of praise, such a celebration of his patience that Sam ended by being impressed with himself. Thereafter he cultivated a quietness that was always self-protective and might sometimes be genuinely meditative, though Wally Wheeler's referring to it as "Oriental" was somewhat off the mark. Li Hum was so passionately in pursuit of the American dream that his children had never heard of Buddha.

So by keeping hidden and moving fast Sam managed to travel generally in striking distance of food and water. But of course it didn't always work. The main arteries of travel ran north and south. Sometimes the east-to-west veins dead-ended in a village of three adobe shacks or a single *hacienda* and its fenced ranges. Then Sam would stock his pack with whatever he could steal and set off across a dry basin or a sunbaked mesa.

At the end of the second week he was forced to climb a mountainous scrubland. A maze of arroyos and ravines sent him doubling back on his path. He thought the vegetation would increase, but it did not. He expected the elevation to offer some relief from the heat, but it did not. He expected to find water, but he did not. Shale split under his boots and sent him sliding hour after hour of the meaningless climb; the sun shimmered low mirages from every shelf of the rockface. He drank the last of his water, then ate the last of his jerky, remembering too late that the salt meat would sharpen his thirst. This failure of common sense discouraged him more than thirst itself, and to dull its pain he set about finding a barrel cactus. He squatted on a miniature mesa where the fat plant was rooted in a crevice, took out his knife, and decapitated the upper third of the barrel, then carved out fibrous chunks of yellow flesh and sucked them. The cactus water was acrid to the point of pain. He knew it would sustain him, but he tasted alkali on top of salt.

Now his discouragement took physical form and declared its force. Salt and acrid, nauseating. Sam stumbled forward, letting himself know that there was not much likelihood he would survive this trip and that he did not much care. The less he cared, the less the likelihood. He climbed aimlessly as the sun fell, willing himself to give up, the taste of salt meat and acrid fiber deep in his throat. It would be a relief to quit. He kept on in the dark, cut open another barrel cactus just to reinforce his anger, sucked the stinking water with a vengeance, and kept on going.

For two more days he climbed, on nothing but cactus water and mesquite beans, lying awake in the dark and rising on feeble, vibrating bones. On the second afternoon his anger failed him and he sheltered when the sun was still high. He lay on his side in a shallow hollow of rock that fit his body even to a gentle rise between his rib and hipbone; and another under his hands, which were folded under his neck. A pillow of rock. His hunger was a hole in his belly, but if he concentrated all his mind on that scoop-shaped void, why, then, he could lie in that as well, live inside the hunger as he lay inside the rock, and it was tolerable; more — a companion. His thirst was fierce, but if he sucked on the round sandstone pebbles that lay within his reach, after a little time his mouth would miraculously make water, so it was as if he were sucking water from the stones.

He was drowsy, and images of his life passed drowsily through his mind, as if dying was a slow drowning.

To be the first Chinese in that school. Later he found out that there had been talk against it, and some had tried to block him. They said it would be Mexicans next, or the Navajo brats in cowhide diapers. But they could not keep him out because his father was not a lowdown, even to them, and Wally Wheeler made a speech saying he laid track once himself, and who did it the American way if it wasn't Li Hum?

Because Li, Sam's father, had been a track hand when he was a boy. Like so many thousands of Chinese he had walked America from east to west, one railroad tie at a time all the way to Los Angeles. But whereas the railroad had dumped most of the Chinese at the ocean's edge and left them there, Li Hum had another idea, of making a place, of fitting in. He had looked at how the desert people along the new railroad lived on everything canned and dried, salted, smoked, pickled, anything in a box or barrel that could come from where the food was because nothing would grow in this coals and ashes of a desert. So Li came back and planted in the foothills of Dos Cabezas, and then higher, carting the water up in barrels every morning before dawn to where the soil was richer and the nights gentle. Two hours up the trails, anywhere there were fat flowers or succulents, anywhere roots had fingered the soil or worms dug, there he planted. Lettuce, onions, carrots, beans, tomatoes, peas, peppers. Sometimes watermelons or cantaloupe, in scattered patches over half a mountain where the soil sat between the boulders. He went there earlier than anyone else would have gone for a few fresh vegetables, dug harder, flung more rocks down the ravines, and killed more rattlesnakes, scorpions, centipedes, rhinoceros beetles, black widows, Gila monsters, than anyone else would have killed for a few fresh vegetables. But what they would do for a few fresh vegetables was to pay — so little at first that they hid their mouths behind their hands, thinking they were cheating the poor Chinee. But Li knew what he wanted: steady customers, and only enough to get by and enough to put by; and after two years of selling from his cart at dusk, calling through the town like a rag and bone man, there was enough saved to go to Los Angeles Chinatown and bring home a wife who knew how to live that way for good enough reason.

Now the people would not go without fresh things, and bragged in Safford and Benson that they had a fruiting desert; they paid fair prices now. Li and his wife, Su, lived in an adobe hut with a sheet metal roof two years more, burning greasewood and tumbleweed, but one by one there was a shed for Su Hum to sell from, a real wood house, then a boy, a brickfront store, a daughter; and now Li Hum did food business with the railroad, and hired mestizos to climb the mountain before dawn and water his beans.

Of all this, Sam was proud. Still, to be the first Chinese in that school was a greater trial than his father could understand. His father said he was American, American; but at school they were not impressed by legalities. There had always been a scapegoat, always been someone littler or afraid. If there wasn't somebody with crooked teeth there was somebody with overalls handed down and patched, too small. Anything would do because somebody had to be It; if they hadn't learned their alphabets and their multiplication tables they had learned by the time Sam came to school how to torture the first Chinese. They started just with names: Slant, Slit, Squint, Snake Eyes, Chinkie, Chinee Hiney, Yellowbelly, Bilious Boy, Cooliekins, Yaller. Everywhere he passed, as soon as he had passed someone would put their thumbs at the corners of their eyes and pull back to make slit-eyes and the rest would snort, not real laughing but like a cough pushed out their noses, the girls just as much as the boys. One spring he hid every afternoon in the leanto between the livery stable and the station hotel until huge Mr. Vandercamp, roaring, caught him.

There were bargains: If he stole a cantaloupe they would not beat him, if he got three hairs off a Mexican girl or out of a bronco tail they would not tie him to the tracks. They stuffed his mouth with salt tamarack while they took off his pants and switched him with tamarack switches; they put his pants high in the tree because they knew he was afraid to climb but more afraid to go home without his pants. They threatened him with Sheriff Robinson, who would lock him up and serve him *habeas corpses*.

They would tire of him. He never knew when they would tire of him and when they would take him up again. He would go free a whole spring, and on the first day of summer someone would knock him down and stuff a caterpillar in his mouth and then for the whole of summer it would be funny to make him eat caterpillars and watch him retch them up with his father's peas. All through sixth and seventh grades they ignored him while they turned their attention to jeering at girls, to swinging at baseballs in the bare yard; and then in the eighth grade they found him again, to make him do what they wanted to do and dared not. He was still the smallest for his age, still had the bird bones and the thinnest flesh on them. His voice had broken and still it was high.

There was almost no place to hide in that town — no cleft in the earth, and the vegetation scattered so sparse you could count the branches to an acre. There was one boxcar on a siding, abandoned when an axle cracked, and lost track of in somebody's ledgers at the SP offices in Tucson. There was the brace of tamarack and cotton-wood that had grown up around a ditch between the track and the Mexican village. There was a prospector's shack in the foothills halfway up to Li Hum's garden, full of pans rusted half through and wood so rotten you could squeeze it in a fist and watch the termites run over your knuckles.

That was where they took him, afraid themselves because his father was above them on the mountain and might come down. Buck Hoskins and Aldo Nene brought the girl, a scratching moun-tain cat for only eight years old, never stopped scratching even while she sniveled till she saw the rest of them in the shack, seven in all, not counting Sam, who was held by four of them, one each to his ankle and wrists, though God knows two would have been enough. Sam never looked at her. They held her and him and then they decided to tie Sam, an ankle each to the andirons and his wrists to the rings over the fireplace. There were two whole bird nests and the skeleton of a bird in that fireplace. He didn't look the girl in the face. They pushed her forward and pulled up her skirt, hooted when they saw that she wore nothing underneath. Buck Hoskins put his huge hands around her hipbones, and Lloyd Wheeler took Sam's little dead cock in his hand and held it out till it touched the girl in the bald crack between her legs. They hooted some more, jostled the girl up and down, Lloyd jimmied Sam's cock in his hand, and that was all. There was nothing to it, not juice enough to be worth the trouble or the fake laughter.

They didn't know what else to do or how to do anything. They let the girl go. She cried and ran, but before she was down the hill she was screaming at them, Mexican words hot as chili.

Sam they did not let go. They said they would leave him tied there and he could call to his daddy if he chose. By this time the

Hums had a house, so they said they would burn down the house if he told his pa. And they left, but Sam did not really think they would leave him tied till his father came down. He had been in the school eight years by now, his sister had been there five, and she was not teased or hurt as he had been. The Hums went to the Methodist church. He did not think they would dare.

It was Lloyd who came back, crying, although he had not been any kinder to Sam than the others. Lloyd was breathing hard, and he began to untie the ropes, clumsy and slow, crying, saying he was sorry, sorry. He put his face against Sam's neck from behind, and when Sam shied away he touched Sam's shoulder with his fingers and cried. *Sam. Sam. I'm sorry. Please. I'm sorry.* It took him so long to undo the ropes, he was so clumsy, he cried so long, he said "sorry" so many times it was a drowsy litany, so when Sam finally was free he felt too spent and tired and full of tears himself to go anywhere. He just buckled down onto the hearth and let Lloyd circle his shoulders with his arms: *Sorry Sam Sam sorry sorry Sam.*

They heard Li Hum pass down the mountain with the mule and cart.

Sam lay in the hollow of his rock like a mussel in its shell, and was so still with memory that the sounds and smells of the desert came singly, powerful and sweet. Mesquite. Cicada. Cricket. The way Lloyd used to clack his tongue when he was figuring something out. Nights on the long way down from home that they used to huddle under the saddle blankets. Coyote cry. The smell of cholla burning.

The smell of cholla burning.

That was the first thing that roused him, even though as soon as he knew what it was, he heard the loose-lipped blowing of a horse and knew it wasn't the first time he'd heard it. And a dead metal sound that would be pots or mugs. Even, then, voices, low but not whispering. Voices with the habit of keeping low.

Sam sat up reluctantly. The idea that he might yet do something to save himself was not quite pleasant. His muscles were full of tiny tremors. His stomach hurt with a metallic hurt. He could scarcely swallow, and when he managed it he almost swallowed his little stone. He listened again, judged that the voices, the clanking, were about a quarter mile away. A coyote, farther, howled again. It would be easier to lie down.

He stood, though, his knees vibrating like plucked guitar strings. Stealthy, shaky, hand-over-hand from boulder to boulder — he saw the smoke before he saw the fire. He took the pebble out of his mouth, bent, and set it carefully on the ground. They had nestled themselves cleverly in a twist of the rock such that you had to enter and double back to come upon them. He waited in the corridor to judge how many. He figured four.

"*Andele, Juan, ¿es tu turno?*"

"*Tu madre, Io hice porti dos veces la semana pasada.*"

"*Si que lo hizo.*"

"*Y aun cuando estás la guardia, tus pedos no noj dejan dormir.*"

"*Ustedes todos son unos cretinos.*"

Coffee, bacon fat. The smell of them made him stagger and lean his whole weight on his palms against the rock. It was not as if he had any better odds. He said "Peace" and put his hands up as he stepped into the firelight. All the same, there were four guns on him before he had focused enough to count. He'd been right: four.

"Peace," he said again. There were three old ones, one of them barely bigger than a midget, and the young one was fat. One of the old ones had on a uniform jacket much too big for him and hanging open on his slack chest. The young one spun a string of their language at him. It ended in a question mark, so Sam put his palms up in the universal gesture of incomprehension.

The little one prodded upward into the air with his rifle. "*¿Quién coño eres? Te corto los huevos si vienes acompañado.*"

The young fat one, wearing over his blouse a cowhide vest that was hung with animal teeth and cracked around the armholes from dry sweat, put a barrel at Sam's belly and forced him back against the rock.

"*So chingado, ¿quien eres tú?*"

The little one grimaced as if he were smelling fun, and Sam took a breath all the way to the sinking pit of his stomach. He figured fifty-fifty was as good as he was going to get. He turned his shrug into a heaven-reaching gesture of innocence.

"*¿Viva Villa?*" he guessed.

6

THE ADVENT OF THE Poindexters stirred scant interest on the Mexican side of town, where there were more urgent arrivals and departures to be dealt with. None of the Mexican inhabitants supposed they would be needing a bank anytime soon, nor would it have made much sense to them that a bank was a sign of prosperity and expansion.

From their point of view, times were bitter. The earliest of them had migrated from the border in the 1890s, when the railroad first staked its claim to this piece of the flatlands. Chinese laborers had laid the track and followed it west, but Mexicans had built the station, the pump house, the hotel, and eventually the town. Some had brought cattle or construction skills with them, others had learned how to dig foundations and hoist roofs, how to get sweet water out of the ground or sewage into it. At just about the time the building slowed, Frank Wheeler had opened his quarry and taken on a couple of dozen men and boys. But when the quarry went broke, those men were thrown back on the paltry wages of their women, which devastated morale. There was more malaise than fury; desertions were more frequent than fights.

A few among the men still had steady jobs, chiefly those who maintained the station and the pump house. It was the purpose of this pump to draw water from the aquifer for as many miles around and to as great a depth as necessary, to hoist it skyward through a six-inch pipe, and to dump it into the engines of the day's dozen trains, which would then convert it into steam, to be dispersed into the air for a hundred miles east and west. Neither the Mexicans who performed this feat nor the moguls of the railroad who paid their subsistence wages made any connection between their labors and the standard prison exercise of moving rocks from one pile to another — even though one function of the railroad had been, for a time, to shift blocks of marble from Bowie to Los Angeles.

Apart from that, most labor was either part-time, such as housework or the tending of Li Hum's garden; or occasional, such as construction, cattle branding, the maintenance of lawns, and laundry. Nearly all of the Bowie Mexicans had learned English. The reason for this, accepted on both sides of the track, was that Spanish was a "difficult" language and therefore presumably too demanding a task for those busy running business and the church. A few of the ranchers had picked up Spanish out of impatience with the pidgin of their cowhands, but most people assumed or asserted that it was the employees' business to speak their employers' tongue. The laws on schooling for Mexican children were in flux, and if the Mexicans had insisted on a school, then the Bowie fathers might have had to provide one. But neither side had any taste for such an encounter, and the Mexicans did not ask.

One consequence of this piecemeal state of affairs was that there was no such thing as a schoolday or a workweek around which to order time, and Mexican life was structured on the things that could be counted on: birth, sickness, death, saints' days, and the Christian calendar.

On the afternoon of the Poindexters' arrival, for example, the town was occupied with the grief of Carmen Acosta, the adobemaker's wife, who had given birth to a stillborn girl. There was widespread sadness mixed with foreboding — it was the second stillborn in a year — but there was also a dispute between the priest and the midwife, he having pronounced the baby alive in order to perform extreme unction, she insisting the child was dead two days in the womb, to forestall the suspicion of some error in the birthing. The midwife went for confirmation to Soledad Iglesias, who had laid a hand on the still womb the day before, but Soledad was nowhere to be found, and her witness was tainted by the rumor that she had sneaked off with her Apache lover. In the end Father

Vicente absolved the child, and Gabrielo Acosta, the mild-mannered adobemaker, absolved the midwife; and a thin band of mourners laid the newborn corpse in the ground at just about the time the Poindexters' Pierce-Arrow was being unloaded in the station yard.

Apart from a few truant boys who went to watch the crowd, and a few youths hoping to be hired for the unloading, there was only one Mexican at the station, and only one for whom the arrival held any personal interest. Maria Magdalene Iglesias was fourteen, daughter of Soledad Iglesias and a husband long ago departed but who had claimed to be, or whom Soledad had claimed to be, the direct descendant of a *conquistador*. One Manuela de Reyes — now also departed but an early inhabitant of the town — had with kind intention embroidered this story when Maria was of an age appropriate for fairy tales. Manuela meant only to give the girl a sense of the past, and perhaps (because she had herself come from a better life) indulge her own nostalgia. But from toddlerhood Maria had fiercely absorbed the myth. It made her known world drab to her, filled her with confused impatience for her mother and two half-siblings, and convinced her that this scratch-and-starve desert was not her rightful place.

Dreams were common, Spanish lineage was generally valued among the Bowie Mexicans, and Maria's baby contempt had been thought cute. By the time she was fourteen it had grown irritating — with the result that the girl was aloof, disliked, and admired in equal portion.

Maria cleaned three afternoons a week for the younger Wheelers, but she did not intend to do so for long. She had been waiting for a sign of her deliverance, and on the day of the Poindexters' coming she had prayed for forgiveness for having failed to recognize the unfolding of God's plan.

For she had learned that the banker and his wife were to be temporarily housed in the old Semple bungalow on Jefferson Street, which she had cleaned after the old lady died and which had never been entered by any Mexican except herself.

Last spring it had seemed to her a curse, a bad God-joke — when she had never so much as traveled the same side of the street as the shriveled old woman if she could help it — that she had to clean around that corpse. It had come about because the old lady's people had all moved away, and nobody had made a plan for her dying. The gringos went along day to day and were always surprised when somebody died, when snakes bit or horses slipped on the shale and flung their riders into the creekbed. Mexicans expected such things, and there were always plenty of people to take care of the living. But the gringos threw up their hands. They never knew anything to do except look to Walter Wheeler to sort them out. Well, he had sorted them out — telegraphed to the Tucson nephews and gotten the body laid out in the dining room in a pine box on top of a cotton cloth. And it should have been Octavia or Inocencia to clean, but Señor Wheeler said no, let them stay at his house and get it ready for the Semple families, and let young Maria Magdalene do the cleaning, and if she did it well, why, then, his own daughter-in-law was looking for a part-time, and it would make a first job for her, Maria.

So she went into the house alone with nobody but the stretched-out corpse that smelled stink-sweet under the powder and dried sachet petals heaped on it. In Mexican Town where people lived six to a room you could not die and nobody know it, so no corpse ever got as sickly sweet as that old husk of dry white lady. And all the same, the smell of her was nothing to the smells she left behind in the kitchen cupboards and under the sink — pots fuzzy with mold, petrified bits of soup or stew, pancakes hardened green and forgotten, milk curdled solid. Maria had scraped and scoured; some of the pots she hid and carried away to the dump, but she dared not do that with all that were crusted and scummed, so she worked sweating the whole day with a kerchief tied over her mouth. She remembered the spiders and rhinoceros beetles, the dry must.

And what for? So Señor Wheeler would say "Hmm! Hmm!" and pat her on the head if she hadn't pretended to have an itch on her ankle and bent down. So she could go three afternoons a week to young Señora Wheeler, who needed full-time help — a baby, two lazy niños, all that wash, old floorboards to scrub — but couldn't afford it, so Maria got to do a full-time job in three afternoons a week.

But now she saw her error. Sometimes God makes a thing look

one way when it is another. For now the *gente sancta* lady would live in the Semple house, and because Maria had cleaned it before, she would be asked again. It would be her right. She would become a *criada* to a rich lady and begin the breaking away from this place that was all she thought about.

On the day of the train she stood in the dirt between the station platform and the track while the engine thundered by her, while the banker's wife lowered herself on a black man's palm. The *gente sancta* was an immediate disappointment, which first depressed Maria and then made her angry at herself. What did she expect, a lasso dancer? The woman was handsome enough, had a slender waist and feathers in her hat. Father Vicente always upbraided Maria for not being satisfied with the lot that God had dealt her. And he must be right. She must be patient now, waiting, staring hard across the tracks, willing the lady to take notice of her while the men hauled down a bandaged piano, a sleek automobile, chairs with skinny legs and arched backs, the trunks and boxes that would help carry her, Maria Magdalene Iglesias, to California when God's will was done.

The house on Jefferson Street was square, bare stucco — the drab, civilized sister of adobe. Like all the houses of Bowie, its shape came out of the corn belt by way of failed imagination. The towns-folk pointed out it was for sale if the Poindexters wished to buy it, though no doubt they would find it too small and plain for their tastes. Eleanor remained noncommittal on this point, which they accurately took to mean that it was too small and plain. The first day the neighbors offered food, information, and their elder children for lifting and shifting; then they tactfully retreated to let the new arrivals settle in.

On Friday, Eleanor woke disoriented in a hard half light. She edged away from Laurel's damp warmth, twisting in her gown. The spillage of garments from her steamer trunk seemed vaguely threatening. She closed her eyes and hung adrift in the atmosphere of a dream that eluded her as she pursued it. Two women on a hillside meadow, or perhaps it was the same woman in two different modes. No, two women — now she caught it — the first younger than the second, though each was dressed in the same handsome homespun, the dark hair and the gray pulled simply back on the nape of the neck. The women were shot as if by firing squad, though there was no evidence of this, no soldiers, no blood, only the knowledge that they had been shot. It was rather beautiful. They dropped on the spot like dancers trained to it, and the young woman gave up and died very peacefully with her hair falling over the grass. The older woman fell back over one bent leg and lay face up in the buttercups. Her features got older and more wizened, but she wouldn't die. Her expression said: I'm hanging on; I will hang on.

What did it mean? Eleanor often played her own oneiromancer, though her interpretations derived vaguely from Joseph of the coat of many colors; news of Freud had not reached her Baltimore milieu. Now she lay torpidly wondering what this dream predicted or portended, cocooned in its atmosphere at once tragic and gentle, misty and determined. Laurel turned toward her in his sleep, and she held her breath as consciousness of her life came back to her.

Her life, her life. Now she opened her eyes on the rubble of her life — her undergarments spilled, her bodices crushed, her shoes squashed, furniture nicked, her precious knickknacks jostled — the rummage of her life, which she was expected to pull out calmly and rearrange in the cramped corners of this dun-colored house of a dead woman.

"My life," she whispered, but Laurel stirred and lifted his hip against hers so she lay rigid, allowing only her mind to twist. The gray kitten stretched and yawned in an open drawer of the steamer trunk. Eleanor envied its animal insensibility. A cat could leave a mother, trade one set of rooms for another, never again see the familiar streets . . . oh, she wanted to go *home* — to wake in that other bed, in that softer light, to rise and step out onto the tree-lined avenue. . . .

The idea of Mass came to her so refreshingly that it was as if it were borne on a literal breeze. To kneel on a cold stone floor, to let go the tiny twistings of her mind into the resonance of an overarching nave, to feel in that reverberation the power of Almighty God, who both cared for her and was amused by her minute agonies. Oh, to feel small herself would be such relief, rather than to feel surrounded by the small, the paltry, the petty second-rate.

She moved from Laurel by inches, but he only stirred and seemed to sink deeper into sleep with a snaggling sound in his throat. She edged from the bed, took corset, stockings, camisole, blouse, skirt, shoes, and hat from their various piles, and dressed in the cramped larder, the only space concealed from the uncurtained windows.

But when she emerged into the street there was no one about, and she realized that in spite of the light it was very early. The mountains to the east were like teeth in the bruised mouth of morning. The Pierce-Arrow sat in the balding yard, but to start it might wake Laurel. She had no sense of the town except for the direction of the station, and she headed that way, her reticule dangling from one wrist. Rounding Jefferson Street to Main, she spotted a spire lifted above the squat houses, but knew it instantly for Protestant by its square clapboard construction, a dunce cap of wood shakes over a brass bell. She headed on up Main Street hoping to find someone awake — and found someone: a small, square Oriental woman sweeping the boardwalk in front of the grocery store.

"Good morning," Eleanor said. "I'm Eleanor Poindexter — wife —"

"*Good* morn*ing*," the woman said musically, with a little bounce of a bow but without breaking the rhythm of her sweeping.

"— of the new bank manager. . . ."

"So," the woman confirmed.

"I wonder if you might tell me where I would find the Catholic church."

Now the woman stopped and turned a gaze on her. She nodded again, that deferential dip of the head echoing all down her body, but her hooded eyes frankly appraising. She stared at Eleanor as if the silence were quite comfortable, which it was not.

"The Catholic church?" Eleanor wondered if perhaps the woman did not speak any more English than "good morning," which would mean she had gotten herself into a *situation* the first time she ventured out in town alone. But she held herself dignified, and eventually the woman transferred the broom from the north hand to the south, and with a precisely pointed index finger indicated the station hotel.

"In the hotel? The church is in the hotel?" Stranger things than that had happened, of course. A little chapel off the dining room, perhaps, for, after all, this was a small town.

"Across." The woman twirled her hand as if shooing Eleanor to the far side of the tracks, where there was nothing but the pump house. "You cross over."

Whatever did she mean? Eleanor thanked the woman, returning a smile that made the muscles of her jaw hurt, and continued on, uncertain whether she had misunderstood or been misunderstood. Her head ached. She had worn a simple hat, a medium-brimmed straw with a cluster of silk peonies and four pheasant feathers, but although it shaded her face it seemed both heavy and tight. Above the binding ribbon her hair trapped heat.

The station platform was empty except for a cowboy with an adenoidal expression, hunkered down against the doorpost. Eleanor nodded in his direction and lifted her skirt into the station. No one. The wire window of the ticket seller gave onto an empty cubicle. Her voice brought forth only an echo. She returned to the platform and tried the door of the hotel restaurant, which was locked. She had lifted her hand to the bell when the cowboy appeared at her elbow.

"He'p yenh, ma'am?"

He leaned over her open-mouthed. He was dressed in an ancient cowhide vest and threadbare gingham shirt, was slightly stooped, and smelled of stale sweat and staler whiskey. She felt suddenly vulnerable and isolated, as well as foolish; but as if this combination of disadvantages were the very one to tap her resources, she drew herself up and said, a little louder than necessary, "Why, yes, thank you. I'm looking for the Catholic church."

"Yenh, yenh," the cowboy nodded above her, too close, a pool of spittle gathering inside his lower lip. Eleanor stepped back. Like the Oriental woman, he gestured (but hugely) toward the pump house, and leaping from the platform, urged her to follow him, grinning encouragement. Some kind of speech defect pushed his voice through his nose: "Thinth way, thinth way!"

She was afraid, but she was more afraid of seeming to be afraid. She descended the steps, picking her way gingerly after him over the rails and between the ties. They crossed half a dozen tracks —

he whooping into the quiet, "Come thinth way!" — then a dusty waste some thirty feet wide. The pump house belched, spewing steam upward. He balanced himself jubilantly on the last rail of the siding, foot-over-foot, heading east; and she clambered awkwardly after, left foot on the tie, right foot on the ground, the heat beginning to trickle from her crown to her ears. "Now thinth way!"

He headed around the east end of the pump house, and when she rounded the corner she found him in the attitude of Balboa or Cortés, one foot on a concrete pipe where packed earth made a bridge over a shallow ditch, one hand outflung toward the north where the land dipped, weed-ragged and rutted with erosion, onto a scatter of adobe shacks arranged in an uneven semblance of a street; and at the end of it, perhaps a hundred yards down the slope, an outsized hut with a mud mound above its double doors, a rude wood cross on top of that, and hanging from a pole poked into the mound, a bell that might serve a cow rather larger than the average cow.

"Theh!" he said. "The Canthulink."

The moment seemed hard and clear, as if caught in a photograph, as if she might have the leisure to study its significance. The cowboy in his idiot innocence still flung wide a hand to present her with: a ditch trickling red water, some two dozen houses made of mud, a few chickens and cadaverous dogs, a hundred yards of rutted dust leading to the one repository of true religion in the brown and blue waste of the world. Between the "church" and the horizon, nothing. Between herself and the church, a woman's voice shrieking in Spanish, and a baby crying. This part of town, at least, was awake at dawn.

"Thank you," said Eleanor, and hesitating only a second, passed over the packed-earth bridge on the water pipe to descend among the shanties. Oh, she was known in Baltimore for her spunk!

The cowboy nodded enthusiastically, lower lip pendulous. She curtsied a little as she passed. She walked between the wheel ruts, barely turning her head toward the squalid doorways but seeing with unwanted clarity all the same. The brown cubes were patched with corrugated metal, cratewood, rags. From one of them the woman's voice kept up its scolding. A rooster with bald thighs scratched at the threshold of the first hut she passed. Across the street a male child, not yet steady on its feet and wearing nothing but an undershirt with a hole at center belly, hung on the cloth door and regarded her without interest. It all seemed remotely familiar — as if, had she been asked what one could expect to find on the central street of a desert shantytown, she might with a little effort have come up with a molting rooster and a baby in a ragged undershirt. To her left, a brown goat tethered to a rusted wagon wheel strained toward her through its own dung.

Still, she went forward, and several thoughts occupied her mind en route. She had time to wonder what sort of sensibility would clothe a child in an undershirt, in this heat, and yet leave its sex exposed. She made room for a speculation on God as a foreigner — an idea she had six summers ago, in the country of origin of the sacraments. Sometimes in Florence, Padua, San Gimignano, her touring party had contained the only English-speaking persons in the congregation, and though it had been odd to share a theology with people with whom one did not share a language, nevertheless it seemed quite acceptable to think of oneself as an Anglo convert to the religion of the great painters of the Renaissance. It was utterly other in a Mexican shacktown, where a — was it really? — yes, a pig, might dart through the dry puddlebeds across one's path.

Further: In the doorway of one hut stood a dark-skinned man naked above a loincloth. His long black hair was bound at the temple with a band of braided horsehair. He was scratching a scar that ran along his collarbone, his muscled chest and thighs gleaming hairless. She saw all this before she had the presence of mind to avert her eyes, and when she did so, the Indian laughed. The voice of the shrieking woman was briefly stilled, then started up again.

Eleanor trained her eyes on the dust-filmed toes of her shoes. As she reached the "churchyard" — a half-moon of jagged stones — two girls of nine or ten rounded the corner and stopped, their arms entwined, their skirts swinging. One of them dipped her dark face close to the ear of the other. The second giggled, her fingers twisting the braid that hung over her shoulder. They turned and scampered between two shacks. The perspiration wound behind Eleanor's ears now, into the neckband of her blouse.

But she had come this far, hadn't she? She lifted the latch, pulled — then when the door resisted, pushed — and entered to a sudden sensation of darkness, cool, and quiet — which was so exactly what she had wanted that her mind skipped and doubled back on itself looking for what was wrong.

The place was still smaller than it looked from outside — the adobe walls must be very thick — with plain benches ranged toward an equally rough altar. There were a cross and a clutter of other objects on it, rather obscured than illuminated by a bank of guttering candles and a hole in the wall behind. From this, a fan of moted rays raked the ceiling and lit the prints of the palms that had stroked the mud into place. There was a splintery confessional to her right. There was the hunched back of a black-clad woman on one bench; no other soul. There was a smell of oleander and cooking grease, and something animal and ripe. Eleanor genuflected, crossed herself, and set her mouth.

She closed her eyes and conjured up the form of a prayer. Our Father. Hail Mary, full of grace. At the center of her mind was a goat, a scar, a mocking girl. *Introibo ad altare Dei.* I will go in unto the altar of God. Unto God, who giveth joy to my youth.

She went forward, fumbling in her reticule. She dropped a nickel in a slotted cigar box, took a candle from the pile, and impaled it on the candelabra, which was a length of two-by-four stuck through with eight-penny nails. Dear God. She crossed to the altar and closed her hands in the attitude of prayer, raising her eyes to the cross.

The Virgin before the cross was a cheap bisque doll, blond, berouged, and ruffled. Her satin skirt was festooned with metal charms in the shapes of pigs, arms, legs; what looked like a liver and a pair of lungs. Once again it was as bizarre as you might have expected if you'd had any expectation at all. But at the Virgin's hem — she made it out in the sputtering half-light — lay a baking sheet, and arranged on it in an attitude of casual precision, paws crossed for sleep or prayer, was the skinned carcass of a very large jackrabbit whose head hung over the edge of the altar and from whose staring eye the blood dripped onto the dirt floor at her feet.

She did not, after all, kneel. She turned and, gathering her skirts against her legs, briskly retraced her steps, out into the blast of sunlight, up the rutted road between the houses, over the earth bridge on the water pipe. The cowboy still stood by the pump house, and at her appearance he backed against the doorway, as if to corral the workmen staring there. He followed her through the gap between the buildings. At the tracks she stopped to catch her breath, to thank him for his time. But what came out of her mouth was, "I can't."

The idiot trained her with a sympathetic stare. Eleanor turned and hurried across the rails and past the station, turned down some other street than the way she had come — there were people up now — slowed again because she had a stitch in her side under her corset stays, but only to a striding walk that would discourage any greeting. At the far edge of town she leaned against a fence and gulped for air.

She tore off her hat and fanned her face. She stared into a cactus with two upraised arms. Its skin was accordion-pleated, grayish-green, with rows of sharp spines at the outer fold of each pleat. It was gashed and bird-pecked, storm-pelted; a headless human, arms raised pleadingly to God.

The sun hurt her eyes to the brain. Yet this was nothing to the heat of hell, eternal and internal, physical but not consuming. It was not a question of her own distaste! The Church is not the Church where they make blood sacrifices to the Virgin, surely? She needed an adviser to let her know what she should do in the absence of an adviser.

She closed her eyes and heard nothing but her own breathing. But when she opened them again she was startled to be facing a tall man and a horse, the horse's mottled nose hanging over the man's shoulder, and both of them looking at her. The man snapped his reins nervously between his fists. He was squarely handsome, but his head was hunched forward deferentially.

"Mrs. Poindexter, are you all right?"

It angered her that he knew her name. Everybody, of course, would know her name. Anger pushed a laugh out of her throat.

"Goodness, yes! I suppose I just walked too fast in this heat."

He scratched his jaw with the fingers that held the reins. "I'm sorry if I startled you. Frank Wheeler, ma'am. I saw you was breathing hard and I thought I ought to check."

She'd spotted this sort of yokel beauty before now. A hat-in-hand attitude inborn. You bring such a man indoors, put him in a good suit, and see a good suit spoiled.

"That was very kind of you; no, I'm fine. I just must let myself adjust to the heat."

"It's very dry heat," he observed.

She agreed with him and angrily walked on. Even with the rising sun behind her she felt the skin of her face burning and coarsening, but she could not for the moment think of that. She breathed as best she could, she sweated, she walked. When she got to the house she let herself in stealthily, as if the place were not her own, which it was not. She pumped water in the kitchen, held a wet cloth against her face and neck, then slowly, piece by piece, removed her clothes and laved her skin with cooling water. Only now the clock struck seven.

"Good morning, sweet! You are up early."

She had stuffed her damp clothes in an emptied box and put on a fresh peignoir by the time Laurel appeared from the bedroom, dressed for his day at the bank, chipper, seeming cool for all his vest and tie.

"Well," she said, "I *woke* early, so I took a little walk." She accepted his embrace, offered her cheek, swiveled artfully away to hold the kettle under the pump.

7

"WELL, I CAME OUT HERE in sixty-three, had seventeen dollars in the toe of my shoe, one set of long johns, and a pair of pretty good arms from loading freight in Elyria. Hired on like a coolie, laying track. Four months' time I was put over a hunderd and twenty men, and every one of 'em just as soon slit my throat as not, so I learned to sleep pretty well five or six winks at a time."

Wally Wheeler sprawled in the oak swivel chair across the desk, slightly more at ease in it than Laurel was in his own.

"I saw there was two ways to make money: one was shipping beef and the other was raising beef to ship. I wasn't famous for my modesty, I allow you, and I didn't doubt but I could work my way up in the railroad."

Walter Nathan Wheeler was the local grandee. Laurel had learned by now that the sources of his prestige could be expressed numerically — he had the most cattle, the most acres, rails to his fence, chimneys to his roof, and so on — but that his real force was qualitative. He was praised for grace *and* guts. He had his shirts custom-tailored in Tucson, and they were only just to the elegant side of ostentation; and he had the only Model T in town, which his cowboys waxed more regularly than they bathed. But when there was a hoof-and-mouth plague in '96, Wally had shot his cattle with his own hand; when Manuela Reyes had stabbed her man, he'd solved a legal dilemma by taking her personally across the border to her family in Agua Prieta; when Miles Shaftoe had defied the new ordinance and opened the saloon on Sunday morning, it was Wally who had excused himself from the choir and gone in among the drunks without any protection but his tongue. Got the bar closed, too. The *Tucson Daily Star* had written him up for their "Citizens Series," and the way they put it was that if anybody was going to tame the West, they'd "give the whip and chair to Walter Wheeler."

The same series had just done a profile of Laurel and had sent a reporter from Tucson for the purpose. Laurel was glad for the publicity for the bank, though as he'd said to Eleanor, the reporter had seemed to be interviewing himself. A great shaggy dog of a man — he'd seemed to want Laurel to say that banking (progress itself?) was inimical to the spiritual values of the land. Laurel thought he knew a thing or two about spiritual values, but he wasn't anxious to be lectured on the subject by a self-styled intellectual from the *Daily Star*.

"I had a friend Zach Cobb tried to get me into go'ment business — he's a big Customs man in Texas now — but 'f I had my druthers I'd always take the outdoor life, so every day's track I laid, I'd look around where we'd got to and think it through: Would this be a good place? Would this be? How 'bout here?"

Laurel shifted, trying to ease the tight place in his shoulders. Not that everything wasn't in order. The gold paint on the glass was outlined in black: *Teller. Manager.* The double-swinging half-door had been made to swing. On the other side of the partition a twenty-two-year-old junior teller down from Tucson — just barely trained and anxious, which was exactly what you'd want under the circumstances — was stamping *Mountain National Bank, Bowie, Arizona,* on every page of twenty-five receipt books, waiting for the next customer.

"There was still plenty of people wandering around looking for gold then, and I got tired of the letters from home razzing me about that, but I always knew the real gold was water. Just water enough, 'sall you need; you don't want overmuch, or you'll get people squabbling about what should you do with the land and building more city than you've got any use for. Look down Maricopa County, it's all lettuce and melons and the cattle folk are darn near chased out. But this land, it's good for twenty acres to a head and it ain't good for any consarned thing else, and the gov'ment'll lease it, so there's no contention. And still you're near enough mountains that Li Hum can keep fresh victuals growing three quarters of the year."

They had been open four hours and they had seventeen deposits, of which the first had really arrived yesterday by draft from Tucson: forty-two thousand, eight hundred sixty-eight dollars and forty-nine cents to the account of Walter Wheeler. The next-biggest depositor was the schoolteacher, Alma Timkin, with nineteen hundred dollars. Laurel was thrilled with the Wheeler money, but the imbalance made him nervous. He was anxious to see the rest of the ranchers follow suit. He was anxious not to be obsequious now and not to be seen as obsequious. He crossed one knee with a black silk ankle. Facing him, Wheeler held the same position with a tooled brown boot, and laced his fingers to make a sling for the back of his head.

"Now, Uncle Billy Sours, that was somebody did make good in the mines, found himself a claim somewhere up around the Wonderland of Rocks, but that rascal knew enough how to cover his tracks; nobody else found it till he bled it dry. There's a Christian moral there, b'cause he made good and never had any good of it. Hated ever' living soul except an old split-palate cowhand named O'Joe, and him he hated one day and fed the next. Five thousand dollars, Uncle Billy ended up with by the time his claim ran dry, and never did a thing with it except roll it up in a coffee can and hide it in his oven."

Laurel laughed. There were plenty of people in Baltimore who kept their money in the mattress or the teapot.

"See, he had a sister thought she was due a share of it, and so ever' six months she'd come clean 'im up and see if she couldn't find out where it was hid. Well, this one time she found it, tucked back in the oven under the plate that held the coals. So she fired it up real hot, thinking he'd have to go in there after it, but he hated that woman enough, he never said a word till the bills were burnt to a crisp. Is that ornery? But I tell you, he came to me and asked would I write him a letter to the U.S. Mint, which I did, and the Treasury accepted those burnt bills and sent him back every five dadblasted thousand of 'em."

Laurel laughed again, and Wheeler slapped the heel of his boot. "Wasn't a bad thing, that. Gave a lot of folks confidence in the United States government."

Laurel stretched his legs under the kneehole and leaned forward across his glow of new beeswaxed oak. Laurel liked Wheeler, liked the pithy mix of vulgarity and prestige, hoped to snag him as a conquest and a character for Eleanor's soirees. "Well, in any case," he said, "your trust is important to us. I appreciate it."

Wheeler cocked his head as he grinned, a surprisingly sweet expression for a hewn face. Laurel saw that his reputation was still a precious thing to Wheeler.

"We need this bank, Mr. Poindexter. I c'n remember the time, if you wanted a horse shoed you'd do all right, but if you needed soles to your own shoes you'd better know cobbling. Now we're growing, got our own glazier, a milliner, the Hinman can seat near a hundred for dinner if need be. It was time for us to have a bank of our own."

"It's true," Laurel conceded modestly. "A bank gives a town a certain weight in the world."

Now Wheeler unhooked his boot, leaning forward with some intensity. "You'll find a lot of faith in this country, Mr. Poindexter, that we're about to embark on an era of" — he cleared his throat — "civilization. I'll tell you, ten years ago it was all we could do to get laws passed against spitting in public places. We had rabble-rousers here, troublemakers, you'd'a thought we were the other side of the border."

"Surely the Mexican situation is a good deal different."

"No argument there!"

"But I mean, the central government in Mexico City is so corrupt — surely the people have a right to a little 'rabble-rousing.'"

"Oh, one thing's just as bad as another with that bunch. President's a drunk, the church is full of thieves, and their great Pancho Villa is a two-bit thug. No, the thing for us to remember is — so to speak — sticking to our own *values*."

Laurel caught the note now. He was reluctant to give up on what he'd hoped was a fundamental sympathy. On the other hand — there was a milky shadow beyond the glass, voices of the teller and a new depositor — the important thing was not to appear obsequious. "Still, we have to respect what they're trying to do in Mexico, too, I think. I'm sure we got a very partial view of it from the newspapers back East. . . ."

"Partial! Partial to a pack of ruffians, yes. Your Honor the Bandit and His Excellency the Rustler. Oh, don't expect too much of the Mexican character, sir. He'll do fine for a hand if he's got a white man to set him an example. Beyond that . . ."

Laurel was surprised by the depth of his own disappointment. "Ah," was all he said, deferring to age, experience, and just under fifty thousand dollars in his vault. Wheeler lowered his boot and hitched the heavy chair forward.

"And speaking of Mexicans, Mr. Poindexter . . ."

"Yes?"

"There was something I wanted to mention to you about that. I understand Mrs. Poindexter is a Catholic."

"She is."

"Fine, excellent. But you see, the ladies are anxious for her to be comfortable, and they asked me to mention to you — she might not have realized that the Catholic church is pretty much Mexican. Well, entirely Mexican. Whereas, you see, the ladies feel that Mrs. Poindexter might turn out to be more comfortable with the Methodists. You see what I mean."

When Wheeler was gone, Laurel set a ledger open in front of him and cupped the left side of his head in his hand, his pen poised in his right. He came to the bank every morning hoping for clarity, or failing that, escape. He would think he could not concentrate on a row of figures, but he trusted his experience that he could, and sure enough, as soon as he physically fixed his eyes on the ciphering he would be calm, he would be in control. He did so now.

What had happened to him was simple enough, and no doubt already roughly paralleled by a dozen members of his Princeton class. He had come home from college full of ambition, and been taken on at the Maryland Warranty and Trust as a man of brilliant prospects. On the strength of that, and a certain social ebullience, he had ingratiated himself into the Kenny clan — to such extent that in spite of the Kennys' wealth (building supplies in a boom town) and the more significant stumbling block of their Catholicism, he married Eleanor. He had seen her — they had both seen her — as radiant executive of a voluminous family and social life. He shruggingly committed his progeny to the One True Church. But no children came. In the first year of their marriage a nephew of a Maryland Warranty's director was inducted in ahead of him, and he was stuck at assistant chief teller for three years. His wife proved disillusioned — though to be fair to her, less from the modesty of his income (she had her own) than from the paucity of romance in domestic life. Now he developed a mysterious rash and started his coughing fits. The Johns Hopkins battery of tests showed incipient pulmonary phthisis, and he was advised to migrate to a drier climate.

Then, just when everything seemed emptiest and darkest, the same nephew of the board member received intelligence from a West Coast banking friend that the Mountain First National was looking for a manager of a new branch in Bowie, Arizona. Laurel's application was accepted by return post. This meant that as regards both title and salary he leapfrogged the original nephew, who, however, was not an envious man and had in any case no intention of living in the desert.

Laurel made perfunctory assumptions about the magic of the Arizona climate, and for a time caught Eleanor's imagination up in the magic. They had pored over maps and magazines; they had drawn together in their sense of averted disaster, of adventure. Some days he thought that the diagnosis of his lung disease let him draw his first free breath in several years.

Now he narrowed his focus to the row of precise figures and willed himself to concentrate. Certainly he indulged her. Certainly he did. All her life people had indulged her. It was because she so matched earnestness with energy, religion with romance. The sisters at St. Agnes had indulged her, the fathers as much as her own besotted father. Perhaps she was more spirited than spiritual, but even this was never perfectly clear, because she so loved to please and because she had so quick a feel for the forms. The spectacle of goodness always moved her. Color and music were her element. You could sometimes catch on her face the abstracted look of ecstasy.

Now suppose he were to tell her she must turn Protestant be-

cause the local cattle baron so suggested. Suppose he should tell
her to give up her religion so as to be socially more acceptable in a
cowtown. Think what she would say!

No doubt there were those who thought him led by the nose,
and would have thought so for no better reason than her height
and her high color. He hoped he earned the good opinion of
decent folk, but he could not live his life hiding out from gossip.
He gave her spirit free rein because it was of value to him; he saw
to her political instruction because he believed all women should
be so informed; he left her to her religious opinions because she
was raised to them. And because . . .

He did not know if he was born to this particular grief, and there
was no one in the world whose opinion he would ask on such an
issue. Anyone who observed *her* for half an hour might conclude
that Eleanor was a passionate creature, but Laurel did not know if
he was a passionate man. He had as a youth suffered the melan-
cholic, angry urges that he supposed were the common lot, else
why should there be such an industry of devil-damning and ethi-
cal exhortation against them? But, those episodes aside, he had
no evidence from a mellow enough youth that he would spend
his adulthood in obsession. Unlike Eleanor, he was distinctly *not*
romantic. He knew — accepted, did not disapprove — many men
who had taken eternal vows and then taken them tongue-in-cheek.
Most men he knew managed their marriages like solid businesses,
and put their passion, such as it was, into affairs of state or trade,
the pursuit of intellect, even cigars and vintage port. Or else they
chafed against the constraints, made off-color jokes, and made it
clear they wouldn't have given their freedom away a second time.
He had known doting couples, too, for whom the dotage seemed
to be mutual. But no one, himself apart, for whom wedlock was
deeply, deadly, the pursuit of pain.

If he had never run into her, for example. If he had settled on
Maude Pierson, her pert little ferret face, her agnostic uncles, and
her everlasting needlepoint — wouldn't he have taken some stout
middle position on the scale of marital felicity? Or anyone else out
of the circles of cousins' friends, daughters of his parents' acquain-
tance — anyone at all except this one particular *belle dame sans
merci,* the line of whose long but no doubt unremarkable torso from

armpit to thigh could fill him with unremitting and unquenchable agony.

It was no one's fault. Sometimes he could step back and view it with the same dispassionate detachment as he viewed a page of ciphering that would not balance. Then he would have, even, a kind of poignant pleasure in the irony that human life is an unbalanced and unbalanceable ledger. Eleanor wasn't wrong, he'd remind himself, or willful. On the contrary, she valued in him exactly those qualities that were his best — his intellect, his measure, his compassion. If she could not touch his flesh without a grimace or *frisson*, no doubt these represented a judicious and discerning aesthetic. It was no fault in her; it was true — he had the sort of flesh that creped even in childhood; he was oddly formed of torso, such that a first-rate tailor could take advantage of his breadth of chest — but without that art, in his God-given poor forked flesh, he was more breasted than broad.

Yet all the same, the anger rose. Far uglier men than he were loved, with fewer qualities to redeem them, yes, and loved by greater beauties, too. Why should he lie aching, eyeing the common female fuzz on her wrist, rationing the number of times he might stroke her mortal forearm, his own heart palpitating over whether she would this time turn to him or stiffen? In his mind's eye he saw her now scuttling from their bed — in Baltimore, on the train, in the littered, not-yet-unpacked debris of their supposed future on Jefferson Street — she rising in a rush, clutching at whatever bit of cloth, sheet, nightgown, peignoir came handiest to conceal and at the same time demonstrate her recoil, the back of one hand against her forehead in theatrical distress — "It's too hot."

It's too hot, it's too late, it's too light. I'm tired, I'm on edge, I'm limp, I'm lethargic, I'm lachrymose. Conjugal duty is a Protestant term for rape. *Don't be coarse, don't be crude, don't be revolting. Don't be disgusting, loathsome, odious, or noxious.* Don't be.

The curious thing was that of all the things he might regret, the only thing he did regret was that she didn't love him. He assumed, of course, that he didn't want to die, but he didn't feel it. He felt the scratch and scrape in his lungs when he coughed, but he did not regret the likelihood of death. No, what he regretted was that she would turn, nostrils flared in petulant self-distress, her fore-head blotched with guilty anger, some tendril or other of her rich hair dangling over an ear, an eye, plastered damp to jaw or collar-bone, pleading, "Not tonight!" Then he would so grieve with long-ing that he had to look away to hide the fact that he was not, as any self-respecting husband ought by rights to be, outraged.

8

IN THE QUIET before dawn, at the signal of a double cuckoo call, the two watchmen at the Mendoza spread were garroted with fine piano wire, and the latches of all eight corrals were simultaneously slipped. The gates swung, the *dorados* at the far sides of each corral set up an ululation, and those on the gate side hallooed to drive the cattle out and back toward the road. The din was instantaneous and terrific; by the time the lamps were lit inside the house there were fifteen thousand beasts in uneasy motion, and by the time the first ranch hands appeared from the patio, cattle were streaming out in a single motion, like a swarm, driven by several dozen *dorados* for whom, to tell by the laughter, it was as much a joke as a job. Dust spread and hung pale in the dark.

Lloyd didn't join in the drive; he'd been told to stay with Guytan Farga around the corner of the main house and wait for Villa. He did what he was told. He tongued his molar, chewed on a licorice lace, and admired, furtively, the efficiency of the roundup. Last night they had camped on the other side of a sandstone butte, the *campesinas* going about their cooking and bedmaking as matter-of-factly as if the sandy clearing were a living room and the butte the town hall. The women ground corn, patted the tortillas in their hands, calling to one another. Lloyd could not get used to this, the hardiness of the camp followers, the offhandedness of the operation. He knew that Mexican women and children traveled with their soldier men, but it violated his sense of what a war was, not to mention what a woman ought to be. He tended to stutter when he talked around the cooking fires, and he suspected that's what made him an object of fun, not seriously guarded, not taken seriously. He smarted remembering his brother Frank, a grown man in his earliest recollection, who made him stutter that way and never took him seriously either.

The *villistas* had given him a mount that must have been a fine cow pony in its day, a gelding sorrel with an off-center flame on its forehead. The horse was past prime now, and a little irritable in the way of old workers. Lloyd supposed that the *villistas* supposed that he wouldn't be able to outrun anybody on such a horse, and yet nobody seemed to be watching to see if he tried. Although he did nothing but follow the rump of the mount ahead, he'd been complimented several times on his horsemanship, with a facetious surprise that suggested all gringos must be city boys. Villa he saw only at a distance, except on the one occasion the *jefe* had passed by Farga's fire and touched his fingers to his hat. "I have a job for you," he called out then, as if to reassure an underling that his preferment had not been forgotten.

He'd been told nothing about this morning's raid until Farga's sister — her name was Concepción, which was nearly as hard to call anyone as Jesus — jiggled his shoulder in the dark and told him to put his boots on. She already had the fire built back up and had a dozen of yesterday's tortillas rolled to push around in the hot beans. They had ridden hard to within a few hundred yards of the Mendoza place, Lloyd behind Farga behind Fierro behind Villa. Then the *dorados* dismounted and walked their horses the rest of the way, spreading silently out among the corrals according to some plan. Farga and Lloyd stayed mounted and Fierro told them to wait by the corner of the *hacienda*.

From which Farga now moved, edging around to get a better view of the front. Lloyd did the same. Farga sat his horse like a jockey, very erect at rest but leaning into the mane and the wind when he galloped. Farga sported a boy's patchy mustache, which he constantly tended with nervous fingers. Lloyd was not sure how old Farga was. Maybe twenty, maybe sixteen. In camp he seemed rather shy, and the others treated him as if he were shy — hugged and backslapped, encouraged — so it was impossible to remember him in the mine, with Sam's ear in his rock fist.

The sky eastward was purpling now behind the sierras, outlining them in their dawn flatness; it would be an hour yet before they had dimension. In the noise of the streaming cattle, the urgency of their sweat and breath, the mountains seemed ethereally remote, part of another world where there was peace. Here the Mendoza people had begun to assemble, the hands and their women from the patio side, curious or sullen or scared. The children came, too, some in arms. A girl of four or five, dark curls jostling down the back of her smock, hid her face in her mother's hip. From the house the grand old *señora* had arrived, standing in her white nightdress with a black shawl wrapped about her that trailed almost to the ground behind, her long rope of gray hair hanging on top of that. The house servants ranged on either side of her, mostly women, a young couple and a boy of fifteen or so who might have been part of the owner's family, it was hard to tell. They all stood in front of the house in a line like people waiting for a train and watched their cattle go.

Now past Lloyd rode Villa, tweed-suited, trotting, Fierro to his left on a richly muscled mount. Fierro beckoned with his drawn pistol, and Farga fell in behind him. Lloyd followed. Villa reined in in front of the old woman, who drew herself up with fat dignity, chins accusing. Villa deferentially removed his hat.

"Señora Mendoza?"

The woman stared at him with haughty hatred. She pulled the shawl across her bosom in fists.

"Señor Mendoza forgot to pay his taxes."

"My husband is not at home."

Lloyd was pretty sure that this was no news to Villa, who shrugged and trailed a hand in the direction of the fleeing cattle. "Well, it is of small consequence."

Fierro twisted in his saddle and called over his shoulder to the nearest man. "Leave him four cows and the bull with the biggest balls. Otherwise he might get discouraged." The *dorado* laughed and trotted on by.

The old woman shifted her weight, and Lloyd noticed that she was barefoot. It occurred to him for the first time that she was frightened, the way he had been frightened, the way Sam had been. Lloyd was not frightened now. If he had been drunk on no sleep riding through a mirage, that would be the way he felt now. He felt as if he had lost touch with who he was except that he was waiting to be told what job he had to do, hoping he would not be told. He could go on waiting forever if necessary, following the rump of the horse ahead.

What he couldn't do was remember the mine, or Sam. It worried him. Lloyd knew Sam wouldn't be able to do anything to save himself, he always needed looking after — but Lloyd couldn't clearly call to mind what Sam looked like back there, curled up bleeding on the floor of the shaft. Lloyd shut his eyes for a second on the gray space where he failed to imagine Sam, and when he opened them the configuration of the line had broken. The little girl in the smock had wandered out and was standing by the foreleg of Villa's horse, her mother kneeling in place with arms outstretched, but whether to pull her back or urge her forward wasn't clear. The line of people held tense.

Lloyd couldn't see Villa's face, but he could see him reaching in his fob pocket, digging for what? A wrapped red sourball. Why did everybody in the Villa camp have candy? Lloyd could still taste the licorice that had come from Farga's sister. Villa reached down, all the way down with remarkable agility — it was like seeing a meal sack do rodeo tricks — and first offered the candy to the child and then, when she had taken it, offered his hands to lift her up. The girl raised her chubby arms, the sourball in one fist, and let herself be swung to dangle over the mane and saddle horn, Villa bouncing her aloft, reaching to plant a kiss on her golden cheek. Farga laughed sentimentally. "*Muchachita!*" Villa crowed, lifting the girl skyward once more and then in a single arc swinging down to deposit her on the ground again, where she scampered back to her mother. It was the second most amazing thing Lloyd had ever seen.

"Now, *señora,*" Villa said as if there had been no interruption, "I would like you to give Señor Mendoza a message when he returns. Please tell him he forgot to pay his taxes."

The old woman said nothing. Villa extracted a second sourball from his pocket and began unwrapping its waxed paper in a meditative sort of way. His voice started blandly and then rose in pitch and force. "And tell him, please, that the forces of the Constitutionalist army will be back, and back, for as many times as we must come back, until the cattle of Chihuahua belong to the people of Chihuahua, and until this land and all the land of Chihuahua is in the hands of the people!"

This rhetoric rang into an applause solely of cattle hooves. The *señora* turned to her servants and said, "Take the children in the house." The non sequitur was brave with defiance. It also served to demonstrate such command as she had left; several women obediently herded the youngest toward the patio. But at the archway the young mother, as if adjusting the weight of the girl on her hip, twisting quickly so that both her own black curls and those of the girl bounced and swung, flashed up at Villa a chin-jutted smile of triumph. Villa saluted vaguely, toward the old woman and over her head at the young one. He popped the sourball in his mouth. Fierro lifted his pistol as if lobbing the bullet toward the cast iron bell over the arch; the bell clanged once, and a metallic vibrato hung on the air. Villa wheeled his horse and doubled back toward the cattle drive and the two dead watchmen gathering dust where they were propped, saying as he passed Lloyd, "Gringo! *Now* I have a job for you."

They pushed due east, a *villista* splinter group of threescore men and fifteen thousand cattle. It was a drive, not a campaign; nevertheless, Villa himself led. They made about twenty miles a day, more when the land was flat and the wagons of the *soldaderas* could move as fast as the herd. When the terrain was difficult and the wagons fell behind, then the *villistas* would stop, mill, and content themselves with sugary sodas and cornhusk cigarettes until the women and children arrived, tumbled out of the wagons, and began building their fires. Sometimes the company would not eat until after dark, in a sweet hanging haze of marijuana and mesquite smoke. Then by moonlight the women would unearth shabby silk *rebosos* and drawn work shawls, someone would produce a guitar, a tambourine; a circle would form inside the ring of fires. Throughout the evening several dozen *dorados* would take women into the wagons — each his own woman, Lloyd supposed, for there were rarely disagreements, and the procedure had a cheerful efficiency about it.

In general the mood was high, and supplies did not run low. Most of the land through which they rode was dry and sparsely vegetated, but occasionally they crossed valleys with water and pasturage, wide fields of ripe corn whose stalks bowed to greet the arrival of Villa's cavalry. At every farm, town, and railroad junction, food appeared: chickens tied in pairs by the feet and slung over bamboo poles; baskets of chilies, onions, beans, corn in fresh ears and dried. They ate chicken dripping in hot green sauce, and only rarely slaughtered one of their own — that is, their confiscated — cattle. Lloyd had begun to put on weight, and now the weight began to put on muscle. His arms were good in any case from the pickax. The *villistas* continued to express surprise that he could rope and ride, but gradually the undertone of mockery disappeared. One day he saved a pair of dogies who had wandered into a ravine, and thereafter he was assigned the dust-choking rear position, from which he could easily have disappeared into the chaparral. But to go where? To escape to where?

There was one other foreigner in the company, an Englishman named Simon Willoughby, who seemed an unlikely sort for an adventurer, though that is apparently what he was. He was about fifty years old, wizened and stubbled, narrow-shouldered but rotund of belly. He smelled like a corral, rode like a professional, and maintained a series of lordly rituals to do with his tea, the knotting of his frayed foulard, the nightly polishing of his battered British riding boots. Lloyd avoided Willoughby as much as possible — it wasn't always possible — not wanting to detail his reasons for being here, and certainly not wanting to suggest that he was here against his will.

For the Briton was an irrepressible Villa fan. "A capital soldier," he would say, dipping a rag-tipped finger in the black wax and rubbing it in little circles on the toe of his boot. "First-rate. Hasn't been a leader with his scope since Napoleon. Garibaldi hasn't got a look-in, not a patch. Scope and speed, you've got to have for the job. Stick a knife in a man's midsection, turn, and wave to the crowd. Not many can do it. Hats off, I say."

Mostly Lloyd spoke to Simon in monosyllables and cultivated a sullen look. Still, Simon could be a source of information. The Mexicans seemed to assume Lloyd knew what they were doing out here in the middle of October nowhere, and always spoke Villa's name with reverence, whereas Simon was willing to chatter facts and tactics. It was from Simon Lloyd learned that the hated President Huerta had killed his predecessor, Francisco Madera, and dumped his body outside the penitentiary. Madera had promised land reform and won the presidency in the first free elections ever to be held in Mexico. Now Huerta had named the traitor Pascual Orozco general over his *federal* forces in Chihuahua and Durango, and all the peasants who had hungered after land and schools were flocking to Villa and Obregón, ready to drive Orozco out.

"Villa never went to school!" Lloyd blurted.

Simon just laughed. "Villa's a prodigy. What's he want with schooling?"

Lloyd shut up, but another time, casual, he asked what Villa had against the Mendoza ranch, and Simon told him it was nothing personal, just a quarter of a million acres. Mendoza's was the kind of wealthy *hacienda* the Constitutionalists wanted to carve up and parcel out.

"Any idea where we're going now?"

"Oh, dear me, we've got fifteen thousand rustled steer, and not guns enough to outfit a company. We'll be headed wherever the cattle buyers are — and he'll know! The greasers've got a worldwide reputation for indolence, that sort of thing, heh? It's part of their cunning, you mark me. Mark if the whole operation isn't arranged ahead of time, down to the pettiest detail. You, now: You'll be trust man, I suppose?"

Lloyd grunted, wondering what a trust man was but thinking that it didn't, anyway, sound too disreputable or bloody. Heartened, he accepted a covert swig of Willoughby's whiskey for his toothache, pretending to be checking something under a saddlebag, because Villa did not allow liquor of any sort in camp. Theoretically, Willoughby agreed with Villa on this as on most things. "Marijuana makes for camaraderie; alcohol for contention," he would say, though when he'd had two or three belts himself he would contradictorily quote: " 'Rum is a fiery liquor that produces madness in total abstainers.' " Now, swilling Scotch against his bad tooth, Lloyd found an excuse to return to Guytan Farga's fire.

One afternoon they came to Cajoncitos, where they drove the cattle in an arc past the northern side of town; and then on a whim of Villa's most of the men doubled back to be cheered through the mosaic-paved central square. They took on supplies again (Lloyd was embarrassed to find himself being hung with a necklace of onions by a giggling *muchacha*) and turned south among olive trees and century plants, outcrops of granite like gray fists, the beginning of the climb toward Ojinaga.

The next day they drove the herd through a narrow canyon and abruptly came upon the Río Bravo del Norte — or, to Lloyd, the Rio Grande. It lay about fifty yards wide at this point, mud-brown and sluggishly churning, its near banks lined with tall grass and stands of cottonwood. For the whole trip they had been passed overhead by flocks of southbound birds, and now as they neared the river they could see mallard and geese waddling in the shallows. Lloyd registered with a catch in his chest that the far bank was Texas.

"Now; did I say so?" Willoughby was at his elbow, reining his horse near enough to lean over and breathe cigar breath on Lloyd's neck. "Damn me if that doesn't prove to be our buyer."

Sure enough, across the river and camouflaged against a low sandstone butte, Lloyd now saw a motionless body of men. It was hard to tell exactly how many there were because they hung back in the shadows of the rock, some afoot and some on horseback. As he watched, a small mounted party detached itself from the rest and advanced toward the river. At the same time Lloyd felt his elbow gently jostled, and he turned to find Villa beside him on a powerfully built dark chocolate mare, not his usual mount.

"Gringo. Come with me."

Willoughby grinned and gave Lloyd a stiff salute. Villa led Lloyd through the herd and into the grass. The geese hissed at their horses' hooves and took ten-foot leaping flights to either side, scolding as they landed. Lloyd began to feel the drumming of the molar that was never quite still in his jaw. He also marveled again how delicately, how much at home, Villa balanced his shapeless torso astride the silver-studded saddle. The general raised an arm to the men across the river, and the lead rider waved back.

"Now, gringo." Villa reined in and faced Lloyd. "You know what it is to be the trust man?" Lloyd shook his head, ashamed to admit his ignorance and wishing he had asked Willoughby when he had the chance. "No? I tell you. We have a simple device for promoting trust and goodwill." He smiled patiently. "Over there is Texas."

Lloyd smiled back through his toothache and wondered for a moment at the simplicity of his deliverance. Was he going to be allowed to cross the river to Texas, and be let go? A trust man? A freed prisoner as a gesture of trust and goodwill to the American ranchers?

"And there are Señor Charlie Alcott and his friends."

Lloyd glanced across again. The lead rider and three hands had come to the edge of the bank; all four carried rifles at rest. Some ways behind them men were gathering on two sides of the clearing, a force of perhaps about the same size as Villa's own.

"You cross the river," Villa said. "Señor Alcott will give you one hundred and fifty thousand dollars in gold. You bring the gold to the middle of the river. Then we cross the cattle. When the cattle have crossed, you bring the gold to me. It's simple, yes?"

Lloyd nodded, tooth thrumming. It was simple, but it had not yet quite made sense.

"If the cattle do not cross, Señor Alcott will shoot you. If the gold does not cross, I will shoot you."

Lloyd swallowed.

"Thus the honor of the transaction is ensured. Do you understand?"

Lloyd understood. Now he would like to have had a question, but he couldn't come up with one. He nodded solemnly and took the hand that Villa held out to him as if in congratulation.

"You will need a better horse," Villa said, and dismounted with that agile swing that always startled Lloyd, so that he himself felt clumsy getting his right leg over the rump of his gelding and to the ground.

"This is Haragana — a joke, eh? Because she is *never* idle. Eh? A joke, like 'Gringo Chink.' "

Villa may have meant this reminder as a threat, but Lloyd only found himself flattered that the great *jefe* had remembered the name of his mine. He could tell Sam that Villa had remembered his, Sam's, joke, and Sam would be proud. No, wait, he was confused. Sam . . .

"When you come back to us, Haragana will be yours." Villa held the rein and urged Lloyd up with a gesture of his free hand. Lloyd put both palms over the silver horn and swung up to the glistening mare. "And the saddle as well!" Villa called up cheerfully. "Which is worth many pesos, and is the work of many hands."

Villa slapped Haragana's rump, and she bolted toward the river, flinging her head back and casting over her shoulder at Lloyd an ambiguous expanse of eyeball: a dare, reproach, excitement, hate? Lloyd dug his heels in and urged her on forward; she went with a will.

The pale brown water eddied at her hooves. The grasses gave her foothold for a little way, then ended in silty mud that swallowed against every step. The way she pulled her ankles free, each with a precise lift and a sucking sound, made her prance like a show horse, and Lloyd knew she could do her job and leave him free for the several that were his. He was part cowboy, gauging the depth and width of the river: *If the water is over my boot twenty feet out, will it be over her head in the middle?* Part schoolboy getting the instructions right: *I cross the river, Mr. Alcott will give me a hundred and fifty thousand. . . . If the gold does not cross . . .* Part cunning victim: *I have the horse in any case. I'll be on American territory, and no American rancher would send me, a kidnapped white man, back to that bandit murderer against my will. . . .*

The riverbed hardened and Haragana could walk for a ways, but then abruptly she was off a shelf and swimming. The current was straighter here but strong; instinct pushed her powerfully across it. There was no way he could hold her steady in the center of that flow, not for a hundred and fifty thousand or fifty times that. But he had no sooner made this judgment than the horse had a foothold again, on a gradual slope of gritty rock that would do; and when he swiveled to look, he was barely halfway across. He checked the reins to see how obedient the lady really was, and sure enough, she stopped and stood stock-still, to the depth of her shoulder in a current the color and grain of milled cedar, with themselves as a knot.

Well, perhaps he could do the job first. Mr. Alcott would not like to lose his deal. But if he delivered the gold to Villa he would then have to cross again as he was just now doing. Under fire, or not? Would Villa let the horse and saddle go? Lloyd knew Villa had shot men because he didn't like their boots. Maybe after all he should throw himself on the mercy of Mr. Alcott right away. . . .

The water was cold, and that felt good; he'd forgotten how hot and gritty he'd been for the whole damn drive. Haragana was responsive to the least touch of heel or rein. Lloyd stole a glance at the silverwork under his right thigh, elaborate shell shapes and etched scrolls snugly cupping the leather edges. Shuddering the water from her flanks, the lady climbed, on hard bedrock this side, prancing now for no reason but her own spirits; and by the time they were clear of the water, Lloyd had begun to wonder if there wasn't something a little heroic in his situation, if there wasn't a way to present it as just a small mite noble.

What Lloyd needed was something big enough to wipe out nineteen years of fraternal ridicule, a lifetime of his father's condescension. He'd hoped to take home copper, or the cash made from a copper profit. Would a horse and saddle do, if they'd been earned at the risk of his life in a grand adventure, the horse and saddle that a copper baron might have chosen?

The possibility of freedom and the certainty of American soil so elated him that he half expected Charlie Alcott's face to look like his own father's — but he didn't realize he was expecting this until, spurring Haragana the last ten yards, he pulled up and found himself confronting four faces of differing age and color but identical obduracy.

"How do," Lloyd said in the onrush of his hope, not checking it fast enough. Three of the four faces were kin, father and sons or uncle and nephews, not a spare ounce of flesh among them, and that flesh stretched over windblown stone like the butte behind. Their eyes were weathered into permanent squint. The fourth man was a bull-faced black who now sniffed and whose nostrils flared so that a sniff had unfriendly connotations.

"Lloyd Wheeler," Lloyd said. "Originally from Bowie, Arizona . . ." But the four men did not seem inclined to return the introduction. The oldest of the related three, therefore Charlie Alcott, spat left over the neck of his horse, which may have been some substitute for talking because the other three now dismounted and began lifting cowhide saddle sacks from their horses. Charlie Alcott stayed aloft.

"Dun-no," he said contemptuously, with gaps between the syllables, "what makes a white man go into this line of work."

The black man flung one of the double sacks across Haragana's neck and bound it by a thong to the saddle horn. If he found any offense in Alcott's remark, you wouldn't have known it from his face. You wouldn't have known anything from his face. He went back to his horse, and one of the younger white men threw a second set of bags across, securing it like the first. Another set landed on Haragana's rump and was sawed forward till it was wedged between saddle and blanket. The horse sidestepped and found better purchase; Lloyd began to have some notion how much a hundred and fifty thousand dollars in gold would weigh.

"Well, it isn't really my line . . ." For another second he flirted with the idea of asking for asylum. But one more look at that blunt boulder of forehead, igneous chin, and he decided this was not the sort of man you would say your prayers to. A fourth sack landed on the horse's neck, a fifth on her rump again. Alcott backhanded a gesture at the black man.

"Show him," he commanded.

The black man unbuckled one saddle sack and flipped the lid back, pulling at the opening with a beefy hand to display a jumble of coarse gold coins the size of ginger cookies.

"Unh!" said Lloyd. The sound came out with a satisfying force that surprised him, and he looked up at Alcott with a sardonic grin. "Nice," he said, thinking about his late mother's ginger cookies. "Delicious," it occurred to him to sneer. At ten dollars a head, Alcott would make 200 or 300 percent profit on the American market.

Alcott regarded him warily. "Do you want to see the rest?"

"No, thank you," Lloyd whined, which he thought sounded quite a sarcastic contrast to Alcott's basso. "General Villa will be more than happy to let you know if there's any missing." Then it oc- curred to him that the trust man was probably supposed to count the money. But nobody had given him any such instruction, and besides, he felt inspired. He whipped the reins right so Haragana wheeled back toward the river. She lurched a little but, bless her, didn't stumble. Lloyd's moods had been flipping over one another like pebbles in the bottom of the river, and the one that washed uppermost for the moment was that he could *love* this horse. She waded in.

The weight of the saddlebags made their progress careful and solemn; solid. There is nothing for sitting tall in the saddle like hanging the saddle with a hundred and fifty thousand gold. By the time the water was over his stirrup the cattle had begun to cross, three to five abreast, four *dorados* directing them about twenty yards downstream. Lloyd carried on till Haragana was shoulder deep — a little less, but near enough the middle that he didn't think either side would fault him on it — as deep as he judged the horse could hold. The water hit them heavier than it had on the way over. Haragana snorted and pulled impatiently at the reins, but stood against the current. He wished there had been room in that Texas exchange to ask for a cup of coffee. His tooth hurt. Two *dorados* on the bank he faced raised their rifles and held him in their sights. He turned his upper body back to see the black man and one of the younger whites in the same position. It astounded him to think that they were going to hold their arms like that for — how long? The first cattle reached him now, the lead hand signal- ing encouragement by cuffing himself lightly on the chin with the heel of his hand. Haragana adjusted herself, bracing against the current, and one of the sacks of money rolled heavily against Lloyd's leg. He tongued his tooth. He wished he had a molar's worth of Willoughby's Scotch whiskey. He looked at the dust clouds forming between the canyon and the river, at the four blue barrels trained to meet at the center of his brain, and he began to feel how long it was going to take to ford fifteen thousand steer.

9

WHEN MARIA IGLESIAS opened her eyes it was on a string of little red ants, the kind like two connected pinheads, so near that when she focused on them she could see her eyelashes, too. The sack that covered the doorway was looped back for air, but the air was thick and promised storm. Moonlight fell just on the corner of her pallet and the ants' stretch of floor. The ants gave no clue why they were going wherever it was; they carried nothing. Maria hiked up on an elbow to follow with her eyes where they turned a corner around the cornshuck bag so sharp you'd think they were *federales* doing drill. They marched back from there to the wall and up it in a line like a crack in the adobe. There *was* a crack in the adobe where they came through. If you went outside you would see them marching up the wall to where they got in, the same as you saw them marching down the wall this side. And what for? Why did ants do what they did? Why did anybody?

Nobody had said a word to her about how she had cleaned the Semple house last year, or asked her to be *criada* to the banker's lady. She had not seen Señor Walter Wheeler. Fatima Paralta said the new *señora* came in the church, but Fatima might lie; what reason would a white woman have for coming in town if it wasn't to look for a *maid*? Yesterday Maria had crossed over the tracks to the Semple house, carrying a package of nothing — her little sister's husk pillow wrapped in a cloth — to justify being on that side of town. She circled the block three times, but the *gente sancta* did not appear, and no one took any notice of her. She wished she had asked the midwife for charms to help along God's will. She wished she had taken something from the house when she cleaned it. This time she peeled a splinter from the fence and carried it back across the tracks to church, where she stabbed it, paint side up, raw side down, into the skirt of the Virgin for a *milagro*.

When Maria was a little girl, Manuela de Reyes had told her about the lasso dancer in the bull ring at Hermosillo. This woman danced with castanets over her head. Her tall body was wrapped in red taffeta tight to her knees and blooming out in ruffles to her ankles. One by one four picadors and then four caballeros entered the ring and roped her with their lassos. When they were done she stood with ropes from hip to bosom, castanets over her head, still dancing, eight men and their eight horses pulling out from her like spokes on a wheel.

Now Maria felt those ropes. Now she knew what it was to be pulled this way and that way and have to dance carefully and strong.

She thought all of this, every bit of it, before she let in her head what had waked her up, before she let the sound come to her of Mama and the Indian. Now they had the blanket over them, Mama's fingers clutching at it, but for what? In a minute Mama would forget about the blanket and it would slide. The Indian was breathing like a bellows at the Wheelers' fire. He was not Mexican Indian, not the sleepy peon sort that drifted over the border from Sonora, but a sneak, a savage, a crazy Apache turned out of the mountains by the gringos when they made the border laws and gave the Nations parcels of their own land. Mama said he was her man but he was nobody's man, he came and went as he pleased. Mama moaned.

Maria twisted her neck and looked across the ants' little valley to the mattress that Azul and Ramón shared. They were still asleep. Or still pretending, as she used to pretend? No. They slept, because they had slept through it from the time of their birth, and because they were dim-eyed mestizos. She, Maria, heard, she saw, she had to pretend, because she was Spanish, her full-blood father long gone before this Indian or any Indian came to make the others in Mama's bed. Mama's hands let go of the blanket, off it went, and the Indian breathed like a bull. Two legs high up, two long legs down, hers the paler with blue veins like armies of blue ants crawling a crack shape up her thigh, his balls slapping hard as agates in a deerhide sack.

Maria clenched her face into the dry-paper smell of cornshuck and watched the ants, a few zigzagging crazily against the flow. She remembered watching Manuela Reyes making fine wax figures for the Christmas crèche, pouring wax in and out of plaster molds, painting the eyes of Mother Maria with a one-hair brush. That was half her life ago. Manuela Reyes had pale skin and a Castillian lisp, and had grown up in a great *hacienda* in Agua Prieta, with a *zaguán* wide enough to drive carriages through to the corral. Now Maria could barely remember Manuela's face, but she remembered the wax Jesus and the curly lamb, more Wise Men than the Lord needed, whole herds of stable beasts. And she had never forgotten the miracle of Mother Maria's tiny eyes, opening straight at you at the quick end of Manuela's blue-tipped bristle.

Mama whimpered and Azul stirred. What Mama and the Indian did was poison like the thick milk of oleanders. Or it was like the time those years ago that the gringo boys had caught her and dragged her to the old prospector's shack on Dos Cabezas, had held her naked to the Chinese — a smell of dead things, dead birds fallen down the chimney, and even the wood spoiled so it smelled like food gone bad.

She twisted on the cornshucks, pulling against the ropes. If it was God's will, why did He do nothing about it? She watched the ants. This afternoon she would take a Del Monte can from under Señora Wheeler's sink and dip kerosene in it to bring home and pour along the whole line of ants. They would drown burning, like the damned.

Eleanor stood in the parlor surrounded by trunks and crates, half-emptied barrels spewing excelsior. The walls were a mustardy dun color, and sun from the windows seared them with yellow squares that traversed from the front door to the hallway as the day wore on. Through one of the windows she could see a windmill — a spindly tower and a bright tin wheel that perched hour after hour without stirring. She remembered the slow-turning Dutch mills she had seen on her European tour, their burden of clear water, their shape substantial with the weight of centuries, and she felt deeply homesick for Holland, in which she had spent six days.

The memory of houses haunted her — the breezy verandas of her grandmother's Colonial, the flocked walls of the dining room where she had eaten as a child, so that a certain red was imbued for her with solemnity and surfeit; the dear dark panels of her house with Laurel on Peabody Place, which she had disdained as merely rented.

It was her particular genius that these dun desert rooms mocked. A cardinal had remarked on it once, and once a senator: She knew how to dispose a space, the objects and the edibles and the people to consume them. She could take the measure of a room and arrange it for a soiree, so that the mere positioning of the drink in relation to the seating in relation to the canapés brought people into communication. Well, all right. A trivial, womanly talent, then. But why was it trivial? If people valued the flow of water through a pipe, sound through a dome, traffic through a grid of streets; if these things were engineering, acoustics, architecture — why should the flow of people matter less? And as for architecture, she would never have placed a door to impede entrance to the hall, like this one. She would have seen better than to aim a fireplace at a cul-de-sac. And who was she supposed to make flow through these stingy spaces?

Leaden, desultory, she took familiar bits of glass and metal, cloth and wood, and put them on rough-cut shelves in strange corners. Day after day she moved objects aimlessly, moved them back again. One morning she transferred her undergarments from the steamer trunk to the chest of drawers from which they had been removed three weeks before, but having done this she found that the chest stood at an inconvenient angle to the door, and although she was strong enough to move it, she was not prepared to commit it to any space where it might plausibly stay. Things were getting to the point that it would foster gossip if she did not make order, but she could not. She — who had had so much energy that her mother admonished her to be still, her friends raced laughing to keep up — now napped morning and afternoon, slouched in the chairs stroking the kitten and staring at the boxes and the trunks. Perversely, she called the kitten Baltimore.

She would rouse herself with a great solitary show of bustle, give herself dressings-down as if she were her own wayward child. In more somber moods she prayed, kneeling at the little mahogany altar that had been her father's gift on her seventeenth birthday, at the height of her religious fervor. The Virgin in its triptych had downcast eyes, as if she would forgive but would rather not hear of specific sin. Impatient with such meek censure, Eleanor would set herself penances of multiple Hail Marys, but before she had accomplished them she would forget why she cared and let the rosary hang from her hand. Staring into the space between her eyes and the nearest object, she would feel that she was staring into the emptiness of her own mind. Every afternoon, before Laurel was due to return from banking business in the town, she would hurl herself into an agitated hour of unwrapping pots and stacking them on the sideboard, unearthing linens to drape over crates, as if progress were being made. Laurel urged her to hire help but seemed to find no evidence of insanity, and was quite content to turn around and take her back to town to dine at the Hinman Hotel.

One day there was a dust storm. The sky darkened at noon, the wind howled out of the mountains. She had the sense to shut the windows, then sat while the house was pelted with several million particles of reddish sand that sifted in through cracks in the frames. She held the kitten against her neck, sipped a glass of wine, and watched the windmill, now whirling with manic speed. From out of the empty land behind it a dust devil grew, carried its funnel in an irregular arc around the windmill and toward her, picked up a chicken, whirled it briefly in a stir of feathers, and disappeared at a rough right angle to the way it had come. The chicken flopped to the ground and staggered drunkenly away. The storm continued for no more than an hour, but when it was done there was sand in the shredded excelsior on the floor; red shadows lay in the folds of her dress, shifting when she shifted. She raised the piano lid to see the keys dulled with dust; it must be deep in the works as well, clogging the hammers, grating in the moving joins. The *nouveau* carving on her little altar was outlined with grit, and when she blew on it, the stuff settled in the votary candle cups.

Now memories of ordinary objects came to her in pangs: a willow tree, her grandmother's chocolate pot, the petit point on her mother's footstool. Over the globe in her father's den there was an etching of the Angel of Death, his hair wild, his wings stretched out on brittle bones, which as a child had riveted her with fear but that seemed in memory dear, a familiar. Frightened at the force of her sadness, she made herself rise, shake the dust from her dress, and walk through the town. People greeted her, jubilant with the disaster. Had she ever seen the like? Wasn't it a horror how the sand got in? The schoolteacher in particular, Miss Timkin, who said she had sent her charges home at the first signs of storm, pressed her with solicitations.

"It's a baptism of dirt," Miss Timkin said with a laugh. She wore an abundance of auburn hair caught into a doughnut at the crown. Her pitch lilted, and her vocal chords trilled. "But you'll soon take it in stride."

"I don't know," Eleanor allowed herself to say. "I seem to be so dreadfully slow at the unpacking . . ."

"It's always a gruesome business, moving house."

"I suppose that's so, but I seem to despair of . . ."

"And you aren't used to this killing heat."

Eleanor marveled at how the accurate words played at hyperbole: *dreadfully, gruesome, despair, killing.* She hurried home, sat in the littered rooms so weighted with loneliness that she could not stand. The inertia was like an armor, shielding her from feeling but weighing her down. She could not unpack.

She picked up and read again the one letter that had come from Mama so far: The mums were out, the Barhytes were building a gazebo, Amy Whitney had her eighteenth birthday party with a canary tethered to her wrist.

At a little after four she was roused by a knock on the door. She checked herself in the mirror, saw that her neck was lined with red grit, her hair askew. Anger flushed her — she simply wouldn't answer. But she moved toward the entry hall, tucking and fiddling at the pins in her hair. She took a breath deep enough to face a committee.

And opened the door on a Mexican girl who stood in a state of charged quiescence. Her fists clamped her skirt where they fell; she stood as if rigidly still but also somehow swinging minutely from side to side. Her bare toes rhythmically grasped at the soles of her cowhide sandals.

"Señora Poindexter?"

"Yes?"

"I am Maria Magdalene Iglesias. I know the dust storm have dirtied your home and I come to help you."

She was no more than fifteen, a girl just on the cusp of womanhood, bare ankles below the voluminous skirt and unbleached camisole affected by the local Mexican women, her hair in a single thick braid from nape to hip. She had high cheekbones under eyes the color of bruised plums.

"I'm sorry, I don't understand. Who sent you?"

"I send myself. I'm a good worker, I know how to clean after these storm."

"Well, I don't know."

"Oh, yes. I have work for Señor Wheeler and Señora Wheeler, you ask them."

Eleanor hesitated, unprepared to deal one way or another with bald assertion. Then, inspired to buy time and establish her authority in the bargain, she commanded, "Come round to the kitchen door." The girl dipped her limber body in a rudimentary curtsy that may have hinted at insolence.

Eleanor took her time getting to the back door, running a cool cloth over her face and neck first, rearranging her hair while she arranged her thoughts. She longed for a black woman to hire, someone comfortable and warm, whom she would know she could trust. But it was no use thinking that way, it would only lead her back to homesickness. No doubt it would be grossly irresponsible to take on the first Mexican waif who presented herself. Eleanor didn't know what to pay. Suppose she should be cheated? Or even stolen from? On the other hand, finding out about all these things would require debilitating social calls, and here was ready help.

There was something else, though Eleanor didn't bring it into focus. The girl was disconcertingly beautiful. She exuded an almost violent self-confidence. The combatant in Eleanor was ineluctably roused. In the next two days the red sand was expunged, the house given order and a measure of grace, the trash taken by mulecart to the dump at the edge of town. Maria Iglesias was quick and meticulous beyond her years, but, more than that, for the first time Eleanor had a reason to pretend she wanted the job done. Pretense was a form of energy.

10

THE DAY OF THE DUST STORM Jessie Wheeler hid under the house, which was built up on stones in the four corners. Coming back from the outhouse, she saw the brown cloud curl down from the mountain, and she ran to the back steps and pitched herself underneath. You were always supposed to go indoors when there were dust devils, but she thought it was safer to get as close down to the ground as you could get. Seth Vandercamp knew about a man in Benson that was in his backyard and his sheet metal roof flew off, whirling around, and sheared his head off. They found his head in the next-door feed trough.

Ma's feet came down the steps against the wind, her skirt blowing back. She called and called, but Jessie lay flat to the dirt and pretty soon Ma went back in. There were old bottles under here and straw from the chicken house, old baling wire, just junk. Jessie used to come here to hide and be alone but now it was Jasper that did it. There was a couple of his toys, a mud pie in a rusty tin and a baseball that had lost its cover and was nothing but a half-unrolled ball of string. The dust was whirling, but she backed up against the steps and was pretty well sheltered.

After a while she looked to the side of the house and could see a hen that had run under there, with the light behind her like a black paper cutout you get at the fair. At first Jessie thought the hen was scared because she kept puffing up, lifting her wings like shoulders, the feathers ruffling. But then when her tail lifted up it started to swell and change shape like the tail end was growing into the head of some other animal. It was an egg.

It took the hen a lot of tries to get it out. She would lift her shoulders and then quiver her tail and the lump would ooze out and then the whole thing would collapse back again and start over. Jessie had never seen a hen lay before. It looked exactly like it feels when you have got a piece of liver in your throat that you know you have to swallow, but you can't do it on one try and every try is harder. Really it looked like a big BM, but Jessie wouldn't think that. She watched every second even though some dust blew in her eyes. Finally the hen made it, straining like she would blow up, Jessie blowing her cheeks out, and the egg got past the widest part and all of a sudden slipped as if it was slippery. It dropped on a rock and broke and then the wind took the shell along another foot or two while the dirt glommed onto the egg jelly. The hen clucked and cooed like the whole operation was a success. Jessie went in the house.

First Ma smothered her and cried, then she scolded and made her wash. Lunch hadn't been cooked because of it all, and Jessie was to stir the scrambled eggs. She looked at that stuff in the pan, it was like glue and cow's eyes and snot; she gave it a whip or two with the fork, but that didn't improve it any, and she went down sick for the afternoon.

It seemed like after that she was sick half the time. It seemed like the day of the dust storm was when it started that things sat in layers inside of her, a layer of corn relish on the bottom of her stomach and ground-raisin icing on top of that, then cod-liver oil, with a pool of blackstrap about as deep as she breathed and pickle brine just under her throat where she swallowed. If she let the layers slosh together they would make her sick. She walked carefully. Smelling burnt things was dangerous, or people yelling at you. Some days she sat and thought how when she was a child she believed there were two little men with a meat grinder inside your stomach. One of them picked up the food off the floor where it fell when it came down your throat, and threw it in the grinder top and tamped it down with a wood pestle. The other one worked the handle, which was near as tall as he was so he had to stand on tiptoes and bend right down to the floor. That was your digestion.

Miss Timkin said your digestion was really acids in your stomach, and Jessie knew it's not good to think about acid in your stomach, it could make you sick. It wasn't good to think about May Nene's breasts, either.

Jessie felt sick all the time. Sick and hate. She hated the scuffs on her lace-up shoes, she hated toejam between her toes and lines of crooked red sand in her elbow bend. The only mirror big enough to see herself was in Ma and Pa's room, but sometimes Ma took Jasper away somewhere in the afternoon and left her to look after Deborah. If Deborah was sleeping, Jessie took her clothes off and wrapped herself in Ma's plaid bathrobe so if anybody came she could say she was playing dress-up. She held the bathrobe open and looked at herself in the mirror from top to bottom. It was all terrible. Her hair was thick near her head and then frizzed out at the edges as if it had been scorched. Her face was square and plain as a shovel, her body was worse than sausage. Ever since she could remember, Grampa Wheeler would take her by the arm or leg, or take a handful of her bottom or her middle, and say, "Look how solid! Would you look how solid!" When May Nene had a stay-over party for her birthday everybody else put on their nightdress under the blanket, but May took off her middy and sat down at her dressing table to brush her hair with nothing but her petticoat on. She had her own room she didn't have to share with a brother or sister, and her own dressing table with an oval mirror; honey-glazed, and brass handles. She was so tiny around the ribs you could have put your hands around there, touching thumbs and little fingers, and her skin was smooth as butter cream. When she brushed her hair, her shoulder blades worked like little bird wings, and in the mirror she had breasts. They were little flesh funnels, they had pink cones, they made you sick at the stomach and tight between your legs. Everybody pretended not to look, and May Nene pretended she was just brushing her hair.

Mama's mirror was square in a plain wood frame. Jessie's body was all one thickness from her shoulders to her hips. Her nipples were brown raw spots. She swiveled in the robe and took a handful of bottom flesh like Grampa, but it wasn't solid, it dimpled up in your hand like a plucked goose. Her belly button was a hole in her middle, not like May's, which was a real button when she slipped down her petticoat to get into her nightgown, like a tiny mother-of-pearl shank button. Another time May had to sit down on the school steps at recess so she wouldn't faint, and whispered to Jessie that she had the curse. She said, "It's such a flow I can hardly get through school on one rag!" Jessie shrugged like she knew what May was talking about but wasn't interested. Now she knew about it from the other girls, and knew about the squares of stained sheet Ma washed out and hung.

Days she looked at herself in the mirror she couldn't eat supper. Ma would feel her forehead and let her go to bed, but later Jessie would wake up starving and go stuff herself with whatever she could find left over. What she ate would settle in layers with acid inside her; she would be thick as a sausage and lie there awake, hating so much that sometimes she did really think she would die. She felt sure you could hate your own body until it killed you. Nobody knew about this. At school she bossed Seth Vandercamp, which made everybody laugh, even the other boys, and she won every spelling bee.

But after the dust storm it seemed like things could always invent one more way to keep on getting worse. One late afternoon — it was late, because Jessie and Jasper were already home doing their sums and Mama was feeding Deborah in the high chair — Pa came home in his suit and collar that made him look pinched up and scratchy. He slammed in the front door so it swung all the way back on the hinges and hit the wall, and when Ma said, "Frank!" he hit it with his fist so it smashed into the wall again. Mama made a high, wailing noise. "He said *no*?" Which meant did the banker turn Pa down for the quarry loan.

Pa said, "Pie-faced back-East pantywaist!" Which meant he did.

Mama said, "Frank, the children."

Pa thrashed around the room taking his clothes off, his hat and jacket and collar. A collar button rolled under the log boxes, and Ma went after it on her knees. He said, "Sits there in a silk shirt and a pair of sissy spectacles. You seen those half-moon things he wears? Mr. Priss-ass Banker."

Ma said, "This isn't fit for the children to hear."

"Hear what? You want to hear?" Pa took a marble paperweight out of his pocket, a piece sliced flat but rough around the edges like a map with rivers all marked in veins. He started slamming it down on the table across from Jessie so the stuff in her stomach turned, but Pa was making his voice squeaky to sound like Mr. Poindexter.

"He said, 'A pity it's not gold, isn't it? I mean, it's rather *cumbersome,* isn't it?'" Pa smashed the piece of marble down again, and Mama said to her and Jasper, "Go to bed," even though they hadn't had any supper yet.

"You want to hear? He said, 'Well, but Mr. Wheeler, I would be lending you your *father's* money, *in effect.*'"

Ma said, "Oh, Frank."

The next day was the third time Maria did not come to work, and when they got home from school Mama was boiling the diapers herself in the big washtub, crying into the stink. Jessie had to make biscuits and gravy, and supper was after dark. Maria didn't come Friday, either, and at church Sunday Maybeth Newsome asked them had they passed on their girl to Mrs. Poindexter because she saw her hanging out wash behind the Semple house. Ma said, oh, she supposed the work was lighter at the Poindexters', and you know you can't expect much loyalty from the other side of the tracks; and Mrs. Newsome said she supposed that was so and she admired Mary Doreen's Christian spirit. But, home, Mama took the octagon pottery tureen and dropped it accidentally on purpose into the sink, where it smashed. Pa said that was cutting off your nose to spite your face, and Ma said she would not be needing any lecture on spite if he pleased.

Now Ma had a bright tin voice and Daddy said almost nothing; if you did something wrong, he stomped out or slammed around. Every night they talked in the parlor instead of going to bed, and Jessie went to bed too early but could not sleep. Sometimes Pa would say, "It's a fortune just *sitting* there," and Ma would murmur to him like she did to Jasper when he had the stomach cramps.

You didn't have to be smart to know what was going on, and everybody said Jessie was smart, especially Mama, but all the same they lied about it every day, about things that didn't need lying about, it was just like they lied to shut her out. When Pa slammed around, Ma would tell her and Jasper that he was worried about the drought (it wasn't any drier than usual for October). And Mama said Jessie was getting to be such a big, strong girl, so helpful; she never much cared for Maria anyway, and soon she would find a really dependable older woman, like Rosaria used to be. (When Jasper was a baby they had caught Rosaria mixing flour and water in his bottle and taking the milk home — did she think Jessie would not remember something so famous?)

One day Jessie was in the henhouse candling the eggs. It made her stomach dangerous to candle eggs, she dreaded to see a blood spot through the shells, but she would not tell Ma that. She said to herself: *I'll be damned before I'll tell her.* Sometimes she whispered it out loud, at night when she knew God was listening: *I'll be damned if I will.*

So she was candling the eggs, and Pa had slaughtered, and he and Mama were out in the yard cutting the beef in strips to hang over the barb wire and dry into jerky.

She heard Ma say, "Well, you give up too easy, is all."

Pa said, "You can't argue with a prig."

Ma said, "I don't suppose it matters one way or the other whether you *like* him." Her voice had a pout in it, although Jessie was not allowed to pout. Neither of them said anything for a while except breathing from the work. Then Ma spoke up again, "I daresay you could beat him with one hand tied behind you, but it's still him that has the money. Sometimes you have to go about things . . . the way they have to be gone about."

"Such as?"

"Well, I think, back East these things are done with a lot of politeness, and society. *You* know what I mean. I think you've got to do it their way." Pa snorted and Mama said, "Well, if you want the money!"

Pa said, "I haven't give up yet. I'm going to do the figures over."

Ma said, "Yes, but I think I must go calling on Mrs. Poindexter. I'll take her some molasses bread."

He was sneering: "Molasses bread," but Mama went on, "Yes, and I'll take Jessie. You remember how she gave the cat? Well, we can go to ask after the cat. And I was thinking, if it seems the right thing, maybe Jessie could learn the piano from her."

Could there be anything worse? Pa said, "What makes you think a back-East lady would want to give piano lessons?" which was Jessie's question, but Ma sniffed, "I *said* if it *seemed* right."

Is there worse? Jessie saw herself going to the door of the hen-house and saying: *I won't. You can boil me. I won't.* Yes, and if she did that she would be whipped for spying, as if she *wanted* to be in the henhouse looking for specks of rooster blood in the slime inside the shells in front of a smoke-stinking tallow flame. Oh, everything is so stupid!

And worse. Because Ma meant it. Jessie knew everything Ma meant and didn't mean — sometimes better than Ma knew herself, so that every time Ma said, "How sweet!" or "No, you may not go to May's today," or "Jesus loves us all" — *every* time, Jessie could have said *Ma means that* or *Ma doesn't mean that* and been right every time. Pa was a mystery, you didn't even know what he cared for outside of that stone hole up the mountain. But Mama was just telling the truth or either she was lying, and didn't always know herself; but Jessie knew.

So they went to see Mrs. Poindexter, Jessie in her voile middy collar with her hair steamed and brushed around Ma's finger, which was called sausage curls and made her sick to look at. Ma wore her pin tucks and the basket of molasses bread over her arm. They walked to the edge of town in lace-ups, and then Ma put on button shoes and set out Jessie's Mary Janes and hid her Buster Browns in the knitting bag. It was just another way of lying.

The first thing that happened was that Maria opened the door, with her hair done up on top of her head and a cloth in her hand with a little tatted-lace edging to it. Jessie could feel the shock off Mama as if Seth Vandercamp had punched her in the middle the way he did to somebody in recess. *Nobody* would let their Mexican open the front door. Nobody had ever thought of doing it. You kept your maid in the back, doing the wash and such. If you made up in a school quiz, *What would be the rudest thing you could do to your friends?* one right answer would be, *Have your Mexican maid open the door on them when they come to call.* Except that nobody just ever thought of doing it.

Maria took in her breath, too; she didn't know whether to be ashamed or sassy, you could see that, the way her purple cow eyes dipped and then flashed and decided to brazen it.

"Come in, Señora Wheeler. I will tell Señora Poindexter."

Maria did a sort of curtsy, as if she had never mucked out their henhouse or boiled their diapers — and Jessie's own drawers, she realized, sick — and gave the sofa arm a little flick with the cloth, like it was her own sofa that she had to fuss over.

The furniture was more beautiful than church. The covers were made out of tapestry in dim colors, with men in old-fashioned suits lolling on a tree, or castles and ruined bridges. The legs on the settee and the chairbacks were curved and carved, glossier than a pew. There was a spinet piano, and cabinets with belly-fronted glass and, inside, things it would take you three visits to look at. There were dark bottles right out on the sideboard where anyone could see them. She and Ma sat on the edge of the settee for a long time, waiting.

When Mrs. Poindexter finally came out, though, she was even more splendorous than she had been in the station, she was all glowing and laughing and getting them settled. She exclaimed over the bread and took it to the kitchen and said they would all have tea, though she didn't rush to make some. All grown-ups looked alike inasmuch as they were grown-ups, but Mrs. Poindexter looked more like a girl than a girl. Her blouse was not that different from Ma's, it was beige and pin-tucked, too, but the sleeves fell soft instead of stiff, the color had lilies in it instead of asafetida. Jessie thought of the word "raiment." Her skin was pale; it was *lit*. So was her hair, near dark as an Indian's but in thick waves, combed up and caught.

"Ah, you'll want to see Baltimore!" she said to Jessie, who knew the Poindexters came from Baltimore but didn't know what answer she should give to this, so she said, "Yes, ma'am," and Mrs. P. went and brought back Mercy, who she had renamed Baltimore and who looked all of a sudden expensive, like Mrs. Newsome's fox neckpiece. Mrs. Poindexter put the cat in Jessie's lap and Jessie petted it for a minute, but soon it jumped down and went over to Mrs. P.'s lap, which Jessie didn't blame it for.

"I thought I would name it after home, in case I get homesick sometimes," Mrs. P. said, laughing to make sure you didn't believe her, and Ma made a clucking sound in her nose.

"How are you settling in?" Ma asked. They talked about the dust storm for a while. Mama gave her advice how to stuff the cracks and cover the food with damp cloths. Mrs. Poindexter reached her face forward on her long neck like she was listening carefully — but listening to something that was not exactly what Ma was saying.

"And you must advise me what sights I should see. I'm most eager to learn about the area."

Jessie tried to think how to talk in this conversation, too — she wanted Mrs. Poindexter to notice her. Wanting it made her jumpy. It came in her head that she could tell about seeing the hen lay the egg, and then the thought took her breath away. You couldn't tell a thing like that. You would be disowned.

Jessie counted the bottles on the sideboard, seventeen of them: red, amber, brown, green; tall, squat, square. She wanted to get up and go look at the peacock feathers in the bell jar, but if she did, Ma would tell her not to touch, as if she was a baby. Jessie didn't want to be treated that way in front of Mrs. Poindexter.

Maria came in, carrying the tea. She must have made it herself, because Mrs. Poindexter had not budged from here. It was on a silver tray as big as a washtub, and Maria carried it by one handle each side with the edge against her waist the same as she carried a washtub, so for a second Jessie imagined soaking diapers on there instead of cups and silver. Maria set the tray on a low table — the molasses bread was sliced onto a pink glass plate — and Mrs. Poindexter murmured, "Thank you, Maria," and Ma ignored Maria and kept on chattering.

"Well, and then we have the 'spring rains' in January, which lots of folks from back East find a joke. I was born and raised in Wickenburg myself, so it's all I know, but I'm used enough to folks remarking on it."

Maria backed up and stood behind the sofa while Mrs. Poindexter wiped Baltimore off her lap and poured the tea through a little strainer into cups with gilt curlicues and roses. Ma said, "Make Jessie's mostly milk, won't you? She's not allowed tea or coffee, only on Sundays, but, well, my, this is a special occasion, isn't it!" Maria held her head very tall and smoothed her apron, and for Jessie everything was backward as if the world tilted, because Maria belonged to the silver strainer and the cups with the roses, whereas she and Ma belonged to clodhoppers hidden in the knitting bag. It would not have made any sense if she'd said this to Mama, but it was so, and Maria knew it just as well as she did.

"Don't you, Jessie?"

"Ma'am?"

"Land's sakes, child, didn't you just hear me? I'm telling Mrs. Poindexter how you love music."

Jessie did not love music any better than the next person. She liked "The Old Rugged Cross" when Miss Timkin sang it in church, and she liked sitting around with Grampa's cowhands when they sang old ballads from their cattle-driving days. She wished Daddy would sing "Sweet Rosie O'Grady," but mostly because that meant he was in a good mood, and she hadn't heard him sing for a while.

She said, "Yes, ma'am." She took a swallow of milky, lukewarm tea. She felt Maria looking at her. Maria's apron was eyelet that came out of back East, not out of shantytown. Her waist was near as small as May Nene's, her neck was near as long as Mrs. Poindexter's. Jessie had heard Pa say once that somebody, one of the cowboys, "had a taste for the *señoritas*," but it had never come to her mind before that a Mexican could be handsomer-looking than a white girl. She took another mouthful of tea and felt it drop through all the layers from her Adam's apple to the bottom of her stomach. Tea had tannic acid, which was the same as you tanned a cowhide with; Miss Timkin had learned them that. Maybe if you drank tea every day of your life the inside of your stomach would get as tough as cowhide. You could make shoes out of it. Your stomach would be tough as clodhoppers and you could kick somebody with it.

"Wouldn't you, Jessie?"

"Ma'am?"

"It would be *such* a pleasure if you would play for us, Mrs. Poindexter. My, to bring your own instrument all this distance! Well, it just takes my breath away."

But Mrs. Poindexter knew how to turn the talk around, and answered by saying how she thought the *real* talent was to make such bread as that. "Ah!" she said. "We must have some of your strawberry jam with it! Maria, would you fetch it, please? It's in the pie safe — a mason jar with red jam," as if Maria didn't know what

Mama's jam looked like, or anybody in the county, when it came to that. Ma sat tight quiet while Maria went off to the back of the house, and Mrs. Poindexter took another bite and said, "Mm-mmm! Really, you must give me the recipe."

Mama clinked her cup down in her saucer. "Well, you'll need six cups of whole-grain flour to six tablespoons of blackstrap molasses."

Mrs. Poindexter smiled.

"And a tablespoon and a half of fresh beef suet. You can use bacon fat if you have to, but fresh ground suet is the best."

Mrs. Poindexter said, "Would you mind copying it out, and I'll send Maria by for it? I'd like her to learn cooking, and your molasses bread would be a *fine* place to start!"

Maria was coming back with the jam, and she heard this. She set the jam down in a pink bowl to match the bread plate. Mrs. Poindexter was smiling, and thought she had paid a compliment. Ma rattled her cup against her saucer, not on purpose, and Jessie could see into Ma's mind as clear as spelling. Ma was going to bring up the piano again; she was thinking that if Mrs. P. could teach a shantytown Mexican to make her molasses bread, then she could teach Jessie to play the piano. Jessie felt shame, and angry, and loyalty, and sick, and sorry for. But most of all she felt she would not let herself be forced onto Mrs. Poindexter. She would not. She'd eat sand first. She opened her mouth and said whatever had been fuzzing around her mind ever since Mrs. P. asked about the sights.

"Everbody will tell you to go see the Wonderland of Rocks, Mrs. Poindexter, but it's a day to get there and a day to get back, and what I think is the marble quarry is just as much of a sight and can be done in a afternoon. We take a picnic up there sometimes on a Sunday. Mr. Hum lets us pick fresh vegetables whenever we come up on them, and it's cooler up there, and prettier'n anything down here in the flat. Sometimes there's wildflowers."

Ma gaped at her and said, "Jessie!" but Mrs. Poindexter was laughing the same as when Jessie gave her the kitten.

"What is this place? It sounds a miracle."

"It's Pa's marble quarry up the Old Camp Road."

"Marble!"

"Yes'm. It used to be Grampa's but he divided it up between Pa and Uncle Lloyd to make their fortune."

"Jessie!"

"How does there come to be marble there?"

"Nobody knows, ma'am. It's a miracle, like you said. Most people was hoping for gold, but this, it's" — she searched in her mind to remember Grampa's phrase — "it rivals the finest *Car-rara* of Italy."

She could feel Ma's eyes glaring in the side of her sausage curls, but she would keep saying anything that came into her head, and if she suffered for it later, well and good.

Mrs. Poindexter said, "Well! I'd love to see this marble of yours. I've been to Carrara." And turned to Mama, "And wildflowers as well! Would it be possible?" So Ma was blushing and stuttering, "Well, yes, gracious, anytime you please."

The piano was not mentioned again because they made plans, how Mr. Poindexter would drive his auto and Jessie and Jasper go up with a cowhand and the picnic in a mulecart.

"If you want to see the spirit of the West, Mrs. Poindexter," Ma said with her breath all up in her bosom, as if she was going to end up in tears over the quarry, "you should watch two men and a dozen laborers set themselves against that mountain." Jessie remembered, though, that Grampa didn't call it *the spirit of the West*; he called it *mule-headed* and *cussedness*.

"My!" said Mrs. Poindexter.

"Why not this Sunday, after church?" Ma said, still flustered some it must have been, because she had told Papa she wasn't going to mention church in any way, shape, or form. And Mrs. Poindexter said that sounded lovely, she would speak to Mr. Poindexter and "confirm."

So it was settled, and Maria took the tea tray back to the kitchen, and Jessie and Ma took their leave. But as soon as they got on the street Ma started walking hard and fast, the knitting bag swinging heavy at the end of her arm. Jessie had to skip every third step to keep up. When they got to the edge of town Mama didn't stop to change their shoes, she kept charging forward over the scrubland, never minding if she scuffed her good kid toes.

Once Mama mumbled, "A parlor maid! A parlor maid!" as if this was a surprising phrase she had just heard of.

Jessie said, "Ma? Could we slow down? Ma? You know? Mrs. Poindexter doesn't know she stole Maria."

"What?!" Ma stopped dead and rounded on her. "What are you talking about?"

"Mrs. Poindexter doesn't know Maria was our maid, or she wouldn't have said what she did about the molasses bread. Maria must have done it on her own."

Now Ma faced her square with her eyes small and her mouth small. Her breath came out onto Jessie's face in hot, dry puffs.

"And you! Butting in where you have no business. Let me tell you, young lady! I'll thank you not to be handing out invitations and messing in things you don't understand!"

Which was lies and nonsense six ways from Sunday. Because getting the Poindexters up to the quarry was the exact thing Ma would have paid six months of piano lessons to make happen, but would never think of saying it straight out.

Jessie skipped every third step to keep up, thick and damp in the flimsy voile, hating the sun and her body and her life. Hating Ma.

11

SAM WASN'T TORMENTED, because they took no interest in his pain. He was a convenience to them, as it would have been a convenience to come upon an extra burro tethered in the rock, or a spare goat wandering. He was made to carry things and to build the fires, to dig when there was digging to be done, and to hunt for wood when wood was needed. Sometimes he would be hit if he was slow, or shoved aside if he was in the way, but there was nothing sexual in their touching him, and they took no enjoyment in hurting him. He might have been a pack ass or a goat, he might have been an old woman.

They were crude and dirty, their voices were boorish, and their feet blunt hammerheads against the desert floor. Their clothes were soiled down the front with spillings of grease and beans, coffee, gravy, wine when they had it. Sam watched them eating teeth foremost, hands in whatever could be handled, tongues used for spoons and napkins, teeth for forks, and he thought of them as animals until the day that he noticed the animals ate rather delicately, the burros chewed, chewed, the way his mother had taught him repeatedly to chew, and the horses gently shuddered the flies away, accepted a carrot with spread lips, lifted their tails when they shit.

Now he saw that they were not animals but thoroughly men; they manufactured their own crudity and understood each other mostly through their mouths. It was he, Sam, who was the animal, who lived for preservation, cared for nothing save food and drink and safety. All he wanted from them was to eat, to drink, to lie down and sleep in safety, and, awake, not to take too many blows. Like the animals, he sensed their moods in their movements, he read what they wanted by their gestures, pointings, pokings. He smelled the bustle of their departure, he felt in the vibrations of their footsteps when it was time to camp. He learned to sidestep the blow or shove he felt coming behind his head.

There were four. The youngest was the leader, a youth with spindle legs and a soft belly but powerful heft in his arms and shoulders. Young-Fat, Sam named this one in his mind. Young-Fat had a face like a melon, and when he opened his mouth it always seemed full, like a melon, of seeds and sticky liquid. He was fond of teeth, and wore a necklace of them; he collected them from any skull they might find along the way. Once in a village he pulled a child's tooth and paid the child to keep it.

There were two in their fifties, or perhaps not so old because their hard habits and hard way of life might have made them look older than they were. The one Sam thought of as Eight-Fingers had gnarled knuckles on powerful long hands, but on the left the index and middle fingers were short stubs. The other, Lazy, was thicker and duller-eyed, always the first to drag his saddle down, and the last to saddle up in the morning. The last, the little one, was almost normal in the size of his head and arms and even long in the jaw, but short below his neck. The others slurred and never completely closed their mouths, but Little spoke in a high, tight whine. None of them laughed much. They generally got through the day as if it were something due them.

Sam made not the slightest effort to learn their language, any more than he had when Lloyd used to admonish him it would be a help in the towns, provisioning. It was a principle of his father's so thoroughly absorbed that it had become an axiom of his own: Li Hum did not want his children learning Spanish. He and Su had not spoken Chinese at home. They spoke English. If the sons of Wally Wheeler wanted to talk like Mexicans and call it learning, well and good, but Li was not going to have his son — nor his daughter, either — confused with the servants of shantytown. And to Sam this had been made clear, and clear again as his sister learned it. So it was second nature now, not to hear what the words meant, only to read animal-like the wishes of his captor benefactors.

Benefactors they were, because he built his strength. They had a horse and a packmule apiece, and one goat, and they rearranged the gear so that one of the mules carried Sam. They would not have hesitated to make him walk, but a man had less endurance than a mule, so they gave him the mule. They kept the best of the meat for themselves, but there was plenty of strength in the stringiest. They wasted food prodigiously, whereas Sam wasted none. He scraped the pans with tortilla scraps, sucked bones. He upended the coffeepot in his mouth, drank the dregs of the goat milk. When they found a spring he drank until his belly distended, and let them laugh at how much he pissed. He wasted no energy. He carried what he was made to understand he must carry, fetched the wood, little by little took over the cooking duties as they saw he was capable and as he insinuated himself into usefulness. Little by little, husbanding his strength and hoarding morsels, he grew back to health. His overalls began to fit again.

The only trouble was, they were going south. Once he got oriented, Sam realized that he had found them, or they him, somewhere between Esqueda and Angostura — which is to say, a day and a half from the border, not so far this side of it as Bowie was the other side. Now they meandered back and forth, purposeless or with some different apparent purpose each day, south to Bacoachi, west to St. Ignacio, south again skirting around Magdalena and St. Ana to Llano, east to Arizpe, southeast to Los Hoyos, northwest to Cucuerpe. Traveling south, Sam felt the backward pull of home. He imagined that Lloyd, heroically escaped, was already there and waiting for him. The other possibility he would not give room to root.

The *villistas'* behavior had no more apparent direction than their path. In St. Ignacio they unpacked hard candies and sold them — or pretended to sell them, because they didn't work as hard at it as at ducking in and out of the *bodegas*. At Llano they made a show of stocking up on supplies — wine, bacon, beans. At Arizpe they got drunk, but not so drunk that Eight-Fingers could not hold a late-night chat with a clean youth in a sombrero and serape, who saluted him with some respect and gave him a folded paper. Eight-Fingers was the one who wore the *federale* jacket, wore it with open disdain for it, spilling his wine and drool down the front of it. Yet before the next town, Los Hoyos, he took it off and turned it inside out, hid it in the saddlebag before they went into town, where Young-Fat pulled the *muchacho*'s tooth with his fingers and gave the boy ten centavos, and then followed the boy into a house, where he stayed several hours. When he came out he was drunk, and still not so drunk as he pretended. The next day Eight-Fingers left them, hard-riding east.

It was through the hiding of the *federale* jacket and the hard-riding of Eight-Fingers that Sam finally understood he was traveling with a band of Villa's scouts. They were tracking the movements of Pascual Orozco's *federal* forces, finding out where *villistas* could be recruited and where the villages and the *hacendados* remained loyal to Huerta's general and his government. They knew in advance where a stolen or captured uniform would be safe to wear, the right signal. They knew how to talk, to whom to talk, to find out what they needed. When Eight-Fingers left, Sam knew with certainty that the man was taking information back to Villa, and yet while Sam rode with the three remaining toward Pozodoro, he surfaced just enough to wonder how he knew. Jealously he felt in the bib pocket of his dungarees to make sure his identity card was still there, folded around his ear. The ear no longer had a smell, but it was as supple as worn leather. He cupped it in his fingers. He kept it safe from them, as he kept his mind. He had made of his consciousness an animal lair, remote; but as he rode toward Pozodoro he surfaced from it just enough to wonder how he knew that a man who saddled and rode away was going to Villa. They camped outside the town, and Sam went in to fetch water.

Pozodoro was an oasis rimmed with crucifixion thorn and desert willow. Its plaza was an oval of yellow stone, rough octagons set edge to edge like the pattern of a turtle's back. In the center was a fountain of adobe paved inside with flat, gray pebbles. Everything was chipped and crusted with age, but it was restful to Sam, things that had been made a long time ago with care. He had a clay jug that he filled from the fountain, the water splashing cool over his hands so that he stood longer than it took to fill the jug, dreaming the drift of the water. It was so plentiful that it didn't need pumping: it must have been fed by a spring. It flowed over his palms, and on one side of the fountain it flowed over a red tile lip into a gutter that intersected the courtyard and ran away between the church and the *bodega* to the south. Sam wore a sombrero now, sweat-stained and soft with age. Lazy had given it to him off the back of his burro where it hung, maybe because they would not want Sam to call attention to himself, his lopsided head, or his Chinese face. In any case he wore it, the shade was welcome, and he had gotten used to the weight of the brim, which made his head feel a little unsteady.

He felt cocooned, almost, in that shade. He had his senses, but he put away deduction, language, memory, prediction. He did whatever he was doing, which was now to hold a full jug under a fountain spout so the cool water spilled over his hands while the old women hawked corn and stringy meat from stalls, the children played stone-throwing games, and the men spoke in important tones of transactions worth less than a peso.

Between the church and the *bodega,* along the red tile trough that carried the water to a cistern somewhere out of sight, there came a man with a Gila monster on a leash. The man was small and wizened, with a leering smile. He came into the plaza calling a guttural, thick sound like a sung cough, urging the Gila monster along with little tugs while at the same time he fended it away from himself with a stick to which a small horseshoe had been wired or tied, a shoe for a pony or a miniature mule.

He came into the courtyard cough-calling, and when they saw him the children squealed, ran in his direction or away, the men stopped their talking and rose to go toward him, the women yelled to him in taunting voices. He tugged the lizard across the court until he had covered half the distance to the fountain, twenty feet from where Sam held his jug.

"*Hghck, hghck, hghck!*" he called. One boy shoved another toward the lizard, and the second flung the first off with an angry gesture. Then the first showed off by stepping in toward the Gila monster, slapping the toe of his huarache on the yellow stone, nearer,

nearer. The man spoke angrily and, hooking the Gila monster by the neck with the horseshoe, feinted it in the direction of the boy. The boy fell back.

Now the man swiveled from his hip a basket shaped like a fishing creel, hung by a strap of horsehair. Braided horsehair also made the leash that circled the lizard's neck, and although everything about the man was ragged — his basket, his rag-wrapped head, the layers of shirt, the rope-belted baggy pants — all the same the leash on the lizard was new, its colors sharp, the work fine, such as a careful hand would make for a favorite horse. The man was tooth-less and he kept his mouth open in a leer that said: *You'll like this, and liking it will show you for what you are.* He said: "*Hghck!*" to every side. The boys and men fell back in a crooked half-circle. Sam pulled the jug out of the stream and tipped some water out, turned to go, but after all he stayed a little, watching what the man with the Gila monster was going to do.

The man reached into the basket and, gaping straight ahead of himself at the boys, stirred his hand around, as if with difficulty finding whatever was inside. The Gila monster, nearly two feet long from the tip of its black and yellow tail to the fangs that overhung its warty snout like a drooping mustache, sagged in the sun. Its belly slung low to the paving stones.

"*¡Caltetepon! ¡Caltetepon!*" the boys chanted. Crust lizard. Crust lizard.

The lizard watched them with a dull, discouraged eye, but when the old man reached out and dropped in front of its snout a writhing garden snake not much bigger than an earthworm, the Gila monster struck, and the snake froze into instant stillness. The man dragged the Gila monster a few feet to the left and kicked the snake away. Sam closed his eyes and turned to go. Turned back.

"*¡Caltetepon! ¡Caltetepon!*"

Now the old man dangled by one rear leg a lean green frog that folded and thrashed its body repeatedly. The women muttered from their stalls, the men and boys murmured, urging.

"*Hghck! Hghck!*" the old mute scolded now, and after a little, after a murmured or a whined resistance, the men and boys pro-duced centavos, which they clattered on the ground around the Gila monster, pitched them underhanded toward his head, or flipped between their fingers so they landed on his back. The frog clenched and opened like a hand.

When the tinkle and clatter of the little coins died out, like the last few popping kernels in a pan, the master of the Gila monster looped the creature by the neck with the horseshoe, poked it away a few pokes, tugged its head up, and poked it again. Then, letting the leash go slack and at the same time reaching across the lizard with the frog that he held by the leg, he half lowered, half dropped the frog to the far side of the lizard's head.

Sam did not really see the strike, although he was watching now, and not pretending not to watch. He saw the frog hit the ground, saw it crouch and spring. Then it hit the ground again, this time with a full wet thud, and Sam knew the lizard had struck it with his fangs, knew the frog was paralyzed and had fallen from its leap, but could not really say he saw the strike. Everyone — men, boys, master, lizard, Sam — watched the frog, because it wasn't doing anything. It lay hardened into its crouch, tilted sideways. The men and boys stared, waiting, as if in imitation of its paralysis. The lizard was in no hurry. Sam took his jug and left the square.

At camp he set the jug on the ground, felt in his bib pocket for the comforting touch of his talisman. They had corn flour, bought ground from a woman in Arizpe, and he mixed it nimbly into a paste, added more to make it behave between his palms, pinched a ball of it and rolled it between his fingers, patted, turned it, lay it in the bubbling bacon fat. He kept thinking of the lizard, its helplessness, and its power. He scooped bitter coffee into the pot and poured in water from the jug.

Young-Fat, Lazy, and Little sat at the fire and paid no more attention to him than if he were a goat for milking. They talked their tongue. They were planning to go south again, to Huepac, where there would be a runner from Juárez with figures on the new recruits. This news troubled Sam. He went to sleep troubled, slept troubled, and dreamed of the lizard, dangerous victim, vicious prisoner, circling an aimless threat in a darkly shining place. "¡Caltetepon!" voices called out of the dark. Crust lizard. He woke early and only then, on waking, woke to the knowledge that he had understood what the three men said.

12

ALMA TIMKIN BODE her time. There was some arrogance in it; she would not be like the others — the ladies of the Eastern Star, the youths of the Epworth League — who would call on Mrs. Poindexter with faces of forced goodwill and loaves of sourdough. Alma was able to take pleasure in the anticipation of things. She would come to know Eleanor Poindexter, but in her own time, when Mrs. Poindexter's glitter had begun to pall for them and when, for her, the novelty of their mere openheartedness had begun to thin. Then Eleanor Poindexter would need a friend with culture, sensibility. Already there was gossip in the town that the newcomer had lured a maid away from Mary Doreen Wheeler (paltry nonsense, with half the Mexicans out of work and a dozen maids to be had for the asking any afternoon of the week). A month and a half had passed, and the Poindexters had not been seen in church. It was said she snubbed Reverend Newsome when he came to call.

Alma came from the church now while the recessional was still thrumming inside, under the October sun straight into the flat hardpan beyond the Semple house. She attended church with faultless regularity, and she sang a passable contralto in the choir, richly moved by the music if not by Reverend Newsome's missionary zeal, nor his sanctimonious insistence on the suffering of the little children — she suffered the little children quite enough. Apart from the music, church performed a purely social function for her. That she acknowledged this would have shocked her fellow parishioners, especially those for whom church performed a purely social function. For Alma, worship was attended to among His Works and not among the hats and hymnals.

Alma was forty-two and still lived in two poky rooms behind the barber shop. She had come west from Akron, Ohio, ten years ago in search of a husband, and had found one beyond her most extravagant expectations — but at the last minute had turned him down. Nothing in her memory so astonished her as this feat of bald selfishness, and sometimes she luxuriated in regret, understanding pretty well that to luxuriate in regret is a different matter than to repent at leisure.

She was known — knew she was known — as a practical woman, forthright. Romanticism of a sort they granted her — romanticism and practicality being two qualities a spinster could combine without contradiction — but on the whole a woman who had accepted her lot with gruff good humor. And yet in the classroom — it was hard to get ahold of this exactly, but it was powerful — the very dreariness, the dogged sullenness of the ranch-and-railroad offspring in front of her, the fingers searching out boogers in the snub noses — thrilled her as if she had been called to split their minds with light. Half a generation of them ghosted that little room: the Humbles, who had memorized snatches of "Hyperion" and gone back to the cows; the Eickenberries, who learned algebra to barber; Lloyd Wheeler, who disappeared off into Mexico with Sam Hum; and Sam's little sister, who had regressed to some West Coast Chinatown. It was as if she should have in her care a little pinpoint of shining, not in a darkness, which would be grand of itself, but in an immense, dusty void. She knew she was extraordinary; she had always known it. What use was it to be extraordinary if she ignited no one else? It had not seemed to her that she would do any igniting through wifery; she was not *called* to it.

October. The temperature had dropped into the sixties at night, so there was a hint of autumn in the mornings, dew on the sills before the sun climbed. Now when it was at its zenith the temperature peaked in the upper eighties, not too bad. Alma made for an empty streambed that was a favorite spot for her private time. The bed was so long dry (decades? centuries?) that there was nothing to indicate there had ever been water here except a rill of uncovered stones and the wandering depression itself, which allowed her to sit a little below the landscape. She unearthed a newspaper from her carpetbag and spread it on the dirt. Then, skirt tucked around her legs, hat tilted so the shade fell on her forearms as well as her face, she sat on the paper with her hands in her lap and recited a few random prayers.

"I lift up mine eyes unto the hills from whence cometh my help. As it was in the beginning, is now and ever shall be; world without end. Thou hast made me for thyself, and my heart is restless until it finds rest in thee. Amen."

This was ritual only, a mantra or the telling of beads, a way of stilling herself. There was more ritual to it, too, involving two memories. She now closed her eyes on the first: a certain Miss Terawney, who wore bombazine dresses and smelled of lilac water in the damp-plaster-smelling basement of the Akron Baptist Church. Miss Terawney carried her New Testament in a protective wrapper made of butcher paper. She had a bosom and, usually, a bunch of false flowers somewhere about her amplitude. She had a Victorian notion of the demands of intellect on young scholars, and she considered Sunday school a *school*.

Miss Terawney used to lecture them on St. Augustine, who was so much her favorite that the deacons eventually intervened, suggesting the lessons were too popish. Meanwhile, however, she had thoroughly indoctrinated Alma regarding good and evil. *Causa efficiens* and *causa deficiens; incausale*. There was, said Miss Terawney, no such thing as evil. Evil was simply an absence of The Good, which alone had substance. Evil was no more than a monumental drought of the spirit, and in the desire of our hearts for good we were like poor sinners wandering the desert, ever thirsting after righteousness.

Alma, aged eight or ten, tried to imagine such an absence. She set herself to supposing that her fingernails were not dirty but that there was an absence of cleanliness under them. This was not successful. No more could she suppose that Mr. Bates next door, who beat his wife, was more empty when he was full of alcohol. The trouble was that evil seemed to have so much juice in it, the fattest spiders the most poisonous, the wet laughter of the lowest boys in the schoolyard whispering behind their hands, the crazy black man she had seen once in the Elyria rail yard, who cut himself and stood bleeding just to spite the passersby. She would have liked to believe that evil was a Nothing; it was beyond her capacity.

Still, the notion had bred a habit in her. It stayed in mind. Once after she had been in Arizona several months, she had gotten lost. She had come out for a stroll, somewhat defiantly, because she had met with too many admonitions against walking in the desert. Wally Wheeler had irritated her with one too many warnings about snakes and sun. She had been lost in some thought or other, perhaps about whether she should marry Wally (astonishing *that* should be the thing she could not remember, what it was that had her so lost in thought), and looked up to find herself out of sight of the town, at some angle to the familiar mountains that was not familiar, in some angle of sun such that west could have been a full forty-five degrees to either side of its descent. She had walked not knowing whether she was heading deeper into the unknown or would suddenly orient herself. The trouble with that infinite-seeming horizon is that you have an infinitude of ways to go. If you're lost in hill country, you always hope as far as the next rise. If you're lost in a maze, you hope to the corner. But here there was nothing to attach a hope to, just the dull fury that, being able to see to forever, you could have walked out of the sight of town.

Her head had begun to pound, and she'd kept her eyes on her feet as she walked, noticing the shine of her leather toes under their dusty coat until the dust itself had begun to shine in that unrelenting sun. She was entirely without water. She began to know that she could die, a few miles from habitation, in a walking dress, her last meal a lunch of bacon and Del Monte green beans. She had knelt down under the shade of her hat and prayed, her mouth so parched that the words hurt, and yet she felt she must say them aloud to keep herself company, and in case God should be listening.

She prayed and prayed. She fixed her eye on a crack of shade under a fist-sized lump of quartz, and gradually, as if she had called it forth with the fixity of her prayer, the shadow formed itself into the shape of a horned lizard, whose wary eye held her eye. She fixed her prayers on that point of light and held it, mesmerized. Then it seemed that from the one glistening pinpoint in the raw universe, wet light expanded. She looked up into the undulations of a mirage, wave on wave of shimmering, the cactus looming plump in it, the desert floor cresting at her feet, the quartz so winking that it seemed to trickle. She caught a dry breath in the dazzle, and everything was *water! water!*

The mirage lasted a few moments, and when it dissolved she saw at its center the thin gleam of the railroad tracks, which she followed back to town. She never mistook the appearance of the railroad tracks for the miracle; the miracle was that His absence was so full of Him. She had never thirsted quite the same again.

Neither — though she had seen dozens of mirages and seen them for what they were — had she been vouchsafed another such vision. But the desert was tinged for her with that one glimpse of grace, and every Sunday after church she came out to sit in the shade of her own hat and relive it a little. Now she looked up to the mountains south, so like waves in their stillness, a conduit for the idle, ecumenical sort of thought that would, in the pews she had just come from, be considered heresy. She remembered that the Indians of India give their gods the form of mountains while acknowledging that gods have no form. She remembered that the Eskimos call their mountains Mother and Father, Grandmother. The Mexicans say Sierra Madre, too, and it's a fact that at the tips of the Chiricahuas there are little streams seeping as from an aureole. Mother Mountain. Even a volcano is a breast flowing fire. These were not things she would say to Maybelle Newsome. She wondered if Eleanor Poindexter had read St. Augustine.

13

FRANK JOINED THE POINDEXTERS in the Pierce-Arrow while Mary Doreen went with the children in the buckboard, driven by an old cowhand named Johnny Fousel, who had the astonishing ability to hold the reins with one hand, open a pouch with his teeth, roll a cigarette, light it, and replace all the gear, never using the hand on the reins.

"I wouldn't want to saddle Johnny with this bunch all on his own," Mary Doreen told Eleanor with an air of self-deprecation, gesturing past the baby's face to Jasper, a shy child with a sweet, rather adenoidal smile. The daughter, Jessie, seemed aloof, much concerned with the crossing of her booted ankles.

In the touring car, Frank sat in the back with his knees bent to one side, his shoulders too wide for his suit. He spoke a shade more politely than he need have, and Eleanor judged that he was likely to agree with something he didn't agree with.

Eleanor was fighting torpor, trying hard. There had settled on her such a dull hatred of the place that she had that morning literally prayed to see some vista, some vegetation that could stir her to life again. She wore a scarf around her neck, as was fashionable back East for motoring; but the air was dead still, and their progress so slow up the narrow switchback that the silk hung limp in her lap and trapped a ring of suffocation around her neck. Laurel spoke to her anxiously. She knew he was appalled by the narrow hairpin turns, the steepness, the split-log bridges across which they rattled, but that he would not show anything that could be interpreted as fastidiousness toward his motorcar. He was also for some reason behaving rather sternly and closed toward Frank Wheeler, as if wary of him. It seemed a hefty burden of emotion for a picnic.

"Your daughter promised me wildflowers, Mr. Wheeler."

"Yes'm, there should be. Anyway, we'll see plenty of cottontail a ways higher. We'll get one, more'n likely."

"Get one?"

"For our lunch."

"Oh!" Eleanor thought him sadly hampered by his gaucherie. At the same time she felt herself to be too tall and clumsy, too strong-featured.

They passed the prospector's shack, half its roof caved in. Laurel winced over a stone slide in the road.

"There were Indians here up to fifteen, twenty years ago," Frank said.

"My. What sort would they have been?"

"Oh, all sorts. Papago, Apache. Now we're shut of them, we'd better look we aren't overrun with *colorados*."

"Surely —" Laurel mumbled, but the rancher had clearly spoken at random and was already pointing out the water pipe, no more than an inch in diameter, that ran from the well in the foothills and climbed beside the road, sometimes propped on lumber Y's, sometimes threaded through holes drilled in the rock. Eleanor remarked how small the pipe was, and Frank bragged that it had supplied a camp of thirty men, and steam engines for both coring and hoisting the rock.

"We had an engineer work out the angle of it," he told her proudly.

They rode for an hour, till the baby got past fussing and was lulled to sleep. The temperature dropped five degrees. Johnny Fousel shot a cottontail through the eye and roped it off the wagonside so it would bleed clean as they climbed. Soon the crevices were filled with the red hung heads of bottlebrush, or lush succulents with leaves like lima beans. They came upon the Chinese grocer's scattered garden plots and took a loose young head of lettuce from one, bright radishes from another. Laurel laughed at

the chicken wire in trapezoids and parabolas around the plots, but
Frank insisted it was needed.

"The varmints get your produce same as on a farm," he said,
loosening a little and even hazarding a grin in Eleanor's direction.
A breeze rose now and floated her scarf. They passed a field of
white bouncing buttons, then a cliffside of purple fringe; she
teased him that he didn't know their names.

"On your own mountain!"

"You'd have to ask Mary Doreen; she's the one for flowers."

"I suppose you think it's sissy for a man to know about flowers."

He rubbed the bridge of his nose confusedly. "I'm more interested in things that have a use."

"Do you think that beauty has no use, then, Mr. Wheeler?"

Clearly out of his depth, he blushed through the clear bronze of
his skin.

They came to another bridge, over an impressive chasm where
the earth had simply split. Jagged layers of rock matched on either
side. The pipe leaped across with no support and had been bowed
by the water's weight into a catenary curve. Johnny Fousel drew
deep wizenings in his face as he took a last drag on his cigarette,
and he flung it into the abyss, where they all watched it arch and
disappear. The horse, dull and docile up to now, picked up speed
and nudged at the back of the automobile. Jessie had been standing
on her dignity, but now she shouted simultaneously with Jasper,
"We're comin' to the bend!"

When Wally Wheeler divided a mountain between his sons on the
eighteenth birthday of the elder, he had meant it as a handsome
gesture — recognizably his kind of gesture. He knew that there was
marble there, and that the quality of it was startlingly fine, and that
nobody else had found marble anywhere to speak of in the Southwest. He knew that cutting stone is arduous, but that as long as it
can be done men will be stubborn to do it — core through strata,
crack open the adamant, make it into something else. He had in
mind that sometime in the future, when he was dead or old, his
sons grown substantial on cattle and wise with age, they would
work out how to get the marble down out of that unyielding coil of
hills. It had never occurred to him that they (Frank, really; of

course, it was the big brother who had bullied the younger into the loss of his patrimony) should try to make a primary fortune out of it. It was too hard, you could see that. Problematic. Yet Wally had gotten caught up himself in Frank's vision, the audacity of it, and had fronted the money for the road, the first steam engine, hoist, and tackle. Then he had watched Frank sink every bit of profit back into the camp — housing, commissary, more drilling and polishing gear — putting nothing by in case of bad times; and Wally had pulled out in disgust, finally, when he found that Frank had left a railroad debt hanging and bought Lloyd out with money that ought to have gone to pay the men.

It was true that the marble rivaled the finest Carrara. It was also true that marble came from Italy free, as ballast on the return trip of American merchant ships, and that it was loaded onto the major railroads straight from the Atlantic docks. Here it had to be cored, split, and hoisted all by horse- and steampower, the water mill-pumped up through the little pipe, the stone hauled down one two-ton block at a time by wagon, loaded on flatbeds at Bowie, and so sent on to the Coast. The whole process was so arduous and unlikely that even in Los Angeles, Italian marble had proved cheaper than the Wheelers'. But Frank would not give it up. He said he could not. He said it plucked at his brainpan like a puzzle. He said his faith in it kept him going.

He said now, echoing his children in a tone that Eleanor had not heard since she sat among her father's client entrepreneurs, some-where between greed and reverence: "Coming to the bend!"

They rounded a curve like a dozen others they had rounded, not as steep as some and not as sharp as others, promising nothing in particular; and suddenly it shot out at them in a horizonwide blast of sun. There it was! — a pyramid of two hundred blocks, each block twenty tons of solid shimmer. They stood at the edge of the quarry from which they had come, a pit fifty by a hundred feet and a hundred deep, a perfect rectangular white void.

Eleanor was more taken aback than she could have said. She had expected something vaguely like the Maryland gravel pits. She had mainly wanted wildflowers, and envisioned the marble as slabs for bureautops. But each of these abandoned blocks was higher than a man and the length of a flatbed wagon. The glittering pit could have been a cellar to the palace of a Colossus.

She gasped. "Why, how do you . . . ?!" Frank was matter-of-fact in describing the process of coring — "If you've an apple corer, ma'am, that's the principle" — and how a pulley works so a horse can pull many times his weight to crack the cored rock from itself.

They tied the reins to the automobile, and Johnny Fousel unloaded while the rest of them toured the perimeter. Jessie stood a ways back from the edge, her eyes plunging to the shadowed shine at the bottom as if she felt the vertigo. Jasper tormented his mother by racing up a little rise and down again toward the edge. This was clearly dangerous; there were shaley patches at the rim, and a sheer drop more than twenty times his height. Frank caught him by the upper arm and whacked him seriously once across the backside.

"Don't you!"

The report of flesh and the round words boomed an echo down the pit, embarrassing them all. Jasper colored, scowled.

"Frank's marble is on the front of four buildings at the Coast," said Mary Doreen. "Well, front or inside, I don't know which. One of 'em a hotel at Long Beach Pier. I tell him I deserve to see it in its final resting place!" She chattered kittenish, and it had a paradoxical effect of making her seem less young.

"Did you know," she went on, "the final polish has to be done by a hand? They turn it and buff it and what-all by machine, but the only thing that'll give it the luster finish is the oil out of a palm of a human hand. Don't that beat all?"

"Wonderful," Laurel agreed. Eleanor glanced at him, saw no irony. She was glad they'd both been lifted out of their doldrums, though it seemed too bad it had to be a hole in a mountain that did it, and not the mountain itself. She *had* underestimated Frank Wheeler. Who wouldn't? Uneducated, inarticulate — this very moment success had made him self-conscious, and he stood half a head above the rest of them, pinching the bridge of his nose with a hand like a small tree.

They mounted the rise that Jasper had run from, and from here they had a panorama of the marble pile and the breadth of the pit. You couldn't see all the way to the bottom — Frank took a stone and lobbed it and it disappeared from view. Waiting for the sound of its landing, they hung suspended in a silence that prolonged, prolonged — so that Eleanor was convinced the stone had already hit and they'd missed it somehow — before they heard the clear, echoing clatter.

Eleanor felt suddenly ashamed. She had so manufactured enthusiasm that now when she was really moved it seemed false to speak. The group wandered back, and she fell in between Frank and Jessie.

"It's hard for me to understand." She tried to say what was in her mind without any affectation of simplicity. "I can understand how cities and cathedrals come about. You start with any sort of shelter, and then ideas and — materials, techniques, will accrue to it. But mining a mountain . . ."

Jessie pressed in close to her, looking up in her face, and breathing heavily from the climb.

". . . I can't imagine putting such effort into it before you have anything to show. Just an *idea* of it."

"Well, yes and no." He looked at her straight for the first time, caught off balance maybe. "I'd seen a lot of other kinds of mining."

"I admire the vision of it."

He accepted that. "Yes, it wants a vision." But having said so, he was shy again, lowered the eyes that were the exact color of the sky behind his head. "We'll need more wood than that, Johnny. Go on get some and I'll do the cottontail."

Johnny Fousel saluted and started foraging over the hill, bending bowlegged to retrieve a stick of dried cholla here, a scrap of rotted lumber there. The children were sent to help him. Eleanor settled herself on a boulder beside Mary Doreen and the baby, crossed her ankles, and spread her skirt. And then as Mary Doreen provided the names of plants — palo verde, ironweed, lantana, manzanita — Eleanor watched Frank skin the rabbit.

He chopped off the hind feet with a cleaver. He took a slender knife, slit the fur around the haunches, and slipped a finger in to help him nick out with the tip of the blade two little pale pods that for some reason unknown to her he didn't want. He swiped the tip of the knife on the edge of white rock, as if to clean or sharpen it, and — all of this with easy, unthinking skill, intent but careless — slit the belly skin like silk.

"Four states and seven counties," Mary Doreen said, "on a clear day. And we've come a good time of year for that!"

"I've never seen a day clearer," said Laurel.

The blood leaked on the white stone ground. Frank severed the intestines into a slippery pile. He stepped on the nub of tail, tucked his fingers under the cut fur at the haunches, grasped, and peeled the skin back as one peels off a glove. The sinews of his hands, the muscles of his forearms lifted under his skin. The fur continued to strip off over the rabbit's head, but held fast at the end, as if it gripped its own skin in its teeth. Frank jerked; the pelt tore at the lips. He lay the naked body on the rock to hack the tail off, then impaled it on a skewer, smearing the blood around the rock with a gunny sack and laying the carcass on the same sack, while her heart beat hard.

He had taken his jacket off to do all this, laid it across the wagonside. Now he took a jug and tipped a little water in his hands, washed them methodically, and shook them dry. He looked up and smiled at Eleanor, and the smile shocked her, as if she'd been caught at something.

"As different as they can be," said Mary Doreen. "And seems like she's the tomboy and he's got the delicate nature of the two."

Awareness of the blood confused her, where to put her eyes. His hair fell over his forehead. He, who moved at ease as long as he was killing and cutting, now was clumsy again, kneeling by the pile of wood as if it hurt his knees to kneel, erecting a spit with several false tries, laughing at himself.

"Well, it'll be enough to feed a platoon," said Mary Doreen, fussing over the basket. She kept altering its position under the shade of the wagon. "Now, I look to you men to do right by me." The baby slung easily in the crook of her arm, she shoved the basket yet again to a spot behind the wheel and glittered a smile up at Laurel. "Leftovers wouldn't keep to the bottom of the hill in this heat." She fanned the basket with its lid, revealing a mountainous pie, jars of jam and pickles. Eleanor longed for her stylish picnics in Provence with cousin Peg: bread, cheese, and *du pays* on a grassy hillside. She wished that Laurel had let her bring along some wine. He insisted they'd be offended by a bottle of never-mind-how-fine a Bordeaux. She wished she had one all the same.

They built a fire and left Johnny to turn the rabbit while they climbed above the quarry. The children ranged in every direction and back again with treasures that then they tossed away; and once Jessie, that lumpish but rather touching girl, surprised Eleanor by taking her hand, swinging it for the space of two strides, and then relinquishing it with a little toss.

From the highest rise beyond the pit, the desert stretched infinite (or a number of miles for which Mary Doreen knew the precise number in each direction), the horizon torn here and there by a peak, the plain neatly severed by the silver rail. Bowie lay in shining squares at the center of the valley. The tracks sealed the valley like the teeth of a metal zipper, but she would say this to Laurel later because she wasn't sure the Wheelers knew what a zipper was.

"It's like a patchwork quilt," she said instead, and Frank and Mary Doreen laughed. Frank set his hand lightly on his wife's far hip while Mary Doreen interlaced her fingers in his. This was accomplished in a single gesture. It bespoke such easy congress that Eleanor's eyes smarted.

"What magnificent country!" Laurel said. She turned irritably away and seized on a white shape in the distance. It was a rectangle neither so regular nor so bright as the marble behind them, but in that expanse of silt it stood out as if one of the blocks had been lifted there by some wasteland *deus ex machina*.

"It's a Spanish mission," Frank answered her question. "Seventeenth century, they say, but o' course the land's gone to the government and it ain't used for anything now."

"A mission! I should like to see that. Is there a road to it?"

"Not so you'd know it."

"It's a ruin anyways," said Mary Doreen.

"All the same." She turned to Laurel. "I must learn to ride a horse."

An exasperated expulsion of breath escaped him. "You must take the car. Then you and Mrs. Wheeler can go exploring however you like."

"Oh," said Eleanor, "I don't want to go where the road goes, in any case."

The petulance of her own tone rang raw on her ears, and she saw that she had mainly rejected not Laurel's idea but Mrs. Wheeler's company. Frank said defensively, "Mary Doreen don't care for horseback riding," and Mary Doreen added, "I'm not *afraid* of horses, I just don't *care* for them." Eleanor replied inanely, "Ah?" as if this were interesting, but blushed hard in the heat and did not know how to put it right.

Later this moment came back to her, as embarrassing moments will, and so was lightly etched on her mind, and so much later came again with greater force. It was all there, she would remember, in the moment: Mary Doreen Wheeler with a stung look to her cheeks, Frank Wheeler with his hand lightly on his wife's far hip, and the daughter taking it all in with her voracious eyes; the mission off in the distance over Laurel's shoulder, and nearer behind them where they were just about to return and descend to lunch, the smear of carelessly cleaned-up blood on the quarry stone.

PART II

❖

Quarry

14

LLOYD WAS A HERO. The first night, Villa reached into one of the saddlebags and dealt out five gold pieces into Lloyd's palm. The second night they adapted his name into a riding song. The third night Guytan Farga made an incoherent speech, the drift of which was that the gringo had become one of them; and they foisted a marijuana cigarette on him, on which he choked. They laughed. Guytan hugged him. Lloyd felt no immediate effect and so took another drag, at which they set up a chorus of warning hoots. Nevertheless, two nights later they got him soundly stoned, and Cesar Santos pulled his rotten molar with a needle-nosed pliers while Farga and Willoughby held him down. Afterward Lloyd couldn't remember whether it had hurt or not, though he remembered a ferocious determination, later dissipated, to get even with them when he could stand again. Now he carried the tooth in his pocket and his tongue in the tender empty space.

One evening they camped at a railway siding below Ciudad Juárez, and part of the troop rode north with Villa. In the night there was the clanging arrival of an engine and four freight cars, and a lot of shuffling and shifting of men and goods, into which Lloyd did not inquire. From Simon Willoughby he already knew that Charlie Alcott's gold had gone straight back over the border to buy American guns, which would be smuggled back across the river or bribed through El Paso customs. The number of *villistas* and *campesinas* was growing every day. By now they were in the hundreds, and from what he'd overheard among the men, volunteers were headed from all over northern Mexico to scour Orozco's forces out and push on to the capital.

Next morning — at little Farga's invitation, and with no one offering objection — Lloyd went into Juárez with half a dozen others, including Simon Willoughby. The streets were speckled with frogs smashed under wagon wheels, and the city smelled like a standing pond. Lloyd took the precaution of an unfavorable exchange on one of his gold pieces, so as not to be flashing it around town, and all the same he got an American shirt, a pair of stiff twill trousers, a gaucho hat, a haircut, and a shave — and still had fifteen pesos left. He bathed in the back of the barber shop in a tub filled scalding by a solemn, harelipped boy. He lay slack, feeling the grit float off him. The boy's narrow bones threatened him with a memory of Sam. The harelip, a sore-looking off-center slash right to the gum, made Lloyd avert his eyes.

He said to himself that he'd make a plan, but the water lulled him, and he got to thinking about how it used to be his mother who brought the Saturday tubful, bucket after bucket off the stove two rooms away, and soaped his hair and his back. His brother, Frank, was already a grown man and laughed at the notion of a boy liking his bath. But Lloyd always sat hunched over his knees and begged her to scratch her nails up and down his spine in the slippery scum till the water sogged his fingertips and his arms got cold. He'd been eight the year she died.

After the bath he got the shave. The barber was a bald man, pate draped down around the back of his neck, but he was neither gregarious nor amusable, and it struck Lloyd that the mood in Juárez generally had not the same high hilarity as among Villa's troops. A bald barber in camp would have drawn perpetual jokes.

It felt fine to have a jaw again, to run his fingers up its tender undershelf while his tongue inside sought the hollow membrane still tasting of salty blood. He decided to keep the mustache, which had got thicker and coarser than he'd ever thought it would. Afterward, his face, lean under the flat-crowned hat, pleased him in a way he wouldn't have let on to anybody. The part where his beard had been, slightly blue, contrasted to the dark leathering of his upper face, but even that he liked. He felt altogether a little tough and a little dashing.

He paid the barber and walked sidestepping frog bodies to look over the bridge across the Rio Grande. He bought a tamale from a vendor's cart and strolled up and down, peering at the tired vegetables and nickel-silver jewelry spread out on serapes alongside the road, then across at the long, low roof of the El Paso customs shed. A heavily laden donkeycart passed through the checkpoint and over the bridge toward Mexico; two glossily got-up *señoritas* shuffled north. He had his four gold pieces rolled in a bandanna around his shin, and his horse and saddle were stabled two streets up beyond the barber shop. He hung his fingers in the slats of a stacked chicken crate, bit into his tamale, and looked at Texas.

He could cross; it was easy. He had taken horses back and forth over the border at Agua Prieta for his dad a dozen times. If there was any problem, well, it just so happened that his dad had a friend in El Paso Customs — Lloyd remembered meeting Zach Cobb as a kid, or else remembered being told he'd met him. Now Lloyd could take Haragana back home to Bowie, a better horse than his brother, Frank, had ever sat; a fancier saddle than his father owned.

Not enough, not enough. Even now, when he thought about the two of them, Frank and his father, the sweat started out of his follicles and his hackles raised. Staring into the scummy mud of the riverbank he remembered himself as a kid, clumsy, effete, a mama's boy without a mama and too much a boy to handle the ropes, the distances, the branding iron; his efforts dismissed season after season, and no way to drive a wedge in that blank few-words alliance between grown father and grown son.

No. A horse and saddle weren't enough. What would be enough was to be respected among men his father despised, a provable *dorado* of the revolution, rich *and* a rebel!

It was not intended, but when Rudolfo Fierro swiped that knife down the side of Sam's head, he had cut Lloyd off from whoever it was he'd been up to then. His history rewrote itself. He was reborn, except that *reborn* sounded like you automatically got a better life the second time, whereas being here among the Mexicans was just another chance, no special advantages, hard and slippery-footed like the first go-round. By the time he got back home he was going to be somebody else than he always thought he'd be. It wasn't clear yet just exactly who.

As soon as he turned away from the riverbank he breathed easier. He finished his tamale, licked his fingers, and wandered back inland to meet the others.

"Yaii, yaii!" called little Farga, fingering his own inferior mustache. "What a horseman, what a lover!" Lloyd laughed and thought how Farga had looked to him in the mine — cunning and strong as a needle-nosed pliers — and how he looked now — anxious, silly, innocent.

Cesar Santos, riding on the other side of Farga, grinned. "You'll need a woman tonight, gringo-my-brother."

"*Chingo su madre,*" Lloyd said affably.

"Alas," said Santos, "I left my mother back in Hermosillo. But Farga has a sister . . ."

"Keep off my sister."

"I wouldn't dare take a woman named Concepción," Lloyd swaggered, and after a second's hesitation Santos laughed and passed the joke to the rider on his right.

But it wasn't quite the right joke; Lloyd felt the way it sat at angles, foreign. It was all right to talk about conceiving children, especially sons. It was even all right to get thick-throated about it. Or it was all right to talk about having women, doing them, poking, plowing, turning their furrows. But you didn't talk about shoveling women and conceiving sons in the same breath.

"Maybe there'll be no need," Cesar said. "Maybe there'll be fresh supplies tonight."

Lloyd didn't ask what he meant. Santos probably knew something, he always seemed to know what was going on before the others. A clear-eyed intellectual with a delicate, straight nose and sallow skin, Santos had left the priesthood and renounced the Church to become a *dorado*. He had something of the saint about him still. He came from a landed family, so if he was reborn into the revolution it was because he chose it. His force came out of a calm center, and he'd become their storyteller, their orator, second to Villa himself.

"Fresh supplies," repeated Santos, and offered Lloyd a drag off a fat juanita weed. Lloyd took it, managed to ape the way the others gulped a breath and held it in. His throat burned fiercely, as if Doc Hoskins had scraped to check for strep.

Santos did not offer the marijuana to Willoughby. Willoughby was drunk. He rode paunch bulging over his saddle horn, swaying a precarious distance either side of the reins; and he kept emitting a refrain of belches, mutterings, and mumblings. Drunk beside him rode a curly-haired new recruit named Luís, with negroid features and gullible, soft eyes. Seeing Willoughby lurch now, Farga whistled softly through his teeth, a troubled sound. Santos laughed, but cursed laughing, and raised his eyebrows over at Lloyd. Lloyd got down and readjusted Simon's saddlebag so the neck of a Texas malt bottle wouldn't show, then climbed back on his horse and maneuvered around to the other side of Santos. Willoughby stank of sweat and malt.

"He'll sleep," suggested Farga doubtfully.

Lloyd took the weed again. "It's none of my business what he does."

They picked their way along the track. At first glance it looked like camp was set up on a middle-of-nowhere siding, with a trickle of creek in land flat and nondescript for miles around; you could imagine the *federales* charging over the plain to wipe them out. But in actuality this was the central north-to-south railway system of Mexico. They would have to take Pascual Orozco out of Chihuahua in cavalry skirmishes to the east and west, but once they did that, they could push by rail south through Torreón, Durango, and on to Mexico City. They kept predicting the United States would lift the arms embargo, and the men said that when they got cannon on the forward cars, the "*niños*" would cut a trail like machetes in a jungle.

A couple of hundred women were cooking and milling on the east side of the track, and their men squatting, smoking, or else piling sandbags on the west. Some families had pitched their gear and started their fires on top of the boxcars. Children were playing a kind of hopscotch in the dirt. While Lloyd and the men had been in Juárez, the train had grown by two cars and a caboose — seven in all plus engine now — and one freight car had been set up as a supply store. Santos said that Villa would have moved headquarters inside the caboose.

It was nearly sundown, the flat bottom of the western cloudbank glowing orange. The group dispersed toward their bivouacs. Lloyd was behind Willoughby and young Luís, but when the Englishman lurched against a car, Lloyd gritted his teeth and put his horse between Willoughby and the train.

"Simon," he hissed, "you're drunk. Go sleep it off or I won't answer for you." Then thinking this a weak thing to say — he meant not to answer for him anyway — he walked his horse to the western rim of the camp and unsaddled. He found a clump of chaparral to set his back against, and curled down on his saddle blanket to wait for supper.

When he woke, nothing felt familiar. He could smell wood-smoke, chicken, and *frijoles*, each scent distinct from the others — hot, sweet, salt. It was dead dark, three or four hours into dark, and the air had a feel to it, like foam or velvet. There was sweet female singing coming from somewhere, and from somewhere else the shouts that meant Cesar was on his soapbox. Lloyd was stiff and a little foggy. He relieved himself behind the chaparral and went in pursuit of the chicken smell. He picked his way among the *solda-deras'* fires, aware of his hat and his mustache and, resentfully, that he caused a little wake of amusement. Concepción, eyelids sagging tired in her plain round face, gave him a plate of food and turned back to tend her fire.

"*Gracias*, sister of my brother. Where is Farga?"

"Gone with Cesar and the others. They ate many hours ago."

Lloyd scooped the chicken into the tortilla, rolled it, and handed back the plate, cocking his head to bite from his *burrito* as he walked back around the train, catching the sauce in his other palm while the women laughed.

"Why must we take Huerta? Why must we give our lives if it takes our lives to overthrow Huerta?"

Santos stood beside the sandbags in the dark. The men sat and hunkered in concentric rings, the air hung with sweet smoke and onion. Somebody had set lanterns on the bags, and their light threw patterns upward on the faces, making them skull-jawed and strong. Santos had a voice that he could play with, volume and vibrato; he could stir the men to a joy of rage. He could make connections you wouldn't ordinarily see, between the *hacendado*'s whip and the bleeding soul of Mother Mexico; he could tell a story so that at the end of it you would know why the *federales* had to die.

"I will tell you why," Santos told them. "If you have a nail in your shoe, it will not be enough to stanch the blood. If you have a nail in your shoe you waste your time to heal the wound. No, I tell you, the nail must come out! The nail Huerta must be pulled once for all from the foot of this weary nation!"

Dark Luís — the curly new recruit — giggled. The sound was shrill and inappropriate. For some reason it made Lloyd look behind him, and he noticed that Villa had come down to stand on the outskirts of the evening crowd. He sometimes did this, when the men had left their women to clean up after supper and had come to smoke by lantern light.

"For thirty-five years the poor have been robbed," said Santos, "the innocent have been jailed, the peace-loving have been shot down in the street. They killed Madero; they slaughtered the only man we had freely chosen, the only man to promise us the soil of our motherland and the futures of our children. They have taken our lands away piece by piece, and when we had no land they called us slaves."

Sometimes Villa walked among the men, calling one after another by his name. At such times he was dignified, even stately, his bulk balanced on his booted legs as if he had a straight line to the center of the earth, his own personal gravity. Each time Villa appeared (and afterward, in the space between weariness and sleep), Lloyd would imagine that Villa was going to come over and speak to him. *Gringo,* he would say, his brilliant animal eyes trained on Lloyd's face alone. *Trust man.* It would be clear to everyone that Lloyd was not to be forgotten, that he was counted on.

"Most of us have not had much schooling, but we know that when all the talk has failed, then you must fight for what you want. And when you fight your own people, then you must know what is worth dying for, and killing for. We want not to be cheated, not to be murdered, mutilated, humiliated. We want homes, we want schools. We want land where we can set our feet and say: 'I pledge my heart here.' We want land!"

"Land!" shouted the men. Santos always moved them, even if afterward they mainly talked rivalry and cunt.

"Let me tell you a story of our general." Santos stepped up to balance on the sandbags, slender legs apart, at an orator's ease. With his face underlit he seemed older than he was, burnished, as if he were covered in something more durable than skin. Down to the left Simon Willoughby was doing contortions with his mouth, sucking air between his molars.

"I rode with Villa once to Hildalgo del Parral, on the day word came to us of the treacherous assassination of Francisco Madera."

"Huerta! *¡Muerto!*" called the men. Lloyd shouted with them, rolling his *r*'s like Santos, sitting loose in his haunches with his shoulders hung forward careless over his knees, like Farga sat.

Lloyd had grown up understanding that Mexicans were second-rate, not quite clean either of body or of soul. Their religion smelled of perfume, which belonged to women; they loved Jesus in a sloppy way that would embarrass a white man. They lacked "diligence," which his father reverenced; they had "bad taste." All the same, he could tell from the time he was allowed to go among the hands that the things it was good for a man to have, the Mexicans had most of. The Mexicans laughed easier at pain, moved easier in their bodies, fought quicker; they could go longer without food. They could drop anywhere and sleep; they could pick up and leave without goodbye. All this was what a white man wanted more than he dared.

And now Lloyd was one of them, a revolutionary. He was ashamed that he had grown up under roof enough to house a village.

"*¡Muerto!*"

Simon Willoughby yelled a bit late, eyes swiveling around the ring. As Lloyd watched, he leaned sideways, shoving an arm along the ground toward Luís. The dark boy had a silly grin on his face, curly lashes on his heavy half-moon lids.

"That day we knew we would have to pledge our lives for the people of Mexico, and the land would be bought with blood. We rode long hours, the *jefe*'s heart was weary, and as we came into Hildalgo his head was aching."

Santos's voice had softened like the voice of someone telling a *cuento*. The Story of the *Jefe*'s Headache. The men held their cigarettes still in their hands and leaned forward to catch what Santos said. Lloyd trained his eyes on Santos and hoped that nobody supposed he had any interest in Simon Willoughby.

"A poor woman came from Hidalgo del Parral, a woman in clean rags with a ragged *rebosa* over her gray hair. She had heard that the great liberator was in bitter pain. She came with a bowl of hot herb medicine for his head.

"She said, 'Great general, that people are poor does not mean they are stupid. That people dig in the ground for their food does not mean they are weak. This is a tea of herbs and roots, a secret of my mother and her mother before her, and there is no pain it will not ease. Take it and be well. It is a gift of an old woman of Hidalgo del Parral.'

"Now, my friends, you know that our general is not a gullible man."

A shout of laughter went up. "¡*Viva!*" Across the ring Luís's head disappeared below the sandbags, then glossily reappeared. Lloyd glanced back at Villa, who was listening to Santos's story with his head laid on the side and a soulful, remembering expression. It came into Lloyd's head that he was a part of Villa's story like the old woman of Hidalgo now. He remembered the Gringo Chink mine the way he'd seen it last, with the burro tethered to the stake off of which Villa had wrenched the claim sign and, inside, the thin boy curled knees-to-chin with his hand clamped flat against his head so his hand seemed to be bleeding from the palm. He calculated the time since then, and came up with seven-plus weeks. It felt like seven centuries. It felt as though it wasn't really him that it had happened to — not that or any it of since he first knew Sam — not his true self. It's a strange thing to say that a whole chunk of your life, nearly a third of it, could *not count,* but all of a sudden he remembered other people hinting at the same thing if only he'd understood it at the time. Alma Timkin used to confuse him by claiming Ohio was "on a different planet." One Fourth of July at home Johnny Fousel had made some remark, how Lloyd's mama'd never let them lay the table so piecemeal for a holiday, and his dad had got a set look to his jaw when he answered, "That's another lifetime, John." At that moment Lloyd had hated his dad blind, and the spareribs went greasy down his gullet; but now he understood how your life can change so much there's hardly any connection between this part and that. Now he understood he was never really the sort to take up with Sam; it was exactly because so many things made him feel weak and mad when he was a kid that he had wanted to protect the littler one, the Chinese. He'd gotten temporarily sidetracked from his destiny.

Across the fire the men cheered up at Santos; their necks were thick and gold. Farga punched a fist in the air.

"Our general keeps his eyes open and his back to the wall," said Santos. "But from the hands of this poor woman he took the brew and drank it down. And the woman turned to the people who had gathered there and said: 'Truly this is a man of the people. If the great Villa trusts me, a poor peon, I may trust the flowers of my life to him.' She turned back to the *jefe* and she said: 'I have seven sons who wish to join you. I deliver them into your hands, for the people of Mexico.' "

The men broke into cheers. "*¡Viva! Viva! Viva Villa!*"

Villa came forward smilingly. He circled the sandbags, but not greeting the men who reached up, fists clenched, to renew their pledge to him. He just kept walking in a circle, toward where Santos stood and then past Santos. Lloyd cheered with the rest.

When he had come three quarters of the circle, Villa stopped behind the kid Luís, whose black locks caught the light. The cartridges on Villa's belt shone like curls of brass. Villa reached down between Luís and the sandbags, rooted among the boots and spurs, and stood up holding a bottle of Texas malt by its neck. He swung it by its rim between his thumb and finger, which gave him a fastidious look, somebody holding a soiled thing.

Villa reached across his vest and took his ivory-handled .44 out of its holster, touched the barrel to the tip of his nose as if he had an itch there. The men shied either side, and now the silence was more profound than it had been for Santos's story, except that from the other side of the boxcars there came the flippant rhythm of the women singing a *corrida*.

Villa turned the gun so that he was oiling the sight on the side of his nose. Slowly he lowered the muzzle and set it against Luís's dark neck, and the boy folded his arms over the top of his head and spread his hands down the bent nape, not so much protective as accepting — as if, if he was going to lose his head, he'd want to lose his hands as well.

Villa stood thoughtful a moment, then bent his elbow sharply so his hand came up to his shoulder and the barrel pointed straight into the black sky. He walked the bottle, swinging it back and forth, over the heads of the men toward Santos and then, turning with a light step, almost coy, walked it over their heads back again, past Luís, to where Simon Willoughby sat spine-straight, his hands hung limp over his knees. Simon was staring, scowling, at an unlit cigar stub between his fingers.

Villa raised the bottle over Simon's head and put the pistol to it. The shot blasted, and the bottle shattered in the lantern light. The singing on the far side of the train cut short. The men in range slapped their hands to this and that part of their necks and arms like they'd been hit by a mosquito swarm. Simon sat still in the middle of it, whiskey dripping from his hair, and after a second the little pricks of blood began to sidle down his face. He shuddered the collar of his shirt. Villa tossed the neck of the bottle into Simon's lap and put his gun back in his holster and resumed his tour of the circle, back to the caboose in no hurry and without a word to anyone. When he was back inside Simon shook, flipping whiskey from his head like a wet dog.

Lloyd slipped off back to his bivouac. He didn't need to go messing with Simon. Not many stuck around, to tell the truth. Lloyd learned next day that he was not much hurt, just had to have a few slivers tweezed out of his forehead and his neck. He was mainly hung over, or scared, or both, so bad that he fouled the creek, and everybody had to draw water upstream of it.

What was surprising, though — they found the kid Luís next morning with his throat slit, laid out between the wheels of the car just behind the engine.

15

IT COULDN'T LAST. That excursion buoyed her like her scarf end in the breeze, no use when they touched down on the plain again. There was little to do. There could be no pleasure in the keeping of that house, ugly as it was and holding mainly the traffic of Maria and herself.

Who invented such places to live in? The big porch was on the west, where the afternoon sun fried you to leather. The bedroom windows faced the street and needed curtaining for even the most idle passage there. You had to U-turn in the hall to get from the kitchen to the dining room. Really, it was very instructive how to make a house, living in one so badly planned as this one.

There was a story, central to Kenny family lore, of Eleanor's having been given a dollhouse lavishly appointed from newel post to chandelier. Christmas afternoon she was found on the library floor arranging little sofas, braided rugs, and carved clocks into a construct of empty boxes. She said the dollhouse was "stupid" and got her mouth washed out with soap. But she remembered the frustration of the narrow rooms, the awkward position of the stairs. Here in the Semple house the space had been cubicled and parsed into grimy little pokeholes. She would like to have blown the whole thing up. She would like to have blasted passages and razed walls.

Laurel urged her to begin thinking what sort of house she wanted, to take the car and go scouting for a site. She said she would. He suggested gently that she should bestir herself to make friends. She knew this was so, and his saying it drove her to bottled rage.

"I'll start a literary circle, shall I then? A Renaissance discussion group?"

"Eleanor."

She repented at once; she had never belonged to a literary circle in her life. She had used to talk ruffles and romance with Cousin Peg.

That week she lay unprotesting while he made love to her, feeling the poignancy of his desire, aware that its poignancy arose from her indifference. The nuns had made the girls bathe in heavy pinafores so they wouldn't be tempted by the sight of their own bodies; she knew that flesh was terrible and thrilling. But embarrassment and envy were all she felt, while he worshiped at her belly, breast. She could see the sincerity of it, she could see that when he ran his tongue along her collarbone, pooled his spittle in the hollow, carried on to lick a ring around her breast and settle in finally sucking, moaning, at the nipple — what he felt was ecstatic and profound. There was a prickling sensation just short of pain in her aureole. She watched him, bemused. Concealing her aversion. Angry. Almost tender because she saw he meant it. She would so have welcomed it, could she have lost herself like that.

And then after a time she was frightened by his need. His illness was sad and somehow rich with sadness, but it was not frightening because it did not undercut his authority, and it was this to which she owed her duty. Duty had carried her across a continent. If she had followed his need instead of his authority, confusion followed. Who was she then, and why was she here?

When he was done she washed herself, put on a clean peignoir, and while he slept she took a glass of brandy out to the porch where, now that it was November, at least a little relief stirred up at night. The sky was imponderably soft and black. Sometimes if she couldn't sleep she'd have a second cordial or liqueur, even a third, varying her choices for the variety of it, and only a little because Laurel might notice if she drank a bottle entirely up. Sitting in that vast dark, she felt herself more profoundly naked, at once exposed and stretched. She remembered the veranda in Baltimore, the air like cotton and the ivy swathing the trees. There, the seasons tumbled past; the ivy would blacken and renew, the leaves of the sweet gum drop and sprout. Here the barren plain and mountains bespoke a temporal vastness, a nakedness in time.

But when she came to write letters home, she found herself describing sunsets in terms of taffeta colors, exclaiming like a traveler at the heat. The local people appeared as quaint. She had no truth to tell about her life, or else no one to whom she could write the truth. Mama, Cousin Peg, even once Amy Whitney, wrote details of upholstery and picnics — letters that struck her, like her own, as scribbled trivia, even though they made her sick with longing.

It wore on her. One day she couldn't rouse herself, and the next she feared she was going mad with cabin fever. Then she would briefly pump herself up with resolve: She *would* choose a house site. She would make a round of calls.

What she did, mainly, was to play her piano. It was the only thing that gave her any peace. The nimbleness of her fingers was a substitute for exercise. Bach let her remember home, and even sadness was an advance over that sour lethargy. Baltimore would jump up on the bench beside her, sometimes Maria would stop in the doorway and listen. Eleanor, aware of the girl and disembodied from her own hands — watching them, wondering at the mechanism that should allow her fingers to remember what her mind did not — was grateful for the audience. She pretended not to know that Maria was there, so that she shouldn't be forced to send her back to work. Once she said something, a throwaway apology, about the fact that she was still in her wrapper at two in the afternoon. "My mother should say I've been corrupted!"

But Maria shrugged. "These corset are not for our weather here. We Mexican women have known that always."

One morning the weather broke. Or rather, a cloud came over, which, like Maria's basket of wash, got wrung out on the thirsty ground. Eleanor went from window to window, listening to the wonderful, rich rumble of thunder, watching raindrops the size of scuppernongs fall out of the scarcely dimmed dome of heaven. Afterward the prickly pear and the palo verde looked polished, and the foothills took on violet shadows. Eleanor put on stout shoes and the lightest cotton skirt and blouse she could find.

"I won't be away long," she said to Maria, while she pinned on her hat. It was what one always said to servants. She had heard her mother say this even when she planned to take a train to Washington.

"Be away long," Maria said with a laugh. "It will do you good." Which was an impertinence, but Eleanor decided to laugh, too. She had a sudden impulse — which she stilled — to tell Maria about the marmoset she'd smuggled onto the sleeping porch at school.

She stepped out into the fresh world. The air smelled alive and green. The rain had retreated instantly into the ground, and the surface was shellacked into a skin of soil through which every footstep broke to powder.

Eleanor struck out onto a ranch road and headed toward the Chiricahuas, peering east until she saw the shimmer of the Spanish mission like a chipped tooth on the scoured plain. She sighted it along her thumb: about the width and half the height of her nail. Someone, she supposed, would be able to tell from that how far it was, or how big, or both. She knew that the desert distances were deceptive and that it would be foolish to try to walk there. She decided once more that she would learn to ride.

She headed toward a ranch house to the south, unpainted clapboard weathered gray — the one that had been pointed out as belonging to the younger Wheelers. The road wound around boulders and gullies between two barbed wire fences; cattle inert in the scrub paid no attention to her. She became aware of an immense stillness, and at the edge of the ranch yard she stopped, hearing only her own blood coursing, as if she were the sole disturbance in the universe. She was hot, dusty; she took off her hat. Now there was a sound like a whistling lariat coming from behind the house. She would ask Mrs. Wheeler for a glass of water.

Frank Wheeler's thoughts were miles away. He stood in the backyard in his undershirt, swinging the chicken around his head, his hand backtracking in its path to produce the precise clack of the neck breaking (the method that Johnny Fousel had taught him when his hands weren't strong enough to twist a pullet dead, but that he still used because he thought it more efficient and somehow less *personal*). His thoughts were six point seven miles away, to be exact. The sound had taken him there. He was watching the whirring wheelsaw shear a three-quarter-inch slab of marble from the block like a slice of bread. The block fed through on greased rollers, the steam pistons pumped a tune, the slice toppled over prettily into the buck-gloved hands of two Mexicans poised to catch it. The light hung in its veins. Anywhere you sliced you opened up something God-hidden in the earth for a million years, a stone snowstorm swirling turbulent like weather and, like a snowflake, not exactly repeated anywhere in creation.

There were not many saw the quarry as he did. Most men headed for the water pipe after they made the climb, and only a few refreshed themselves at the sight of the pit, dived into it with their eyes, buoyant like it was a watering hole. That's what it did to Frank. Lloyd it never had. A sunny, game kid, who always wanted to please him — but Lloyd never loved the rock. Mary Doreen wanted it for Frank's sake, which was the right feeling for a woman, but she didn't raise it up out of there with her eyes, she didn't flex her muscles wanting to get at it. Wally had looked at it that way for a time, before his angering caution got the better of him. A workman could see it sometimes, even a Mexican, and that man would hitch himself to the pulley if he had to.

Frank dropped the newly dead dominicker on the pile, where it thrashed. There was a wire pen of the creatures beside him, and at his feet about a dozen limp bodies. He reached into the pen for a leghorn, swung it up — and saw her poised demure and large at the corner of the house, straw hat held in two hands in front of her skirt like something out of a back-East magazine. For a second she was superimposed on his daydream of the marble, together with a subterranean sense that she had something to do with the quarry that he could not now recall.

"Oh! Mrs. . . ." Her name wouldn't come to mind.

"I'm sorry," she said.

He snatched his shirt from the fence post, conscious that his shoulders were bare and sweaty. He dropped the leghorn back in the pen. The dead dominicker flapped its wings, and its scrambling set the rest of the pile in motion. Frank did his buttons.

"I'm afraid you've caught . . ." he said just as she was starting, "I knocked in front . . ." They both stopped. She lifted her hands, palms up.

"I always seem to see you at your slaughtering," she said.

He didn't know what she meant, and not knowing suddenly annoyed him. She stood there so cool, so sure she had a right to be wherever she pleased — his private yard for a start — because she was back-East folk, eddi-cated, up to her ears in bank money. It embarrassed him to be tucking in his shirt. He shook his head.

She said, "The rabbit, up on the mountain."

"Oh, Johnny shot that. I just dressed it." This was stupid, literal-minded; now he resented that she made him stupid. He said testily, "I suppose I do put food on my table one way or another by slaughtering."

"You put food on all our tables."

"Yes'm."

"I don't suppose we should eat meat if we're not willing to watch you at it."

This was a funny thing for a woman to say, and altogether she struck him as unwomanlike. She was like somebody running a temperature on purpose.

"You'd get an arg'ment from my wife about that. She says she don't mind any amount of cutting up and cooking, but she doesn't want to see things die." He put a hand down to still the last throes of the chicken on top. "She's gone into town about some dry goods."

The Poindexter woman (the name came back to him) wafted a hand to say it didn't matter, and he felt inhospitable now. He didn't seem to be able to feel the right thing no matter what he felt. If he didn't get those chickens plucked straightaway he'd be after the pinfeathers with a pliers till dark. "I could offer you a cup of coffee, though . . ."

"Please don't bother. What I'd like most is a glass of water, if I could trouble you."

"No trouble at all." He held his hands over the trough to pump water onto them, dried them conscious that the towel hanging there was none too clean, and headed for the back steps.

"Really — a sip from the ladle would be fine."

"No, no, now. Mary Doreen wouldn't let me hear the last of it if I didn't get you a glass." He held the door for her. "We got a pump indoors two, three years ago."

"But I know you're working."

"There's a dozen chickens'll thank you for the delay."

"It's so beautiful after the rain," she said climbing past him, smelling of heat and flower water. "But a thirsty walk all the same."

A square divided half for living room and eating, the other chopped into bedrooms — Frank never particularly looked at his house, but this woman made him see how plain it was, scrubbed splintery. A long pine table gave off an odor of linseed oil, a row of black iron pots hung on a beam by their handles, smallest to biggest. He was aware at the same time how proud Mary Doreen kept things and what poor things they were to keep. Eleanor Poindexter looked around with a bright, too-cheerful look.

"Ah, you have your own marble on the sink. It's beautiful."

From an open shelf he picked a heavy-bottom glass tumbler and primed the pump. "Thank you."

"When Laurel and I build, I want our house to be full of your marble. Floors and pillars of it. A whole built-in vanity." The water came out in a rush and sloshed his cuff. He glanced at her warily. "I mean, of course, what we can afford. I've a lot to learn about building prices. But I do know it's a first principle of architecture to use the native materials. So I'm lucky to have landed in a place that has such beautiful stone to work with, am I not?"

He did not know what to say. He felt that she had somehow read his thoughts and come upon cupidity. Or Mary Doreen had already gotten to her, that's why she's here? The banker had changed his mind? He handed her the glass, and she drank greedily.

"Well," he said, "I hope I get the quarry open again so we can accommodate you."

"I'm sure you will." Her breasts took up a lot of the space between them, a little edge of lace crisped out at the level of his own chest. Sometimes he cornered Mary Doreen here by the sink, but now he was in that corner. He was too tall to get past the pots on the beam without bending, and he didn't want to bend. A trickle of water ran from the corner of her mouth down her long neck, and she ignored it, kept on gulping back the water like a man.

"Well, but I didn't come about that," she said when she finally paused. It struck him this was probably true after all. Poindexter wasn't somebody that would talk about his business with his wife. Over the linseed oil he could smell her, musky-sweet. "I really do mean to take up riding, and I wondered if you'd have time to help me."

He turned back to the shelf and took a pewter cup, pumped himself a drink. This was just what Mary Doreen would have wanted, but he stalled, pretending not to understand. "That's a hard one. There aren't many of the town ladies that ride, and the ranch wives, they ride western. The trouble is, I don't know anybody'd be able to teach you sidesaddle."

"Oh." She tilted her head at him. "Do I want sidesaddle then?"

He wiped his mouth with the edge of his hand. "I couldn't say."

"What would be the advantage of a sidesaddle? Apart from fashion."

"You can't wear a skirt and ride western."

She laughed. "That's what I mean. But otherwise, what's the difference? Isn't western faster?"

She was somebody that would want to go faster, or think she did. He wondered would she have as much grit as she credited herself.

"I haven't rode sidesaddle myself," he said. She smiled at his joke, and this pleased him out of proportion. She was friendly enough, and it couldn't do any harm to court her favor. Still, part of him would have liked to pin her against the wall just to shock her. "But it's my observation," he said, "sidesaddle you sit *on* the horse. Western you go *with* him."

"Well, then" — she handed him her glass — "I'll get some culottes made. Will you have time to teach me?"

A pushy woman and a man who won't be pushed. Too cumbersome for a small ranch kitchen. He upended her glass on the drainboard and led her back outside.

"I might could. Or else think of someone to do it." At the steps he felt obliged to add, "Mary Doreen will be sorry to have missed you." He meant to put her off till he could have time to think it through, but something like curiosity or swagger got the better of him, and instead he beckoned her around the pile of dead chickens, stuck his arm inside the shed, and came out with a fistful of hay, which he handed her.

"Let's see how you like a horse close to." She hung her hat on a post to take the hay. Frank put a foot on the lowest rung of the fence and whistled through his teeth. Digger, a short-legged pinto mottled like spilled molasses, came lifting his knees in a lope.

"Hold your hand flat out."

She did. Most of the hay fell on the ground, but Digger put a nose in her palm, chomped on the rest, and looked at her out of one eye like a chip off midnight. When the hay was gone, he went on nuzzling her palm, and Eleanor Poindexter shivered and laughed a clear bell of excited laughter.

"That's it," said Frank. She lifted her free hand and ran it down the pinto's face. "His name is Digger," he said.

The horse reached with his head and hooked his chin over her shoulder, his upholstered brown face against her face, dark eye to eye. Eleanor Poindexter stood steady against the horse, her look scared but talking low in her throat. She didn't flinch.

It surprised him. The way — he remembered now — it had surprised him how she took to the quarry, how she dropped her airs. Now she surprised him again because she was afraid and not willing to be afraid. Mary Doreen claimed not to be scared of horses, but if she got herself touched by one she'd shy away cute as a foal. This Poindexter woman would stand her ground.

"That's it," Frank said again. "You'll do just fine."

16

FOR MOST OF THESE PEOPLE life was dour and small. The first batch had come late in the century, after the gold fever had died down, from Iowa farms and Ohio industry, from land too small or wages too low to feed them, because the Southern Pacific required a dining stop at intervals of four or five hours along its track. The second batch had come to provide necessities for the first; and after that the town grew by each amenity and service it could afford until, as Wally Wheeler had observed, there were soles enough in it to support a family just on the repair of them, heel and toe.

They had come from less than they thought they were coming to. They wanted decency rather than fame, comfort in place of wealth. They were resilient and optimistic and had chosen as their mission to tame the West. All the same, they found marriage disappointing, God remote, the land unforgiving, and the money always hard to stretch beyond shoe leather to some few little pleasures.

They hardly ever spoke the truth about these things to each other. Why should they? They spoke a good deal of the weather because it was so much the same, and a case could be made out for its being superior to the weather wherever back home was. They spoke a good deal about the Mexicans because the Mexicans' lot was demonstrably worse than their own, and a case could be made out for its being the Mexicans' fault. They spoke a good deal of the future because comfort seemed to recede always further into it.

What entertainment they had was of their own making, and gossip often stood in for erudition. If Josef Vandercamp had said, "I hate my life," this would not have been considered information; but if he said that, according to the old split-palate O'Joe, Mrs. Poindexter had been down in shantytown and gone into the church there, his authority grew a little. If Jo Hannah Robinson pointed out that O'Joe was tetched in the head and drunk more than half the time anyways, that had to be taken into account. If May Nene said there was religious music coming out of the Semple house, it had to be considered. And if Selma Eickenberry, who lived next to the railroad tracks, kept an eye out without ever acquiring any corroboration of O'Joe's claim — well, the case came around to no conclusion, the same as any other learning.

They were intense. It was a matter of some moment. Every Sunday that the Poindexters did not show up in church was a rejection greater than Sunday last. The excuses that could be made for them were fewer. The evidence grew more inescapable that, just as they had always feared, the Poindexters were between them atheistical, popish, and uppity.

But as soon as the Poindexters appeared, it was all forgiven. Once let her come inside the church under a blue felt brim, rich hair wound into a French knot that poked it up to a tilt in back, dark ribbons streaming; let her augment the angle of it bowing her head over the Wesleyan hymnal, and both of them join in the Doxology! Well, the Reverend Newsome had the inspiration to change the morning reading, and did the parable from Matthew, about getting the lost sheep back in the fold.

The Bowie Methodists were modest, but not as regards Methodism. It didn't seem strange to them that a Catholic should undergo such speedy and apparently painless conversion. Catholicism, like higher education, no doubt belonged to the murky mores of the East Coast, and could be sloughed in one transcontinental train ride, like a snakeskin against the desert scrub.

Laurel ended by concluding, as he so often did, that he had underestimated his wife. At first he dreaded that she would ask about the Catholic Church, and was grateful when she didn't. Then he began to watch uneasily her routine of solitary "Mass" at the little altar, which he thought eccentric, outside the healthy function of worship. He worried about her failure to make social calls or announce herself "at home." He feared that if they didn't go to church it would be read unkindly, on the just grounds that Mrs. Poindexter thought herself too good for them. Worse, he feared that the townspeople would infer the state of his health. He kept hoping the right time to bring the subject up with Eleanor would present itself.

It didn't, but all the same, one night he broached it. She had gone out to the screened porch, and he poured two brandies, took out the little silver tray, and sat at an angle to her, looking at the cool blue rim of the horizon between dark desert and dark sky.

"I hadn't *quite* foreseen," he began in an ironic tone, "how visible I would be in a town this size."

"And I would be," she said serenely.

"You, of course." He shifted his weight and glanced at her. Her hair was combed back off her face to catch the breeze, knotted at her crown, and tumbling free from there. "It's immensely interesting," he said, "the convolutions of the power structure. Money is paramount, of course, but there's so little education and so little government that the other counters shift. Moral power is real — the moral forms in any case: church, charity — and the perception of one's virtue by the others. The schoolteacher — a maiden lady of faultless character, so far as I can determine — is rather suspect in that she reads Keats for recreation."

Before supper Eleanor had pulled from a drawer some bit of needlework begun and abandoned in Baltimore (a good sign?), but it was too dark for that now, and it lay in her lap while she let her body take the lazy V of the wicker chaise. He knew that he was inviting her to laugh at the town with him, and that this might defeat his purpose, but he had no other inspiration. "Whereas Walter Wheeler, who has the money in the first instance, secures his position by teaching Sunday school and introducing a spittoon ordinance. Did I mention that?"

"Laurel." She held her glass by both hands under her nose, mouth hidden, eyes cool.

"Yes?"

"I love to hear you spin a theory. But I have been married to you for four years now. Why don't you just tell me? We need to go to church, is that it?"

He was forced to know he underestimated her. And yet there seemed something almost perverse in it. She stood on ceremony, she lived well concealed within herself, until once you'd twisted yourself into a knot trying to play the game aright, she would turn on you a look of frank simplicity — she did so now — and say, for instance, "I've seen the Catholic church. It's a mud hut in shanty-town."

As if it were he who were disingenuous and not she. Relieved and angry, saying nothing, he sipped his brandy.

"Let me set you a conundrum, though. Say we attend the Methodist church. If I admit my behavior is hypocritical, is it? Or does it become honest the moment I acknowledge I'm a hypocrite?"

They went to church and she, who might have given the small version of herself, marched expansively down the aisle. Afterward he remembered that there was a complicated stitching on the yoke of her suit, which reminded him of chain mail. She walked, hand on his arm, a little armored.

Mrs. Vandercamp, in a resonant alto, sang "A Mighty Fortress Is Our God" with such contortions of her face and neck that half the congregation closed their eyes, affecting a look of rapture. Reverend Newsome read from Scripture regarding lamb and fold, and then sermonized on some unrelated topic, either the ten talents or the talent hidden under the bushel basket — or perhaps it was some clever cross reference that Laurel's biblical scholarship was unequal to. The Nene girl, curls crowding each other horizontal to the height of her crown, kept turning to ogle Eleanor and getting kicked in the shins for it. Wally Wheeler and Murray Robinson passed the offering plates, which were pewter and must have cost four times the morning's take.

Afterward, outside, the people addressed themselves to Eleanor while looking at each other. They offered a dozen logical justifications why the Poindexters had not been seen in church till now: the unpacking, the heat, the settling in, the storm. They stood on the periphery of a palm tree too low for shade, chatting in clusters while the damp gathered on the upper lips of matrons and under the collars of brash-faced young men. The children played tag, or hung curious in the crowd. This, Laurel thought, was where health lay: one foot below sea level, seventy-eight degrees at a November noon, humidity about one and a half. He felt the damp exuding from him while he took in the baked air.

"Have you met Sheriff Robinson? Jay and Mona Nene? Ruth and Josef Vandercamp? Pru Hoskins?"

They would have been quick to find a reason to dislike her, but in the meantime they wanted to establish a claim. Mary Doreen Wheeler tucked a hand around Eleanor's elbow.

"We did manage to get them up to the Chiricahuas, and let them see the valley view. Frank says you haven't been to Bowie till you've seen it from up there."

Frank Wheeler, tentative as ever, let his wife speak for him. He took hold of a palm frond and methodically split its blades to the tip, which would have looked like a nervous habit in anybody with smaller hands.

"Eleanor" — Mary Doreen flung a small glance around to register the use of the first name — "is going to learn to ride." She drew an arc in the dirt, dancelike, with the toe of a buttoned shoe too clumsy for such a motion. She dimpled at Eleanor's presumed accomplishment. "Frank's agreed to teach her."

It was the first Laurel had heard of it. He was taken by a surge of anger that she had let it emerge this way, in public, from a relative stranger. It was a trick she had. He'd seen her win over her father more than once with a *fait accompli*. Whether she rode horses was her business, but he didn't like her incurring an obligation to a man he'd refused a loan. Eleanor couldn't have known about that. All the same, she blundered in without thinking.

At least she had the decency to be embarrassed, giving him an ironic little grimace and not looking at Wheeler at all, who in any case continued to split his frond with scholarly concentration.

"How do, good day." The Chinese grocer in a bowler hat and his wife in gingham joined the group. They were a square couple, faces broad and flat, he solid, she sleek and cushioned. Hum's brim sat low to the brow, shading eyes that conveyed both sadness and strong will. Wally Wheeler barely touched his Stetson; Laurel saw that the Hums' tenure in the group was conditional.

"You haven't heard from Lloyd," Li said to Wheeler, a statement. He took his glasses off and polished them with a blue bandanna.

"Not yet; I don't *expect* to *yet*."

"I also haven't heard from Sam," Li said, and the exchange had the rhythm of ritual. For a second the two of them shared the look of tired old men.

Then Wheeler clapped his elder son on the shoulder and announced more generally, "I don't expect to hear from Lloyd until he rolls in here in a silk suit and a li-mou-zine!"

Frank grinned. Li shook his head doubtfully. Several laughed.

The clumps of folk had milled and shifted vaguely along gender lines, to form a ring of men, an oval of women, the Hums tangential to both. The women were now pressing Eleanor with invitations, while the men moved on to talk of the Mexican troubles.

"You don't worry about Lloyd down amongst those gangsters?" somebody asked, but this was a question so tactless that Wheeler didn't have to join the chorus: *No, not him, he'll stay clear of that bunch!*

Laurel smiled at genial random and took another breath of the dry air, willing it to work its benefice. Too deep an inhalation made him cough. Still, it was a dry cough, calling no attention to itself, producing nothing but dry sound. Not for him the spongy lung lining, the sputum, the blood. One doctor at Johns Hopkins had described the process of recovery as pearlmaking. The microscopic rods of the bacilli lay in his lungs like grains of sand in an oyster. If he ate well, rested sufficiently, took in the clean, dry air — then layers of calcification would coat the bacteria, lock them away where they could do no harm. Deep in the tissue you could manufacture your own defense.

Behind him the women still fussed over Eleanor while the men went forward, comfortably in consensus, vilifying Villa.

"Now, you must be sure to join the Thursday circle. It's being held at Jo Hannah's house this week."

"What do you think about this buildup in Chihuahua? They say they're swarming like flies down there."

"We pick a new subject each month and read up on it. It's a wonder to learn what they're doing in the Congo missions!"

"I think it's the banditry he likes. This ree-volution's just an excuse."

Around him the men laughed wisely. Their fundamental values — civilization, living standard, education, sanctity of life — were those that Laurel shared, without necessarily wanting to put them into the hands of the Bowie elders.

"You hear there's talk of lifting the embargo? The fool president is going to *arm* those hooligans."

"No, you watch, Wilson'll invade."

"Who, him? He hasn't got the stuffin'."

"Not *against* the bandits, I mean. He'll go in on their side!"

Now without warning he was tired. Tuberculosis often presented itself as a malaise, but this sudden downturn of his spirits did not feel physical — a moral fatigue, rather, a social disenchantment. It flashed across his mind that a man is unhappy to the degree that he disdains his neighbors.

The women were taking their leave, still giving off small vibrations of anxiety in which Eleanor basked, bright with nerve. "Well, we should love you to give us a talk about Baltimore. We're powerful ignorant of the East, ha, ha!"

"Join us Thursday, mind."

The Poindexters climbed into the car. The curly Nene girl still hung beside them. She reached toward the handle of the door, but Jessie Wheeler shoved her hand away.

"Goodbye! Goodbye!"

Frank Wheeler finally left off destroying his palm frond to crank the car, giving it more muscle than it would have needed. Laurel and Eleanor left in a wake of goodwill. She turned to wave. She shone the way rock becomes translucent under pressure.

Or else he was wrong. When they got home she went into the bedroom and closed the door. He heard her long after, pacing, rocking, he would almost have said thrashing, before she napped in the stifling heat.

17

THE FIRST THING to be dealt with was attire, which proved so difficult that she nearly gave the whole project up. Mr. Dan Riggs at the dry goods store asserted that she could not get a pair of culottes made in town for the simple reason that nobody had ever seen any. She would have to go into Tucson, and even so she might not find them. In the meantime, the ranch women wore dungarees the same as the men, and he could outfit anyone in those up to a two-hundred-and-fifty-pound hand, which he'd had to one time for the Humble ranch.

"I felt mighty sorry for *that* horse!"

Dan Riggs was small, slight, rubbery in his ambling around the dry goods counters. He had a corrugated brow, brushed over with his few last gossamer strands of hair. His mustache hung in two perfect points. A vain man then, with, moreover, an acerbic tone. Eleanor did not trust him.

"You know, what the Mexican women do to get on a mule is, they take the back hem of their skirt and pull it up between their legs and tuck it in their waistband. It makes a pretty decent pair of trousers, and it's a whole lot cooler."

"Is that so," Eleanor said coldly.

There was humiliation in it that could only be borne by a show of carelessness, because proprietor Riggs did not know much about the size of women's hips and did not know anything about hers. What she ended with, in the curtained space beyond the counter of

Horlick's Malted Drops and licorice twists, was a pair of dark blue twill worsteds that called itself a "waistband thirty," whereas her waist, she knew perfectly well, was twenty-one. She did not trust Mr. Riggs either to understand the odd shape of a man's trousers or to keep his counsel in the town. She had a moment's stinging vision of the ladies standing outside the church of a Sunday morning exchanging misinformation about the size of her waist. However, the boots were some recompense. When she slipped them on, the tooled tops hugged her calves, the strength and pitch of the heel threw her forward into a natural stride.

At home she fretted in the mirror. The shallow rise of the trousers lost the advantage of her slender waist; her blouse boxed straight from bosom to hip. However, a fitted linen jacket with a long peplum gave her a certain equestrienne dash. Her wide-brimmed straw hat was trimmed in artificial iris that picked up the indigo of the worsteds. She would not have pruned roses in such an outfit in Baltimore, but given the cow-town context, the improvisational nature of the assignment, and the reckless mood with which she chose to meet it, she was not altogether displeased.

Laurel was displeased.

It was on a Saturday morning that she went for her first riding lesson. She came to him in the parlor, where he sat sorting a box of books he'd fetched from the station. He said without looking up, "Here's something that may interest you, Eleanor. The new Jack London just out. It had rave notices in the *Sun*." Then he peered up over the half-moons of his spectacles, that anxious smile that always seemed to be at once pleading and remonstrative — or perhaps she was a little primed for his disapproval. In any case he stopped, exaggerated a look of shock (clowning was never his forte), but said nothing, so she supplied, "Isn't it dreadful! But it's the nearest thing I could find to jodhpurs." She wanted to use the word *jodhpurs,* to remind him that, on horseback, women of wealth and rank wore trousers.

"Hmmm. Well. Perhaps we could send for jodhpurs for you. And you could delay your riding lessons until then."

"It would be summer before they got here. No, I'll do as I am." She smiled archly. "The horse won't mind."

"As you wish."

So she did as she chose and he let her, as usual. Then why did she leave him feeling humiliated, while he stayed behind full of wronged righteousness?

Frank Wheeler, however, laughed. He said she would swelter in that jacket, and that the wind would take her hat if she succeeded in making the horse move at all. Then he saw he had offended her, and became so awkward over it that she ended by reassuring him, laughing it off herself. He produced from his own house a sort of Mexican-looking hat with a flat crown and a string to keep it around her neck if the wind caught the brim. Mary Doreen Wheeler came out and offered her a cup of coffee (declined) and said with a face of fixed goodwill that Eleanor looked simply scrumptious. The girl Jessie peered out through the curtains.

Had Eleanor undergone such a tedious and contentious preparation for anything at all in Baltimore, where there were a dozen activities to choose from any hour of the day, she would have scrapped the whole idea. But that was not the case. What else was she going to do? So she approached the horse from the left as she was told and lifted her boot to the stirrup and her hands to the saddle horn.

What combination of attributes was it that made her good at this? There was no way it could have been predicted, although afterward you could list factors enough, guessing merely, to account for it. She was, like the pinto, a little short in the thigh and long in the foreleg. Was that an advantage? She had the habit of upright posture and the habit of persistence. She had a sentimental love of dumb creatures combined with a quick response to challenge. She was exhilarated by speed. She was always anxious to please a teacher, and she never knew, as her parents had indulgently said of her, when enough was enough.

"Sit into the saddle. That's it. Heels down in your stirrups. Feel the horse through your spine. You've got it, yes, ma'am! Don't touch that saddle horn, lift his head by the reins. That's it. Now, go!"

At first she was diffident of Frank Wheeler's time, but once he had decided in earnest that he would teach her, she learned, much to her astonishment, that cattle ranching is an undemanding job. "There's always fences to mend and gear to be seen to. Accounts to keep. But the cattle find their own way to the food. Except when they want branding or slaughtering, they pretty much keep themselves. It's not like farming. The chickens are more work."

His own land was only a fraction of the cattle's grazing; he shared a twenty-thousand-acre lease of government land with his father, and when he needed a hand he hired one from Wally, too, usually Johnny Fousel, who had taught him to ride when he was four.

All this he told her between instructions on blanketing, cinching, mounting, trotting. He was a willing talker once he was on steady conversational ground. Now and then he was even gallant. She found she was startled from time to time by his flattery, and wanted to believe him wittier, perhaps, than he was.

"This horse has a good eye for a lady. You don't want to take any nonsense from him. But put your foot firm and he'll follow you half to Kansas. He's got taste."

And indeed, Digger seemed to be in love with her. He had that habit of hooking his face over her shoulder when she came near. Once she learned to stand still for it, he would touch his nostrils to her neck, ruffle his lips along her collarbone, the velvety damp forelip quivering. There is no accounting for the fact that she liked the horse's nose in her neck better than her husband's. It was simply so.

The Poindexters continued to spend Sunday mornings among the Methodists — "bread pudding religion," she called it to Laurel — but the riding lessons became her Mass. Mondays, Wednesdays, and Fridays she dropped Laurel at the bank and drove the motorcar out to the Wheeler ranch, discarding the hot jacket as soon as she was out of town. As the year closed, the days turned balmy. Frank would halloo to her from his chores. If Mary Doreen was about they would exchange a few words. Then she would uncouple the corral gate and stand, shoulder against Digger's neck, murmuring to him while she curried him with a worn wood brush that fit the cup of her palm. She stood smelling his hide, feeling the light on her crown — not thinking, yet in the only contemplative state she had known since she left the church.

Then they would ride. Around the corral first, then around the ranch, Frank beside her on a more mischievous horse, a roan who would wipe him off on a cactus or a cottonwood if he let her, or

skid to a cattle grate and try to pitch him over. This horse was called
Sally, a much too homey name for her. She had a little Arabian in
her, and patently knew herself to be superior to pied Digger of the
short haunches. Digger, though, by virtue of muscle and a dogged
spirit, often outran her. This was a pattern well established between
the horses by the time Eleanor came to ride, so she was simply the
beneficiary of it. But it exhilarated her, she was more than willing
to take credit for it, and Frank was more than willing to watch her
run and win. So they raced across the flat, and within a short time
were jumping railroad tracks or dry streambeds.

Frank Wheeler could listen as well as talk, although more or less
as a tourist of her conversation, constantly surprised — or else he
pretended surprise as a way of mocking her — at the idea of traffic,
factories, a river through a town, a staircase in a private home.

"You had a houseful of servants."

"Hardly a houseful. A nurse, parlor maid, cook, a gardener."

"That's a houseful in these parts."

They would dismount for a rest, a drink from the canteens. She
would lean back on her hands, aware of her knees, the difficulty of
disposing them modestly, and carefully, too, to avoid the little rocks
and roots that, all the same, would leave her palms pitted with a
three-dimensional mirror of the desert floor.

"Didn't all that noise drive you loco?"

"No, I loved it, I loved the rush and bustle."

"Well, like I said . . ."

The Maryland landscape he found exotic without irony. Land
interested him purely. She told him of the unimaginable density of
vines, edible wild things growing along the roads — she tried to
describe the taste of scuppernongs, the tough hide of the fruit and
the shock of sour-sweet — and trees so dense you could clapboard
a house with the wood you had cleared to build it.

One afternoon she described the lot that she and Laurel had
chosen for their house — overgrown with grass and creeper, the
sky half hidden and the ground dappled by the oaks. How they
had spent a full Saturday, Laurel and a gardener and she in a hat
veiled against the midges, scything the ground so that she would
be able to string out the plan of her house.

"You yourself?!"

She ignored this. "There were hundreds of wild poppies, it seemed a pity to cut them down, except they spring up again so fast. They lay there like a carpet of flowers and grass. I gathered armfuls of poppies, armfuls, to take home."

Tears sprang to her eyes and she sat still, facing him, defying him to laugh. He didn't mock her, but he also didn't offer any sympathy. All he did was stretch the point of his chin a little at the air, the tender underskin bobbing as he swallowed. Afterward they mounted and rode themselves out of awkwardness, rubbed it off against the wind.

She learned to pace herself so she could gallop without getting a stitch in her side. She learned to canter. She could pick her way down an arroyo and up the other side, reins lifted above the saddle horn, reassuring Digger with her knees, her low praises, a gesture directing him to this side or that.

"You didn't knock a pebble out of place," Frank would approve. Hat back off her face by its cord because it was too much trouble to keep on, her face pinker than was good for her complexion — with sun and exertion, maybe with the praise — she exulted. She tapped Digger with her heels and rode.

Even Laurel had to admit that Eleanor's spirits rose. She had her energy back, her color, her enthusiasm. Some days she would ride by the bank just to let him see her new acquisition of a skill — trotting, cantering, galloping. At night it seemed to him sometimes that she was really trying. She would turn to him, run a tentative hand up and down his back. Hide her eyes in his shoulder, certainly, but nevertheless, with her hand, explore.

18

MORNINGS WHEN HE WOKE before light, or afternoons when they lay in the mesquite bosks for siesta, Sam conjured the Gila monster in his head, made a brother of him. Sometimes he twisted the bandanna around his neck until he could feel the tug of the leash, or he slipped it over his chin and held it between his teeth to remind himself that he had no language. He imagined himself with a tongue that could paralyze Young-Fat, Lazy, and Little, whose names he knew as Juan, Cortillo, and Gervaso but of whom he chose to think in the mute language of his reptile self. More than once they referred to him as *el sordomuto,* although they had heard him speak and they still gave him orders he followed. When Eight-Fingers returned (his man's name was Octavio), Sam imagined that his poison tongue paralyzed the man in the stub of his hurt hand.

He found a thong in Lazy's saddlebags one day when he went for coffee, a slender cutting no wider than a string and three feet long. He tied it into a single loop, and now daytimes he would sit and play cat's cradle with it, hour after hour, often as he rode along on his mule. Watching the string take the same pattern over and over stilled his mind, and he backed up to the place of his lizard self. Nights sometimes he would tug the thong around his neck or twist it into a quadruple loop into which he would slip his wrists, practicing immobility, as if his prison was of his own making and in his control. He remembered how, when he had sat through recess in the shadow of the schoolhouse wall hoping to be forgotten, they had called him Lizard and made a taunt of his trying not to be taunted. Now he promoted himself. *Cal-te-te-pon,* he whispered.

And yet the *villistas* let him range from them, gather mesquite for the fires, fetch water from the rivers or the towns. Sometimes he found treasures to add to his pocket with the thong and his soft ear. He found a spoon with half a handle and a needle with a scarlet thread. The best thing he found, embedded in the mud of a watering hole, was a compass without a glass. Even though its glass was broken, it pointed north. He put it in his bib pocket with his ear.

More important, by staying still in the shadows of courtyard walls and bodega corners listening to the women, he learned how to roast the hearts of agave, the century plant, for winter food. From the pods of the *hediondilla,* the "little stinker" creosote, he made a tea for Young-Fat when he got a chest congestion, and then for Little when he caught it in his turn. He watched the women weaving sotol and desert palm, and began to make baskets. For the first time, the men made comments about him.

"Smart puppy," Young-Fat said, his mouth dropping sticky seeds. "Clever little fucker," Lazy said: *chingadito.* Chink-adito, Sam thought, cleverly, and thought of Lloyd, of those days when he had slept in the mine and not known that he could nest in the earth like a lizard, that it could be his true home. *Cal-te-te-pon,* he whispered to himself at night, giving himself a name: Caltetepon.

They went south again, to Querobabi on the Río Zanjou, to Cornelio in the foothills of the Sierra del Viejo, and then to Utres on the banks of the Sonora, where the nights were so cold that Sam and the men, too, took turns chopping greasewood and heaping the fire all through the watch, and where sometimes they could see the firelight in the eyes of bobcats on the hills above, attracted and kept off by the hissing light.

Sam had seen cold weather and hot, high country and low; he had lost all track of time, but he studied his compass and carried the conviction that Lloyd had found his way home. Was waiting for him. Sam strained northward as the Gila monster had strained away from his master — that is, in perfect stillness, body sagging submissive, with no appearance of a wish toward flight. They went east again into the cold February plains. For four nights they encountered no town, the food was scarce, and Sam roasted mescal hearts and ground mesquite pods into flour.

The scouts gathered information about the *federales* whenever they entered a town, information given them by sympathizers, or bought, or tricked out of government partisans with whom they pretended drunkenness. This information they sifted and discussed around the fire while Sam scoured their metal mugs and earthen pots with sand, or while he played cat's cradle, or lay curled under his blanket with his bandanna in his teeth, his thong twisting in his hands. The government forces were nearly all gone from Sonora now, and Villa and Álvaro Obregón were routing them out of Chihuahua. Most of the *federales* had retreated to join Orozco at Mapimi. What worried Young-Fat was that Venustiano Carranza, the rebels' "first chief," was planning to move his whole troop south. Carranza claimed this was because there were no east-to-west railway lines, and communication was inefficient with his great generals Villa and Obregón. But Young-Fat was suspicious: The move would put Carranza between Villa and Mexico City, closest to the seat of government if Huerta fell. Worse, Carranza was leaving in charge in Sonora a colonel named Plutarco Calles, who was bitterly hated by the Yaqui Indian forces under José Maytorena. Villa had appointed Maytorena as governor of Sonora, and that pitted Carranza's men against Villa's, straining and threatening to splinter the revolution before they ousted Huerta from the capital. When Lazy and Eight-Fingers talked of Huerta they called him *sot* and *mother-mutilator;* but they had scarcely kinder words for Carranza, who was supposed to be their ally, mocked him as bookish, called him *little pubic hairs* and his troops *the girlies.*

Such talk was of no use to Sam, but the women in the plazas had useful things to teach him. It was useful to learn how to spot the soft, flat caps of sandfood near the roots of certain bushes, how to dig in a circle around them and lift out the succulent parasite to bake in an earthen bowl. This he learned by watching and listening, curled like a lizard sunning against the walls of a courtyard in Mazogahui while the women chattered.

And again they went south, camping for a length of days in the hills above the dam at El Novillo. Nights he lay half listening to the scouts, he wished he could dredge up the words that Lloyd had used, which he didn't then understand, to plead for him with Villa. *I will go with you if you'll free my friend.* Something like that. Sam longed north to Lloyd and felt his leash dragged south.

At El Novillo they made their camp in a pie-wedge depression between limestone ridges. The *villistas* always tried to find a rock to set their backs against if they were able, and chose for preference shapes of land that had only one easy access. The men had been into El Novillo for two days without learning anything, and Little was quarreling with Eight-Fingers about some officer among Carranza's men whom Eight-Fingers thought was a spy and Little said no, no, he could be trusted. They were bored and irritable and they had bought three leather pouches of the mescal brew from a desert man with a half-buried still, so they drank, and after the others slept Sam watched Little, who was supposed to be on guard, fall asleep as well, with his pistol under his neck. This sometimes happened. They were as sloppy in their watches as in their eating; it made quarrels among them every day. Sam thought nothing of it as he pulled his blanket over his head and curled himself into his mind (*caltetepon, caltetepon*) before he fell asleep.

But when he woke in the deep dark of his blanket cave and middle night, he heard sounds that were not the animal night noises of the desert, not kit fox or packrat or the wind in the million leaves of a mesquite. The sounds were a feeling in the ground, the heft of a human foot, its twist against the rock face with a weight that would grind a few grains into sand. The feel of the grit below Sam's cheek and the whorl of his naked eardrum told him that there were weight and stealth only footsteps away. Then his other, the still-petaled ear, heard another sound. He curled back in his lizard space and felt his blood course in and out of the slow pump of his heart. What was that sound? It was the sound of — cheese. It was the sound cheese made when a knife was drawn across it, and the blade having sliced through soft stuff came to wood. Sam listened for the making of sand between boot and rock, the shudder of the earth trampled by a human foot. He lowered his chin and, without using his hands, bit the edge of his bandanna upward toward his mouth until he had worked it between his teeth. His upper ear heard the sound of cheese being sliced closer by, and this time the gurgle that a chicken makes when you grasp it by the neck. He heard liquid seep into silt.

Sam's mind kept back against the earth nest where a lizard lay while his hands did their cunning human task, slowly, slowly drawing and twisting the thong into a quadruple loop into which he slipped his wrists. His forehead was wet and he rolled it gently against the ground to sponge the sweat and smear his face. Now a footstep encountered a mesquite twig or a bit of charcoal so that there was real sound, and Sam heard Little's sleeve scrape against the silt, and his mouth say, "Ahn?!" before the cheese was cut, and the gurgle and the flowing soaked the earth under Sam's earhole with sound. He bit, pushed his tongue into the salt dirt taste of his bandanna, he slowly twirled one hand in a full circle so that the thong was figure-eighted between his wrists and his wrists bound tight against each other, pulse to pulse. He waited for the fourth cheese to be cut but heard no such sound.

Now his blanket was pulled from the foot and the cold air struck his face. He remembered that in the mine his blanket had been flipped first from his head. He opened his eyes wide and wrenched his head left and right against the bandanna, his heart pumping hard now but at the same time calculating that the bandanna would that way look tighter in his mouth than it was. He rolled his wrists against each other to strain at the thongs but still hide the twist between them. A boot came in his field of vision, then another. They were black, round-toed. *Federal* boots.

"*Mira lo que encontramos,*" said the owner of the boots. Look what we have here.

They sat him against the rock while dawn came, while they went through the *villistas'* saddlebags, ate the beans left from supper and a chunk of roasted agave, sipped but spat out the mescal in the leather gourds. There were only two, both younger than any of the *villistas,* one with a broad Indian brow and a pair of glasses over wide-eyed boy's wondering eyes; the other with a cunning, mean, and jackal look to him. This one unfastened Sam's bandanna and dropped it to the ground. Sam had a pang of regret for it, like a friend he might not ever see again. The *federal* kept asking, "Do you speak Spanish? Do you understand? Can you hear me?" But

Sam held himself absolutely still, staring into the jackal face as he had seen young dogs do, as if he were trying, trying, to understand and could not.

Through this, Young-Fat, Eight-Fingers, Lazy, and Little lay where they had slept. Each offered his own pool of red wine to the earth beneath his chin. Young-Fat's necklace of teeth arched in front of his face, rising out of the wet as if the earth had sprouted a wounded jaw. Eight-Fingers's face was under his blanket, and the corner of the blanket sponged darkness toward his head. Little's arm was flung over his saddle, reaching back, although his pistol was under his neck where he had slept on it, the barrel full of blood. Lazy was sweating in his death. Drops like oil glistened on his forehead, though his red wine was thin; it had run into a rivulet in the rock and drained away. All four were there; Sam could not explain why he had heard only three being cut. Perhaps it was the first cut that had waked him.

When the *federales* were done eating and rifling through the saddlebags the wide-eyed one asked, "What shall we do with their prisoner?" and the jackal-face took out his knife again. He held the flat of it to his nose like someone about to bestow a knighthood, then stretched it out to Sam, blade up. Sam had crawled into the shadows of himself to watch, and was not afraid. He held his hands out, knowing not to part them and show the figure-eight of the thong between his wrists even when the *federal* set the blade below and between them. The *federal* jackal sliced upward. He said pompously, "You have your life as a gift of Victoriano Huerta, illustrious president of Mexico!"

The pieces of the thong sprang from Sam's hands like worms. He scrambled over the rock and ran north, away from the river and into the nearest bosk. He had his ear, his identity card, and his compass. He regretted his bandanna and his mule. As he ran into the great desert, and as he walked when the sun climbed, he began to grieve for Lazy, Young-Fat, Little, and Eight-Fingers. He was not afraid of the desert now, or the long trip north, but he was lonely. He dreaded learning to live again without a leash.

19

IT WAS HARD to go home after school now. Three days a week Ma would be boiling the diapers, standing over the washtub crying while the steam crimped up her hair. She said the lye hurt her eyes and made her cry. In her head Jessie called this the Lye Lie.

Sometimes the cup of lye would be sitting on the sink, which gave Jessie a shiver because of Buck Hoskins's aunt in Morenci that had a little boy die from drinking laundry lye he mistook for milk. That boy had the pitiful strange name of Birdsle, she remembered, and he was four years old. He lived a week screaming while the lye ate his insides out and Buck's aunt sat wringing her hands, and afterward she had Birdsle's little button shoes dipped in copper from the smelter in Globe.

It wasn't the lye that watered up Ma's eyes, because when she didn't boil diapers she cried all the same. She would be rolling the biscuits or cutting up jerky for the gravy and she'd just go in her bedroom and close the door, lifting it careful on the hinges.

Ma kept finding new chores for Jessie to do. There was all Maria's work, and Ma said how the riding lessons for Mrs. Poindexter were really just one more thing than poor Pa could handle and they'd all have to help out more. The way she said this, she was blaming Pa and Mrs. Poindexter both. Now Jessie had to churn the butter, which was mortal boring and made her back hurt low from the strain. All the chores got later and later; it was dark regular before they ate. If Pa was out on the range Ma would find something else that had to be done, a drawer in a mess, or a coal scuttle that hadn't ever been scrubbed and had to be scrubbed right this minute, so when Pa came in, supper was still not ready. Jessie asked Ma why didn't she find somebody to take Maria's place, and Ma stirred the diapers with the long wood paddle. "You may not realize it, young lady, but we have to save every penny now, because your daddy may not get the loan for the quarry."

This was something you would say to a stupid person, or someone too little to do arithmetic, because Maria had cost a dollar and a half a week and it would take you four thousand six hundred and sixty-six weeks to save seven thousand dollars, which is eighty-nine and a half years of boiling diapers, approximately.

One day coming back from school, Jessie saw Maria in town. Maria nodded her head and gave a curtsy in the middle of the street, smiling with her eyes looking down past the side of her apron like somebody that knows something you don't. Maria tucked her white ribbon-tied parcel under her arm and swung around onto Jefferson Street, and Jessie had to stop and swallow down the throatful of her envy.

Another day when she went into town with Ma she stood fidgety and trussed up listening while Ma talked to Maybeth Newsome, and Mrs. Newsome said she had seen O'Joe come out of the back door of Shaftoe's saloon with a whiskey crate and load it straight in Mr. Poindexter's touring car. "Well!" she said. "I just stood there with my stomach churning!" As soon as Mrs. Newsome said it, Jessie's stomach knew what it felt like to be butter churning. It was like a punishment.

Jessie did not know what she had done to be punished. She had started to get bosoms, and pushed up on them while she looked in the mirror. She had watched a chicken lay, she had envied a Mexican. These did not seem sins that would be serious to God. It was more serious to know your mother was a liar. It was the only thing she could not imagine telling anybody, and that was a good test of sin, even if the sin was thinking something true.

The next day was butter day again. Jessie stood churning while Ma went into the bedroom and lifted the door closed — a complaining, mournful sound. The thin, sour smell of whey swelled up Jessie's palate. She could feel the separating going on inside the churn, and she could hear Ma face down across the bed muffling into a pillow so Deborah wouldn't wake. The churn turned in herself, vomit rose in curds on the thin acid of her belly. Every wrenched circle she made with her fists put a pain like metal across the base of her spine.

She gave Jasper a saved-up nickel to finish for her, and she sat in the henhouse till her stomach stilled. She knew Ma would yell at her — Jasper was supposed to be feeding the horses then — and Ma did. It gave her an ugly feeling knowing she was right, a dark joy. She looked Ma straight in the face. But afterward she watched Ma mashing the baby's canned beets through a sieve, and it came into her head, then, that her own life was not going to change. Something about Ma's mashing down on the heel of the spoon, the red brine running in the rusty porcelain sink, made her realize she already knew everything about her own life that she was going to know.

The next morning she felt such a sick hollowness that she asked Ma could she stay home from school even though asking made her feel like she was giving in to something. And Ma said no. Then Jessie walked so slow up the ranch road between the barbed wire that Jasper whined at her, so she told him to go on. The metallic taste and the dull pain in her back were worse this morning, and she hadn't got halfway to town before she felt her drawers rubbing sticky in between her thighs. It frightened her without surprising her — she had known it would come one day — it made her feel all at once downhearted and important and misunderstood.

There was no place to hide, so she turned back away from town and scanned three hundred and sixty degrees around the barbed wire and the scrub. There was nobody, only cattle. She pulled her skirt up in front high enough to get her fingers inside her elastic, and pulled on it so she could look. The blood was spreading in a red circle on the white cambric, a color clear as the circle on Johnny Fousel's pouch of Bull Durham tobacco. It was the same color as chick or rabbit blood or bleeding a steer, but she thought of tobacco because sin was in her mind. Just while she looked in her drawers more blood came down one leg, and when the feel of it made her jerk, a drop fell in the dirt. She let go of her skirt and hung on to the fencepost for a minute, pain in her back, shame in her mind.

She didn't want to give Ma this, but she didn't have anywhere to go but home. A cow a ways off from her chewed its cud and looked at her indifferent. Cows, sheep, and goats are called *ruminants* and have four stomachs each, Miss Timkin learned them. They cough the grass back up after it's part digested and grind on it some more, and by the time it gets to the fourth stomach the roughage is broke down and makes them food. One stomach is not enough to live on grass, so people would die from how cows live. The drop sat up fat on the ground in front of her toes. Powdery specks of silt climbed it and swirled, and then all of a sudden it sank and disappeared. Jessie let go of the fencepost and went home.

And then it was not anything like she had supposed, it was like being the baby again, who has maybe fallen and cut herself, and Ma must cuddle her to make it better. Jessie had been ashamed to tell Ma that she knew what was happening and ashamed to tell her that she didn't, but she didn't have to say anything at all. She came in the back door and leaned against the frame. Pa had gone, and Ma was tidying the drainboard, Deborah sitting on the floor in her check pinafore, banging a spoon in the telescope cup. Ma rubbed her hair off her forehead with the back of her hand. Jessie's back and belly gave a little leap while she tried to think what to say (*It's not my fault! I'm sick. I am!*), but Ma looked once at her, she had the dishcloth in her hands, and she dried her hands in one wringing of it.

"Jessie. What is it, child?"

This was so much the lovingest tone that Jessie could remember hearing from Ma that it bent her at the knees. She slid down the doorframe and sat on the floor. She didn't want to do this, but she sat and sobbed.

"Jessie! Sweetheart!"

Ma put her to bed, and washed her, herself, and cried a little with her, and once she said, "It's so hard!" She put Deborah in the other room in the canvas folding cot and let her cry herself to sleep. She put a steam rag on Jessie's head and bound between her legs with a square of fresh-tore sheet. She brought Tabatha and petted her till she curled up at the foot of the bed, on the blue quilt that Pa's ma had made when Pa was little. Jessie didn't know what she had done to make such a change, only bled between the legs, but it was as if they shared a trouble. Jessie sat up awhile against Ma and let Ma rock her and stroke her knee, and she felt spent and still. Ma's forearm was freckled, the veins rose high on her hand like squash vines on a stone. Jessie lay back down, and Ma stroked her forehead. The hurt in her back relaxed against the bed, and Jessie dozed.

When she woke, Ma was still sitting there, rocking in the old cherry rocker she had pulled up to the bed, but her manner was more stoical and remote. Ma's face was thinner than the last time Jessie noticed, her eyes were young and blue, but all around them were wrinkles fine as if a mesh of little hairs had been pressed into her flesh and pulled away again.

"How are you feeling now, Jessie?" But as if it was time she should be feeling better.

"I'm awright."

"You're a woman now," Ma said, and smiled, but not as if this was anything to be celebrating.

"Yes, ma'am."

"I should have talked to you before, I know, but I swear, I've been so busy life is just getting away from me. And you youngsters grow up so fast these days. Do you understand what's happening?"

"Well, yes, ma'am. I know some. A lot of the girls have it, they have names for it."

"The curse?"

"Yes'm. And falling-off-the-roof and Gramma's-comin'-to-visit."

Ma smiled, then squared up her body and folded her hands on her knee. "Well, there's things we must talk about."

Her voice made it important, women together, but Jessie wanted to hold it away as long as she could and fall against Ma again and rock. Please, she wanted to say, could we just let it be until tomorrow? Could we just let it *be*?

"When you have your monthlies," Ma said — and although her mouth was firm, her eyes cast down and up so Jessie could see this was unpleasant for her to say — "it means your body has become a woman, and there's certain responsibilities that go along with it."

More chores, Jessie thought, dismayed, but now Ma fetched a deep sigh while she traced the brown thread in the gingham on her knee — down one side of the square to the blue thread, across to the yellow, and back up again. "Do you know how babies are made?"

It was not a fair question, it made you ashamed to know and ashamed not to know. Jessie knew that babies were made when a man and a woman got married and kissed lying in the same bed. Mexicans did it not married. She didn't know exactly what the bed had to do with it except that to think of it made you hot with sin. She supposed the babies were night creatures (*nocturnals*, Miss Timkin said), like a skunk or a kit fox; but when she thought of this her mind brought up a picture of a tiny human critter no bigger than a bedbug running across the sheet from the man to in between the woman's legs and climbing up inside her. This was so silly she would not admit to it. "I know some," she said.

Ma frowned and rushed. "Well, the most you need to know is that when you have your monthlies, it means you're making eggs now, and your body is able to have a baby, so you must be very . . . circumspect." Jessie knew where the egg was, it was in the hot knot of muscle just at the base of her spine. She did not know what it was to be *circumspect*. The thought that she would lay an egg was so alarming that she clutched at the sides of the bed, and Ma started up red-faced.

"You haven't let a boy touch you, have you?"

"Ma'am?"

Ma took a breath and settled down again. "You mustn't be wrestling with boys anymore, or letting them touch you. You mustn't be alone with boys after dark, or go off alone with them."

"Why not?"

"Men can't help themselves."

Ma was miserable saying this, and Jessie felt miserable. The loving between them hadn't lasted but an hour, and now Ma was angry like she always was when she was lying, her eyes restless and her voice gone a little hollow, like a preacher. What did that mean, that men can't help themselves? Help yourself, Ma said to company at table. That was not what she meant.

"You mean kissing and such?"

"You must understand, Jessie, men are made different — not just their bodies, I mean, but their whole makeup is different. You can think a man — or a boy — is nice and Christian and well brought-up, and all the same you can't trust him. You aren't ever safe."

"What do you mean?" She wanted to cry out, to bring Ma back to the way she had been a while ago. The deadweight of hating Ma was in her again, like heavy emptiness inside her. "What do you mean, 'safe'?" Her voice was sneeringer than she wanted, Ma would call it smart aleck, they would back off from each other like cattle pawing. "You don't mean all men! You don't mean Reverend Newsome. You don't mean Pa!"

Now Ma's eyes flashed to mean that Jessie had gone too far, and this was so unfair that Jessie went wild inside herself. She saw she had struck that spark off the blue flint in Ma's eyes, and she sat up hot-faced and fisted. "You don't mean Pa! You don't mean Pa!"

Ma slapped her smart across the cheek.

Then they both sat staring in each other's laps, Ma with one fist curled inside the other on her gingham knee, and Jessie feeling the hot trickle, not from where her cheek stung but between her legs onto a square of soft old sheet that had sat soaking in a tub of lye every washday for years on end, until it had gone soft enough to sponge up blood. In the other room Deborah started crying.

"Get ahold of yourself. Of course I don't mean your Pa. Who said anything about your Pa? I swear, you try me, Jessie. Now just calm yourself and try to rest, and we'll talk about this again when you can be reasonable."

Ma folded up Jessie's petticoat and hung it over the back of the chair. She picked Tabatha up off the bed — why did she have to do that? — and went out, pulling the door to. In a minute Deborah quieted down again.

Jessie lay and looked into the hot dark on the inside of her eyelids, and the strange thing she saw was the brain of a steer that Aldo Nene had scooped out and brought to school one day in the winter, when it wouldn't spoil. Some people eat them scrambled up in eggs, he said, and that made the girls screw up their faces even though nobody believed him. When Miss Timkin came up on them in the play yard, Aldo tried to hide it, and some slime had got smeared on Leroy Newsome's bookbag, but Miss Timkin just said it was a very interesting thing, and looked very like a human brain that all of them had inside their own skulls. She said how all your thoughts are caught in the little twists. Ginny Robinson asked her was it true that people eat them and she said it was.

What Jessie was thinking about now was the little twists, how people are caught up in their twisted brains. For instance, when Ma said she was not talking about Pa, it was a lie. But if she meant Pa "couldn't help himself" that was a lie, too, damaging to Pa in some way that had to do with kissing, and with bleeding in between your legs, and with teaching Mrs. Poindexter how to ride a horse. But she couldn't contradict this lie because she couldn't figure out what sort it was or why Ma should want to tell it. It was too twisted to undo. She fell asleep, and when Pa came home that night she went up to him and hugged him, in front of Ma, on purpose. He seemed surprised, he seemed pleased; but later at supper he was awkward with her, too grinning and hearty, so she knew Ma had told him that she got her monthlies. She prickled with shame. She couldn't swallow. She felt there never is an end to all the twisting.

20

ON THE EARLY TRAIN, Laurel read from Bowie to Tucson a *Daily Star* that had come from Tucson to Bowie on a still earlier train. He remarked on this, marveled at the apparent resolve of science to fill our lives with trivial convenience.

"Transport and information," he enthused. "Between them they'll dwindle the globe." He knew how many trees per year were consumed in newsprint for a daily of middle size; and he speculated how many more must fire the boilers of the trains to shunt the printed pulp to all the venues where it was wanted. "Profitable employment for as long as trees last," he said, meaning by it *forever*. It occurred to Eleanor that trees were in short supply on this horizon, but it seemed a churlish objection in the flow of his bravado.

A meeting with managers of the Tucson bank was the ostensible reason for the trip. Mainly Laurel was going to see a specialist in pulmonary disorders, because he didn't want his condition known in Bowie. Eleanor thought Dr. Hoskins ought to be informed, but Laurel said she had no understanding of small-town gossip. Society was full of people who would not sit down at a meal with a tubercular, he said, or thought they could be infected by a handshake. There were some who would not take money from his hands if they knew.

"Speaking of newsprint, Eleanor: You should drop by the offices of the *Star* and let that reporter interview you."

She mimicked her mother's drawl: "It's vulgah for a woman to be interviewed."

"Nonsense; not at all."

"In any case, I shall stop by there, only because I want copies of the article about *you*. For Mama, Cousin Peg . . ."

She was anxiously fond of him this morning. Perhaps because he was wearing the dark blue herringbone she used to admire in Baltimore, when he went off to some confab of import and mystery. Perhaps because by wearing this suit to the Tucson doctor he betrayed his own anxiety. His nonchalance had the studied bravery of a little boy. She was reminded of her astonishment when she had learned that, at Princeton, he used to roll an iron hoop down the quad with a stick. It was, apparently, quite a popular pastime for young scholars.

She thumbed through a *Woman's Home Companion* that Mama had sent from Baltimore. There was one of those bluestocking articles, about a woman who would rather be a stenographer than a wife. She described Sunday mornings lying abed with a penny dreadful and blueberries and cream. She made it sound almost licentious, whereas Eleanor could scarcely imagine anything more dreary than stenography. Another article was about a woman who had planned her own Cotswold cottage, a feat reckoned to be remarkable. "Many women can draw plans, but few women, when it comes down to it, want to be responsible for the exact location of a closet."

Resentful of this judgment, Eleanor glanced up at the passing desert, better aware of its changes now that she was attuned to it. The mesas, for example, all showed a ragged incline to a flat top, but they came in different moods, a shallow amber one with a soft sand texture, a brittle, formal gray one. It was like the Mexican faces, which all looked alike — deep-set eyes, wide cheekbones — until you came to know them. In fact, features differ as subtly as a clef; you have to learn to read the notes to recognize treble, waltz time, semiquaver. Laurel had a Bach face, orotund with intelligence. Frank Wheeler's was a reel, direct and rugged, taking you by surprise with its wit. Maria's face was nothing Latin — Chopin, rather, energetic but restrained, a prelude. Peculiar notion.

"Here, Eleanor. This might interest you. There's an article about the women who travel with the rebel armies. A convenient way to feed their troops, eh? Can you imagine bundling up your babies and your goods to tramp after your husband over the scrub?"

"I can imagine."

"This will reassure you, though. It says that Carranza made a mistake to set up his provisional government in Hermosillo, because there's no railway line direct to the capital. He's apparently thinking of moving his troops south again."

"Oh, yes."

Why should he think she would be reassured by this? Did he think the proximity of the First Chief frightened her? On the contrary, she had seen pictures of Venustiano Carranza and was taken aback by his European, even Victorian demeanor. By contrast with Obregón and Villa, who were stocky and blunt-featured, Carranza stood stiff-backed in celluloid collars and pin-striped suits, he wore reading glasses and a full blunt beard. Curious name, Venustiano. Could anyone imagine holding up for christening a baby with the name *Venustiano*? But then she herself had an Aunt Premelia. What would Maria say to a *Hortense* or an *Abigail*?

She brushed soot from Laurel's knee. "Maria says the Mexicans in Bowie scarcely pay any attention to what's happening south of the border."

"Well, they should. They'll be peasants until they have a base in their own homeland, and their own democracy."

Perhaps. But *their own homeland* put the lost house in her mind again. She propped her elbow on the windowsill and stared out. They came to the outskirts of Tucson: an ostrich farm with the birds stiff-perambulating; a sweep of sparse grass around the new university; in the middle distance, a city of tents — which Laurel did not tell her housed the hundreds of tubercular poor who came here to get well or die.

Tucson exhilarated her from the moment she stepped through the graceful arches of the station. The new Santa Rita Hotel was similarly arched, simple and sumptuous in a taste Eleanor declared genuinely Continental. In their room she played the *grande dame* for him, sweeping the drapes back and drawing one fringe theatrically over her shoulder. Laurel, delighted at her delight, loosed her into town for the morning while he went to do business at the bank and clinic.

The core of the city was an old Spanish town, and its architecture had been taken up in newer buildings so that everywhere she looked her eye rested on, or was arrested by, a whitewashed opening in the shape of a parabola, or a wrought iron grille, or a barely sloping roof tiled with handsome half cylinders of interlocking terra-cotta. For a while Eleanor walked drinking in the sight of these buildings. Oh, it wasn't Baltimore; half a block down the side streets the adobe mud showed through the paint, and a cart was abandoned on a wheel like a turned ankle. But something here struck her eye with force and freshness. Adapted from Spanish buildings, these had evolved to hold the sun at bay, and at the same time to mirror the desert's flat colors and bold shapes. The houses in Bowie had come from the Midwest, the East, and beyond that from northern Europe, where they were meant to huddle against the cold and let the snow slip off their steep-pitched roofs. She tried to imagine the Semple house in a landscape of English hedgerows. And really it looked quite charming in her mind's eye. She thatched it, let ivy climb on it. She stood staring at a burden of ripe oranges on a potted tree, pondering this image of the appropriate. Then she imagined a whitewashed, flat-roofed shape around a patio in the spot where the Semple house now stood. No use. It would stick out doubly awkward among the dour gables.

She walked on. An open blacksmith shop agitated the air with forge heat, the sounds of metal, and male laughter. She laughed herself, a little drunk with the freedom of the sidewalks. The sidewalks were poured, the streets paved; an electric streetcar clanged up and down. Some of the shops were dressed for Christmas, and substantial women deliberated inside them. On the pavement an Indian squaw in voluminous tiers of calico sat impassively on her blanket with half a dozen pots. Eleanor entered one of the dry goods shops and bought a yard of ribbon just for the joy of purchase.

Culottes she found ready-made in the trading post, which called itself The Emporium. She also bought a pair of gaucho pants in cool hopsack, and a Mexican silver belt to wear with them. She

chose a pair of beaded moccasins for her father, and for Cousin
Peg a turquoise set in silver rope. She bought a version of the
scoop-necked blouse Maria wore. She bought a new riding hat and
a second pair of boots. Giddy with some mechanism of consumer
physics (a body in motion tends to remain in motion), she chose a
pair of jet and coral thunderbirds for her mother, which her
mother would surely never hang in her ears, and — having arranged for these items to be delivered to the Santa Rita — in a final
anticlimactic impulse bought from the squaw on the sidewalk a
shallow red-earth bowl, which she then carried in the crook of her
arm to the *Daily Star*.

The newspaper was housed in a shedlike building off of Congress Street. Mechanical fans stirred the smoky air. At a long reception counter she made her request of a young woman whose face
was pinched together by her glasses.

"I'll just slip back to the morgue," the woman said pleasantly,
and disappeared behind a glass partition. Eleanor had never heard
this expression, and although she understood it in a general way, it
had a depressing effect.

There was nowhere to sit down. She was suddenly tired, deflated,
with a sour sense of self-dislike. The word *morgue* hung there. She
glanced at the clock, saw that Laurel would be at the doctor's
exactly now, and took superstitious alarm at the coincidence. Beyond the glass partition sat some dozen men typing away in the stir
of haze from their cigars.

She set her bowl on the counter and fanned her face. Now she
sent up a prayer for Laurel's health, but cloyed indulgence sat like
a taste on her tongue. She was thirsty. She looked vaguely around,
hoping for a water cooler.

A man swung in from the outside door, ponderously large under
a nimbus of grizzled hair, a flapping sheaf of papers in his hand.
Intent on his reading, he passed her, shoved through the swinging
panel, stopped at the partition, turned, put out a hand for the
rebound of the panel, and only then looking up, asking with an
intensity quite out of tone with the question, "Are *you* taken care
of?"

"Yes, I am, thank you."

He continued to look at her, pencil protruding from his hair, straggle of papers in his hand, rapacious eyes above a jaw jowled like some animal of the mudhole sort.

"Temple of Music Friends' Society?" he asked, pinching ruminatively at his broad nose.

"I beg your pardon?"

"No. Horticultural Congress."

"I'm afraid I don't —"

"Not Temperance Union . . . ?!"

She shook her head.

"Oh, well." He grinned a grin of sudden and bogus boyishness, whipped the pencil from behind his ear, and tapped its blunt end on the arch of newsprint. "I'm a student of human nature, not a master. You'll have to tell me."

He was just a little ahead of her, a little headlong, so that even as she reflected that she was under no such obligation, she was answering, "I came by for some copies of an interview with my husband."

"Of course. And your husband would be . . . ?"

"Laurel Poindexter. Manager of the new Mountain Bank in Bowie." Now she was truly annoyed with herself. He'd get no more out of her. She picked up her bowl, was taken aback when he groaned, flung up a hand to agitate his hair.

"Jesus! How do you stand it?"

"What?"

"Where are you from? East Coast, must be. What can you find to do in Bowie?" He continued vigorously to rub his scalp, dislodging a few flakes of dead skin that drifted to his shoulders. "I'm sorry, you love it. Tell me you love it, I won't say another word. Do you want a cup of coffee while you wait?"

He turned as he slid a hand along the swinging portion of paneling, holding it open at arm's reach, one leg flung forward in the air like a music hall comedian. She opened her mouth to refuse, thanked him, and passed through.

As soon as they reached the newsroom, he turned hard left and led her into a cubicle like an oversized teller's cage. The lettering on the door said *C. Emmett Rollstadt, Managing Editor*, but as soon as he was ensconced behind the desk he put out a hand to her and introduced himself: "Ben Dargen."

"How do you do," said Eleanor, confused. Ben Dargen pulled a bottle of Old Grand-Dad from under the desk that he treated as his own even if it wasn't, and took from the stove plate a blackened tin pot from which he poured a liquid even blacker. He had his shirt-sleeves rolled back and secured with bicycle clips, his eyes were restless, and his face was rumpled, but he moved with a shuffling suppleness and a hint of comedy, as if he were about to break into a soft shoe routine. He poured two fingers of the whiskey into a spotted glass and raised it to her.

"Seriously," he said, as if that was the toast. "Bowie, Arizona. And you're from . . . New York? Boston?"

"Baltimore."

"Baltimore. The wide reaches of the Patapsco. I never understand how women do it."

She did not know whether it was especially sympathetic or vaguely insulting that he thought Bowie would be harder for a woman. She took a sip of coffee and winced at the taste of scorch.

"No milk here, I'm afraid; it won't keep half an hour. I mean it; I don't know how you do it. It's another thing for men. At least we can pretend we're tapping into some kind of adventure — even if it comes down to seven days a week behind a blue pencil. But you — intelligent, sophisticated. I can't see why you don't just pack up and go home."

She could have said, "I don't see, either." She could have said, "I think I will." It would have relieved her profoundly. If only Cousin Peg were here, or some woman friend who would say, "It must be so hard" — to whom she could say, "I want to go home." But this was not a cousin or a friend. His hands roamed the desk, flipping pages, snapping paper clips, and all the same he trained his attention on her, a man and a stranger whose profession was curiosity.

She took the other possible tack. "What makes you think I'm intelligent and sophisticated?"

He said at once, "Well, for a start, you've bought a bowl from Th'a Juhki, and not a bunch of dudery."

"Oh." She settled the bowl more securely in her lap.

"They're an amazing people, the Papago. Every time Th'a Juhki makes a pot she thanks the earth for the clay." He filled his glass again and, following her eye on the bottle — what kind of man drinks two whiskeys at his desk in the middle of the day? — he said, "I'm sorry. Did you want some?"

"Certainly not!"

At which he leaned back in the swivel chair — for a second she thought he was tipping over — laughed in a basso an octave lower than his speaking voice, and sucked the rim of his glass. "Well, tell your secret. What do you do with yourself in Bowie?"

"Nothing you could print for news. I play the piano. I'm learning to ride horseback."

"Is there any compensation for you? Anything you can like in this Final Outpost of the Philistines?"

"Oh, yes," she said, but cautious; only what she'd not mind seeing in print. "I very much like the old Spanish buildings."

"Wait till you see the new sections out north, though. They've had wagonloads of topsoil brought in so they can have front lawns the size of Rhode Island. Every one of them'll take enough water to keep a tribe of Papagos. The desert's getting chewed up till it won't be one thing or the other."

"There seems to be rather a lot of it," Eleanor murmured.

"Oh, but the desert is very vulnerable; it's more easily despoiled by people than other kinds of land."

Here was an arresting idea! "How so?"

"It stands to reason. You put a row of houses in a desert basin and, good, everybody has mountains out his window. But you put another row of houses behind it, and the mountain's obliterated. You have to walk to the edge of town to see why you came."

"Yes, I see."

Into his stride, Ben Dargen filled the little room with heat and noise. What sort of music was that face? Something ambitious, maybe overweening; Beethoven if not Wagner. "You can tuck houses away in the crannies along a mountain or the vegetation of a riverbank, and when you look at them you've got houses on a mountain or a riverbank. But you put houses on hardpan, and it disappears. You build a city in the San Simon Valley, and whatever you make it out of — wood, tin, glass, masonry — that's what there is."

"Surely it would revert to scrub in a few years' time."

"No; no. That's what you think. Forest reverts and rots. This air preserves. That's why the lungers come."

The meaning of this new word registered with a sting. *Morgue* and *lungers*. Perhaps one should expect to have one's vocabulary expanded in a newspaper office. She smiled coldly, just as a rap on the glass announced the morgue-lady, who excused herself for coming in, handed Eleanor three copies of the relevant *Daily Star*, and excused herself, backing out.

"I must go. My husband will be waiting for me."

This made no impression on Dargen, who beamed that boyish grin at her again and gave her one boom of the profundo laugh. "So you've developed a passion for the local architecture. What then? That will hardly fill your days."

His fidgeting hands made her uneasy, and the hard focus of his look made her even more so. She didn't know how to take her leave. She didn't know whether he intended a flirtation or an interview. Her only clear impulse was to contradict him. "It might. I was just walking through the streets thinking that I want my own house in the Spanish style."

"You won't find that in Bowie, unless you build."

"I'll build." He shot her a look. "I mean *we'll* build, of course, but I'll do the plans. In my marriage I'm responsible for domestic matters."

Dargen looked politely doubtful — his face was better formed for the doubt than the politeness. "Domestic matters like architecture. You're talented!"

"I don't know about that, but I know where to put the closets."

"I'm damn sure you know a hawk from a handsaw."

"And a hacksaw from a coping saw."

"Ah!" he said, ironic.

"Houses are a domestic matter, Mr. Dargen."

"Well, I wish you luck. But I'll lay odds you won't end up with a Spanish-style in Bowie, no, ma'am. At least in Tucson we've got the upper class and the Allianza. Down in Bowie they'll let you know you've picked the wrong side of the tracks."

"And you think I can't stand up to them?"

He ran a heavy finger down the crease beside his mouth, appraised her. The image of the adobe church flashed through her mind; she was glad she had not said anything about the Methodist church. She raised her chin.

"Well, as I said, I'm only a human nature student," he apologized. "But if you'll pardon me, I'd have to say no. They'll wear you down."

She stood, folding her clippings inside the bowl. "Thank you very much for the coffee and the fortune telling."

Which ought to have been a dismissal, but Dargen tapped his cheek open-mouthed with a percussive thwack. "It isn't just a question of architecture, either." And he was off again as if he hadn't insulted her and she hadn't answered his insult and gotten up to go. "There's a ludicrous quarrel going on in town here — the mayor says we'll be a metropolis in fifty years, and the sheriff calls him a public laughingstock. But neither of them questions that a metropolis would be a fine, brave thing. Whereas — why, you said it yourself — the desert is beautiful, but the Anglo-European Establishment has no business here."

She had said nothing remotely resembling this, but such is the power of our desire not to be counted among the Philistines that she stood for another five minutes cradling Th'a Juhki's shallow bowl, letting Ben Dargen hold forth about the sins of humanity against the desert.

21

IN MOST PLACES, Christmas represents fecundity in winter, a promise out of the year's howling belly. In the San Simon Valley the season offers more immediate salvation: It gets cool. There might be a shower, or even that spectacle, a frost. By noon, most of the days would pass for summer in most of the world, but in Bowie the women brought out wraps with cat or canine strips around the collar; the men built evening fires and carried lap rugs in their buggies.

The pyracantha bowed under its berries, and housewives loaded their mantels with it, pretending holly. There were roses and hibiscus on the altar. The 4-H Club draped a tinsel garland on the saguaro at the corner of Main and Church, and every family donated a bell, reindeer, dwarf, or similar evidence of theology. On the Mexican side of town those who had a pig or a goat prepared to slaughter. The sense of Christian brotherhood reached even to Shaftoe's saloon, and the cowhands got drunk more often than usual, and drunker. O'Joe the split palate could be seen weeping in the mornings hunkered down beside the swinging doors; but evenings he'd perk up again, and tell the story about Lew Dane, who was taller by six inches than the coffins they had in Benson, so when he died unexpected, they sawed his legs off at the boot top to fit him in.

It was not a place where people gave soirees without a reason; most gatherings required an occasion and a public potluck. But in this season they made more calls than usual. Wally Wheeler called on Mrs. Hum with a whole hind quarter. Su Hum called on Mrs. Newsome with a salted cod. Mabeth Newsome called on Alma Timkin with a *John 3:16* in cross-stitch. Alma called on Eleanor Poindexter with a copy of Handel's "Water Music," which Eleanor had mentioned one morning after church. They drank a cup of tea and promised they would get to know each other after the holiday fuss died down. There was such a sense of community in the mild air that Sheriff Robinson began to talk of running telephone lines, though everyone accepted this as a sort of Christmas fable. On the other hand, Alma Timkin told Wally Wheeler she was going to buy herself a motorcar, and because he scoffed, she did it — went into Tucson, laid cash down for a Model A, got herself instructed, and drove all the way back, eighty-eight miles in a little under five hours.

Eleanor continued to drive the shorter distance to the Wheeler ranch, three times a week, though with Christmas coming Frank had extra to do; there were beef and poultry orders from the Coast, family coming from Wickenburg, and the children out of school — Mary Doreen apologized more than once for needing him to cart goods or beat the rugs. So in this period Eleanor took Digger out to ride alone.

Meanwhile, she scoured Laurel's *Daily Star* with the fear that she would find herself impaled in print. No interview appeared. There was also no retribution in the matter of Laurel's health, for the doctor had pronounced him no worse and possibly a little better. Apparently, apart from culottes and a Papago bowl, all that came of the Tucson trip was that Eleanor acquired the habit of skimming the *Star*.

Some of the news was good: On the twenty-third of December Congress passed the Federal Reserve Act — a Christmas present, Laurel said — which would stabilize banking forevermore. Some of it was bad: In Dublin the Ulster Volunteers had armed, and there were bloody clashes between police and strikers. News about the nearer conflict across the border was either inconclusive or contradictory. In early December the Constitutionalists seemed to be pushing the federal forces out of Chihuahua, and then in the middle of the month Orozco recaptured Torreón and the rebel offensive came to a standstill. When Pancho Villa won a skirmish, the wire services credited his tactical genius; when he lost, they blamed it on the weapons Huerta bought with ruinous taxes, and called for the lifting of the U.S. arms embargo. While Villa and Obregón fought on the same side, their appointees in Sonora, Calles and Maytorena, squabbled with each other. In Mexico City, business interests, the banks, and the Church endorsed Huerta's regime, but American diplomacy was tilting toward the revolutionaries. Woodrow Wilson said we would never on any pretext seek a foot of Mexican territory; unidentified State Department officials said we would invade. Villa praised all Americans as his brothers in liberty, but when Eleanor mentioned this to Walter Wheeler one Sunday, he cordially replied that Villa should be strung up by the thumbs.

As an early Christmas present, Laurel gave Eleanor a horse of her own, having sought the advice of the elder Wheeler. It was a quarter-Arabian mare, a pale buff color prettily marked with a drift of snow down the center of her nose. The mare could not be kept on Jefferson Street, so Eleanor boarded her at Frank's ranch and continued her schedule as before. She found herself, toward Laurel, tossed between gratitude and obscure resentment. The mare was beautiful, broken, obedient, and fast. But Eleanor had come to love Digger for his workaday devotion, for the miles they had covered. She felt *untrue* to him. She also felt this was a foolish conceit, and it added itself to the things she could admit to no one.

She seemed unable to find a name for so elegant a beast, and the failure bred a pointless panic in her, so the fourth time Laurel referred to the mare by her pedigree as "the quarter-Arabian," Eleanor began to call her "Quarter." Laurel behaved as if offended. He said *quarter* was an ugly sound and a diminishing notion. She said *quarter* was a perfectly serviceable American word. He said that insofar as it was *American,* it merely meant twenty-five cents; and besides that, it was not a lady's name. Eleanor countered crudely that they were talking about a *horse.* He replied more crudely that that *horse* had cost him ten shares of B&O; and he put on his hat and went to the bank at eleven o'clock at night.

He was home in an hour, and both of them badly frightened. She had drunk most of a bottle of Burgundy and could not stop sobbing. She declared she had never meant to insult the mare — the most beautiful gift anyone had ever given her! — and he, though he was the more shaken of the two, held her, stroked her hair protectively, and avowed that it didn't matter two figs, he couldn't imagine what had come over him. He then wanted to solemnize their reconciliation, but she was exhausted with crying and begged off, which he allowed with stilted grace, and the quarrel dwindled without closure so that, as with the trip to Tucson, very little came of it except that the nobly begat horse now had the name Quarter.

Then an odd note was introduced at the Wheeler ranch when Mary Doreen refused the three dollars that Frank and Eleanor had agreed on for Quarter's boarding fee. Mary Doreen was hanging wash in the yard and she passed the back of her wet hand over her forehead, waving the bills away, scrubbing at her curls.

"But she'll cost you feed," Eleanor protested.

"No, now, I mean it. You've more than paid for the lessons, it don't seem neighborly to take any more."

Frank came up and mumbled something neutral. It was clear that Mary Doreen was contradicting his arrangements and that this embarrassed and displeased him.

"Really, I don't see why —"

"Because I say so!" Mary Doreen actually scuffed her boot at the powdery dirt, then passed it off with a charming laugh while Frank studied the knot of the rope he held.

Eleanor supposed this was some matter of pride on Mary Doreen's part, but it didn't seem to make much sense, and it left her feeling uncomfortably obligated. Although Frank continued to treat her with the same easy, kidding manner, underneath he seemed remote or angry. More than once she saw him working at the fences when she turned onto the road, keeping an eye out, though by the time she got there he would be at the corral or the coop. Sometimes he visibly hovered, as if she stood in the center of a circle he didn't want to cross. She guessed he was avoiding her perfume. Once after her ride he stepped sharply back from her, and as she got in the car she saw him at the trough, as if washing off a contamination.

The only time his mood expressed itself aloud was when he

disapproved her riding out alone on Quarter. "There's too many things could happen to you," he said, stern toward the chicken he was plucking. "Your husband would thank me if that horse got spooked, and reared or bolted."

She brushed it off. "I'll take full responsibility." But this made him set his mouth and rip at the feathers.

And she didn't know, after that, whether it was his idea or the girl's own, that young Jessie would ride within sight of her, or be sitting on a boulder by the farther-out fences, Digger nearby with his reins dropped as if she'd just walked him out to graze.

On days when the *señora* rode, Maria's work was done in half the time. She blued the sheets, she boiled the dishwater and the *señor*'s handkerchiefs, she dusted with spirit of ammonia — all the things Señora Eleanor pretended were ordinary cleaning, but that Maria knew belonged to a house of sickness. Maria did all of it exactly as she was told, and then she sprinkled water out of a vinegar bottle that had been blessed by Father Vicente. Even so, days when the *señora* wasn't in the house she had time to spare, and in her spare time she taught herself to read.

It was difficult and slow. Books and magazines discouraged her so she studied mainly in the larder, where she couldn't be seen from the windows, and where the shelves were better than picture books: *Del Monte beans, Heinz pork and beans; Del Monte peach halves, peaches in syrup; Heinz pea with ham soup, Armour ham, Heinz peas and carrots; Avondale figs in heavy syrup*. It could be done. The labels that had no pictures were the things she could see anyway — crackers, tea, flour. The goods they got from Señor Hum's garden were not written anywhere, so she was short of greens and roughage, but sometimes in one of the *señora*'s magazines she could match a picture to a word in the recipe.

She had to be able to read because if she couldn't read she would never leave here; the ropes would pull tighter and tighter around her until she couldn't breathe to run. Things were not good at home. The Apache was gone, the way he had gone two dozen times before, except that Mama seemed to know he was gone for good, and this was not the kind of knowing Maria doubted. Mama squatted in the dirt, her hair dragged on her shoulders. She could not so much as boil a pot for beans; or would not. Maria would find little Ramón trying to scrub clothes on a glass washboard higher than his armpits, Azul patting Mama's neck with the flat of her hand: pat, pat. The women asked, "Soledad, how do you know he will not come back?"

It was not the question Maria would have asked. She would have asked: *How can you let this happen to you? Where is your pride?* At night Mama moaned and Carmen Acosta slapped on the doorframe with a huarache.

Maximo de la Luna had taken to waiting for Maria after work, where she crossed the tracks from town. When they passed over the packed-earth bridge he pretended the space was more crowded than it was, swinging a dance-walk, swiveling his hips. One night when she came to throw the washwater out he was there under a sliver of a moon; he caught her against the wall of her own house, his thumb sliding over her nipple while his other hand held her against the wall. He wet her mouth and pressed it, and even as she fought him, her throat ached; the saddle of skin over her spine began to loose and tingle, just the space that ached when she bent over the washtub, just there. The pan was trapped between them. She broke from him and hit him on the thigh with the pan, but this only made him crow with laughter.

So she stayed later at the *señora*'s and looked at pictures of faraway places, of trees and the ocean, and high-stacked buildings made of quarry stone. She found the word she wanted and traced it with her finger: *California.* She learned to read the names of the magazines from hearing them asked for and read out of. From the stack of newspapers on the sofa table she matched the word *Baltimore* to the postmark on an envelope. (She said to the *señora*, "Here's a letter from Baltimore," but the *señora* seemed to think she had done nothing remarkable, and Maria's disappointment passed quickly to scorn and then to triumph.) Mostly she memorized words, but now and again she strangely understood something without knowing she had learned it. She saw not only what linked *peas, plums, and peaches (Poindexter, Papago!)*, but also *Tabasco* and *Nabisco;* she went about the house the whole of one washday with her mouth screwed up like a lemon: *"sc, sc, sc."*

By the third week of December she could read seven fruits, six vegetables, fifteen staples, four cleaning compounds, and six kinds of liquor. She had eight colors, nineteen brands, and seven magazines. She had the days of the week and the months of November and December. She had numbers, if she took her time; and to describe things: *large, small, light, heavy, best, delicious, young, crisp, new, evening, daily,* and *wholesome.* She took a *Sun* home, but the type was so cramped that she still could not recognize more than a few letters in the headlines, and a few days later the midwife put the pages to better use birthing Constanza Laredo's healthy boy.

Maria took other things home, too, both waste and theft; it was not always possible to know which was which. Both the Poindexters wasted sinfully. Señora Eleanor would throw out anything left in a can after they had eaten part of it; she talked about "spoilage" and "taint" and "bacillus." Wherever she sat there would be garbage left: the parings of a piece of fruit, half a cup of tea, or a lettuce leaf. Maria fed Ramón and Azul on ends of ham, chicken backs. Her mother's soup had costly bones. She took a jet button from the *señora*'s sewing box and hung it on the Virgin's skirt for a *milagro.* Now she was able to contribute to the tin sheet on the altar by which Father Vicente was fed: meat bought not shot, bleached wheat flour; and once a can of Del Monte apricots in heavy syrup, which Gabrielo Acosta was invited to share with the priest because he had a chisel.

There were other thefts, things you couldn't see or hold. Sometimes Maria stroked the keys of the piano (very lightly; it wouldn't do to be overheard by someone passing by). Sometimes she sat on one of the tapestry couches and scratched Baltimore under the chin, angling her head, and turning the pages of a magazine. Sometimes she kneeled down at the little altar and prayed to that private and expensive Virgin.

In Christmas Week a boy appeared at the front door with a cottontail by the ears. He was one of the scruffy Ruffinos from the ditch end of town, and had no English but "feefty cents, feefty cents," which he kept repeating as he gestured at the rabbit's skinny limbs and belly.

"Oh, dear," said the *señora.* "I don't have anything to keep it in. And it will eat all the grass in the yard."

"*¿Qué dice?*" the Ruffino asked, and Maria scowled at him. "She says Señora Nene had one twice as fat for twenty-five cents."

When the boy had gone with his quarter Maria offered to show how to skin it, but Señora Eleanor said she didn't want to watch. For Christmas Eve Maria stewed the filleted meat in canned milk and pimientos, with fresh parsley out of the Chinaman's gardens, and Señor Poindexter said, "Rabbit *à la king*, a wonder." The señora said, "It tastes just like chicken."

Maria had heard white ladies say this of rabbit before, and also of rattlesnake and chipmunk. It made no more sense than if one should say cornmeal tastes like wheat or tripe like kidney. Yet it was always said prettily, as if it was clever to say it.

Maria craved this language; it was why she needed reading. Yet she would feel exasperated. Not at all fragile, the *señora* seemed defenseless all the same. She knew how to lay the crystal, drive a motorcar, which spoon or smile to use; but she did not understand the ordinary things you had to know to keep alive. She didn't seem to know how to make a rich man happy, get a baby, get friends around her for when she needed them.

Then, sometimes, the *señora* blundered fantastically. On Christmas Eve, after the dishes had been shelved and the rabbit bones tucked away for Mama's soup, the *señora* gave Maria, in a piece of satin paper and a satin bow, a pair of Zuni thunderbirds. To her! As if a three-quarter-blood Castilian with an ounce of pride would hang reservation things in her ears! Maria thanked her, first bashfully, in her shock (she had hoped for money); and then turning that confusion to account, with a shining lift of her eyes. The consolation of it, afterward, was that she had done the thanking as well as Señora Eleanor did herself, for the fat church lady's awful soup and the preacher's pamphlets. She gave the earrings to her mother, who had no such pride, and who boasted through the Christmas Mass how much her daughter earned; and who waited almost three weeks before she traded them to Fatima Peralta for a rooster and a length of wire.

22

AN EASY TROT on the flat to where the dry streambed cuts a shallow, winding trough; gentle into and out of that. Pick up speed with the sun full at the back, heading east; double around the jacaranda to meet the streambed where it curls; squint into the sun and leap. Back again; and leap. Full gallop to the arroyo with the scatter of stripling mesquite on its brow; and now, and now, and *now!* Hit the far bank with a jolt and scatter of quartz, sweat cold on forehead, heart thumping hosannas, every breath a laugh.

All the same, Eleanor never seemed able to accept as adequate that she was happy now, was reconciled to the desert for the moment. Oh, no, she must always think she had found the whole answer at last, understood herself finally, would henceforward live in this second's exultation. Unfortunately, this was true of bad moods as well: Then desiccation was general and eternal, life was tragic in all times, places, and aspects; people were treacherous and also wasted, damnation loomed, etc.

Wine helped. One of the light, dry whites at the top of her joy could keep it humming there, prolong it for an hour, another. A Bordeaux in the dark mood would settle that mood out like sediment, to leave her listless, vague.

She was twenty-five, four years married, believed herself born into original sin. She had her first orgasm drunk on a Friday afternoon, standing, hanging on to a bedpost, pressing a curl of four fingers into her dimity petticoat, thinking of somebody else's husband.

He had said only, *"Don't* get hurt," with a look in his eyes that was pleading, though, for something else, which she had seen in other men's eyes and was not surprised to see in his. But she was surprised to see it in the wind in front of her as she rode, in the sky over the Chiricahuas; and later — agitated beyond containing, the rhythm of the horse still in her — in the sanguine swirl of her claret glass.

Her first reaction was terror. She did not immediately connect it with the fumblings and pumpings of married life. Before she recognized ecstasy she thought she thrummed in the blind grip of retribution. Afterward she washed shakily, the smells of horse and toilet water and her wrung body potent to her. When Laurel got home she was in bed in a different layer of dimity and eyelet. She said she must have had too much sun.

And she did feel ill. She had the tentative, woozy viewpoint of convalescence, overlaid on an intimation of catastrophe. She felt fragile. She didn't think she should move too much. She had a sense, long since outgrown, that God was on the ceiling. At the same time, she was curious and defiant; she touched the skin of her forearm tenderly. She felt her thigh with new respect.

By Sunday she said she was well enough to go to church (true; she felt fine) because she did not want to miss her ride on Monday. She sat in the hard pew restless and reckless, while Reverend Newsome tediously droned on about a frugal, hardworking God who bore no resemblance to *her* vision of astounding glory; and afterward heard herself charging forth in chatter to poor Alma Timkin, whom she planned to like because she was the only person in town with any culture but, oh, dear, what a hearty, simpering soul she was, such a spinster, when it came to the point.

On Monday, after Laurel had left for the bank (the Tucson doctor said he should walk whenever the temperature was endurable), she packed a picnic into the motorcar: bread, cheese, and wine, like those on the hillsides of Provence with Cousin Peg.

It was now just after the new year, but work at the Wheeler ranch was still heavy, and she did not expect to share her picnic with anyone. Did not want to. Did not particularly want to see Frank, and once she got there made no effort to find out where he was. Perhaps she made a little effort not to. She called Quarter to her; both Quarter and Digger came. There did not seem to be anyone about — the children had no doubt gone back to school — and she breathed easily at this. She gave Digger a long, murmuring caress, saddled Quarter, put her picnic in a saddlebag, and left the ranch.

As soon as she had closed the barbed wire gate, she felt a surge of rebellion and — what was it? — truancy. She rode excited for half an hour, not thinking of Frank Wheeler or his warnings or his desires, occasionally observing that she was not. She cantered a little, perfecting her form, or rode in an easy lope toward the horizon, looking only to the horizon, that reach of land as sere as an abstract thought.

After a while she dismounted, spread on a slab of convenient sandstone the cloth she had brought, broke her bread, and poured the wine into a tin cup she had found in the Semple larder. She lay back on the rock and watched the sky. Frank Wheeler's face appeared magnified in the expanse, eyes ether blue.

When she sat up again she felt a little dizzy. She hunched cross-legged in her gaucho trousers, angled her hat for shade, and stretched her eyesight once again to the horizon to steady it. And saw, oh, for the dozenth time, the irregular white slice that was the old Spanish mission.

It was still not noon. Nobody had seen her leave the ranch. Laurel wouldn't be back until evening. All of them would be shocked to know she'd go so far alone, but she didn't care. She took great pleasure in assessing that she didn't care.

She was practical, assured herself that her water canteen was full and her cinch secure, that the little watch face on her brooch was ticking. She spoke encouragingly to Quarter of extra rations when they got back. Several times after she took off, when she got a stitch in her side and the mission looked no nearer, her determination flagged and she thought that, after all, she could turn back now, nobody cared. The thought reassured her, and she continued at a gallop. The sun was straight overhead and the two of them made no more shadow than the patch under Quarter's belly. She crossed northeast at an angle over the railroad track. The scoured earth was so much the same that once she stopped and turned just to make sure there would be landmarks for the return. Then she tested her progress by counting to a hundred with her eyes on the saddle horn. When she looked up, the pale square was appreciably larger; she was encouraged, and did it again, twice more.

And after all when she slowed, panting, on a curve of what had once been road — a scattered outline of rocks the size and texture of underdone bread — Quarter's shadow scarcely preceded her, and the little watch said only three quarters of an hour had passed. The mission took its irregular shape from a ruined bell tower, or perhaps the beginnings of a bell tower never finished. The wall stood roofless and ragged four feet above her head, interrupted at intervals with the arched shells of windows. Eleanor respected the ghost of a road and wound with it to approach the building from its southern end. She passed a box elder and two olive trees. Rounding the corner under the bell tower, she came upon a massive arch, where one thick door of bolted beams still hung by a huge iron hinge, although it was parched brittle, and its wood beetle-eaten to lace. The remains of the other door lay scattered on the ground. Above the emptied space hung a cascade of bougainvillea, a waterfall of scarlet so violent it burned the eyes. Gingerly, not dismounting because it seemed safer to be high off the ground, she bent to pass through.

At her entry there was a scurrying of lizards from their sunning spots. A pair of cactus wrens lifted and settled again on a burr sage. But really she need not have worried; the whole east wall was crumbled to the height of her knees. A few mesquite grew in the sheltered corner, a pile of tumbleweeds tangled into them, and that was all. She turned slowly on her horse. She was standing in an open nave, one transept stretching east at the end of the crumbled wall, the other ground down to its outline, so that what remained formed a footed L. Her heart began to pound. She could see the Chiricahuas through the high arches, and, now no farther than they to the south and east, mountains that had been her horizon, so that she sat at the center of the potter's wheel from which the mountains had been thrown.

To the east a tumble of the stone loaves outlined a patio or cloister, and in the center of it sat a well — not a windmill, but a proper circle of mortared stone, which once had had a roof (the uprights protruded from the mortar) but now was overhung with a gnarled fig tree. The tree heaved its roots against the circle, which it both cracked and held together.

She walked Quarter to the edge of the nave and stepped over. The stub of wall was a full eighteen inches thick. She registered that this much mud, and part of a skin of paint, had held together for more than two centuries. The patio was laid with flat shale, but the nave interior was dirt-floored. Where the erosion was deepest you could see that the walls had been set into foundations, but there wasn't even the ruin or rubble of a floor, just packed earth.

She dismounted at the well and tossed in a stone, which landed not with a plop but with a rustle and a scurrying. Still, there must be water, or there would be no fig. She climbed on the broken wall and slowly turned in the spare, centrifugal beauty of the spot. She stood in one of the arches on the western side, a saint in a niche, and measured the nave with her eye. Sixty feet by twenty? Seventy-five by thirty? It had taken her three quarters of an hour from wherever she had eaten her picnic. The Wheeler ranch was south of town, so she was probably no farther from Bowie here than she was from the ranch. By horse this place was probably less than an hour from the bank, by car not much more than thirty minutes. And there must be water.

Water; she drank from her canteen, poured some for Quarter — and then in sentimental impulse also splashed a handful at the root of the fig tree.

She mounted and toured the place again, broke off a spray of bougainvillea to tuck in her hair, then took off straight south to the railroad track, followed it at full gallop — the way back was surprisingly short — turned west across the flat until, just as she came in view of the Wheeler ranch she also came upon Jessie, out on Digger, and she called to her, "Come on back to the ranch with me!"

The girl broke into a startled smile and dug in her heels, galloping after on the serviceable little stallion. The two of them stirred up some dust skidding into the chicken yard, Eleanor shouting when she saw Mary Doreen Wheeler plucking chickens on a stool, and then when she saw Frank standing back of the coop with a coil of barbed wire in his hand.

"I've found my house! I've found my house! I've found my house!"

23

IT WAS SAID that Villa wanted hangings because there was no wall to stand the men against, and he thought it was wrong to shoot a man without a wall behind him. Fierro held out for a rifle squad. There were also no trees, he said, and if they were going to build scaffolds they might as well build a wall. In the end they did neither, just took the prisoners out at daybreak and set them against the dark part of the sky, beside the sandbag ring where the cocks fought in the afternoon and that looked a little like a wall and maybe satisfied the need for a wall. The ground was so parched there that an hour after the last kill you couldn't see there'd been a cockfight in that ring. The morning of the first execution Farga milled among the men, excitable, but Lloyd stood back as near the tracks as he thought he could stay and not have anybody remark about it. The prisoners, four *federales* who had been taken on one of Fierro's night raids, were led out from the boxcars, each one in most of a uniform, although one was missing his jacket and one had his feet wrapped in place of boots. All four took the blindfold, but after the blindfolds were in place, one of them kept turning like he was looking for something behind him. There was nothing behind him but the last place the sun went down. There were eight in the firing squad, in clean whites with cartridge belts and sombreros because this was the first execution in this camp. They went down on a knee, some left, some right, and when Fierro gave the command the shots rang ragged; but the prisoners all sank at the same time, like they'd been drilled for it. Three went face down, but the other fell backward over a bent leg and lifted his head up off the ground a few times before he died. Four *villistas* ran up with stones to knock the gold out of their teeth.

Lloyd got up only the one time to watch, but every morning afterward he'd wake at cockcrow and lie listening for shots. The funny thing was that if he heard them, he'd go back to sleep. If he didn't, he'd keep waiting for them until the whole camp staggered to its feet.

By the turn of the new year recruits arrived in roundups, more than could be fed. Sometimes whole villages came to deliver boy volunteers; old men in flat black hats embraced them, mothers wept; they departed like families seeing young scholars off to school. Other soldiers, older, arrived quietly with their women and children in tow; others appeared alone in the middle of the night with one serape for bed and coat. Villa's hundreds swelled to thousands. New boxcars came down from the north full of horses who bolted from their sides, men racing in the dust to lasso them, their *viejas* already scrambling up the ladders to claim camping space on top.

All of a sudden Lloyd and Simon were not the only Anglos. There were mercenaries and volunteers from Texas, California, Tennessee. Journalists came and went, making use of a little bloat-faced interpreter bald as a coot; "Moon Mullins goes to war," said Simon. The Americans would ask Lloyd when he'd joined with Villa, and he would say, sometimes, as much as that he'd come down meaning to get rich on copper and changed his plans. It got a laugh. But he was never sure if Farga was going to tell more of a story, and generally he stayed out of their way. Sometimes the older *villistas* would cuff his head and ruffle his hair — was that good, or not? Sometimes when a new man joined them, they would say, "The gringo's all right; he was trust man at the Ojinaga ford-ing." But sometimes they'd just say, "Never mind the gringo."

One morning an airplane came down and landed on the desert, silver struts gleaming. The men crowded around it, polishing the underbelly with their sleeves. A photographer took a picture of Villa in a bear hug with the pilot. Afterward the plane sat on the desert, one wheel squashing a prickly pear, while the trains pulled out toward Yermo and Conejos.

Every week or so some semiofficial American diplomat would arrive and disappear into the caboose with Villa and the interpreter; afterward Villa would praise Woodrow Wilson and hug the agent for the camera. After a month of these negotiations the U.S. arms embargo was lifted, and grenades and rifles came down, legal, from over the border. All of them had to be hoisted into the supply car. Lloyd's muscles sang at night. His throat had a permanent thick husk of dust. There were two *niños,* as they called the flatbed cannon, and by mid-February ten miles of train stretched back over the single track toward Juárez like a centipede. Nine thousand men camped on the flats in a mile-wide swath along the train, each with his horse looped to a scrap of chaparral, his women and children huddled anywhere there was an empty lip of boxcar or a cattle catcher. Nights now the cars etched a fiery line across the desert.

The centipede undulated forward toward Torreón, the repair car first with its cargo of cannons, crossties, and a Chinese crew. Huerta's general, Orozco, sabotaged the track as he retreated, and where the rails were mangled the crew piled out with picks and new iron, swaggered over by a foreman with a wide sombrero. Six *dorados* walked before the train, measuring their distance from it with skinny branches, peering at the track for mine wires. When they were relieved they came red-eyed and squint-wrinkled back to their women for *frijoles* and old coffee. Then the train would catch up in stages over the repaired track: water train, officers' private cars, feed, supplies, hospital, Villa's red caboose, more horses, water, men, and goods.

Every few days a troop would ride off, their *campesinas* after them, children wailing or mute and the women urging them along, bundles slung from one shoulder. The men would go off shouting and laughing, the women dogged, but when they came back the next noon, a day later, two days later — always longer as they traveled south — the men rode with their eyes on nowhere, slumped in the saddle, the horses rocking on their haunches. One part of the company always came back a half day later than the rest, the ones that had stayed behind to "raise the ground" and stick the dead ones under it.

Lloyd and Simon were assigned to the supply train, toward the end near the hospital cars. Sometimes they assembled weapons from the shipments, sometimes Farga brought them gear to clean up for Villa and Fierro. They were supposed to make sure the barrels were clean, blades sharp, saddles soaped, reins supple, sights true. Anything that swiveled must be free of grit. Anything that fastened must hold. Anything that shot must shoot. They sat with rags and brushes, whetstones, legs dangling off the edge of the open car, looking over a patch of trampled desert while Simon itched for action.

"You ask him, why not?" Simon would say. "You're his golden boy."

"Stop that," said Lloyd.

"Ask him when you and me are going to get into it."

Simon had acquired a dog, a Mexican hairless he claimed had a body temperature of a hundred and four degrees — "topping for a cuddle" these chilly nights. It had perfectly bald grayish skin that wrinkled around every joint like the fell on a raw ham. It was not a whole lot bigger than a rat, and a rat was winsome by comparison. It generally slept the day away burrowed between a greasy rag and Simon's crotch.

"Do, now," he said. "Just saunter on up and poke your head in and say: begging your bloody pardon, *mi general,* but could you give Mr. Willoughby and me a general notion when we're going to be deployed?"

Lloyd checked the clip spring on an old Lee-Enfield. The work had a squeejaw familiarity about it. After Lloyd's mother died he'd lived in a family of men — his father, brother, Johnny Fousel, and other hands who came and went. A woman took away the laundry but a man did the cooking, men cleaned up, men made their beds and lay in them, one man to one narrow bed. Evenings in the bunkhouse or on the back porch men would sit oiling metal and leather like this, measuring oil on whetstones drop by drop. Now he tried to feel as if he was a crucial cog in a war machine, keeping it slick, two steps away from the *jefe* himself. But it was housekeeping, really.

"I expect he'll tell me what he wants, I won't have to be putting any questions to him." In fact, Villa hadn't spoken to Lloyd since the cattle crossing.

Simon held the disgusting dog to his neck. "Touch of the lily-liver? If you can't tell the man you want to fight, how will you manage to fight when the time comes?"

"Shut up, Simon."

Simon had a way of hitting too near the bone just at random, scattershot. For all his fervor, he'd soured since the incident of the bottle, and it tickled him when somebody slandered Villa. "Bloke from the *L.A. Times* — says our general is dedicated, with the single-mindedness of a saint, to a bunch of illiterate, half-baked humbug." Then he'd rub his stubble and wheeze. Somewhere back in the straw under half a ton of Springfield rifles he must have had a bottle still, but Lloyd judged it was wisest not to know anything about it.

And Simon had this way. He'd sit half a century running his mouth so pointless you could doze off at the ears, and then all of a sudden he'd stumble into your guts. Because it was true. Lloyd was waiting to get into the fight; of course he was. There was no point being here if he didn't fight, marking time at work he could be doing as anybody's cowhand and have a mattress under him at night. But whenever Farga showed up with a load of materiel he wanted cleaned, Lloyd would be sure he was going to be told to saddle up, and he'd have his stomach in his gullet for a half hour after. He knew for a fact no Mexican ever felt that way. They laughed at hurt and death. And here was Simon, slump-shouldered and splay-gutted and old, picked out by Villa for public shaming, and still he couldn't wait to play the hero, saying yet again, "He can count on this old gun, you tell him, no mistake."

But in February the mood in camp changed. It was bitter cold. Every night there was a quarrel over either a cockfight or a woman; all the kidding had bite. They sang only the *corridas* that ended bloody and unjust. When they talked about women it was with a shove of the lower lip, meaning women had it too soft and knew nothing. It was not as easy as it had been to get food, and what there was was mostly beans and flour. Concepción dished up stingy where she had been free-handed, and Lloyd thought she resented him. The afternoons followed one after the other bright and cold, and Lloyd felt a dull space between his eyes and the saddle or the barrel he was working on, his mind a blank while the train inched down the middle of Mexico.

One Sunday they camped by a water tank with no more than a foot of dirty water at the bottom, and Lloyd noticed there were half a dozen priests wandering around the camp. Farga came by with Villa's pair of Smith and Wesson .44's with the full scrollwork and the Mexican eagles carved in the ivory handles, snakes in their mouths. There was also a Mauser Lloyd hadn't seen before, and Fierro had personally asked for a dozen hand grenades.

"Summat's up," said Simon.

Monday morning a troop headed south in a flood of dust, and in the afternoon another one followed after it, a third to the southwest. Farga went off with Fierro, so important he didn't say goodbye. At least four gringo greenhorns rode with Villa, men who hadn't been here long enough to scuff their boots, while Lloyd was left kicking his legs in the dust they raised. More cavalry took off all evening, pushing one way or another, though generally south. It was Simon who pointed out that the women hadn't gone with them this time. Simon speculated the companies would meet up later and head somewhere no one but Villa knew about. That was the way he kept the advantage of surprise, said Simon, not letting even his own captains know what their objective was till they were on it.

"Is it Torreón, do you think?"

"No, not yet. Too far south still. Any road, they'd take the *niños* for Torreón."

"Where, then?"

"Mapimi, I shouldn't wonder. It's a big one."

By dark there was nobody left but the repair crew and about two hundred men to guard the train — and some of those arthritic, or kids, or missing one or another piece of their anatomy.

"And here we sit," said Lloyd, to get in with it first.

"Hurmph," Simon said in his throat, testy.

That night and morning the place was eerie for its stillness. You wouldn't think several hundred women and babies could be quiet enough to give you the creeps. The *campesinas,* who usually kept up a cackle over breakfast, sagged over the plain like a piece of faded cloth.

But when the sun got high the plain warmed up more than it had for weeks. One woman, loose-legged under her skirts, climbed the water tower for a lookout. A boy guard teased her, waving his pistol, and then on purpose or by accident, his gun went off and shot a hole in the tank. It made them laugh to see that tower pissing on the desert in a thirty-foot arc. A girl still in braids held out her skirt to catch it, and then a woman made a bowl of her *rebosa,* one corner in her teeth and the sides stretched to arm's length. The boy got full of himself and shot half a dozen more holes, and women held pails underneath, another and another, any kind of vessel they had with them, till everyone was carrying off water, sloshing and splashing it. They washed every spare piece of cloth in ten miles and spread it on the chaparral where the men had tied their horses, while a few hundred naked children ran around in the dust flats in the sun.

Lloyd washed his clothes, too. Concepción gave him a pair of Farga's peon whites, and while his shirt and trousers dried he wore those around camp, his bony shins sticking out below the loose *calzones,* his wrists four inches beyond the sleeves. Then the women laughed! But he shucked it off. He hoisted crates of .22 shells (made in Oklahoma and Kentucky) from one end of the boxcar to the other, just to keep busy, while Simon went off to see what he could find out. Lloyd watched them down by the horsecars slapping each other on the back, Simon and a couple of Mexicans more grizzled than himself, and the kid still full of bluster for shooting up the water tower.

But when Simon came back he hunched over his awful dog and talked British, in riddles.

"A revolution is the same as women."

"Oh, yeah."

"Yuh. You always think it'll be different this time. But once the chase is over, then the fight begins. You watch, once they get Huerta they'll start carving on each other."

"Wha'd they tell you?"

"They wouldn't tell me if I had a copperhead in my boot."

"They seemed friendly."

"Did they now. What would you know about seeming friendly?"

"They were laughing."

"Jesus Mary, you amaze me. You think because they laugh they're happy little children. How long have you been living with these people, that you think they laugh for fun?"

The dog yawned. Lloyd took a handful of .22 shells and started tossing them overhand like darts at a forked stump of greasewood ten feet away. "What's eating you, Simon?"

"These people laugh for revenge, and when they're sick to death."

"I don't know why that should make you mad at me."

"Because I'm sick to death of *you,* stuck here and you in a major whinge all day long every day. You make it a bit of a trudge, I can tell you. You make it a bit of a slog." He rubbed on the dog like it might have had a hair or two after all that he had to get rid of. "I'd like to know what you care for."

"What do you mean?"

"I mean what you care for! You sit here in the middle of this cocked-up continent in the middle of the greaser army, and you don't give a pom diddly whether they get their land or not."

Lloyd set one shell right in the fork of the stump, and rewarded himself a notch in the wood of the boxcar with his fingernail, surreptitiously.

"You've got no taste for a fight," said Simon. "You don't like one man more than the next. You don't think. Who are you? Why won't you talk to the Chinese?"

Lloyd sat up. "What do you mean?"

"I mean, when the repair crew comes by you don't have the time of day for them."

"You don't know what you're talking about!" Lloyd lobbed the rest of the handful at the stump and shoved off the boxcar, landing in a squat. "Leave me alone." He stalked off and spent the rest of daylight with one eye over his shoulder to avoid Simon Willoughby.

But that evening Simon disappeared. When Lloyd went to feed Haragana he passed by the bivouac Simon had staked out beside the track, and it was just a wiped space in the dirt and a little pile of sifted ashes. Lloyd asked around and, sure enough, a couple of the men had seen him headed north. Kitted out? *Sí*. And the dog? *También*. So.

Lloyd squatted down and poked a stick in the dead ashes. He couldn't figure it out. Willoughby was a mercenary, an old hand at the slaughter junket. He was piss-boring, but he wasn't scared. He stank and he had queer foreign habits and he talked world without end, but he'd been chasing wars since he was a boy for nothing but money and kicks. Now he was gone, took off just as easy as Lloyd always knew you could. Well, good riddance to his boots and his bootblack and his high temperature hairless monster. *Tanto mejor*. No skin off my nose.

He was used to warming himself by Concepción's cooking flame before he bedded down, but tonight he pulled excelsior from the machine gun crates and made a nest in the boxcar. He was surprised he hadn't thought of it before. The car kept the cold night wind off of him and it insulated him, too, against the laughter of the other men, which gave him bad dreams that made him sweat although he couldn't remember them when he woke.

In the morning he dragged himself up out of sleep one layer at a time, through the wool of his blanket and the scratch and rustle of the straw into the sharp cold, hearing sounds again, plodding steps beside the car, and a general rumbling from the ground. He shoved back the heavy door and swung his legs over the side so that his stockinged heels hit painfully. Straight on, the sunrise was a flaming orange ball just at the level of his eyes, and he blinked away from it while it burned in his eyelids. As soon as he took a breath he ate familiar alkali, and he had a pang of regret that he hadn't noticed, yesterday, how the wet laundry had held down the dust.

From the south they were coming back in a rolling surf, the several troops at once, men on foot leading their horses, or walking horseless, or slumped in their saddles, or lying in the wagons; and here and there a complicated machine with three heads and five legs lumbering to support a stump in the middle. The horses stepped carelessly. One ancient passing the supply car raised to Lloyd a federal spur, the spiked wheel red in the sun, tied by a bit of torn cloth to his shattered hand.

"Did we win?" Lloyd shouted.

The old man stopped and looked around, found Lloyd in his

focus again, and flopped the spur against his wound. "We won," he agreed. He shook his head as if to clear it. *"Viva Villa,"* the man said, and went on.

Behind him a horse dropped and spilled his rider between two dead fires, the horse keeling from the ankles in a dancer's roll. The man leaped back as it hit the ground and jerked his leg out of the way. The horse lay still, breath heaving. With an expression of brusque efficiency the man pulled the pistol out of his belt and shot the horse. Blood sprayed out of the ear onto his shirt. He replaced the pistol and with the same brusqueness took hold of the saddle to wrench it free. But it would not come free. One stirrup was caught under the weight of the dead belly. The soldier pulled at it again and again with a monotonous sameness of force, with monotonous failure. Finally he stood up and strolled away.

The wounded walked like drunks, and for a time everyone who went by was wounded. A boy passed swinging a branch over his head, beating himself in the back as if he were his own horse in need of urging. Another had made a sling out of an empty cartridge belt, and he carried his arm like something precious, crooning to it. They headed toward the hospital cars and lay higgledy-piggledy on the ground, some noisy but most silent, while over the next few hours the medics made room by lifting the wounded into the near side of the hospital cars and lowering the dead out the other.

Lloyd huddled against the cold. No one asked for help, and there wasn't any help to be given. He watched the troop for maybe an hour before anyone took notice of him, safe enough in his space that he started when there was a shout at the level of his knee.

"Hey! *Chica!* Gringa!"

It was the young captain from Utres, the one they called The Tireless. "Go to the repair car and get a spade. Now you will help us raise the ground."

Lloyd struggled to put on his boots and did as he was told. At the head of the train the Chinese crew was handing down pickaxes and square shovels to a silent group of men. Lloyd pulled down his hat in a gesture simultaneously deferential and concealing. He was thinking how convenient Simon had seen fit to bolt before he got assigned to the only action left at this end of the hero-making.

Thinking of Simon, Lloyd touched his brim to the man who handed him his shovel, a small, aged Chinese with a queue tucked down inside his shirt. The man ignored him. Lloyd held the handle in his fist across his chest, cupping the blade stiff-armed like a rifle as he followed after the others; but no one thanked him for the joke.

For four hours, maybe five, they dug a trench about a mile from the track, Lloyd and two of the Chinese crew, and four others that had all been in the fight at Mapimi and therefore had a certain stink and a certain tenderness in common. Three of those were seasoned soldiers, but one was a handsome kid whose hair was paler and redder than his face. Nobody talked except to swear. The ground was cold and hard. The two Chinese went along with pickaxes, marking the sides of the trench six feet apart, and the others followed after with their spades, scooping the axed earth out and then trying to dig between.

Lloyd struck the ground with the square blade, where it sat without making a dent. He set his foot on the blade and stood his weight on it, and he made just as much impression on the ground as a lizard claw or a little scratching bird might make. He had heft, he was no lily whatever Simon said, so he slanted the spade to get a corner into a crack, slipped the point in, made a shuffling jump onto it either side of the handle, and in it went to a depth of an inch, inch and a half.

He battled the ground one lift of his weight onto the blade at a time, the whole planet pushing back at the bottom of his foot, which got a groove worn in it, a callus on the arch, a raw, scraped ache in the heel. They dug to a depth of three feet, no more, and Lloyd didn't like to ask whether they never went deeper, or whether it was because this ground in this spot was so goldarned hard.

It got no softer as they went down. He had dug before where the crust was hard but after a foot or two gave way to clay, where a shovel would go in clean for a good dig. But this was hard all the way down, overbaked like a roast left in the oven till it had gone to leather and past that. Sweat ran like tickling insects down his ribs. At first he was cold, and then his body hotted up in the brick oven of afternoon, so he took his shirt off and tied it around his waist by the sleeves and dug in his undershirt, and then he was hot and cold at different times and places on his body with no reason to it at all, arbitrary. Sometimes his chest was chilly but his fingers burned.

They came upon some bones — Lloyd thought maybe tailpieces from a cow or a spine of a large coyote, but then a couple more that looked too much like a human armbone not to think of that. It seemed odd and somehow unfair, in all the packed expanse of this desert, that they should have come upon somebody's old battle-ground or burying ground here where they were trying to make their own. If the spade struck a bone, then the bone crumbled easier than the earth; the bones were just leaven to that hard loaf. Lloyd tossed up a couple of femurs no bigger than a small child's, and when the blood rushed to his head from too many swings of the shovel without a breath, the earth's undertow pulled on him, the legions of the dead swam up. He thought, *If we waited long enough we'd find the whole earth packed with bones just as deep as we dig. The dirt'll eat us all.*

They brought the dead in a mulecart from the infirmary car, and when about eight feet of trench were dug, the two Chinese laid them in by the hands and feet. Lloyd kept his eyes on his spade and let two others go down to fill the trough behind them. His breath was still frozen when it hit his lungs. The fingers on his spade were numb and sore at the same time. The Chinese were catching up to him, on this side the old man with the queue tucked in his shirt, too small-seeming for the deadweight he had by the armpits, on the other side a heftier crewman with bootheels in his hands, the two of them gently swinging the corpse over the dirt mound to lower it in. Lloyd backed up to let them get a foothold and found himself looking into the face of Cesar Santos upside down.

He squatted for a moment with the wind knocked out of him. Santos's mouth was open and his eyes were closed; his face had a grayish cast. He had died in the standard way, a couple of bullets in the shirtfront and less blood than you might expect, although he landed in the shallow pit with a certain loose sag that made you think it might be otherwise in back.

"Cesar the Mouth," one of the men said fondly, and reached over to press Santos's jaw closed, but it was already stiff. "He wants to tell the devil a thing or two."

Lloyd reached around in the dirt and picked up a pair of small bones. "Hey, look!" He formed them into a cross and placed it on Cesar's chest. But at this the largest of the Mexicans crossed himself and turned away with a disapproving sound. The kid shook his copper hair, and then like a motor somebody had cranked, he began to vibrate through his torso, haywire. He made no noise, and none of the men paid any attention to him. Lloyd set his heels back on his spade.

They had covered Santos and half a dozen more when The Tireless came back and tapped Lloyd on a shoulder.

"Gringo. *El Jefe* wants to see you."

Lloyd barely grunted for an answer. He dropped his spade where he stood and turned on his heel. Walking sent the pain from the ball of his foot through the arch to the knuckle of his ankle, and he covered the mile back to the train as near tears as he'd been since he could shave. He wished he'd followed Simon Willoughby. He wished to God he'd gotten out before Villa had a use for him.

He knocked at the door to the caboose. A grinning guard let him in, past officers lounging on the bunks, one soaking a foot in a bucket, cocooned in smoke that smelled of cowhide and burned applesauce. This caboose had been retired from the SP, and he'd probably seen it pass through Bowie — dingy gray paint, little fluted globes to the lamps, and heart-shape velvet chairs like a girl's. On one of these at the far end of the car Villa sat facing this way in dirty blue underwear, playing an index finger on a gold piece on a table, round and round. He stopped this long enough to upend a soda into his mouth.

"Gringo. Sit."

Lloyd sat, gingerly in his thighs.

Then it was over in less than a minute.

"How does it go for you? You like it here with your *dorado* friends?"

"Yes, General." As soon as Pancho Villa turned his attention on you, those sad, alive dark eyes, you knew you were special after all. There was something touching in how his hairline receded, like an ordinary man.

"You are a good trust man, eh?" Villa laughed.

"I hope so, General."

"Good, good. I want you to do a little something for me."

"Yes, sir."

"An American boy, you know about mechanical things, yes?"

"Yes, General . . . ? Mechanical things?" The hulk of the *niños* came into his mind, the oily guts of the machine guns, the flat-pegged tops of the grenades. What was Villa going to ask him? Blow up a train? He nodded stupidly.

"I am going to send you a very long ways to do me, personally, a favor. Are you willing to do this?"

"Yes, General." Lloyd swallowed dry. Villa shuffled among the papers beside him and spread out a page of torn newsprint that said *Times Picayune* across the top. It was a crumpled ad, all swirls and curlicues. He stroked the wrinkles carefully out.

"I want you to go to New Orleans and buy me a Packard," Villa said.

24

MARY DOREEN HAD FELT the impact of her husband's infidelity long before it occurred. By now, if she had not absorbed the shock, at least she had learned to jolt less under it, and rode her days no rougher than the Pierce-Arrow arriving three times a week on her potholed road.

It was Eleanor and Frank who were deceived. The space around them had always been charged, but also hedged by rules and clear permissions. Frank had a stubborn, unexamined belief in marital fidelity. He knew Eleanor troubled him, but that feeling did not in the least amount to an *intention*. Besides, his wife was as hungrily eager in bed as he could have asked for. As for Eleanor, flirtation was her element, not lust. She certainly had him in her consciousness, but for the moment her attention was all on the bent speck on the horizon, how to make it whole, and hers. Laurel was dubious about living so far out, but he had been dubious before; she bent her efforts to convincing him.

She rode out to the mission twice a week through January, timing herself on the little watch that hung upside down from an opal brooch. She had underestimated some; her best time was just over an hour from Main Street to the mission gate. She reasoned that an automobile could cut the time by a third. A breakdown on the way would present a problem, though; perhaps they should also keep a room in town. She noted with satisfaction that Li Hum was installing a gasoline pump in front of the grocery store. She had no sense that she was inventing suburbia.

The winter rains came, and on the days they kept her in, she began sketching plans for the renovation. She was only dabbling, but once she started, it was always in her mind. It now seemed to her that placing walls was not a task wholly different from arranging furniture, although she had supposed it was, since it came under the name of "architecture." In fact, she seemed to know quite a lot about where it would make sense to put a door, and how the light would fall. Perhaps she would be proven wrong. Maybe these were very great secrets known only to men who had studied abstractions beyond her capacity. She didn't think so. She knew she had things to learn. What is the principle of a cesspool as opposed to a septic tank? How many beams, how close together, do you need to bear a roof? But such things seemed to be a matter of information, no more difficult than the sums and measurements of a recipe.

Frank was cautiously encouraging. The land was in the parcel that he and his father leased from the government, and they would make no objection to her homesteading it. Mexican labor was cheap, and Gabrielo Acosta was said to be good at adobemaking — of course, it was the Mexicans who said so — though she might have to ship her roof tiles from the Coast. It was hardly the place he would have picked to live, but he knew plenty of ranchers who lived farther out than that. In Mary Doreen's hearing Eleanor had spoken of marble floors. He felt entirely justified, in late February, in going along to see the site.

But they shot straight out from the ranch as if released. They both felt that. They galloped as far as the railway tracks, he ululating, she laughing from time to time for no special reason. February is not yet spring, but the air was balmy in a literal way, an unguent against the skin. Spectacle pod and Coulter's globemallow were in bloom, not wonderful flowers close up, but in the expanse and blur a bright spattering of white and orange.

Beyond the track they slowed, picking their way through fishhook cactus. Frank said, "It feels like a long time since I've had a good run like that," at which her breathing had to be controlled.

His need to say anything at all, the hesitation and lurch of his speaking, woke the danger. He was very large. He had on a jacket of some animal skin worn supple. On Digger she had sat below him, but Quarter and Sally were matched for height; she felt their mutual vantage point as power.

They stopped once, briefly. She drank from her canteen. He drank from his. He said, indicating the clear sky with a tilt of his head, "Nine months of the year, heaven offers no inducement." This was half of a local boast about the weather, of which the other half was, "Three months of the year, hell holds no terror." He would not have said *hell* in her presence. Still, there was something wrong with having mentioned heaven, and especially *inducement,* which was not a word he used.

They walked the foaming horses. Sally flushed a pair of road runners from the creoscte; the birds panicked south, and Frank cleared his throat with a cough.

"You've got good mesquite browse on the way to your house," he said, swiping a gesture toward the bushes. From anyone else, she thought, *your house* would have been ironic. "See how the grasses are clumped under them? There's half a dozen kinds of grass under a mesquite tree. Do you know why?"

"The shade?" she guessed.

"No, shade'll hold a little water, but then you got more competition for it under a mesquite. No, it's nitrogen. The plants are hungry for it, and mesquite sucks it out of the ground for feet around. Then when the pods fall, they're dumping little nitrogen pellets."

Nitrogen! Who had ever spoken of nitrogen to her? People thought a man who worked the land was ignorant because the things he knew weren't taught in school. She felt protective against his hypothetical detractors.

"Will it be very expensive for me to build a road?"

He glanced sideways at her, quizzical; comical. "The way we mostly make a road is: Drive a wagon from where you've been to where you want to go. After you've got wheel ruts, that's your road. You might have to fill in a few ravines. One Mexican, one shovel, if you've got time to wait for him. Or a team of them for a week — either way, about thirty dollars."

And that was thrilling, too, a kind of hardpan *savoir faire* whose nature was deeply masculine. She had a glimpse of the perspective from which *back East* meant *effete*.

They mounted again with a rush of energy, and as they neared the mission, Eleanor's uneasiness and her coveting became one thing. No one had envisioned this ruin as a dwelling place. Laurel was troublesome. Frank saw it only as a curiosity. Now it was urgent she should win him over. She led him with the winding of the road, toured the perimeter. She wheeled Quarter back and forth, pointing out the depth of the transept walls, the beauty of the arches, the cascade of bougainvillea.

"My notion is to keep the nave as open as possible," she said. "One *big* room with a mezzanine for a library — where the choir loft might have been. The bedrooms could be in the transept — or else it might be a chapel. I'm not sure. It partly depends how much it would cost to rebuild the other transept."

She had a riding crop with which she indicated the shape of the rooms, reaching down as if to draw with its tip in the dirt. Watching her, Frank was uncomfortably reminded of men he had known: entrepreneurs; his father planning the route of a cattle drive. The mission, for shape and color, could have been his quarry turned upside down, not as big as that, but bigger than any project he'd ever seen a woman take on.

"You'd have a chapel in your house?"

She lifted the rein in a shrug. But turned, head angled back as if defiance were in order. "Really, I'm a Catholic."

"I know that." Apologizing for knowing it. "I just don't know anything about it." Apologizing for that, too. "It is allowed, in your religion, to make a house out of a church?"

"I don't think anyone ever asked."

For some reason this struck him funny, although it troubled her. She bossed Quarter up the nave.

"See here. The kitchen can come off this end; you don't want afternoon sun on it, anyway."

She dismounted, looped Quarter's rein on a palo verde, lifted her basket and cloth from the saddle where they hung. Frank slowed her with a gesture, to take his saddle blanket down. He let Sally's rein hang while he ran a toe along the base of the wall, checking for wildlife, then shook out the blanket. Eleanor spread the cloth on top of it and set her basket down.

"I'm afraid it's just fruit and cheese — a far cry from your wife's kind of picnic feast."

"It will be . . ." He shied at the mention of his wife and could not finish his sentence. She had the heady, sudden certainty of being with a man who desired her.

"Well, I'm afraid my kitchen table is a little low to the ground." She spread two napkins with a flourish, inviting him to play. "But it saves on chairs."

"And besides that, you've got a tree growing in your larder."

"And lizards in my parlor. Look!"

She ran to the lowest wall, hopped over it into the cloister, and tossed a stone into the well. She waited for the rustle of leaves, but what she heard was a thick *plop,* the sound of mud struck. She wheeled around to him with a look so momentous that he took fright.

"What is it? What happened?"

"It's water!" she said.

He had seen that look before, but he had not seen it on a woman. It was ambition. It dislocated him. It had greed in it; it was how he felt about his quarry; it meant you would spend any effort the thing would ask.

She raced to the far side of the nave again and climbed up into the center niche. "There's water!" she shouted, sang. Turned, playful. "Well, there's mud." She raised her arms and put her two hands on the sides of the opening, leaning back in the arch so the sky outlined her as she swung, her loose hair grazing the adobe; and probably that was the moment of no return, although for her part she was thinking about how to sink a well (send a man down with a shovel? or do you need some kind of a drilling machine?) and intended less provocation than at several score other moments in her life.

Frank followed after and put his hands up to help her down. She did not need help, but she took his hands. On his forearms below his folded sleeves the veins rose blue. She slid down in the space between the wall and his leather jacket, the heady smells of hide and ambergris. Yet when she closed her eyes and lifted her face to his she remembered, once, bicycling full tilt into an old man on a sidewalk. Helping him to his feet, brushing him off — she remembered the dismay: It's too late, now, to go back and brake; there's no choice, now, but to deal with this, somehow.

He pressured her behind the knees with a forearm to lay her on the picnic cloth. It was broad daylight. She looked past the horses' heads through a palo verde to a piled cumulus, the horses mildly chomping hay. She put the vaulted ceiling of her living room in place above her eyes. Frank managed the buttons and opened her blouse to bare her shoulders. Even in that temperate air her skin was brutally exposed. There was so much of it; so much skin and so much air.

"Frank," she said. "I can't. Not here." But this form of protest was in itself a promise. What did *not here* portend but *somewhere?* What was *not now* but *sometime?*

Maria had finished and was only waiting for the miles-around petticoat to dry where the gathers were so tight at the hip. She had spread it flat over the tin table in the backyard, and now she was kneeling in the bedroom before the altar, the *señora's* little wooden rosary beads between her fingers, praying the strange penance Father Vicente had put on her. Father Vicente had found the *señora's* hatpin stuck through the Virgin's skirt for a *milagro.* He said that Maria's sins were pride and greed, and that to want the life of the *gente sancta* was to deny the will of God. Her prayer was not a sincere prayer, and she raised her eyes to the Virgin, worshiping rather the fine patina of pale paint, the graceful curve of eyelid over downcast eyes, than any mother-of-godliness captured by the painter.

She heard nothing until she heard behind her the swipe of twill against itself, and one, two bootheels where they left the hall carpet runner and hit the bedroom floor. By the time she turned, Señora Eleanor was already hand-upraised. The hand held a glass of wine that was spilling into her cuff. The cuff turned slowly red. At the same second as Maria's heart began to pound, she thought, "Quick, salt." She watched the hand reach out and slam the glass on the bureautop. Señora Eleanor still had her hat hanging back off her neck, her culottes were smudged and crushed, and her mouth was open with anger. She reached, grabbing toward Maria, but Maria raised her hands to protect her face, and so what the *señora* caught was the rosary. The little carved teeth of its wood beads bit into Maria's palms before the string broke and flung beads like pellet shot. Some pinged against the window on the far side of the room.

"How dare you!" the *señora* said.

Maria, still keeping her hands between her face and the angry eyes, turned in a half crouch, scrambled from the kneeling pad, and tried to see some way to escape through the only door. The *señora* blocked it. Trapped, Maria watched the beads roll and clatter, and come to rest; several under the bed, two in the pin dish on the vanity, another in the center of the pillow whose slip she had just changed (the gray cat standing wary, arched), and others back on the floor by the little altar, around the Virgin, who cast her eyes down at them in a mood of mild forgiveness.

"How dare you!"

The *señora* turned aside to fling off her hat, and doing so made a space through which Maria could escape. But once in the living room, she paused. She did not know what to do. She had a leftover sense that it was her duty to pick up the beads. The petticoat was still drying on the table in the backyard, a good place to dry, but unorthodox, and if she left it there, she might lose her job.

That was the point, what stopped her: To be without a job was to be no better than her mother, trapped and crumpled. It might already be too late. Maria had always known it was an arrogance to kneel at the altar, dangerous to be caught. She stood in the belly of the dark red paisley on the living room rug, her fists full of skirt, torn between the scattered beads and the petticoat, as if these were the poles of her dilemma. As she stood undecided, the *señora* came out of the bedroom doorway. All changed.

"Oh, Maria, I'm sorry!" she burst out, she almost yelled, and she flung herself on the floor at the curled tip of the paisley pattern and began to sob.

Alarmed, Maria looked out the three windows to make sure nobody was passing by. Señora Eleanor was on her knees. Her hair had sand burs in it, and her blouse would need scrubbing out tomorrow.

"Maria, I'm sorry. It's your God, too. Forgive me!"

Maria watched her cry, shoulders rising and falling, bent in the same position as Maria herself had taken before the Virgin. Maria did the only thing she could think of to get out of that position: She backed up a couple of steps and sat on the couch. It worked. Señora Eleanor swiveled sideways to let her weight fall on her hips, and so sat on the floor, still heaving dry sobs out.

"My most grievous fault!"

Maria pulled out a clean handkerchief and pushed it at the *señora*.

"I'm sorry, Maria. I'm sick. No, that's not true. I'm unworthy and confused. Please, use the altar whenever you want to. Will you?" She did look ill. The tantrum draining out of her eyes had drained them dead. Her face was streaked with salt and sweat; curls frizzed around her face. Maria's subsiding fear swelled in two directions — a wave of contempt, a wave of protectiveness — for this so-large and unmanageable creature in her care.

"Let me make you a bath," Maria said. At which the great baby began to cry again. She hiccuped and used her handkerchief and hoisted herself onto the sofa beside Maria, who shifted away to make room for her.

"I would like that. Would you do that for me? It's time you were getting home, but I'd like that." She brushed her hair back off her face, she took a deep breath and seemed, a little, to take command of herself again. "Is there anything I can do for you? Are your — conditions — here all right? Is there anything you need from me?"

The place stirred in her that Father Vicente labeled greed. She looked at her mistress now, to judge how far it might be safe. The *señora* was spent as a dog after too long a run.

"I need to play the piano," Maria said.

When out of Señora Eleanor's face there came a surprised laugh, she pursued, "And I want to learn to read." Then this baffling woman, who made more fuss of suffering than Carmen Acosta, and for less reason, went into tears a third time, taking both Maria's hands and lifting them to her hot face, where she held them till they were wet.

25

WALLY TOOK TO COMING by the bank whenever he was in town — almost, Laurel would have said, on any pretext. He talked mainly business and politics, but when he left, he left behind him a stale air of lonely old man.

He would hang his boot on his knee and his skull in the hammock of his hands. He would aim his glance over Laurel's head at the diploma on the wall. "Let me tell you what a pickle Wilson has got himself into in Chihuahua," he would say (always assuming that Laurel shared his scorn for the president; he never asked a question that might have taught him otherwise). "Old friend of mine runs the custom house down on the El Paso border; Zachary Cobb — Corn Cobb we called him back in the railroad days, because he fancied himself a bit of an orator. Really, he was a Roosevelt man, though I think the roughest riding he ever did was shooting gophers from a cow pony down at his mother's uncle's place in Vera Cruz. Anyhoo . . ."

Sometimes Laurel was busy but he never tried to shut Wally up, get rid of him. He wasn't sure just why. The more he saw of the older man the more he missed the company of cultivated peers.

"Always thought he'd go into politics, Zach. I think he always meant to, but he had too many mouths to feed. Too risky, so he ends up in Customs, and now he claims there's no more del-i-cate

spot for diplomacy in the U.S. go'ment. But that's Zach. Back
before the track was finished laying, he worked in a greasy spoon
in Lordsburg, had some old sort of a cook — Rumanian, Hungar-
ian, one of those. To hear Zach talk, that place was the Ritz for
food; he'd spin you a tale about con-tin-en-tal this and goo-lash
that, and have your mouth watering for what wasn't but a bit of
greasy steer shin in salt water. He could talk that convincing.

"Had a letter from him this week, he's busy rubber-stamping
firearms over the border. Fool go'ment. But he's got his orders.
Here's the comedy of it, though. Wilson's all in favor of helping
those cutthroat Mexicans. But he can't always do it official. Villa,
for instance — he *isn't* anybody. He calls himself a general, but
what he is, is a general nuisance, hah. No — what I mean, he hasn't
got any kind of position you can send an ambassador to. So they
keep trying this and that sort of special agent, and Zach thinks —
this is really why he wrote, he can't stand me not to know this — he
thinks the State Department might use *him* as go-between. He'd
give his eyeteeth. Not that he says so, I mean — I'm reading between the lines."

Here Wally would pause and shift some portion of his anatomy,
stretch to his arm span, spider his huge hands on his knees. "I tell
you, though, that man's a pushover for his women. Three daughters he's got, poor devil, and a wife with a mouth on her . . ." His
laugh would boom hollow. "Treat 'em rough and tell 'em nothing,
I always say. . . ."

But sometimes he would add an observation personal or melancholy, a change of subject with no apparent link. "Funny how the
older you get, you have to have order all around you. Little things;
the way your tack hangs on the wall. Don't know if it's the same for
a man has his woman outlive him."

Or he would drop in so its ripples widened a reference to his
younger son: "Lloyd's the one will roll in here one day rich as a
lord. Lord Lloyd, we'll call him." Or to Frank: "I know he'll come
right in the end, but he has to make his own way."

Laurel suspected there was a plea hidden in this last, that the
bank should go ahead and front Frank the loan for his quarry. No
doubt Wally had figured out that everything would go to his off-

spring anyway, and was too hardheaded to buy himself a little family tenderness with it in the meantime. When Laurel looked at Walter Wheeler, it struck him that people are as immovable as rock. The force it takes to move them leaves them scarred; as many end up rubble as learn how to build.

In any case, if Wheeler looked to Laurel to underwrite the quarry, he didn't want to deal with it. The bank was on solid ground now. The SP had opened an account out of which it paid wages from Olga to Wilcox. All the ranchers in the same radius were customers. Laurel had agreed to half a dozen business loans and mortgages, and his books were showing a healthy 4 percent; he wasn't going to risk it because Wally Wheeler was lonesome.

Leaving, Wheeler never failed to leave behind a gallant reference to Eleanor, usually to her riding: "I saw your missus out on the range last week and I swear I'd've thought she was native-born."

Every time, after he left, Laurel spent a heavy hour. Wheeler's blatant attempt to conceal his emptiness under talk of money and power was discouraging. Laurel wondered if he was equally transparent.

But Wheeler was aging, failing inexorably in small ways, whereas Laurel's health was improving, that much was clear. His appetite was back, he could time his cough at less than once an hour; he hadn't had a night sweat in the new year. The doctor in Tucson had felt free to make a joke: "If this was galloping consumption back in Baltimore, Mr. Poindexter, out here we'd consider it barely a trot."

No one would have understood had Laurel said that Arizona didn't "work" the way he'd hoped. And as for what that way had been, he now realized that he'd had some vague image of Eleanor "wasting her sweetness on the desert air," blushing not altogether unseen because he would be available as witness.

Instead of which, what he was watching, powerless, was a general coarsening of her fiber — or, to continue the analogy, the metamorphosis of a rose into a zinnia.

The petal softness of her skin was gone. She scarcely bothered anymore to shield her face from the glare, and it had darkened and begun to grain. The tanned flesh ended at her collarbone, where her shirt blew open to the sun, and you could see these unsightly edges now even as they were subsumed in others, because more and more she was wearing the low-necked peasant blouse she had bought in Tucson. She went uncorseted till evening. Sometimes she wore pants and boots for an hour or more after she was done riding; and even in her own proper shoes her walk had taken on a striding rhythm beyond buoyancy — which he had always liked in her — into the area of self-assertion.

He could say nothing, because such freedoms were but an extension of the spirit he had always lauded. And if that prohibition held against boots and blouses, how much more did it apply, after his stance on racial harmony, to her making a familiar of her maid! For that is what she had done; he had come upon them one afternoon laughing over some magazine — Eleanor on the sofa holding the page up at shoulder height and the Mexican girl leaning over, one hand deep in the tapestried stuffing, the other lifting her hair off her neck with a hand that held a dustrag, the two of them lacing laughter over some picture and providing for all the world a tableau of giggling schoolgirls. To give her credit, it was the maid who saw the inappropriateness. When she became aware of Laurel she evaporated into the kitchen; whereas Eleanor merely shot him an arch look from under an arched brow.

And now this insanity of the Spanish mission. He was stupefied by her enthusiasm, because it was not remotely possible that she believed it remotely possible, that they should live in a renovated ruin so inaccessible to his place of business that she could not show it to him until she built a road there. Yet she was asking in town, in public, about the composition of adobe, the availability of construction workers, the deed rights to government-owned land. She sat sketching little maps, which one might have believed some harmless pastime except there was no evidence that she saw the fantastical nature of the plan. He cautioned himself with the memory of her father, who had been cajoled to the point of letting her marry a non-Catholic; for he had to wonder, now, whether to live away from town was not analogous to marrying away from one's faith.

"Eleanor," he had said weightily, "I have no doubt it's beautiful, your mission. But it's too *far*."

She faced him with solemnity of equal weight. "Laurel, I have no doubt it's far, my mission. But it's too *beautiful.*" Then she laughed, lifted his two hands, preached patience at him, an open mind, promised she would have him driven out in a buckboard, her cheer feverish, on the edge of hysteria.

If that were all. That was not all. Though all of it had to be of a piece, how could a man look at the other thing? How could a man — who had in his field of vision a varnished fine oak grain, a ledger linenbound and filled with pale green grids, vertical stacks of neat black and scarlet figures in the calligraphic order of his personal competency — how could such a man look at the probability that his own wife drank?

He could not, in fact, look at it. When he looked at it, it slid away, and he was left blaming himself for fantasies and lack of faith. She was short of friends and occupation, that was all. She was modern. She had more appetite than most. See how she always had a cup of tea in her hand, a pencil in her mouth, a slice of fruit at table, a blade of grass outdoors. She was an *oral* creature; it was a physical manifestation of her hunger for life.

Such a line of reasoning was good for half a column. Seven and six is thirteen, times nine is twenty-seven, carry the two is one-seventeen. But when his focus was steady on the numbers, his peripheral vision sickened. She stood just out of sight topping up a wineglass that was never allowed to get as much as two thirds empty. If he came upon her doing this, her gestures minutely altered with the consciousness of his gaze; they became — not furtive, not at all; the opposite of furtive — careless, demonstrative.

The same freedom informed her flourish at table as, meal after meal, she produced in a travesty of accommodating him "something to relax you," a "refresher" because "he must need it." They had never used to drink wine at meals, at home, unless there were an occasion, a guest, or — he owned it — an attempt on his part to introduce romance. Now if the evening turned chilly she would be mulling an *ordinaire.* If his cough was in evidence she would prescribe buttered rum for both of them. A headache of her own required cognac. Exhilaration called for claret.

When he woke before her in the morning he lay close to her face, breathing the strange new odor of her breath, a fermented scent that took him back to childhood, to the orchard at his grandfather's farm in West Virginia, the apples so profuse that it was never worthwhile picking all of them. Grandfather said the ones that fell were "gone back to feed the ground," and in October the house and fields all smelled of that rich rot.

Laurel sat at his desk, in the orchard, the green grids of the autumn grass, the neat verticals of black and scarlet apple trees; and just out of sight again she began to wander, restive. Her eyes were just a little bloodshot. The sun, she said. She was up half the night. A coyote howling kept her awake. They were low on sherry and port again. Yes, isn't it astonishing! — she noticed the same thing of flour and sugar just this morning. She was prone to tears, to swift tempers, to laughter at a pitch half an octave above mirth. Then her father must come to mind, and Laurel saw with chilling clarity what had been obscure to him before. Erin Kenny, who became expansive at nine of an evening, oratorical at ten, argumentative at eleven, and maudlin at midnight; who amused his friends with volleys of quotation and bragged of his hangovers. . . .

But a woman.

He recalled one Princeton professor with a scandal in his past, a young beauty not his wife whom he had coddled through an awesome repertoire of debaucheries. Or there was in his own family an aunt at several removes, a widowed crone, who could not be counted on for coherence at a holiday gathering. These were embarrassments at the periphery of things, and left alcoholism in precisely the space it otherwise occupied, in the alleys of existence. They left at the center still utterly unimaginable, himself, Eleanor, in such grotesque relation.

In this town every idea he held was suspect as progressive. If he was liberal with his wife's freedom and she repaid such liberality with personal negligence; if he was egalitarian and she mocked that principle to consort with her inferiors — well then, well and good. He would pay for his convictions.

But where "temperance" was an axiom — more, an ax to bludgeon that style of life he saw as fostering grace, intellect, the growth of global empathy — where morality was so simplified and self-satisfied that you could go to hell on the fingers of one hand (smoking, drinking, gambling, dancing, card-playing — fornication, being unmentionable, was not included in the account) — what layers of diminishing dignity might not be peeled from a man whose wife turned souse?

26

NOW EVERYTHING HAPPENED HEADLONG. From depression she bounded into mania, from lethargy to an impetuous doing she partly propelled and in which she was partly caught. She had taken up, in the same week, Maria's education, architecture, and adultery, for none of which she was adequately qualified. She and Frank saw each other only after church and in the corral when she came to saddle Quarter. Each encounter was paralyzed and dumb. She thought of him incessantly, whatever else she was thinking of, in his most flattering aspects (breadth of shoulder, eyes, ambition, knowledge of nitrogen). She slept badly, often not at all until she had drunk her stuttering thoughts to sleep; and even so she would be awake before dawn, full of plans of which none was more urgent than that she should sleep again, which she could not. By midafternoon she would be so exhausted that she could sleep where she sat, to wake crimped of muscle, aching at the nub of her spine.

Meanwhile, everything also happened backward. She had only meant to inquire, of Walter Wheeler, how one went about applying for a land grant, and of Maria, whether it was true that Gabrielo Acosta made adobe; but now she had her writing table covered with forms relevant to the Homestead Act, and by Thursday she had five Acostas on her front porch, including a suckling child nearly two years old on the breast of the wife who apparently acted as Acosta's agent. He, at any rate, stood smilingly silent while she held forth.

"This place is a great ways out in the desert," Carmen Acosta informed her sternly. Eleanor agreed it was. Its remoteness was a major factor in the government's assessment of its "improvable" value, which was so low that she might have in excess of the standard hundred and sixty acres if she chose. The ordinance maps took no notice of a ruin.

Eleanor said, "I would think it fair to pay Mr. Acosta for his transportation time," but this apparently ran tangential to the reasoning of the woman, who had a face the shape and sheen of an eggplant and whose voice carried that indelible nasal note of unanswerable complaint.

"There are two more *niños* than this at home, and not one of them old enough for working. A poor man has to struggle to put food in his family's mouth."

Eleanor did not dispute this. She had never seen a child at the breast before, and this one was old enough to manage a dexterous and sophisticated kneading. She smiled an appeal to the man Gabrielo, who appeared at once bashful and abstracted, ran his fingers under his chin, and then studied the fingers as if they might have gathered evidence.

"I have seen that mission when I was a girl," said the wife. "It would take many, many weeks to make bricks enough to build it up!"

"Perhaps Señor Acosta should have others to help him."

But this alarmed the woman, or else she was offended at the implication that laborers could do the work, for she quickly agreed to a price of seven dollars a week, to begin as soon as the land had been obtained.

Maria, when Eleanor reported the transaction, snorted impatiently. "It's two dollars too much. You should have called me out to answer her."

"He's supposed to be very good."

"He's very good, and he has no work — except for friends that pay in cottontail."

"Well then, it will feed his family, as she said."

"Five dollars would have fed them well enough."

But this exchange wasn't about money. They were trying out the ground between them. They were tentative and skittish, smiling a lot, vulnerable, quick to hazard and retreat. Maria restrung the rosary beads on button thread, and Eleanor commanded her to use them when she liked. Maria volunteered opinions — "The long collar is better with your face." Eleanor overpraised her. "I can always rely on your taste." They minced around each other, tested each other. Eleanor confided the details of her renovation plans, and Maria offered the lasso dancer of Hermosillo. Neither admitted her skepticism toward the other's dream. Perhaps they were making friends.

A week later, when Eleanor rode out to the site, she found a whole encampment of Acostas, seven this time, and a lean-to of creosote and tin in the armpit of the transept. She was too baffled to protest. They had made a fire pit of the loaf stones, and Carmen Acosta was frying tortillas on a battered griddle. Gabrielo and the smaller children were asleep, flung across blankets under the lean-to. At a distance south, a larger boy wheeled a wooden barrow with two enormous jugs toward them over the sand. As he approached, Eleanor saw that he had his mother's aubergine face — all the other Acostas were sinewy and sharp-boned — and if he was too young to work, he was nevertheless making a fairly good job of maneuvering the clumsy wheels among the rocks.

"Four miles is the nearest water," Carmen accused her, "and we can haul barely enough to drink and wash the *niños*. The making of bricks will take much, much more. We can't bring it by ourselves, Polo and I, and if Gabrielo goes for water, how can he be making bricks? No, it's impossible. You will have to find someone to dig again the well."

Eleanor was astonished to learn there was water within four miles — there didn't seem to be a break in the parched hardpan between here and the horizon. She had not yet made application for the land, and her husband had not agreed to the idea at all. Nevertheless, in the current impetus of things, wasting a little money seemed a minor matter. So she said, "Does Gabrielo know anybody who can dig a well?"

"Oh, what use are they?" Carmen scolded, but the boy, cross-legged on the ground, offered from out of his mother's face his father's bashful smile, and she suspected that she had just contracted for the digging of a well.

Every day that she did not ride, she drew. The nuns of St. Agnes's had taught perspective along with the catechism, and Eleanor had always received good marks for her watercolors. Now she began by imagining glass in the arches, wrought iron grilles, a roof of Spanish tiles sloping low toward the cloister-turned-patio, the well rebuilt under the shade of the fig. She unearthed her easel from the second bedroom where superfluous goods were stored, and set it up in the living room.

Her watercolor elevation pleased her well enough; she had caught the neutrals of the desert, the suddenness of color in the bougainvillea. But when she came to sketch the indoors, both her perspective and her imagination failed her. She could not see sides enough of an interior space that existed only in her mind. Angles did not match, planes went askew, objects seemed to float in the middle distance.

She unearthed her beechwood ruler and concentrated on the floor plan. She'd measured the nave at sixty feet, fifteen inches in quarter-inch scale. The width was twenty-eight feet, which made scaling easy except that she had no paper large enough, and if she glued two sheets together she still had no room to measure out the transepts. She assembled four sheets from her tablet, but this was too large for the easel, so she moved her paints and pencils to the dining room. Laurel, when he came home, nodded by with a look of sullen sufferance that chilled her. After that she was careful to clean up the dining table before he got home.

She was very anxious not to displease Laurel — strange, because she had always lived in the careless certainty that he doted on her. Now that she knew herself to be desired by a handsomer and more virile man, she trod softly and pretended to be blithe. Had he confronted her she might have stood her ground, but he did not, and she cleared the space in front of him to make way. Particularly she cleared it of any evidence of plans for the mission. Yet it seemed to her that only when she was measuring walls and calculating angles could she lose herself into calm.

On Sunday after church she asked Walter Wheeler if she might borrow his buckboard and Johnny Fousel to show Laurel the site. As she spoke, the southeastern quarter of her body was seared by the knowledge that Frank Wheeler stood in that direction. Wally

said she could have any dern thing from him she asked for, only
Johnny had stuck his hand in the fan belt of the Ford and didn't
have fingers enough left over from rolling his cigarettes to hold a
pair of reins with at the moment, haw. No, really, the smart thing
would be to hire a wagon from Vandercamp's livery. If she was
serious about this building, she'd need regular hauling for materials anyway.

So Monday she called in at the livery stable, and after she had
spent some three quarters of an hour corn-sidering, as big Josef
Vandercamp put it, all the posser-bilities, she ended up the out-
right owner of a secondhand flatbed, with permanent free livery
space and cut-rate draft horse rental. Quarter was not trained to
pull, but she could stable Quarter there when it proved convenient.

She had not intended to buy a wagon. (Josef's grandson Seth,
due to graduate from grammar school in the spring, was already
hired for the Nash dealership in Tucson.) As for a driver, Vandercamp said he didn't want any *pepe-pedros* handling his horses, but
O'Joe — no last name that he knew of, though anybody in town
would point him out — would work for no more than would get
him drunk at Shaftoe's. He wasn't quite right in the bean and you
couldn't hardly understand a word he said, but he could drive first-
rate and he'd do what you told him and he didn't have sense
enough to cheat you.

Eleanor was not thrilled with this prospect, but she saw that
Vandercamp was not going to make a second suggestion, so she
crossed over to scan the boardwalk in front of Shaftoe's saloon.
That was he, she supposed, the lone occupant of the spot, a tall,
aged cowboy tipped back on two legs of a four-legged stool, elbows
up on the windowsill. His mouth hung open and his tongue lay in
it like a dead thing. She did not immediately recognize him, but he,
when he saw her, put his heels on the boardwalk, tugged at the
points of his leather vest as if in some aboriginal effort at making
himself presentable, and identified her: "Canthulink."

This seemed to her sobriety and sense enough to drive a flatbed
wagon. She reflected wryly that he had gotten her to one mud
cathedral and could probably get her to another.

"Mr. Vandercamp tells me that you might be able to help me."

He agreed to whatever she suggested; he seemed to require no

advance notice when she would need him — did he even understand what she was saying? — and when she came to money he
shrugged repeatedly, "Whun you think. Whun *you* think."

Tuesday the temperature soared in a sudden foretaste of summer. A leaf of lettuce wilted on the plate before Eleanor's eyes. She
lay down to nap and woke damp from a dream of drowning, the
sense of which she tried to trace and reinhabit because it seemed to
her that there was an important wisdom in it. She felt like the
woman — child? — in an old story — Perdita? Nicolette? — cast
adrift in a casket. She, whoever she was, would have waked in her
bobbing coffin surrounded by the turbulent sea, not knowing her
direction and at the mercy of indifferent currents. The only way
that she could take any control over her own spinning and drifting
would be to leave the safety of the casket and plunge into the
unknown. And which way, then, would she try to propel herself?

On Wednesday at the mission a starving black dog both barked
and wagged at her, and there were two more men, introduced as
Alejandro and Gaspar, bearing a marked familial resemblance to
Carmen Acosta. There was no activity in the vicinity of the well,
nor any evidence of brickmaking, but the men were widening the
lean-to with stouter poles. A laden mulecart was pulled into the
shade beside it.

Gabrielo Acosta volunteered speech to her for the first time.
"You come just at the hour to plant the chickens." She supposed
his English was at fault, but from under a scatter of goods on the
cart he drew two crates of rust-feathered hens. Gabrielo beckoned
everyone to the box elder by the road, where two by two, a pair of
feet grasped in each sinewed fist, he tossed the eight birds into the
air. Two by two they flapped, squawked, floundered, and grasped
a branch.

"This way, we plant the chickens," Gabrielo told her with teach-
erly solemnity.

"You mean they'll stay there?"

"They will stay, go, stay," Carmen answered for him. "Morning
they will come down to lay and eat, but in the night they will fly up,
away from the coyotes." Her tone suggested this arrangement was
more tiresome than efficient.

Well then, Eleanor had as yet no water and no bricks; she had five children, eight chickens, a mutt, a lean-to, and a wagon. It was a relief to think that Laurel probably wouldn't let her build here anyway. But then it seemed more alarming to stop than to go on. She did not know how she would pass the days at any pace but this.

Friday she went to Tucson to make formal application for a land grant. Maria went with her, outfitted in one of Eleanor's skirts and blouses. The lace yoke set off Maria's almond skin, and the gored skirt swayed seductively — but Eleanor had been unable to find a wide enough pair of shoes. Maria sat, whenever she sat, with her huaraches tucked out of sight far back from her hemline. Maria had never been on a train, in a restaurant, in a town, or in a high-necked blouse, but she improvised a stylish unconcern.

Eleanor handed in her forms at the post office, which served as the land grants office and, Maria in tow, went looking for a stationers that would have oversized paper. They found the stationers but no such paper. They headed back to the railway, but on the way they passed the now-empty spot on the sidewalk where Eleanor had bought her Indian bowl. It occurred to her that a newspaper would have very large paper, and they hurried along to the *Daily Star,* where she gave her name and asked for Ben Dargen. The pinch-faced lady disappeared, and for a few minutes she and Maria stood in the din of the press.

"He's a talker," she told Maria recklessly, "and a flirt. We won't let him get started or we'll miss our train."

Eventually Dargen lumbered out, newsprint spewing from his pockets. "Well! We don't usually deal in *pleasant* surprises around here."

Eleanor drew Maria forward by the hand and curled her arm through Maria's arm. "This is . . ." Her mind made its virgin tour into the awkward space of ethnic sensitivity. My maid? My friend? "This is Maria Magdalena Iglesias." A half second's panic had produced the middle name, which she would not have been able to remember. "Mr. Ben Dargen."

Maria thrust her hand at full arm's length. Formally: "I am delighted."

Dargen boomed a laugh; in the same movement he bowed, shook Maria's hand, and performed a side skip of his shambling frame. "How do you do, Miss Iglesias. To what do I owe —?"

"Maria and I have been dealing with the land grants office. I'm planning to restore a seventeenth-century mission, and I wondered if you would be able to spare me some very large sheets of newsprint for drawing paper."

Ben Dargen shook his head to mean she was a phenomenon, and fetched her the end of a press roll himself.

Sunday morning she woke too early, opened her eyes to the moon shadows on the dun-colored wall. With consciousness came a spasm of fear that flowed along her whole curled body. She did not remember exactly what she was afraid of, until she remembered that she would face Frank and Mary Doreen at church.

She dressed in a shawl-collared linen dress particularly demure — a schoolgirl's dress — and entered the clapboard building with her fingers tucked under Laurel's arm. But the younger Wheelers were not there. After the service she heard Wally saying that Mary Doreen's people in Wickenburg had had a death. She listened between the flutings of Alma Timkin's voice, not wanting to appear unduly interested in who had gone to Wickenburg and for how long. But when Wally moved on, she put a hand on Alma's arm and urged, "Could we walk a little bit?"

"Why, certainly."

Eleanor steered her away from the clusters of folk, onto the tough and springy grass. Alma gave off little tremors of curiosity. The weave of her blouse was coarse, and it felt to Eleanor as though her fingers had become sensitized, like a singing tooth.

She said, "I want to ask you a favor. I suppose it's very odd of me."

"Why, anything at all."

"Maria Iglesias — she says you know her? — well, I've agreed to teach her to play the piano, and to read. She's very bright, and she really badly wants to learn, and then, of course, it would be helpful to me if she could read a recipe, for example, without my having to teach her in the kitchen. . . ."

Alma bent her head, eyes alert and round under the auburn wings of her hair, as if she were struggling to comprehend something difficult. Eleanor glanced away.

"In any case, we've agreed that I'll spend an hour a day with her, and then she'll make up the work on Saturdays. She's very hardworking, and I think she's a young person who might be able to make real use of an education if she had one. Anyway, I do all right with the piano, I seem to know how to get across as much as two clefs and half a dozen octaves, but I'm no good at all trying to get her to read, or understand why a word looks like it does. . . ."

Alma said, "My dear child, you're exhausted."

Eleanor shielded her eyes with her fingers. She looked at the tip of her grosgrain toe in the grass, which grew every which way in a pattern gratuitously complex. She said, "No, no, not really."

"I'd be more than happy to teach Maria," Alma said. "But you must rest a little."

"I'm fine." Eleanor worried that she might have invited condescension. "Just very busy is all. But fine." She hoped she had not incurred an intimacy.

Frank sat squint to her daydreams. In imagination she would lift her arms — observing herself doing this and also in reality half lifting her arms — to the space that in her fantasy he occupied. When they touched, he would dissolve. She reassembled him, approached again, lifted her head so, closed her eyes so. But when she neared sex as she knew it in marriage, all buttons and awkwardness, the saliva-thread of connection with romance was severed. She backed up. She began again. She elaborated a locale for their meeting, a corridor of Byzantine design, goatskin rugs before a hearth.

Monday when she drove up to the ranch he was leaning against the fence clean-shaven, in a freshly ironed shirt. She understood from this that he was alone.

She sat for a second before turning off the car, feeling the vibrations of the motor through the soles of her boots and in the tender, tickling base of her kneecaps. It was a flat, bright morning in a dour and dreary patch of land, and she felt that she and Frank were alone alive in it.

Then Digger whinnied, and she turned the motor off.

"I don't know if Wally told you." He handed her down.

"I heard him say there'd been a death in Mary Doreen's family. I hope not anyone . . . ?"

"Her ma's half-sister, not so close by blood, but somebody she grew up with, and it's real hard on her ma."

"I'm so sorry. And Mary Doreen went —"

"She's gone to Wickenburg to help out."

"Yes."

"She'll be gone three days or more."

"And she took . . . ?"

"All the kids with her."

"Ah-huh."

Digger was at the fence, and she turned to let him hook his face over her shoulder. The hide of his long cheek rasped her face.

"Eleanor."

It's hard to know the difference between love and fear. Had she meant to tease him, by embracing the horse? Frank dropped his mouth against her neck. Then he took her hand and led her toward the house.

But inside the space seemed hot and small, the raw beams and boards belonged to an alien cast of mind. These floors were scrubbed for virtue's sake, clean as morality. Beyond Frank's shoulder the bedroom door hung open on its iron hinges, an iron bedstead with a muslin cover tucked tight and square. He smelled of harsh soap. She had the dismaying sense that somebody had ironed his shirt.

Nevertheless, she lifted her mouth into the hollow under his jaw. Why? She was known for being able to flaunt the small proprieties, defy inconvenient curbs and strictures. Why, when she felt herself hesitate and want to think again, did she feel bound by these opposite and particular rules? He pulled her toward the open door but she hung back, feeling guilty of coquetry.

"Frank. Not in your marriage bed."

So he took her into the little room beyond the kitchen, with its splintery pine floors, a rocker in the corner, and a worn blue calico quilt on the narrow bed. He had to dislodge a cat; two others slept in the shelf of the washstand. There was a corncob doll, a bowl of ordinary pebbles, pegs that held dungarees, and a dress sprigged in forget-me-nots. He pulled the flimsy nainsook curtains, and she turned to him with passion — because if she did not, how could it be justified? It would finally be so unendurable if mortal sin turned out to be just not what one wanted after all.

He dealt with nearly all the clothing, somehow. They maneuvered to arrange themselves under the quilt, but the bed was narrow, and the rope mesh beneath the thin mattress whined with
their weight. They laughed uncertainly. The limp curtains barely
filtered and did not dim the light. She looked into the rough beams
of the daughter's ceiling and imagined vaulted whitewash. Frank
stroked her gently. She made the shape of his enormous hand in
her mind and watched it play. He wasn't in any hurry, and gradually she relaxed. Gradually, as if there had been a string between
her nipple and the center of desire, as if his hand plucked that
string, she was stirred; something in her struggled to manifest.
Then momentarily she was stirred to anger. The anger passed,
recurred. He entered her and she strained toward the higher note,
failed of it, slipped again into the minor key. Anger. Where had it
come from? Why that, of all emotions?

She gave it up, in profound disappointment. Disappointedly she
clenched her fingertips into his back and gasped, pretending. The
anger was gone. As she did with Laurel, she waited, compliant,
until he in his turn gasped and shuddered.

Now she was drowsy, and all she wanted was the warmth of his
body against her; she would like to have gone to sleep. But he was
moving strangely, setting his thigh between her legs and playing at
her breast again. She lay inert so he would tire of it. It seemed
obscurely more sinful, his patient rubbing, than adultery itself. He
edged himself down to reach her breast with his mouth and pull
her against him, riding his thigh. She breathed sleepily and
moaned a mild complaint, but the sound of her own voice struck
an erotic note, and the humming, loosening, began again. She
hung in it, followed it, let it take her, and in the second just before
she came, a lucid understanding appeared: *He has been taught to do
this.*

Then she slept. She slept as she hadn't slept for several weeks,
deep in daylight, dreamless. When she woke it was to the poignancy
of the nainsook curtains wilting from too many washings. She felt
deeply tender for those curtains, for their being so useless against
the light. She turned luxuriously, hearing Frank putter in the
kitchen, and building an instant daydream, as if this were the
daydream she had been looking for all along, a lifetime of such

stretching and such puttering. She was wholly happy. She heard
the squeak of the pump handle, and the water gush. She lay delicious in broad daylight, content, in love.

Reluctantly she rose and dressed. She followed into the kitchen,
stood for a moment in the doorway watching his broad back at the
sink, the shoulder muscles working under his shirt. She went forward and put her arms around his waist. "I love —" but she must
have startled him, because he shied.

"I'm sorry."

"No, I'm —"

"What can I do to help?" She saw that he was not fixing her a
meal but scrubbing andirons in the sink. She was startled by the
sight of his face, which had been diminished by the addition of a
pair of spectacles.

"I got into this . . ." he said vaguely.

"Oh, please, whatever . . ."

"I'll get you some coffee, shall I?"

"Let me get it."

She reached for the pot, but he intercepted her arm and
snatched it away. "Sorry."

"Frank?"

"Sorry."

"I didn't mean to —"

"No, no, you just sit down." He removed the glasses, gave her a
smile of the mouth only. "No reason you should be getting your
own coffee. Just sit right there."

So she sat. He pumped the water, stoked the stove, measured the
beans, and poured them in the grinder. She could see he was used
to making coffee. She sat awkwardly at the table with no place to
put her hands. She knew she had been reprimanded; he didn't
want her to touch the kitchen things. But his tone of voice now was
apologetic, nervous. He said what a good sleep she'd had and how
Quarter would miss her ride today. Eleanor sat miserable and did
not know why. It was not his fault. He was shy of her using Mary
Doreen's coffeepot; it was the same as her not wanting to be in
their bed. It was perfectly understandable. It would be different
when . . .

When the floors of the mission were paved with his marble there would be a cool expanse. There would be room to breathe, none of the fidgety, cramped space his family imposed around him. Moonlight would cut through the windows and make high, arched patterns on the stone.

"I know I can do it," he said. "I only need the loan to get on my feet and I can make it go."

She was thinking about the marble and had trouble understanding that he was talking about the marble.

"When I went to the bank I asked for seven thousand dollars, but I reckon if I had as much as five I could get by. The Mexicans need the work, and they know it's in their interest if I start up again."

His back to her, he clattered metal mugs on the counter and sloshed coffee into them. What he said was embarrassing, indiscreet. But you have to make allowances for a person who has had no social training. She knew he was an innocent. Money had been no part of his motive.

"Your husband said it's too bad it isn't gold, but it *is* gold. It's hard to get out of there, sure, but look how far it comes from Italy."

"Yes, I know," she soothed.

"I've got all the figures, they prove it could be done, give it a year and a bit. It's one of those industries you have to carry a loss till you build up your customers, but I know I'm good for it."

"Could your father help?"

"Oh, he could. He might, again, if somebody else showed they had the faith in it I do. I tell you now . . ." He sat and gulped the coffee, gulped in air, letting her know something about his need. "I can't give it up. I never will. Every time I get on that road it lifts my spirits so I almost feel like I could lift off flying."

"I know," she murmured, seeing him soar above the stone, wanting to be part of his desire, wanting to recapture the spoiled warmth. She stroked his forearm to insinuate herself into his vision. "I know." She leaned to him, wanting that hunger wrapped around her.

"Your husband would listen to you," he said, straightening away from her, almost sullen with the reluctance to say this. "He'd listen if you had a mind to ask him."

27

SAM SAW WONDERS on his way.

He crossed a desert that had been scorched by fire. Black sticks stuck up out of the bare ground; black rocks, black bones, black cactus marrow. The earth was like a plucked turkey breast with its pinfeathers singed. After he had walked for miles, the wasteland swallowed him and he could no longer imagine an edge of it. He tried to think forward and across to grass, but the bleak brown peeled back from the edge of sky like a lid. Then he made the time pass trying to guess which trunk of chaparral the lightning had struck first; that would make a center, and after that he would be walking away from the center. But every shriveled stick he chose led to another that he chose again. He imagined a heat that would cross so much bare space to consume the next living thing, wring the fibers of the ocotillo in a fire fist, sear the small ground plants. Such a fire would leap in quick flares, each one extinguished by the ferocity that carried it to the next. His mind watched it leap while he put one dogged foot in front of another, and he crossed the burned basin before the water in his jug ran out.

Another day he passed coral sand dunes where the soil undulated in an imitation of the sea, and lizards swam under clouds stratified like rock; but that day there was no water, and he had to gouge and suck bitter cactus.

One evening when he was feeling durable, walking late, he came upon a ring of *bacanora* twenty feet across, an ancient stand of the century plant that had spread as each mother plant sprouted pups beneath her skirt and died. These agave were in early bloom, they were pungent with a perfume of rotten meat, and they were being visited by a host of long-nosed bats who hung like heavy humming-birds, their shoulders dusted gold with pollen in the moonglow.

Sam woke one morning before daylight, tucked in a curl of dry streambed, to see a tarantula shine in the dark dirt in front of his face. He shook and shouldered his clay jug, his basket, the blanket he had stolen at Empedrado, and went on. As the light seeped, he saw that the ground bristled; hairs raised on its back. A tarantula crushed under his huarache, and when he recoiled from it another brushed his heel. The sun rose on the earth furred with spiders, and all that day he walked through them, stepping carefully. They were ordinary desert tarantulas, heavy-bodied, hairy, dusky. He knew they wouldn't bite a human unless he gave them reason, and that if they did the bite would be no worse than a bee sting. But he also knew that desert tarantulas hide in daylight, and these did not. There were so many that there weren't crannies enough to house them. Sometimes they tried to shoulder under each other. Sometimes they crawled beneath the lizards they were eating. Mostly they marched without purpose. It rained a little, and Sam passed a deserted village of half-underground *huki* roofed in logs and brush, where there was a well, and a good stone pestle left behind, which he pocketed. He found amaranth greens to eat. There were plenty of mesquite pods for tea; and all day, tarantulas. They began to thin when the light began to fail, but he walked all night, risking his feet but unwilling to put his face down among them, till day broke and the tarantulas were gone, and he slept in the sun.

He was traveling in the Sonoran flatlands to the west of Sierra de la Madera, which meant he was at risk for thirst, but it kept him in spring weather out of the reaches of the cold, and it cut the vertical miles. Long, dull days he was drawn on by an image of Lloyd that had become not so much ghostly as abstract, a hieroglyph of longing. Early in his passage he had made himself a basket, using palmetto spines for cordage and split fronds to bind them. After, he found sotol and bright bear grass, and he carried bunches of them in his basket against future need. His huaraches wore through the soles, so when he found water he sat beside it for a day twisting and binding grasses into sandals. Their straps rubbed welts in his skin, and the soles scraped shabby in a matter of hours. He went without shoes over the dirt, but cut the ball of his left foot on a shard of granite and had to stop to let it heal.

The cut was shallow but dirty. He camped in the rocks out of sight of a *hacienda* whose well and coop he raided at night. By day he tended his cut with warm mesquite tea while he sat and plaited baskets. Sometimes when he peered from his hiding place he saw two women come and go on the patio. He made himself a sombrero and a soft pouch with a braided strap to hang across his shoulder. He stripped slender peelings of gray mesquite bark and wove into his hat the form of a Gila monster — *caltetepon*. He stayed for several days, basketmaking to pass the time it took for his skin to knit, stealing eggs and handfuls of chicken corn to grind with his pestle in a shallow depression of rock. He made himself a slingshot from a strip of huarache leather and a flexible forked branch, and once he hit a rabbit with it, on the haunch, but with little force, so the rabbit swiveled comically and ran off the way it had come. Sam plaited a dozen baskets, each surer and stronger than the last, with snub-faced, cone-tailed monsters of mesquite bark worked into their sides; and in the end he bound his foot with palmetto fronds and went up to the door of the *hacienda*.

It was a large house, built around a patio and surrounded with empty stables and corrals. Inside there was no one but the women he had seen, a white-haired giant with a ponderous, fleshy walk, and a sullen middle-aged serving woman in faded embroidery. This one answered the door and, when he offered to barter baskets for a pair of shoes, called to the other, *"Está el canastero,"* as if the basketmaker made regular rounds in this waste corner of the world. Elephantine, draped in dirndled folds of dark cotton, the mistress made toward him and beckoned him in. When he removed his hat she touched his earhole with fingers like rising dough.

"Who did this to you?"

"Pancho Villa." They were the first words he had spoken to a human being in a number of days or weeks that he had not tried to count.

"And to me as well," she said, with such dour conviction that for a moment he measured the shape of her head beneath its binding of white hair, checking its symmetry.

Her husband and two sons had been killed fighting for the *colorados* against Carranza at Hermosillo. The *villistas* had stolen the herd, and her daughter had gone off as *campesina* to a *federal* captain. Most of the hands, including the husband of the serving woman, Juana, went east to join with Villa. When they were left alone, the two of them had made a separate peace. "Aaiee," the old woman mourned between sentences, and her servant, collarbone heaving across the open neck of a blouse decorated for an Indian holiday, mourned after her, "Aaiee."

But their peace had cost them their interest in the world. They asked no further questions of Sam, had no curiosity about him apart from a remote amusement in his accent. He ground them a supply of corn flour and patched a wall that winter had broken, fed the chickens whose meal he had filched the night before. In the evening he sat on the kitchen floor while the mistress sorted beans, weaving again the seat of a chair that had worn through.

He reached for a fresh length of willow and bent it against itself, but the strip was too sinewy to break. The woman touched him on the knee and handed him a yellow stone the size of his palm, with which he cut it easily. The stone, flat and elongated, fit neatly in his grip. It was shaped like a spearhead but chipped for fingerholds, an ingenious piece of prehistory, a stone cut by stone to make a cutting tool. He passed it back to the woman, but she waved with the back of her hand to mean that he should keep it. He thanked her and turned it in his palm, admiring the whetted edge, the yellow darker in the grips, as if it had been stained by use with the hand that held it.

The woman watched him sidelong as she let the beans sift between her fingers. Her skin was like fine-grained bark. He thanked her again, but sensed that this was not all, not enough. He saw that she glanced at the worn bear grass basket in which he kept his belongings, so he opened it, emptied its paltry contents on the table: compass, pestle, identity card, slingshot, waterskin. He was embarrassed when she picked up his ear and bent it curiously between her fingers. He hoped she would not choose it, although it was of no use, a dead piece of himself that he was not ready to let go. She held it to the side of her head over her white hair and laughed. He was relieved when she chose the pestle.

Sam ate canned stew at dinner, slept in a bed, and left in the morning in a pair of laced cowhide boots and cotton stockings that had belonged to the youngest son. Both women cried to see them go.

He had started by stealing all the food he didn't take from the desert, but now he risked forays into the little knots of houses on the edges of the estates, bartering baskets for tortillas and goat's milk, for a hide pouch to carry them. These feudal villages, which he encountered at the rate of one every three or four days of otherwise monotonous wandering, consisted mainly of women and young children. There were scatterings of old men, only a few boys over the age of ten or twelve. But Sam was neither feared nor threatened. *"Está el canastero,"* the women would tell each other, and he developed the habit of announcing himself in the third person, *"Está el canastero."* The women were starving under their pendulous flesh; the children's joints were like the marrow knuckles that people fed to their dogs in Bowie. Sam knew he was often fed because he was foreign and disfigured, rather than because they had any need, desire, or wealth to spare for baskets. These were the landless, the widowed, the left-behind; they lived a war that was out of earshot. They folded pity in tortillas, and he handed it back in baskets; it was a decent barter.

One morning Sam made his coffee in a camp a hundred steep feet off the plain. He had climbed there for no better reason than that his eyes were sick of scrub and welcomed a knobbled mesa. He raised the cup to his mouth and felt a vibration of the earth that was not quite a sound, looked west, and saw a blurring of the horizon that was not quite a cloud of dust. Then he heard a rifle crack, far and solitary, like the crack of a baseball connecting with a bat, and after that a thin spattering of continuous rifle shot. He was bleachered too far from the game to see it. The sound came no nearer and acquired no heft. It crackled for half an hour while the sun rose on a gorgeous sky. His fire warmed his beans. A brown chameleon climbed a sage branch and turned slowly green.

All that day he hugged to the hills, expecting to be overtaken by soldiers, but none appeared. The boot leather had formed to his feet by now, and he felt the ground rise to his footsteps like a hide stretched over a drum. He felt the earth as a continuous stretched skin; he stepped carefully on this piece of it, while on another part the dust bounced on the dead.

He didn't know when he passed into Arizona, and didn't know that he didn't know, because he had always guarded his identity card and imagined crossing, triumphant, at a border town. He envisaged a mounted border patrol, as he had seen when he went in the wagon with his father. Perhaps he even thought there would be a fence, as if a nation were a ranch and deserved an edge. What happened instead was that one day he found the remains of a campfire with an empty can of Heinz pork and beans and a twisted-up packet of Lucky Strike cigarettes. It dawned on him that he might find one or another of these bits of garbage in Sonora, but it was unlikely he'd find both together. He couldn't be sure. He consulted his compass, continued north, and the next day came on a dirt road with a sign: *McNeal 8 miles.*

He must have entered America between Douglas and Naco, then, well to the west of where he wanted to be, so he headed east. He didn't aim for McNeal. The idea of a white town made him uneasy, a trading post and a grocery store. He continued to eat amaranth greens, found quails' eggs, gathered the organ-pipe fruit that was softer and more delicate than figs. He climbed into the foothills of the Swisshelm Mountains and then, perversely, into the Chiricahuas, though they were steep and he knew them to be convoluted, full of cliffs. He climbed fast and blindly, day after day. It was as if, having followed the most sensible path through Mexico toward home, he was now, within striking distance of his objective, unwilling to achieve it. Now Bowie was due north. Lloyd was either there or dead. He still climbed east, as if he needed the higher reaches for the thinner air. There was more water, there were even fish, and he fished patiently, but he was cold at night.

He came to a place where the rocks performed juggling acts. Boulders balanced on slender pinnacles. Needles of stone supported globes and wedges. Inverted pyramids stood on their points, and in the ravines laminate slabs hung over space, apparently dancing on their hanging vines. Then he sat down and wept because he had seen rocks like these, so like these that it couldn't have been far from here, with his father in their wagon when he was a boy.

"Now, you see that rock," Li Hum used to say in the thin-pitched monotone that was Sam's first security and that he only later came to recognize as a *foreign accent.* "That one took me a whole day to put up there. I had the hardest time to make it stay." Or he'd say, "Yes, here. This one was very difficult, I had to haul this boulder all the way from Los Angeles!" And Sam would snigger knowingly, dazzled at the game, pleading if his father paused, "How about that one? Was that one hard to get up there?" Looking sly, never wholly disbelieving that his father built the hills.

Sam stood and reached up to a stone the size of a skull, so precariously balanced on a fist of the same stuff that it looked as if an ordinary breeze would topple it. He leaned his weight up into it. It wouldn't budge. He attacked it with his puny force, he pushed and shoved.

He was a survivor now. He could eat desert itself, he knew bats, bugs; he was at home in war and was friend to the asymmetry of his own head. He'd outlived too much to be frightened by anything.

How could he go home?

28

ELEANOR DIDN'T GO BACK to the ranch that week but stuck rest-
lessly at home, unclear to whom she was responsible, and for what.
She continued her early, twisted wakings, and wondered if these
dark daybreaks partook of the nature of purgatory, since she felt in
suspension rather than precisely damned.

Two futures ran in her mind in channels; she could track down
either one. She could leaf through a catalog, choosing this or that
style of fob for Laurel's birthday, while in a portion of her mind
she wandered with Frank over land they owned in common. The
habit of double vision came more and more easily to her. It brought
comfort and escape; she could not take seriously the consequences
of one course of action while the other played alongside with equal
force.

Saturday afternoon O'Joe drove Laurel and Eleanor out to the
mission. They set out in late morning in glorious golden heat, and
Eleanor was full of optimism. She had decided on a stance of
unconditional normality. For four hours or so, she thought she
could model herself on a western wife, someone capable and hardy,
taking everything in her stride. Laurel had dressed up for the
occasion. He wore a satin tie with pale gray fleurs-de-lis; she did
not suppose this section of God's world had ever before been traversed by a man in such an ornament. She said so, and he smiled.

Even O'Joe seemed relatively spruce, and had a sort of shave. He was as hard as ever to understand — their name came out something like *Min an Minter Hoindecter* — but he seemed to have no trouble at all understanding *her,* either her instructions or by implication. He took a bead on the mission and drove straight enough to it that their wheel ruts might have been the first cut of a road. When they jolted into a ravine she caught at the sides of the wagon, and after that O'Joe got down and led the horse gently through the others. She began to wonder on whose authority he had been pronounced an idiot.

She glanced sidelong at Laurel's profile, which wore an expression of careful tolerance. She was anxious to convince him that the mission would be a gracious place to live. That was today's purpose, although in a variant narrative it was not he who would live there. She smiled winningly at the side of his face, willing him to look at her.

He kept his eyes on the horizon. She was reminded of a childhood trip with her father, from the Kenny warehouse to some construction site. She had wanted to go with the supply wagon, which had a team of dappled horses and a driver with a shy, crescent smile in his blue-brown face. But she was dressed in white silk stockings and a pinafore, and her father said the wagon was *filthy dirty.* These words shamed the driver and humiliated her; she had beat her fists against her father's thigh in a tantrum that even at the time she realized turned the shame to him. He had slapped her on the jaw, which afterward stung as she sat in the carriage, resentful and repentant in equal parts, smiling hard to make him look at her even though she was tight with anger inside the bib of the pinafore. There was no particular reason this memory should have stuck with her, any more than another several dozen trips or tantrums she might have remembered but did not. It was the sensation in her chest that brought it up, like a sour aftertaste.

She talked against the taste. "Look how near Dos Cabesas seems. Could you believe it's twenty miles?" She lay her hand lightly on Laurel's hand, which was on his knee, and breathed against the tightness in her chest. She chatted of whatever came to mind, a chattering ram to break down his reserve. When she repeated something that Frank had told her, crossing these flats on horseback, she began with the words "They say." She informed Laurel about mesquite, its voraciousness for and its spreading of nitrogen, even though he might wonder where she had heard such a thing, and even though it was the sort of arcane trivia that he did not much like to hear from her.

She gossiped on effortfully. Yet the nearer she got to the mission the less the mission seemed to have to do with Laurel, and the more preposterous it seemed that she should be taking him there at all. She felt herself involved in some kind of conspiracy with the Acostas, or some very esoteric endeavor that only they could understand.

The Acosta clan, when they drove up to the ring of stones, stood, apparently awed by the sight of Laurel (his maleness? his suit?), all in a row as if posed for a photograph. The men held their sombreros in their hands. The black dog flung its whole body into a wag, ribs exposed at every arc.

The sight of them filled her with alarm, because she did not know how to explain them. She had hoped they would be at work and would keep at their work. Since they had not, they looked very like *her* workers. To head off the obvious questions, she offered arbitrary information. "The young one, Polo, such a solemn, helpful child; do you know, he wheels a barrow four miles to fetch water, not once but twice a day! I gather Señora Acosta is from Benson, which is reckoned to be a long ways to come for a marriage." She felt him look at her now. He knew that she chattered when she was nervous, but she could not stop to breathe. She was like a swimmer uneasy for the shore, stroking too hard, exhausting herself with the fear of exhausting herself. She turned to O'Joe, told him to feed the horse and wait for them.

She walked Laurel around by the bougainvillea and through the arch. The sight of the hypaethral nave calmed her, and for the first time since they left town she began to breathe in easy rhythm. Here she could concentrate. Her mind did not skitter but fixed itself. The place was the premonition of a home by now — she could superimpose her floor plan on it. You would enter the south end of the nave under a balcony that formed an entrance hall below, library above, leading to the reconstructed bell tower. There might even be a bell. The long shaft of the nave would be the living room. The space where nave and transepts crossed would be an open dining hall, the kitchen beyond in the top end of the T, where the altar must once have been. The transept to the left would be a chapel, the one to the right a series of bedrooms whose southern aspects would open onto the patio. Sun would strike there in the morning, but by afternoon, when the fullness of the light reached the chapel, the patio would be in shade.

"I wish I could paint well enough to show you the way I see it in my mind. The Persian rugs on a marble floor — an expanse of white, but cozy niches for reading and drawing. I'm trying — don't laugh at this — I'm trying to *put* myself here. To bring my Baltimore self and my Bowie self together. Does that make sense to you?"

There were two realities here as well: the rubble and tumbleweeds of the present, the shining Arcadia in her mind. But realities separated by mere *now* and *then* are not in conflict. She tended to think in terms of future possibility rather than the substantial past. For days at a time she had not pictured Frank at the arched window or at the corner by the palo verde tree, having in mind for those spots an arch of leaded glass and a bank of pine cabinets, respectively.

But now as she led Laurel along the nave toward the upper section where her kitchen would be built, she could remember Frank there, the blue veins risen on his arms, as disconcertingly as if it were a memory that she and Laurel shared. There were two presents in her head. Each had the brittle clarity of something seen through glass. She expected Laurel to turn and accuse her when they crossed by the tree where the horses had been tied, and yet her whole attention was on his question — "Have you inquired into roofing materials?" — and her whole effort was to answer so that he would be satisfied.

"You do have it all planned out," Laurel said.

"It's tentative, of course. But I suppose I've spent a lot of my life thinking about houses. I suppose that's what women do."

"It's unorthodox but original. And no doubt cooler than the house in town."

"That's exactly what I thought. Especially if we could have marble floors — think what a difference that would make!"

She was afraid of saying this, yet it had only to do with her desire for a marble floor. She suddenly wondered if there was a way to keep the palo verde alive indoors.

"No doubt."

"I know Frank Wheeler is anxious to get back into quarrying."

"Is he indeed?"

He said no more, and she didn't dare say any more. But he praised the horizon. He admired the fig, studded now with little fists of leaf, and listened to the dull plop of a stone in the bottom of the well. They came back to the wagon, where the men were hunkered in the shade, drinking from a terra-cotta jug. Carmen swung toward them, carrying the two-year-old; a toddling girl hung on her skirt. Carmen had found her voice, and addressed her complaints to Laurel.

"The niños spend all the day finding firewood. This is a hard place, we have to go farther every day. I think you will not want to cook on wood yourselves. You will need to bring kerosene, or else pay somebody to bring you wood by the load."

While she prattled, Gabrielo stood by, watching proudly. He nodded from time to time. From time to time he glanced at Eleanor as if to say, "Can't she talk!"

On the way home Laurel was subdued but cordial, asked intelligent questions, and this allowed her to grant that the distance was a problem, arguing that the beauty of the place would be compensation. She remembered that he had a famously open mind. He inquired about the Mexicans — "Have these people always lived here?" — and she stuck as close to the truth as she dared. "I don't think so. I think they're hoping there will be work." He nodded, apparently satisfied. He looked at his pocket watch when they left, and again when they pulled into Jefferson Street — it had taken them an hour and twenty-seven minutes — but he didn't complain. She had warned him that a wagon would be a poor sort of test; now she joked archly that the Franciscans had a longer way to travel.

They had dismounted, paid O'Joe, held trivial discussion, bathed, and dined, before he forbade her, still quietly and in a reasonable tone, to pursue the matter of construction any further. They were at table, which she had set with cold meats and Maria's spiced pinto beans. She had just reached across to fill his glass. He said specifically, "I forbid you," and before she had quite registered on her weary nerve sleeves this formula of words, he said further, "Do *not* pour yourself more wine."

He had never uttered a command before. He had such an exhaustive vocabulary to make his wishes known, so extensive an idiom of persuasion, approval, preference, disdain. He was someone who elaborated and refined; he did not give orders. She had the bottle on the lip of her glass, and she held it there, neither pouring nor setting it down.

"I beg your pardon?"

"Don't pour yourself more wine! I want your head clear for once."

"What do you want?"

"I think I have expressed myself."

She set the bottle back on its heel with a thud. "Perhaps my head isn't clear. Speak words of one syllable. What are you implying?"

"I just want you to be quite organized in your mind while we dispose of this." But it was a retreat. He dropped his eyes to study the strings of beef fat on his plate.

Her hand still on the bottle, she felt foolish and cowardly. She picked it up again and compromised by dribbling a half inch in the glass.

And drank it, while he rallied and berated her for extravagance. He called her selfish, impractical, self-assertive. "If you *must* have a residence of that size, and if it *must* be made of adobe, very well then, but have the common decency to choose a site at a reasonable distance from my work."

"It wouldn't be the same."

"No, it would be different by the element of reason."

"The beauty of the place is its setting — you said so yourself this afternoon."

"A mud house with marble floors!"

"It's quite common in Spain and Italy. It's cooler, as you said."

"You're a raw amateur."

She crushed her napkin in her lap. "I'm an amateur, but I'm good at it. I *like* figuring where the closets go." She wanted to fill her glass again, and because she didn't dare, she wanted to punish him. "You and I might have had a baby. In that case I would have been an amateur mother, wouldn't I?" The lenses of his spectacles snapped light, and she rushed on. "Laurel, it makes me *happy*. I can find out what I don't know. Gabrielo will make the bricks and Alejandro knows about stress and load-bearing beams. He worked on the Wheeler ranch, it turns out, and his uncle dug the sewage for this house. Isn't that interesting?"

"Have you thought what you're asking of me, that I should spend two hours a day riding in the heat and dust so that you can indulge a whim of living in a church?"

"Maybe you could keep an apartment in town."

"Wonderful! I should advertise generally that my wife and I so little agree on a place of residence that in effect we live apart."

"That's not what I'm asking."

"Is it not? Perhaps you would clarify for me what you are asking."

She stood up. Her chair was dragged upward by the volume of her skirt, threatened to tip over, and then did not. She filled her glass again, showing him how deliberately she filled it. She said, "I have come two thousand miles to live with you. I am asking you to come nine miles to live with me."

She carried the glass out to the porch, to settle in the wicker chaise. She lay back and held the swallow of wine at the base of her tongue. They had been friends once, dependent on each other in small daily ways: Hear what I did, look what I bought, tell who you saw. She let the wine slide down and, moved by the justice of her argument, felt a fullness in her throat. She also knew that she had won.

29

WELL, IT'S WEAK-MINDED NONSENSE believing in a personal Providence. The disinterestedness of the universe teaches us what beauty is. How clever of God, then, to have invented coincidence!

Because here she sat, Eleanor Poindexter's Maria, on the couch beside Alma with the fat blue volume of *The British Treasury* in her lap, and it was Eleanor Poindexter who had come to Alma in the end, bringing, in the form of a favor asked, exactly that elusive gift she had always known was waiting somewhere in the bleak landscape of a schoolteacher's existence.

The girl was bright. She had an intelligence a notch and a half above the average, fairly strong on logic, rather literal in its demands, with, by the same token, a restless curiosity that made her trowel down to the essentials.

And she had what none of Alma's other pupils had: a deep belief that education was in her self-interest. Maria wanted to read with a single-mindedness that Alma had not encountered in ten years behind the desk (fourteen if you counted her apprenticeship in Akron), because she retained what white America had generally shed for its myth of equality, an assumption that the mysteries in sign and serif, punctuation and print would get her *on* in the world. She believed it absolutely, as she believed that cheap Burgundy turned into Jesus' blood.

Maria had come to Alma recognizing the alphabet but without any notion of *alphabet*, or that the letters were arranged in a particular order. The concept, in fact, was foreign. What did the alphabet mean? What did it spell? In what *sense* was *a* the first letter? Maria asked these questions with the musculature of glossy eyebrows. Alma, who had a reasonably humble assessment of her own education, was troubled that she had no answer.

"It makes it easier to remember," she explained, though Maria found it more difficult to learn the alphabet than to memorize words or figure out phonetics. A more honest answer, Alma thought, would have been that human beings fight the void with arbitrary order.

Maria was one of those who fought it with notions of speed, distance; some other place, anywhere but this. When she talked about her trip to Tucson, the train wheels chugged in her voice. The newspaper office had impressed her chiefly for its noise — she spread her arms to show how the rumble filled the air, and Alma had an inkling of how the decibels of the printing press might demonstrate the power of words.

The girl was sleek with beauty and energy. Eyes blue-brown like the dirt mountainsides in the shine of distance, facial bones full and high, making shadows of her cheeks. Her nose, slightly depressed at its tip, prevented her from looking frivolous. If one had been reading Darwin (Alma had), one might be tempted to think of the fittest of the species.

"What do you want in life, Maria?" she had asked.

The girl's eyes opened as if this question were an answer in itself, as if to be asked it were to be handed aspiration. She lifted the limpid gaze to the little slit of sun through Alma's high window. She sighed on the inhalation. "California," she said exhaling, unequivocally. California as avocation, perhaps. California as *summum bonum*.

Alma wondered if Eleanor realized how much that Tucson trip had fed the girl's ambition. It would not occur to Eleanor that it was an odd thing to do, to take her as chaperone on the railway. Eleanor Poindexter had grown up in a place where servants went on trips. It was part of the burden imposed on blacks. Westerners scorned the need of help to travel. So working Mexicans never got to go anywhere.

"And what do you want to do in California?"

Maria couldn't answer that. She lifted her fledgling shoulders. California! She might as well have said the moon. Not because it was far (Alma had no doubt this industrious naif would transport herself one state sideways) but because it stood for something noumenal as moon dust. It had not been altogether otherwise in Ohio.

This evening Maria sat straight-backed with her head bent to the book. The parlor of Alma's little apartment behind the barber shop overflowed with books and magazines, relics of past enthusiasms such as a salted snakeskin and a peeling violin. The lamp lit these objects and the amber arch of Maria's nape, haloed with dark down. She had begun by following along with her finger on her place, but at some point she had given up that practice, as if perceiving it to be vulgar.

> *"Have you seen the white lily grow,*
> *Before rude hands have toucht it?*
> *Have you seen but the fall of the snow*
> *Before the soil hath . . ."*

" 'Smutcht it,' " Alma prompted.

"What is 'smutcht'?"

"It's an old form of the word 'smudged' — dirtied or stained." She was pleased with the choice of Ben Jonson as primer. He had an extraordinary way with one-syllable words, and here and there just the odd esoterica to keep a pupil at the stretch.

"Smutcht," Maria said, with a visible effort at memorization. Perhaps she would immediately begin to apply it in her household. Because she *used* everything; that was the point. All Alma's other pupils shut school away from the business of living, scarcely knew that arithmetic had to do with money, never supposed that the poets could advise them in puppy love. Whereas Maria had already weeded her syntax of all but the most occasional Spanish construction. Her accent was as much Baltimore as Nogales. New acquisitions rooted in her vocabulary like set-out seedlings. Yes, very likely tomorrow the laundry would be smutcht.

"Now, what is the poem saying so far?"

"It's about questions," Maria said promptly.

"What sort of questions?"

"It's about . . . question*ing.* Have you been here and there, have you done this and another."

"It's about *inquiry,* then?"

"Inquiry," Maria absorbed the word, she consumed it in the energy in front of her nose, she ate it by pronouncing it. "Inquiry."

Quite wrong, of course. The poem used interrogation as a device, not as a subject. But it was provocative that Maria should read it that way, and there was a truth to it beyond interpretation. Because while the poem waltzed on through its metaphors of virginity, the questions were supposed to be rhetorical: Have you seen a lily, have you seen snow fall? But for Maria Magdalene Iglesias the answer to both was *no.*

"Very well. Go on."

"Have you smelt the bud in the . . . "

"Briar."

"briar,
Or the nard in the fire?"

Again, no and no. There were thorny plants to spare in the desert, but not a briar between here and the sea, and as for nards in the fire — just what exactly was a nard, anyway? She hoped Maria wouldn't ask — not that Alma minded admitting ignorance, but she was still in the process, here, of establishing authority. Have you seen? have you smelt? No, and that's the point after all, isn't it? There are some who hunger and thirst after whatever it is they haven't seen and smelt, and those are the ones who sit like this, one leg wrapped twice around the other under a skirt smutcht with the palm sweat of effort, frowning into the black figures of the text with infinite patience and desire.

"Have you felt the fur of the beaver,
Or sss——"

Maria raised a couple of fingers off the book, warning Alma to wait while she worked it out.

"Swansdown, ever?"

"Good." No, no beavers and no swansdown, ever. You couldn't blame a girl for wanting to go to California idealized or actual, couldn't blame her for longing after snow and swansdown, lilies and briars, and even a nard or two, whose best hope of life here would be marriage to a ham-handed and imperious laborer chosen from a radius of no more than thirty miles; six children in a decade; varicose veins; the loss of her teeth, her figure, and, if she was unlucky, the job she grew to despise with the passing years.

> *"Or have tasted the bag of the bee,*
> *O so white, o so soft, o so sweet is she!"*

Soft, sweet, brown Maria frowned fiercely at the text — not because she was having any difficulty with the words, however, so Alma asked, "Who is 'she,' do you think?"

Not so prompt, this time. "How should I know who 'she' is?"

"Well, but what do you know about her? That she's — what? '*O so white* . . .' "

"Oh, yes, *white*." This embarrassed both of them. Alma said nothing. Then after a few seconds, sullenly, "Señora Eleanor."

"No, Maria. The poem was written three hundred years ago," Alma said, but realized from Maria's flung gesture that this had been a condescension. Nobody needs to teach a Mexican metaphor.

"Do you mean because Mrs. Poindexter is white and soft? A sweet person?" she amended.

"I am speaking about *inquiry*. Because the *señora* is asking questions, but . . ." The gesture and the voice trailed off.

"What sort of questions?"

"Well," offhandedly, "she is looking for the answers where they aren't."

Far off the mark, absolutely nothing to do with Jonson's metaphorical progression of the senses. On the other hand — perhaps a perception about Eleanor Poindexter? Alma would have to give it thought.

And in the meantime, she had never noticed that before, about Jonson's poem. How, beginning with the praise of his virgin's virginity, he moves in on her. He sees her, he smells her, he feels her, he tells you how she tastes. Till by the end she's quite, quite smutcht.

What *would* Maria do in California?

30

GABRIELO ACOSTA, like all great cooks, freely gave his recipe away because those who used it couldn't make it work for them anyhow. He decided in his bones, each batch, how much of which ingredient was necessary. If someone asked him how he knew, he squinted skyward, palmed his jaw, and explained that it was a question of the time of year, the light, the weather, the will of Jesus.

He could make a perfect form for bricks out of any four scraps of wood, without reference to their length or recourse to a saw, by nailing the end of each into the flat of the next, pinwheel fashion around a rectangular space that, his eye being magically true, never varied by a quarter inch.

He mixed his mud with straw like anybody else, but he also swore by a certain proportion of cholla pod, which he ground himself with a granite pestle and which he said made the bricks *fibroso*. He stirred in a measure of chicken blood for gluten, and feathers, because their spines rendered the material *elástico*. He said the most important ingredient was salt. It distributed warmth in the dough during the drying process, so that the brick baked to its core and would not turn sandy on the outside while it was still mud within. "An adobe mustn't have a slippery heart," was the way Acosta put it. For the same reason he watched his forms as tenderly as sleeping children, judging the moment when they must be waked — the bricks shaken free one by one on the hot ground to finish drying. People who lived in Gabrielo's houses had tough, elastic, staunch-hearted walls. When they meant to praise a thing they called it "salted mud."

Five days a week now, as soon as Laurel was gone, Eleanor abandoned Maria to the domestic round, rode out to the mission, and was back before Laurel got home, often with half an hour to spare for Maria's piano lesson. She didn't mind the long ride either way. On the contrary, the rhythm of the horse, the monotony of the land, the repetition of the same route gave her badly needed coherence. Otherwise her moods surfaced at random. At the mission she was single-minded, even driven. At home she sat, indolent, or engaged in wifely errands. She could fantasize for a week on one furtive glance from Frank, assuring herself that he was an artist on a western scale; a sculptor of marble mountains. Even at some dreary household task she could believe she was in preparation for a larger and more passionate life.

Laurel must know where she spent her days. They did not discuss it. She felt no guilt about either the mission or Frank, because when she was with Laurel these ceased to exist for her. She laid out his dinner attentively, even if she had two hours ago been stringing stakes to mark a wall he did not want built. Once (with the clear sense that the Wheelers were mere acquaintances), she brought the quarry up again.

"Will Frank Wheeler be getting his loan? I'd like to think I could buy marble locally."

"No, I've looked into it. The venture isn't sound."

"Oh? Not sound how?"

"As a business venture that isn't sound would not be sound — you can't make money at it."

"Are you sure? The stone is so lovely."

"It's lovely. But the price of getting it out of there is prohibitive. No, if you want marble you'd do better to order it from California; it'll be cheaper, and it will arrive before the new millennium."

At least this amounted to a tacit acknowledgment that she was free to buy building materials. In any case, she had maneuvered the subject safely.

Otherwise she said little about the mission and less about Mexicans. She didn't mention Maria's lessons, uncertain what attitude he would take. Instead she passed on the news from Baltimore, embroidered such local chatter as she picked up from the ladies after church. The social skills she had practiced at St. Agnes's came into play when she needed to make conversation of her mental scraps.

Laurel, for his part, seemed preoccupied with world affairs. In early March he told her with an exasperated clack of his tongue that President Huerta of Mexico had announced he was giving up the bottle.

"Thank you very much! Isn't it wonderful when we can ask a dictator not to be a drunk!" A few days later he called her attention to a front-page report that the Catholic Church had made massive loans to Huerta's government for "the keeping of order."

"Keeping whose order? The *old* order!" he fumed.

She understood that she was implicated in the excesses of both alcoholism and the Church. But she was not troubled on behalf of God. It was drinking he had rendered difficult. She could no longer so much as sip at wine without defensiveness. She would sit at the table nursing a modest glass, not enjoying it, swallowing awkwardly. Not drinking left her equally self-conscious and cotton-mouthed. Her glass would be half full when she cleared the table, and she would make a vulgar point of funneling it back into the bottle. Later, alone, she would gulp thirstily. Every swallow she did not take, every glass she hid, she built resentment against him.

There was dinner, then, to be gotten through, the night, the waking, breakfast. Then she could saddle Quarter. (Josef Vandercamp, seeing her only at this moment of the day, spoke of her in town as a cheerful, hardy girl.) She could take off for the mission.

For the renovation work itself she seemed to have a natural competence, as she had for horseback riding, though her relations with the Mexicans led to one awkwardness after another. Carmen was always either complaining or demanding, and as Carmen was not her employee, there was no effective way to hush her. Gabrielo worked or did not work without reference to Eleanor's instructions. She had made a mistake to contract him to start when the government assignment of the land came through, because it did not come, and none of them quite knew whether they had begun building or not.

Consequently Eleanor brought O'Joe out more often than necessary, with half loads of materials or some piddling little sack of
nails in the bottom of the flatbed. In her inexperience she sometimes ordered the wrong thing and had to send it back. O'Joe also
brought the Acostas' staples, for which she shopped at Hum's,
because what was she to do? They had sent their borrowed mule
back. Could she ask them to walk ten miles for food as well as four
for water?

Gabrielo made bricks, and erected a more permanent shelter for
himself and his family in place of the lean-to — that is, on the wall
of her house. Appalled, she nevertheless paid him a week's wages.
Next he made an outhouse, then three adobe cubicles extending
south from the transept, for Alejandro, Gaspar, and Felix. Feeling
foolish, Eleanor paid them all. Then Gabrielo seemed for a couple
of weeks done with adobemaking altogether. Or rather, some days
there would be a pile of new bricks, and then for several days none.
Those there were remained in stacks and made no progress toward
the string demarcations of the walls she intended. Deterred by
Gabrielo's very mildness from giving him an order or even asking
about his progress, she would ask Carmen in a conversational tone
why there were no new bricks today. Carmen variously informed
her that Gabrielo did not work on Sundays, on his saint's day,
during siesta, at certain phases of the moon.

Exasperated, Eleanor said, "When *does* he work, then?"

Carmen's eyes widened in the narrow top of her face. "He
works," she explained, "when he is making the bricks."

And in spite of all this, the building began to happen. Though
she was no good at managerial authority, when she sat on the
ground with her plans scattered in the dirt in front of her —
Gabrielo, Polo, Felix, Alejandro, and Gaspar hunkered in a semicircle with her, sometimes even O'Joe — she could explain. Her
hands turned out to be good for talking. Where her brushes hadn't
made it clear, she was able to make them see.

"Look" — the palm of her hand scooped the space in front of
her, so they looked at the space — "the beams at that end can slant
at the same angle as the arches. It'll be a triangle, not an arch, but
the same angle. Do you see? Then we can space the crossbeams on

each side of the arches. That'll work, won't it? That will be close enough together?"

"That will work."

"We can get the tiles in Tucson, but I don't know where to get the beams."

"There is a lumberyard in Wilcox."

"No. We can take the wagon up the Chiricahuas and cut our own trees."

"Will that work?"

"That will work."

These men had all been employed by white men, and had taken orders. They would not take them from a woman. But it didn't matter, because when she failed to order them, they worked anyway. They'd never known a woman to take an interest in this particular stage of a house's life. She spooked Alejandro by knowing the difference between a dado and a slitting plane. She could tell the pennyweight of a nail on sight. As long as she didn't pretend to more authority than she earned, the eccentricity of it impressed them. And days when they worked together she arrived home so exhilarated and exhausted that she went to sleep without a drink. Then she would be up at dawn and back at the mission before the Acostas' breakfast coffee had gone cold.

"I want it to feel as if inside and outside are all part of the same space, you can just move at ease from one to another."

"Like the plaza in a town."

"Yes, that's right. But we want the windows on the patio side about two feet higher off the ground, so there's room for furniture." Her hands arranged the furniture, "And to break up the symmetry. I *think* that leaves plenty of air but cuts down on the sun inside, so it won't heat up so early in the day. What do you think?"

"I think that will work."

They were without well water for four weeks (O'Joe carted ten gallons from town twice a week, in addition to what Polo could wheel) waiting for the pulley she ordered from Sears, Roebuck. Now, the third week of March, it arrived, and O'Joe brought it, together with two creosoted pine poles, an iron crossbar, and galvanized buckets.

Alejandro, tall and stringy to Gaspar's muscled breadth, dug holes while Gaspar drove the poles on either side of the fig's splayed trunk. Gabrielo fed the holes with gravel and a thin gruel of adobe. Alejandro invited the children to pull on the poles, swivel and rock them, working against Gabrielo to make room for more pebbles, more adobe, forcing a tight fit. That was a day's work, they said. Tomorrow it might be set.

But tomorrow it was not set, in Gabrielo's judgment, and the day was spent waiting for mud to dry. Polo scrounged for wood while the grown men played games in the dirt with the littler children. Eleanor, setting an example, pulled weeds from the transept where her bedroom would someday be.

When she arrived next morning they were already at it, the crossbar fixed, the pulley hung, the rope winding onto a wooden wheel. Alejandro was in the bottom of the well with a spade. Each time the bucket was raised, one of them dumped its contents in a heavy basket, and Polo took the dirt to the pit where Gabrielo mixed his bricks. The well dirt, Gabrielo claimed, was of wonderful consistency. "Mud *profundo*," he said, fingering it. "Under-the-world mud."

But for a length of time it was not mud at all, but dry. "Don't worry," said Felix, who was perhaps Maria's age and had a voice of resonant, quick softness like a small animal's passage. "Don't worry, there will be water. He must dig the side down first, to make it solid."

He and Gaspar dumped each bucket and loaded it with branches of mesquite, which they lowered to Alejandro. Leaning in, Eleanor could see his head and hands, but his feet were lost in darkness. He took the branches and wedged them into the interior wall. Then he bent in the tight space to load another bucket with clods and silt.

At about noon they hauled him up. He displayed the soggy soles of his huaraches, and they all laughed at Eleanor, her fervent clasp of hands against her collarbone. Even Carmen, serving tortillas around, laughed — a rarity. Eleanor ate a tortilla, and they all ate Maria's molasses bread. After lunch Gaspar went down, but he was too big, and dislodged twigs on one side while he pressed them into the other. So he gave it up and traded places with little Felix.

"Don't worry," Felix said, "I'll send you mud."

Around three o'clock he did, a whole bucket of it, rich as pudding. This time all of them, not only Gabrielo, turned it between thumb and fingers and pronounced it good. This time all of them clasped hands to heart and laughed at each other. The children laughed without knowing why.

After that she was unable to leave. The mud got gradually more malleable, then the consistency of thick porridge, then soupy. But such buckets were half an hour or more apart. In between came dry, then damp, shavings from the sides, the slow process of pressing the twigs as a retaining net. Felix came up, and Gaspar went down again. The opal brooch read four, four-thirty, five. She was too late to be home by the time Laurel arrived from the bank. In the next bucketful you could see a swirling pattern, almost as if the silt wanted to settle. Supper would be late, that's all. The next bucketful, when she told Polo to set it on the ground and leave it for a minute, produced above the sediment a film of real liquid. They cheered again, but Gabriclo as well as Eleanor looked back through the arches of the western wall to check how low the sun had gone.

That was, itself, reason to live here. The sun had skimmed the earth. There were a few blue smudges of quick cloud. By some trick of atmosphere the setting rays did actually splay like a child's drawing or the fingers of a hand, milky into the eye-searing color that was neither pink nor yellow.

"I'll go when I can lay my finger under water," she said.

"You will be late then," Carmen scolded bleakly. "The sun is down. Your husband will have bad temper."

The men looked embarrassed for her.

"One more bucket," Eleanor said.

Next Monday when she rode into the mission, her bedroom walls were up to a height of eight feet, and a thatch of palm branch was laid across joists made out of the beams of the ancient door. A sheet of tin had been set on stone feet, for a table. On top of it sat a spray of Coulter's globemallow in one of Carmen's pots, in water clear as crystal, clear as water.

31

TEXAS LASTED half an hour short of forever, and when Lloyd passed into Louisiana he was still in Texas, treeless prairie as far as the eye could see. But by evening of the second day (which means nearly three weeks after he'd crossed the Rio Grande), he and Haragana began to wander in among more trees, bugs, and water than he'd ever had any reason to think about. Apart from the girth of it at its middle, he'd had nothing against Texas. The people were friendly and decent, admired his saddle sometimes, gave him directions, and sold him food. He began to feel like he'd done all right. He hadn't made a copper strike and he hadn't seen battle, but he'd run with the *dorados*, trust man to Pancho Villa, and now he sat on silver on the finest horse he'd ever owned, with upward of five thousand dollars in his saddlebag; and Texans who didn't even know that treated him like a man and not a boy.

But Louisiana spooked him. The amount of green things didn't seem natural. He camped at Lake Arthur and the next night at New Iberia, so beset with chiggers and mosquitoes that he was up on Haragana before first light. He followed the Bayou Teche and passed a pillared building he thought must be a courthouse until he passed two more and figured out they were plantations. He'd grown up in the biggest house there was, in the place he came from, and both stories of it would have fit twice in the downstairs of one of these gabled and gussied monuments. Then for a couple of hours, bending down to scratch through his socks one side or the other, he didn't see any habitation at all that wasn't a one-room shamble of clapboard leaned into its chimney — which side held up which was hard to tell. Black men and mules plowed in the cane stubble on both sides of the road for miles. The air had a slimy feel to it. He came upon another bayou with no sign to tell its name, where the stillness of the water reflected the evil height of the trees and their gray moss veils. And when a stick in the black water raised itself up to look at him with a flat eye, he pulled his rein hard right and faced into another swarm of mosquitoes. The bugs hung to his head like they were traveling in a sack around him. He had to close his eyes. Haragana hated them as much as he did, though, and outran them without a nudge of the spur, and they kept going hard till they crossed the Mississippi on the ferry at the town of Union after dark, because Lloyd was not going to put his head down on the ground or ford a river, either one, in such a place as this.

He asked an old, fat, strolling white man in a straw hat if he knew a hotel where a person could find a decent night's rest. The old man worked a jaw of chew for a minute before he said, "Well, now, I b'lieve that'd be the Bald Cypress you'd want, young man." He gave directions with the swinging of his cane, and it wasn't till Lloyd was installed in a stuffy little bare-board room above the saloon that he figured out he'd been insulted.

The Bald Cypress didn't have a bathtub, and it was too late to go looking for a barber, so he tried to take Texas off with a bowl and pitcher's worth of water on the end of a towel, with indifferent success. Cockroaches the size of his thumb crawled over the floorboards, and one of them flew at his head when he lit the lamp. He lay down in his socks and long johns, but he kept seeing the road separating on the two sides of Haragana's head, and he could hear mice in the rafters, and he couldn't sleep; so he slept too late the next day, and it was after noon by the time he got between the Mississippi and Lake Pontchartrain as far as the Vieux Carré.

Then New Orleans turned out to be a terrible town. The buildings looked like women's underwear. You had to take your hat off to see the lacy top balconies, and felt like you were riding down a hallway in the cramped outdoors. There were more motorcars than horses, and the cars acted like they owned the road, sideswiping the buggies and crowding the mounts. Haragana, as steady a lady as ever stood in a river, shied half a dozen times at the beeping and gunning. About half the autos were driven by women, the other half by blacks in smart clothes. Between Pontchartrain and Elysian Fields he saw enough of these men to make up a platoon, and he shook his head at a world where the chauffeurs wore boots and brass while the soldiers went to war in huarachas.

He'd gone too far and had to get himself directed back to Canal Street, where the Packard dealer was. Lloyd was anxious to do his business as fast as possible and head out of town. He'd thought far enough ahead to know that he didn't know just how he was going to manage a motorcar *and* a horse, but he knew he would carry out his commission and the devil take the hindmost. A lady in three hats' worth of hat pointed him the way, and smiled behind her hand when he bowed to her.

He was a man who'd owned half a marble quarry and whose father wore handmade shirts; he'd handled a Ford at barely fifteen. He wasn't some rube or yokel. But this Packard place was more like a porcelain dinner plate than a proper building. The pillars were sculptured tiles that started at the bottom with a pattern of waves, turned into tree trunks as they climbed, put forth china roses, and then at the top turned into clouds. In front of each one was a tub with some kind of February-flowering tree, just as if to prove God couldn't do it half as pretty. Lloyd looped his reins around a branch and pushed inside.

In there, all was light and polish, more ballroom than shop. A crystal chandelier hung over a mezzanine, and the balustrade was draped all along with a blue satin banner that said *Ask the Man Who Owns One.* From the mezzanine a staircase curved down to a floor waxed to mirror like the bayou; it could have been still water. Ranged in a semicircle on this floor were five black limousines shiny as Willoughby's boots; and in the middle of them, in front of him close enough that he could reach out and touch its horn, was a silver-gray shape sleek as a sloop from brass grille to snow-white-sidewalled spare, with solid domed chrome hubcaps, windshield winking, button-backed horsehair-stuffed leather upholstery, folding top collapsed under matching cover, the doors outlined and underlined with loops of black rolled metal like a flourish underneath a signature. He took a deep breath of fresh leather and axle grease. He reached out and touched her brazen horn. He lost the power of speech.

Now a man descended the curved staircase from the mezzanine toward him, a clean-shaven fellow with his black hair slicked sideways in both directions from a part straight as a blade. He had a gray striped sack suit with peg-top trousers and a dark red four-in-hand, and he carried a gold chain that he turned very nimbly so a pair of keys climbed over the side of his index finger and crawled back through two other fingers to his palm.

Lloyd had his saddlebags over his shoulder, and the weight of them made him list. His shirt and twills were gummed into permanent creases by three weeks' riding. He had half that much growth of beard (one barber in San Antonio) and a strip of lily flesh above his hat where the sun hadn't hit. He took off his hat. He supposed he stank. He was feeling about as intimidated as he'd been at any time since Pancho Villa sat down on his kitchen crate, but the fellow made the mistake of opening his mouth — "May I he'p you, *sir?*" — on a tone so glutinous with sarcasm and superiority that Lloyd was reminded what authority he carried in his saddlebags.

He found his voice. "I li-ike this motorcar," he said, yokel.

"A supe'b model, the Forty-eight," the fellow said with a smirk. "A six-cylinder with electrical se'f-starter."

"That so," said Lloyd. He hung his saddlebags gently over the door and tapped the edge of his boot against a tire. It was not a kick — Lloyd had no intention of causing any damage — but the fellow said "Uhn," as if he'd personally had the wind knocked out of him, and another man, bigger, headed down the stairs.

Lloyd swiped his hand along the silver fender, lovingly. He walked to the front and faced straight into the golden honeycomb, blinking at the great brass eyes.

"The gas acet'lene headlamps of the earlier model have now been supe'seded by electrical," the man informed him, by rote and disdainfully, as if the words were sure to have more syllables than Lloyd could follow. Lloyd continued his tour and hopped up to the running board, swung a leg over, then the other, and settled himself into the black leather, which yielded with a gasp and a sigh.

"See heah," the man protested.

Lloyd gripped the wheel. "How fast?"

The man said, "*Sixty* miles an hour on the open road," but he was gently wiped aside by the larger fellow, who now arrived leading with the back of his hand. This one had the same divided haircut as the other, but the hair was gray; his suit was no more different from the oily fellow's than a wider stripe could make it, but he stood half a head taller.

"*I'm* the manager. May I *he'p* you?" this one also asked.

"No, that's all right," said Lloyd, coveting the curve of the burled walnut dashboard while he rubbed the leather underneath his thigh. He sighed. He reached for the rubber ball of the horn and gave it a firm squeeze. The horn blared, and the two men stepped back a step.

"*Now,* see heah," said the manager, and Lloyd, savoring it, turned him a bumptious grin.

"Yes, sir?" he said.

"I'm afraid I'll have to ask you . . ." said the man.

"Oh, that's okay," said Lloyd. "I don't need a demonstration."

". . . to come *out* of theah."

"Is cash all right?"

"I beg your pardon?" The big man hesitated, while the little one smirked again and fiddled his chain of keys. Lloyd smirked back at him and reached across for his saddlebag. He somersaulted back the flap and upended onto the leather sheen a spill of gold coins like a miser in a bedtime story.

He was rolling now, more ways than one. Now for an afternoon of his life he could do no wrong, he was the witch doctor *and* the chief. Haragana didn't want to walk behind him tied to the spare, but he said, "You WILL," and she did, because he had the voice, the bearing, the authority. Traffic parted before him, people hopped to; everything he wanted came to his hand, and fit, and he had taste, and he looked fine, and he was fine.

From top to bottom: a straw boater with a ruby band; a haircut and a shave; a hot bath and a splash of lavender; a shot-silk sack suit, cream just off to the yellow, with notched lapels; maroon-figured ivory four-in-hand with matching handkerchief; mocha gloves and calf shoes with tan spats. Having bought the car, it was no trick at all to buy the clothes, and having bought the clothes, he got a suite at the Hotel Royale without even shaking his saddlebags, in which the jingle was, to tell the truth, getting a little thin.

He wandered along a street with an unpronounceable name, where women hailed him from the doorways and a mulatto took his arm, swishing her skirt against his thigh, kneading her fingers along his bicep.

"Good loving, dickie-bird?" she teased, winding his elbow against her fat breast, but his lust was confounded by the jellied bounce of her flesh, a double chin when she laughed — and it occurred to him that he could talk about her back at camp as *if* he'd gone with her, and much cheaper, so he shook her off and headed back to the hotel.

He slept in ironed percale and breakfasted on mangoes and *beignets,* and was lounging back in his bed about deciding this was not such a bad town after all, when a picture came into his mind that made him stand up again and stare blind out the window into the street. It was a picture of Pancho Villa when he arrived in that sweet, sweet car; Villa with his arms spread for welcome, a wide smile under a gray hat that looked just like Walter Wheeler's Stetson. "Gringo, my son," Villa would say. He would clap Lloyd on the shoulder and gather him in a soldier's hug; the *dorados* would crowd around as they had around the airplane, polishing the fenders with their shirtsleeves. Lloyd looked out on this image, over the heads of crab vendors and chauffeurs, a parasol, a filigree of balcony; and he put his boots back on and collected his still-damp clothes and long johns off the radiator where he'd hung them. He stuffed them in his saddlebag in place of the last gold coins, and headed down to the desk to pay his bill.

But sometimes one day is magic and the next day the sorcery has disappeared. Haragana had had a night in a strange stable to brood on it, and she had decided against progress. He tried tying her to the spare, the bumper, and then the windshield brace, so she could walk along beside him while he encouraged her. He coaxed and threatened. She would let the rope stretch taut before she moved at all, and take a dozen steps, just enough to let him think he'd won, and then dig her heels in suddenly and skid forward while the car dragged back and he had to brake. He'd never known a horse to act so much like a mule. He tried the rope at full length, and less, and tight to the car. It was stout rope, and in one of these contests the windshield brace bent an inch or more, so the glass angled forward. Lloyd bent it back — he found out he was praying — so the windshield stood up straight again, but there was a crease left in the metal rod. Then Lloyd knew every father's grief at the first imperfection.

He had progressed by this time a total of half a dozen blocks down Pontchartrain, and people were looking at him. He wore his hat shoved back on his head like he knew what he was doing, but he was beginning to sweat inside the yellow suit. Finally he decided he had to start over some drastic way, and he left Haragana tied to a lamppost while he drove the car more than two miles to the edge of town. He stopped at a drugstore and bought two five-gallon drums of gasoline, wedged them down in front of the backseat, and left the Packard in front of a livery stable. He paid the stable man a dime to let him go upstairs and change back into his riding clothes.

He walked back. His shirt was dry but his pants and long johns were still soggy at the seams, and the air too heavy to help much, so he was hot one minute and chilled the next. By the time he got back to Haragana he was pretty much fed up and ready to lay down the law.

"I can't get to Mexico this way," he warned her, mounting. "Don't you make me choose." He thought a good run might help, and he drove her through the traffic hard, clipping a streetcart once, and once mounting the sidewalk to avoid a car, never minding a scared matron, he was that mad. He banged his heels against Haragana's sides like she was a drum he needed to keep rhythm on, and thought it might work, because when they came up to the car she was frothing, and stopped docile at the back fender. She gave a snort.

"I mean it now!" Lloyd told her, hoping to catch yesterday's tone, and tied her to the spare again with about ten feet of slack.

She followed him for several miles, although, of course, that meant going at her speed, a fraction of what the Packard could have done. They weren't as far as Union by suppertime, and Lloyd didn't consider the journey had begun till he got across the Mississippi.

And then she quit. They were winding down one of those roads overhung with iron oak hung with moss. Shacks were set at intervals of half a mile back in the black dirt against the blacker woods. He slowed for a one-lane bridge over a snaggled creek, and when he accelerated on the other side, Haragana gave a neigh like a shout of rage. He turned to see the rope jerk taut and her neck jerk with it. The car stalled as he braked.

"Oh, my God." He leaped out over the door, but when he got to her she reared, danced forward a step or two on her hind legs, pawing, and came down with one hoof in the dirt and the other at two o'clock in the silver arc of the right rear fender. After which she daintily lifted her hoof and set it on the ground beside the other.

"Oh, my God," said Lloyd again. The fender looked like it had been given a whack with a ball peen hammer. Lloyd fingered one ragged edge of the dent where the paint had shot off little flakes, the way it does prior to the fact that rust doth corrupt. He sat on the running board, put his head in his hand, and grabbed at a stalk of grass to chew for consolation.

Below him on the creekbank, staring up, sat a black boy about ten or eleven years old with the nap of his hair cropped down so short you could see his skull shine through it. His bony chest was bare, and he was barefoot, with a pair of navy blue gabardine trousers in between. The trousers were plainly hand-me-downs from somebody who could afford them, too big and tied on with a piece of string. They looked pretty much like the trousers Lloyd had been made to wear to Sunday school when his mother was alive, although those had been stiff and ironed every Saturday, and these were limp at the knees and rolled. All the same, it struck him odd. The boy was sitting, not fishing, with one hand rubbing in the mud of the bank, and while he stared at Lloyd — or, rather, at Haragana — he drew his fingers up to his mouth and began sucking, ruminative.

"How do," Lloyd said. The boy continued to stare, at Lloyd and back at the horse, dipped his fingers in the dirt again, and sucked again.

Lloyd sighed and got up to check out his horse. He averted his eyes from the sight of the damaged fender, and he approached

Haragana in the mood you would somebody who's brought it on herself.

"Whoa, now. Steady, you." He stroked down the side of her neck, not sure exactly what he was looking for. There wasn't anything she could have broke besides her neck, and if she'd broke her neck she wouldn't be standing here sawing it up and down like an unrepentant numskull. Tomorrow she'd be stiff from the jolt, that's all.

The black boy raised up on his knees to stare, fingers in his mouth. Lloyd said, "Do you know how to ride a horse?" The boy said nothing, till just the moment Lloyd had decided it wasn't worth waiting for, at which point the kid drew his fingers out so far as his nether lip, to pipe in a falsetto, "I can ride a mule."

"You ride a mule bareback?"

"Yes, suh."

"Then you can ride a horse," Lloyd said, not really sure this followed, though he himself had had a donkey before a horse. He reached under Haragana for the cinch. It was one of those times when you have to act before you think, because thinking will only come in between you and action. He dragged the saddle off and hoisted it into the backseat of the Packard.

"You *want* a horse?"

The boy regarded him suspiciously. Well, that's all right. Lloyd could understand that. He'd have inspected the molars of such a piece of luck as that himself. The boy's skin, no thicker than the leather of a lady's pump, gathered over his frown, and he ate some more dirt. "I mean it," Lloyd said. "I got to get across Texas with this motorcar, and I can't do it in the company of this horse. Her name is Haragana. Do you want her or not? 'Cause I'm going to turn her loose somehow."

"Nah."

"What?"

"You gone say I stole her," the boy suggested.

"Now, what would I get by that?"

The boy shook his head one deep swipe from side to side, as if to say he was nobody's fool. Lloyd started to be irritated — he didn't have time for this — but the boy tried a second time to get it right: one slow swing of his head and a sly, sophisticated look. Lloyd had been on the other side of that, trying to convince somebody he was in control. It struck him that he was in a funny-wonderful position, having a horse to give away and wanting nothing for it. The feeling of it made his chest swell up. "No kidding, you can have her if you want her."

The boy lifted more erect on his knees, half hoping but not yet believing. "What I gotta do?"

"You gotta come up here and climb on her, because I'm going to make it to Union one way or another before dark."

The boy turned and looked over his shoulder. Funny, that. The devil was back there, maybe, or somebody who was going to tell him no. Then he hung back on the edge of belief for a second longer, wiping the dirt in the crotch of his pants, before he leaped up the bank and placed himself thigh-to-foreleg against the horse.

"What she be name?"

"Haragana."

"Hodgonna."

"Close enough." Lloyd gritted his teeth and handed out the reins, which the boy took, avoiding his eyes, and gingerly. But once he had them, he appropriated a fistful of mane and lifted his foot as if certain that Lloyd would offer him a hand up, which he did. The boy stepped in the cup of Lloyd's laced fingers and gave a mighty fling of his right leg over. It was clear he'd done this many times; there was somebody to hand him up, at home, wherever it was he'd now be heading. He left the damp smudge of his featherweight in Lloyd's palm. Lloyd wasn't worried about Haragana getting fed. There was cane, and more grass around here than she'd ever seen, or Lloyd ever hoped to see again.

"Treat her right," he said, however.

The last thing he did see, bottom lip in his mouth but hand on the honeyed dashboard of his car, was the back of the kid, palm beating a tattoo on Haragana's rump, the two of them color-matched, making dust down the only dry lane in the whole swamp length of Louisiana.

32

SHE COULD NOT SEPARATE the clear evidence of his wanting her from the conviction that he would leave his wife to be with her. She couldn't do it. No matter how vague such a course might be, she always came back to the conviction that the one thing implied the other, like the beauty of a young soldier implies his early dying; not things you could separate with an act of will.

She was building her home on land still under his lease, by his leave. When it was done there would be, instead of the ramshackle ranch house, a magnificent solid place for him to fill. He was a big man, tall in body and aspiration, wide-shoulder-souled. The mission would be a fitting place for him to come days after he had struggled with a mountain. Did she really believe any of this? She believed that if it wished itself into being, she could be swept away by it, so that the problems of his wife and her husband would be ineluctably swept before. It was the sweeping away she wanted.

This is why she went to the quarry with him, to see what would happen, to risk a possibility. Perhaps if she was with him once more he would recognize that they must be together and, having seen it, would take responsibility for it. Up to then she had encountered him only in church, and once in the dry goods store where she had gone for nails and he for a bridle; and once when his cattle ranged near enough the mission that he could happen by. On that occasion he was given a warm, oniony tostada and a cupful of the wonderful water, but their conversation was no more open than it was after

church, since the Mexicans were scattered over the site, and talk
carried clear in that clear air.

That was all she saw of him — slim feeding for a fantasy. Really
she had exchanged fewer words with Frank than with Mary Doreen, having gone one afternoon to make a contract for the purchase of chicken blood and feathers.

"The blood and feathers, not the meat?"

"Well, you see" — Eleanor concentrated on her patent toe over
the splintery floorboard, feeling herself to be vaguely attached to
some black practice or voodoo rite — "the adobemaker uses them
in the bricks."

"Oh. Well, we could save the feathers. And I suppose work out
some way . . . but I'm sorry, the blood *will* smell. Had you thought
of that?"

"I think he uses only a little."

"I don't mean in the walls, I mean before I could get it to you. In
this heat, and when it gets hotter . . ."

They sat in the ranch house parlor scrubbed to raw, prideful
cleanliness. They drank lukewarm sarsaparilla and ate salt-rising
bread with strawberry jam and discussed how quickly blood would
rot. The baby crawled on the floorboards. Frank was out somewhere mending fences. The girl's room was shut up tight. In any
case, Eleanor felt as remote from that space as if the door might
open onto sand.

"The feathers are easy enough," Mary Doreen said. "I'll just put
them in a clean sack for you. But —"

"You must let me know what I owe you."

"Not a thing. My land! We throw them away."

"But it will be trouble for you."

"Not atall."

On the one hand her heart beat raggedly and she was conscious
of her breathing. On the other, Mary Doreen Wheeler was a person
of no special significance, a cow town's darling. Mary Doreen
wrapped one hand in the corner of her apron and held her stoutly
shod feet a little pigeon-toed, heels off the ground.

"Perhaps I should buy the chickens live," Eleanor said, "and have
them killed when they're needed."

"Well, yes, that makes more sense! Of course, you'll have to feed them in the meantime, but that way you've got the meat as well."

"We'll eat chicken on the days they make bricks."

Mary Doreen laughed. "It'll be a carrot to the mule, to make the Mexicans work."

And although she had been thinking virtually the same thing — had Mary Doreen not been quicker, she'd have said it — the image of the carrot and the mule annoyed her. She was offended, for herself or Gabrielo she wasn't sure. "The Acostas are extremely industrious," she said primly, which was not exactly true, or not in terms that applied in the Wheeler parlor.

"Well," said Mary Doreen.

There was a little awkwardness, which each filled with a mouthful of salt-rising bread. Then Mary Doreen carried the baby out to the henhouse and helped Eleanor choose a dozen reds and dominickers, which she opined had more blood in them than the paler species. She said this as if it were a fact.

"You'll have to get your hands to build you a pen." She set the baby on unsteady feet, grasped a red, and stilled it between her palms, comforting the feathers into place.

Guilt and sisterhood, Eleanor had felt when she saw Frank in a shirt that Mary Doreen must have ironed. But now the blond-downed forearms feather-smoothing, the efficient wrists, seemed an accusation of a different kind, meant to throw her own uselessness into relief. The air smelled saltily of manure.

"Oh, no; we plant them in the box elder," Eleanor replied, and disdained to explain, and decided that she would learn to pluck poultry herself.

But when they went to load the chickens into the Pierce-Arrow, Frank arrived. He carried the crates around to the front while Eleanor wrote out a bank check that Mary Doreen waved in the air long after it was dry. She held it uneasily, like a piece of tableware she hadn't been taught to use. Frank sent her indoors for some kind of cloth to protect the seats, and Eleanor followed him around the house, her eyes demurely on her feet. Why did she do this, what sort of force turned her into somebody she wasn't, because a man made love to her?

"You're avoiding me," he accused. This was true or absurdly

untrue, or both, it was a small matter whether she was avoiding him. That he accused her was the important thing; it meant he hurt for lack of her.

"No, Frank. But what use is it?"

"No use. Come with me to the quarry."

"Now?"

"Tomorrow."

"It's Saturday tomorrow. Laurel will be home."

"Monday then."

"I don't know."

"There's nothing to know, just come with me Monday."

She felt there was a rhythm to be caught, a play of hesitation and advance, of hope and discouragement that it was part of the rules she should mete out. "You spring it on me all at once like that, I can't say if I will. Why the quarry?"

"We can be alone there."

"And talk."

"Yes, and talk."

He did say so. Wasn't that clear admission that there were things to discuss?

They met at the splayed foot of the mountain where the ranch road ended and the twist began up past the ruined prospector's shack. He came out of the south against the purple Chiricahuas; he grew out of the middle distance until she could see the individual eddies of dust around Sally's hooves. It was when she was out riding that she always thought of him most intensely, so that his appearance was a daydream fleshed. She slowed, and he reined in beside her; they began to climb.

It was full April. Green lay in every crevice of rock and fold of the earth, as if it had been spilled and shaken. Sally and Quarter trotted with controlled skittishness, like horses smelling a race. Frank and Eleanor were both of them washed and combed to a paroxysm of cleanliness — he had a razor nick in his chin and a spot of blood where chin touched collar — even though it was an hour's climb and exertion would undo their care. She felt the sweat already trickling. He trotted with a natural sway that, however, belonged to the habit of his riding; it packaged a rattling dis-ease.

"I thought for a while there I wouldn't make it; it gave me a turn, what you'd think of me if I left you standing."

"What happened?"

"Alma Timkin had to go to some teachers' meeting in Tucson, and she's let the kids off school for the day. Alma set them a project to fetch in plants and such. Mary Doreen says I knew about it, which I don't think I did. She wanted me to take Jessie on the range with me, but Jessie was feeling poorly anyway."

He didn't say "luckily," but it sat there unsaid. They sighed at the averted miscarriage, they sat prickly at the intrusion of domestic fact. They were not people whose daily lives could easily coexist with sins of magnitude, and though for Eleanor the usual trick was a trick of vision or sleight-of-hand, she could not make Frank's solid ménage disappear so easily as her own. His situation was too redolent of Pyle's Pearline soap and dried beef gravy.

Frank said, "Jessie's going to be one of those that has a hard time of it once a month." This was a complicated intimacy, a risk; but also a boast that he took such things in stride. She was embarrassed and impressed.

"Poor child," she said. His face dazzled her. The sun dazzled it. Why should squareness of brow and jaw be masculine? At what level of godly direction or dry biology were such things decided? What should the little network of veins over his cheekbones have to do with shaking in her thighs? His eyes were rather small, or else the habit of facing sun was in the skin that bunched to protect them; but straight on they were underlit, intense as the light in wine.

"Umm, but she can play it a bit, too. It's good for getting out of chores."

See? He had already begun to treat them ironically, declaring his preference for her over his family. He had already begun the process of severing himself from them. He leaned toward her now and stroked, with grave deliberation, the length of her upper arm, shoulder to elbow, drew his fingertips lightly under her elbow, lifted his hand, and did it again. She closed her eyes, the pleasure a sickness.

They climbed. She was used to long periods on horseback now, but always on the flat. This relentless rhythm, the lurch forward, the backpull of gravity, was constant effort, as if she herself and not the horse were climbing. Her grip on the reins was tight, as if she were pulling herself hand over hand. The switchback road seemed to double on itself out of some perversity almost personal, thwarting their achievement of the peak. She worried about arriving tired, and at the same time expected some miracle to crown her effort, if only she could ignore the strain and keep calmly on. They passed a patch of Li Hum's carrots with all the tops razed and strewn around, and this small desolation had a grim quality of prophecy that she did not mention, because she was superstitious and because it seemed female and silly. Below them on a shelf of yellow sandstone a rattlesnake sunned in luxurious coil. A gambel quail with fourteen chicks in a line behind her crossed the road like a complicated pull toy on a single wire.

Later she remembered those. And that Frank talked almost incessantly, this man well known for silence in the presence of his wife (like Gabrielo Acosta, she suddenly and uncomfortably thought), but who seemed to accept responsibility by this means, to use talk like a parent as a way of encouraging her for the climb. He talked steam pressure and tackle strength, cubits and leverage and sawteeth to the inch. He described the hoisting of the twenty-ton block onto a wagonbed, with four men and two ropes, and pulleys no bigger than the span of your stretched hand.

"It gets to be a kind of personal contest. I'm not the only one I know who thinks that; most any kind of miner will say the same. It makes you spit on your hands and go at it, and then spit on your blisters and go again. But that's what it's all about, that's what it's *for.*"

They crossed the narrow bridge over the cavern where the split rock matched on either side, and rounded the bend into the dazzle of the piled marble. In the encampment there were buildings but no beds. A commissary, a vast shed that housed the machinery, a slicing house — but the workmen had lived in a tent camp now dismantled. They rode past a configuration of the massive blocks and around to the shorter side of the quarry. His horse was saddled with extra blankets, and now he dismounted and led her to a structure a few yards from the edge — two board sides and a tarpaper roof, backed by more marble blocks and open toward the pit, facing across its corner a little hill of winking quartz. She had thought they would be inside, somewhere in darkness or half-dark. She minded the sunlight, and too late she thought that they should have devised and brought some sort of tent. With the workmen at her new home and Maria at her old, with his family at the ranch, there was no other option but that they should seek out such a remote place as this. But she longed for enclosure, candlelight. When she timidly suggested this, he laughed at her and praised the view. He spread the blankets so they could nestle with their backs to the marble, in shadow looking out on the transcendent glare of that gigantic hole. She saw that this was part of his joy, and she remembered seeing the roofbeams above his head. She wondered if, making love to her, he saw his quarry as she saw her house. She was jealous of the rock.

"Come." He put his arms around her. The ropey tendons of his neck stood out. There was force in his wanting her, dangerous, and which made her larger because she had caused it. There was no pleading in it as there was with Laurel, but threat; there was no carefulness, and all the same it was held back, fisted in him. The place that was usually void in her turned liquid. He urged her down.

But when he began to undress her she remembered his skinning the rabbit, and her self-consciousness came back. She fought it, invoking the spirit of Cousin Peg, perhaps an unlikely priest but the only one available for the need: Let yourself go. *I will not think. I will be loose and careless. I will let what happens happen.* Not knowing how to throw it away or stifle it, she applied her discipline to itself, willing will away.

He undid her buttons and his belt. He put the belt on the blanket beside them. Her camisole had to come off over her head, and the tatted edge caught on her hairpins, so he took her hairpins out. Each one came out with a little release of pressure on her head as if this piece of her brain and then that was allowed to relax, and that, and that. The rhythm of pinch and release on the surface of her skull lulled her. But he put the hairpins one by one on the ground, and then she began to worry after the hairpins, would they be lost, would she have enough to put her hair back up, what would she do if she arrived back in town with her hair undone? When he had undressed her and himself, and knelt above her, she lay divided into two consciousnesses, one willingly half drowned in sensual pleasure and the other civilized, askance, appalled at daylight and the animal curve of his pale body.

He leaned to her. He put his mouth on her breast. She put her hand on the rope of his spine. He eased himself down beside her and put his thigh against her thigh. He put his hand between her legs to spread them. She put her palm around his sex. How paltry few combinations of the human anatomy there are. She put that out of mind and willed herself to be swept away. When she looked over his shoulder, his face now hidden in her neck as he eased himself into her, she saw on the brow of the little quartz hill across the corner of the pit a horse she recognized as Digger, and the girl mounted on it, the daughter, Jessie.

The girl sat perfectly impassive, clear in the white light at a distance of no more than twenty yards. Eleanor's body flexed and pulled into itself before her mind had registered the sight as anything out of the ordinary. Her body, even, had communicated its clenching to Frank, who twisted away from her to look before Eleanor had quite understood the implication of what she saw: the girl in a pair of faded dungarees and a yellow shirt, her feet toed in against the horse, her chunky face aimed full at them but impassive, registering no comprehension. The red roots of the girl's hair were dense around her head.

Frank's body shrank with shock. It turned in on itself the way a fern curls in hard heat. He let out a gasp that made a prickling sensation against the still damp space he had licked below her ear; and an understanding began to seep into her mind like moisture in the silt floor of the well. Above them a cactus wren called four low, harsh notes.

What happened next could be more clearly seen than understood. Some actions have a core of impenetrable privacy. Once Jessie had deliberately plunged most of a litter of kittens into a bucket. Once she had lashed out at her mother in unconsidered fury. It's hard to tell. What is clear is that she stood on the brow of the hill looking at them without expression. Eleanor tried to raise up, but her hair was trapped under Frank's elbow. The weight of his torso was on that arm, so her effort was checked at once. He shifted to free her and at the same time, instinctively, to put his back to Jessie, but this left Eleanor the more exposed, and she turned her body but not her head, reaching for whatever piece of cloth came handiest, not wanting to take her eyes off Jessie out of some inversion of shame or fear. The girl looked at them steadily, stood in her stirrups, came down hard on the horse's back at the same time pounding her heels into his sides, and flicked her fingers against his rump as you would try to flip free of something sticky. She dug with her heels straight for the quarry edge. Frank opened back toward her at the sound of the hooves and Eleanor arrested her arm in midgesture, Frank's gingham shirt hanging from her hand in the still air.

It is nowhere known whether, at the last, it occurred to Jessie that she did not want to do this. The horse, seeing the quarry drop, did not want to do it. Digger balked and locked his legs against the gravel chips. Jessie hung for a moment above the saddle as the stirrups rose; her feet slipped free, and she catapulted clean into an arc of air. Digger, neighing panic, continued to slide on the rocks, stumbled, and shuffled for a few seconds until it was clear that he could not check his momentum against the unsteady ground, and then he fell, nearer the rock wall than she, in silence.

To the two watching, that silence was of unendurable length. They sat each half upright, exposed, suspended in the anticipation of the end of silence. It ended twice. The girl, having pitched into the void while the horse still fought for purchase, struck first. The sound was both brittle and liquid, magnified by the drum of the space, as if a fledgling bird ejected from the nest too soon had failed to fly, hit rock, and that sound were amplified so as to command the attention of a god enjoined to keep count. The horse exploded. Explosion ricocheted down the mountain, boom after boom.

The silence afterward was fuller than the sound. Eleanor lowered the gingham to the rock, then brought it across her breast. She held — as if shielding herself from exposure but out of sequence — the shirt across her breasts. Frank shifted his weight against his hand and, in stages, stood. He turned toward the quarry and put his hands out to his sides palms out, as if to steady himself against the world. The cactus wren sounded the same four harsh notes. Frank pulled his underwear from the snarl of blankets and put it on. He put on his trousers and then his boots. She handed him the shirt and pulled the blanket across herself, made a little pile of the hairpins on the rock with small ministrations of her hand.

"I have to have the blankets," he said.

"Frank?"

"The blankets. I have to get her up."

"Let me help."

He turned and looked blindly at her. "Go. Go down. You weren't here." He began to pull at the corner of the blanket, so she stood, her thighs immense in her eyes as she fumbled for her clothes.

"You weren't here," he said again.

Still she was busy trying to invent a way that she could help. She pulled at her camisole, which was snagged on the heel of her shoe. She had as yet very little sense of how separate from her concern it was, how little her business it would be, that Frank and Mary Doreen Wheeler had lost a daughter in a quarry accident.

PART III

❖

Prospect

33

Sam made his camp in the prospector's shack below his father's garden. He set his meager belongings under a corner of remaining roof and covered them with old wood. He tied a twig broom to sweep the bird bones out of the fireplace, the litter from the floor.

His shirt had rotted, and he'd crossed into the San Simon Valley in the ruin of his overalls, whose straps had frayed away so the bib hung like an apron. He'd walked the boots to pieces in the Chiricahuas and went barefoot now. His hair was down to his shoulders, coarse with the drying of the sun, and he kept it out of his eyes with a braided strip of sotol around his forehead. He was dark and bony and the muscles of his calves were hard, and still as soon as he was in sight of home he felt tentative, unsteady on his feet.

Here, every morning before daybreak a pair of Mexicans trundled past him with a watercart, and no more than an hour later trundled back again, the cart stacked with vegetables that they would take on to his father's store. No one else passed. There was no traffic to or from the quarry, so it had failed exactly as Lloyd said it would when the brothers quarreled. Sam was proud of Lloyd's judgment, even though their copper mine had fared no better, and he was glad there was so little movement on the road.

His plan was to treat Bowie as he had treated Mexico, watching it from the shadows, listening. He would wander along fences by the railway track within earshot of the gossip of the Mexicans. He would crouch by the door of Shaftoe's saloon, sit in the shadows between the stores on Main Street, follow the cattle grazing on the Wheeler land. Sooner or later someone would mention Lloyd — or, better, sooner or later he would turn a corner, crest a mesa, and there Lloyd would be. He would say hello and Lloyd would take a second to know him in his strange getup and all this hair. Then they would cuff and clap each other, awkward, saying: *So, you made it back. You didn't die, then. I'll be damned. So here you are.*

But he was in no rush to begin this, because to do so was to test the other possibility. First he would provision his camp and rest. He climbed to the garden with a basket, picking the smaller plants of each sort, one here and there so it wouldn't be missed — young onions, a still yellow tomato, waxy pepper bells, a few green beans. He pulled a carrot, remembering the feel of it, its resistance and release, the sweet grit between his teeth. An extra half-acre had been cleared and terraced, planted in paunchy melon. He took a cantaloupe and burst it on a rock, scooped the seeds out, let them pour stickily through his fingers, and thought of Young-Fat. For Lloyd's sake, he wished Young-Fat peace. He felt in his hanging bib for the cutting stone the old woman had given him, which he kept with his ear and which was the size and shape of his ear, an ear turned useful. He used the stone to dig out the cantaloupe flesh and thanked his father for planting, years before his birth, a harvest for his return.

Among the lettuce he found a bucket rusted through the bottom. Patiently for half a day he sat binding a coil of sotol and yucca so tight it would sit wedged in the bottom, waterproof, soaking up a little moisture but letting none through. When that was successful, he carted up one bucket after another from the mill pump at the bottom of the trail, which had once supplied the quarry and which gushed forth like a cow overdue for milking. On one of his trips to the pump he had just let go of the handle, the water sighing as it dwindled, when there was a single booming sound somewhere like dynamite blast far off. He remembered Lloyd, whooping with a sort of kid's joy every time he detonated a chunk out of the Gringo Chink. First Sam thought this explosion must be from the quarry, but that made no sense even in the unlikely event the workmen had gone past without his seeing them; the quarrying was all done by steam and core. He supposed somebody must be making a road somewhere. He forgot it and hoisted his bucket to the shack.

Once he'd filled his waterskin and the iron tank, he had the luxury of water. He laved his body cool, his skin pale under the overalls (*yellow-belly, chinee hiney, yaller!*), he crumpled up the overalls and plunged them in the pail. He squandered three bucketfuls in the joy of laundry. He spread the overalls out on a slab of boulder, and then, the sun being so high, the air so soft with April, he knotted a scrap of blanket around his waist and took a pan of beans out to snap in the sun. He sat against the south wall of the shack beside the road, tipped back with his hair spread out to dry, dozy but still alert to listen downhill on the earless side. Somebody might come up to tend his father's garden.

No disturbance came from that direction. There were unhuman sounds, quail coo and the underground scratch of creatures that would only surface at night. Eyelids dragging, he mostly felt for the tip of the beans and bent them over the edge of his stone until they snapped. But before he realized it there was hoof noise on the nearest bridge uphill to his right, a labored trot, and the rider was on him before he could move any more than to fling his arms out to the sides, catching his weight against the wall, half a bean in his left hand and the scrap of stone in his right.

It was a woman he had never seen before, tall on a tall horse so that from the angle of the road she looked at him in direct perpendicular. Her horse was nervous, stepping high and casting its head against reins held too tight because the woman had them in a fist above her head, mechanically pinning and repinning a dark fall of hair that kept slipping out of her grasp. Sam sat stupidly spread-eagled against the shack, self-justifications stuttering in his mind, but as she passed she looked him full in the face, eyes wide open, without seeing him. She worked at her hair, moved her gaze along with the passage of the horse, and passed down beyond him. The understanding that she had not seen him sat over Sam like a chill.

It was not discretion. He'd seen Bowie women pretend not to see an embarrassing thing; the effort always registered in their mouths, the little muscles of the chin. He'd seen Mexican women ignore what they disapproved, and their stillness was noisy with the disapproval. This woman had looked right through him.

What followed at once was the conviction that Lloyd was dead. Sam was a ghost come home to find a ghost; suddenly he was memory-blind — some trick of the harsh light he'd faced these months — and could no longer bring Lloyd's face to mind. His upside-down impulse was to go inside and hide himself. He carried his beans and pan, the blanket wadded closed with one hand, and huddled on a stool by the hearth, trying to get hold of things. He sat still, pressing on the substantiality of his thighbones, remembering the mule, the mine, the charcoal scrawl on the claim board, Lloyd's boots, Lloyd's long fingers, Lloyd's guffaw, until gradually the memory became real again.

He put the strange woman out of mind and went on with his plan. He settled in. For several days more he wove a mat to sleep on, carried water, patched the roof. He ate and slept, ate and slept. When he could go for half a day without hunger, he ventured out to look for news of Lloyd.

He started at the perimeter of the Wheeler-elder ranch and worked himself in a square maze from the far grazing land toward the foothill into which the house was set. This time he kept alert to every direction for the sound of hooves or human voice. Near the corral where the half-dozen horses were kept, he crouched in the shade of a boulder to wait for the comings and goings of an afternoon. Only the horses, and only two of those, stirred with any regularity. Once Wheeler came out on the porch, stretched, returned by his front door, stooping into the shadow. Sam leaned against the stone that held heat like an animal, and he must have dozed, because when he was aware again he could see old Johnny Fousel fifty yards ahead of him, stringing barbed wire on the posts of a new corral. He watched the old cowhand's movements for any sort of clue, any sign, even of a mood, that he could interpret as news. And though Fousel's back was to him, he thought he saw such a sign: a slow, discouraged downswing to the arm that drove the brads around the wire, the whole set of the body slumped and joyless.

The impatience that overtook him was a rare thing for Sam. He had to know. He had to know *now*. He was eight months on the road toward this moment, and this was the moment it had to be, and he didn't care that it would cost him his anonymity. He shoved away from the rock and set one foot in front of another along the fence until he was close enough to speak normally, and then said, " 'Scuse me. Sir?"

"Goddarn!" Johnny jumped and scowled, sucked on the thumb he had snagged. He flipped the wire defensively and glared at Sam, who waited to be recognized, his heart noisy, while the old man continued to suck on the thumb.

"Sneak up like that," Johnny complained.

"I'm sorry."

"What do you want?"

The man glared without the slightest sign of recognition. If Fousel knew him, he had a fine poker face. But what would be the purpose of pretending?

"I wonder is Lloyd Wheeler home?"

Fousel narrowed his eyes, begrudging. "What would you want to know that for?"

Was this general enmity, or aimed at him? It had not occurred to Sam that Walter Wheeler might blame him for Lloyd's going, but of course it would make sense; they would have known at once that Sam and Lloyd disappeared together. If Fousel knew him, then surely he would want to know whether Sam had news. On the other hand, if Lloyd had made it back, maybe Wheeler would give orders to keep Sam away? And if there was news, and the news was bad?

He hesitated. "I was told there might be work."

Now Fousel gave him a blank long stare, a little tuck of one corner of his mouth.

"Not for your likes."

Which was not, still, unmistakably clear. *Your likes* meaning the one who went off with Lloyd? Or only the old taunt *Cooliekins?* He smarted at *your likes,* but this was a time he had to hold his ground.

"Is Mr. Wheeler at home, though?" Sam persisted.

"*Mr.* Wheeler's home, and he's had trouble enough so decent people leave him be."

Fousel looked away, eyes on the wire brad that he positioned with the bleeding thumb.

"What kind of trouble?"

"That's a family matter."

"A death in the family?" Sam blurted.

Fousel gave him a startled glance and spat over the barbed wire. "Go on now" — he slammed the hammer into the post and raised it on the backswing to demonstrate that Sam was in its range — "leave folk *be.*"

Sam retreated across the hardpan, his recklessness dispersed but not his impatience. *Family trouble.* Was that his answer? And did Fousel know him, or not? *Your likes.*

He went through the town, threading between the buildings and the alley back of Main Street, circling toward his father's store, listening for any evidence that Lloyd might be here. He stepped onto the street side of the boardwalk, caring less now whether he was recognized, passed Dan Riggs's dry goods. Children stared at him, and adults averted their eyes. No one said "Sam?" The women hurried with their bundles.

He stopped outside the post office and stood against the flagpole, looking toward the Hum General Store, the canvas awning whose stripes had faded nearly two years' worth since he saw them last. In the street in front of the store, fat and shiny, sat a new gas pump like an armless human with its single glass eye full to the brim. This evidence of progress in his absence was faintly shocking. Through the Mexican desert he had not thought about his father making improvements to the store.

He stepped gingerly across the walk and squinted in the panes of the mullioned window, remembering the day that the panes had arrived, by rail from Phoenix, the box of shredded strawy stuff with which his sister had played at being blond. On the other side of the window the countertop was set with jars of candy like a brittle skyline; beyond that the pickle barrel, the soda cracker barrel, the vegetables in their neat rows. He stood looking, six feet away from her, at his mother through the glass. She was soft and square, her hands were soft and square, she gentled a pile of onions into place in a slanted box, tumbled potatoes more carelessly. Sam held his face against the wall next to the glass, out of her range of vision and in it, motionless and daring her, until she looked up.

She registered another human presence in a slight recoil of the neck only, eyes almost as empty as those of the woman on the horse. She turned and moved farther off to tidy a pyramid of cantaloupe. He thought: She will turn around now with the surprise of recognition. She will turn now. Now.

But she did not. She sidled one glance at him and moved farther away, toward the back of the store, where Sam now made out his father in the dimness, filing boxes on the shelves like books. Ghosts through glass, his mother and father exchanged some few words he couldn't hear. With his fingers bent like a duck's head, Li Hum drew a horizontal line at the level of his chin, and his mother nodded, her head dipping and then her body echoing the dip to her knees like the shadow of a genuflection as she turned away to do whatever it was he had bid her do. Sam had not thought of either of these gestures for two years, and yet they were so familiar that he would have recognized them across a street, across a continent. He peered into the recesses of the store looking for his sister, but she wasn't there. He drew his focus closer, to his reflected face, the skin sunk between cheek and jaw, the hair lying flatter on one side than the other, his clavicle poking from his bare chest. He became aware of his nakedness, but it was not the lack of a shirt that made him feel naked. The face in the glass was a stranger's face — he caught the word "Indian" from a passerby. And yet if his mother had recognized him, he would have recognized himself.

He ducked down the alleyway between the general store and the dry goods store and headed toward the railway tracks. Who could he trust? Who could he ever have trusted? Not his mother, whose gentleness was weakness; not his father, the mountainmaker, whose love he had longed for but who drew a boundary in the air that said: Go no deeper; come no closer. Voices behind him raised the hairs on his neck, and for the first time in many weeks he remembered the light of Fierro's knife down the side of his head Who? Not the *villistas*, who fed him while he listened for their blows coming. Only Lloyd.

In the station yard the old split-palate was loading curved roof tiles on the back of a buckboard. As a boy Sam had been afraid of this man, O'Joe, who didn't seem any older fifteen years later than he had seemed then. The split-palate hoisted an armload of tiles, looked up, hoisted another. Sam lifted a stack himself, and the two of them fell into a rhythm. O'Joe accepted the help without a word, and when the wagonbed had been loaded, squinted and said in a grudging tone that meant Sam was to expect no pay, "Thank'uh."

"I wonder if you know where I might find Lloyd Wheeler."

O'Joe looked at him, no more interested than before. "Menhico," he said, and climbed into the buckboard.

"Has anybody heard from him?"

"No-no."

"Is he dead?"

O'Joe considered this. He cocked his head and squinted into the area of Sam's shredded knees. He nodded sharply. "Muhn be dead."

And was that it, an idiot's answer, his quest finished, his ignorance over and done? Sam watched the split-palate go. The buckboard pulled out along the track and the sun glinted behind it, showing the rails like silver fillings. Without thinking, without purpose, Sam followed along the track. He put more muscle into it than it called for. Soon the wagon had cleared the end of town. Sam kept his eyes on the ground and realized after a while that he was following a sort of road. In the distance ahead of him the wagon haloed itself in dust, and he kept on after it while it made a smaller and smaller speck, until finally he tired and sat cross-legged on the sand. What he saw in the distance now was not only the wagon, stopped, but a strange and dreamlike bustle, a pale growth sprouted on the desert, and men hoisting whole trees on the scaffolding around that old ruin where, once, he and Lloyd had lain boy-naked to the sun the whole of a truant afternoon.

34

IT WAS NEVER exactly clear what happened, and of course you couldn't ask. Well, you could ask, but you couldn't *press*. Apparently Frank Wheeler had said he was going out riding fence but changed his mind. His daughter had said she was staying home but changed her mind. Frank went up to the quarry (was he thinking about starting up production then?), and somehow or other the girl had found him there. Maybe she followed him without calling out? That was possible; the other children couldn't tell them much about Jessie Wheeler except she was feisty and stuck up (translate: like her grampa). In any case, the horse had lost its footing. Frank had not seen how.

It was somehow more terrible that he had not seen it, and mothers thought about this late at night, or sitting in the hard pew Sunday mornings. Hearing it without seeing it seemed the worst, just as the hard part to imagine, for men who had been involved in quarry work, was that he had climbed down there hand-over-hand on the steel rods that made a palm-punishing ladder into the pit, wrapped her in a horse blanket, and brought her up on his own. Not only that, but instead of roping her over his horse, he had ridden down the mountain carrying her in his arms, wrapped in that heavy blanket, a deadweight of over a hundred pounds. Dan Riggs, who had been the first to see him come in town, said he held her up off the saddle horn. It was more than an hour's ride down

that trail on a walking horse. Nobody ever carried such a weight in
that position. It had to be some kind of crazed grief-strength.

And then they had to haul the pinto up. Old Josef Vandercamp
pointed out it'd be hard enough for Wheeler ever to go near the
place again, without a rotting carcass in the pit. It wasn't decent.
Vandercamp lent a wagon and two pair of horses, and most of the
Masonic Lodge went up to help. When Wally Wheeler heard about
it he said he was going, too, but Alma Timkin gave him a tongue-
lashing that for once he could let somebody else take charge.

The buzzards had accomplished some of it; you could see where
Digger's guts had flung, but they were gone. So were the rest of the
softest parts, the lips, the eyes. The men tied bandannas over their
mouths. The buzzards hung indignant while they harnessed the
horse around the collapsed belly, hauled with pulley and tackle
from the top the way they usually lifted stone. One haunch stayed
behind, and nobody was willing to carry it up the way Frank had
carried the girl. How do you climb hand-over-hand with a burden
like that? There was nobody in the crowd so dull that he didn't
work it through in his mind, the weight, the wet, the awkwardness,
though nobody talked about this aloud. They sent the tackle back
for that one leg.

Then they disagreed what to do with the carcass, bury it or burn
it, how to get the stench off the wagon the fastest way — and ended
up deciding ("Let the birds have it") to haul it back to the narrow
split-rock canyon, where it would fall out of sight. So having lifted
the horse up one sheer edge they unloaded it at another, and
Digger, who had loved to leap a ravine, went a second time over
the edge.

Last, they washed the marble down. The water pump wasn't
running, so they had to carry up ten-gallon jugs. They poured the
water and rubbed it around with old rags, like a housewife who has
cut meat on her marble drainboard, like a stain in a colossal sink.
After that for several days the women found their husbands reti-
cent and slow.

It was a bad time. Families brought food out to the ranch, but
nobody except the baby Deborah ate anything. Most of the time
the baby was in Mary Do's arms, or propped between her knees; or
the mother kept a foot just touching a chubby leg where the child

sat playing on the floor. Already Deborah had cottoned onto this, and now if Mary Doreen moved two steps away would wail and put up her arms. You could see how years from now, when the young men came calling, she'd still be spoiled. With Jasper it was almost as bad; he scarcely left Mary Doreen's sight, and if he did, she started up asking after him. He ran circles trying to cheer everybody up, singing silly jingles through his nose, shoving half-grown kittens in your lap, and only succeeding in irritating the bearers of the casseroles.

All the same, those three seemed to be all right, reeling and taking up their lives. But Frank was like a man who had survived a stroke partly paralyzed. He sat in the same spot on the couch day after day. He answered questions, but it wasn't him answering. He looked at you from somewhere else. It was hard not to imagine that after all the callers had gone home, Mary Doreen had to lift him like a baby, like the lost third child, and sit tucking him in till he slept deep enough underneath his nightmares.

There was nothing much anyone could do beyond those calls. Walter Wheeler offered to have Jessie's name chiseled on a headstone from a proper mason in Tucson. But Mary Do, speaking with some force, said Wally would not need to be laying out any cash for *marble;* and they marked the grave with the plain slab from the sink where Mary Do used to set her jam. She would get another, she said, when Frank opened the quarry up again. They held a service Tuesday for the girl — memorial only. They shut down the town for it. Sheriff Robinson declared a bank holiday, funny as that sounded; it was the first time they'd ever had a bank to close. Laurel Poindexter came to the service and had sent by rail from Phoenix a spray of real roses that they hung down the front of the altar, since there was no coffin. But Poindexter's wife was not there because that was just about the beginning of her flu that turned out to be so serious and last so long. So serious and so long that a suspicion began to form whether they hadn't been naive and whether the banker's wife wasn't in fact a "lunger."

Did no one add two and two in a different column? Was there no one (with the possible exception of a fifteen-year-old Mexican girl who had no reason to distribute her suspicions among the Methodists) who remarked on an odd coincidence? Not one. Which must mean that there was real innocence, or generosity, at the level of the town's subconscious.

Because the intuition of these people was rarely wrong. For example, no one had witnessed Wally Wheeler's proposal to Alma Timkin nine years ago, and neither had spoken of it — he out of pride, presumably, and she out of delicacy — or perhaps it was the other way around. Whichever, nevertheless, it had been widely discussed. Old gossips without a shred of evidence, and guessing from the flimsiest clues, had been amazed that he should choose her and scandalized that she should turn him down. Mrs. Nene said she never would have dreamt and Mrs. Semple that she could scarcely imagine — but if they never dreamt or imagined, how could they have known? However, they knew. And what is more remarkable, Wally Wheeler had understood he was the subject of this gossip and never suspected Alma of being its source. She was a gossip herself, principally of successes and romance; he did her credit that she was not a boaster.

Having once turned down his money and prestige, Alma now accepted the other mantle of wifery: She was there. She guided him through the narrow place his faith had come to. In the first week after Jessie's death he threw himself maniacally into the digging of half a dozen patently unnecessary postholes, on the sixth of which he wrenched his spine so severely that for the next forty-eight hours he couldn't stand. It was the first time Wally Wheeler's backbone had ever failed him. When he could straighten up again he seemed to have discovered a disinclination to do so. His age suddenly sat visible on him, like scum on cream. Calling almost daily at his ranch, Alma arranged and rearranged abrupt domestic noises, brisk pillow-plumpings, and napkins slapped on the table-top. He never broke down, he was not that sort of man, but he was prone to the seepings of age. The creases of his skin showed damp. If he leaned his cheek against his hand, the imprint of his knuckles stayed; the flesh regained its shape as slowly as a pressed hot loaf.

It took her a little while to understand this. His life had been so arduous and full of event that at first it seemed he ought to be able to shoulder one more grief. It was not as close a loss as the death of a wife, the disappearance of one son, a quarrel with the other. But now, she saw, he had decided that the girl had been the "only real Wheeler left." Jessie was the one his hopes had fastened on. "I used to take a handful of that baby flesh — it was as solid . . . !" His grandson was a puny thing; she was the one it had all been *for*.

Would he have noticed this if the girl hadn't died? Never mind; it wasn't Alma who would judge him. Nor old Johnny Fousel, whose hand had healed imperfectly from the fan-belt accident and who stood daily in the door of the ranch house wringing his sore scar, waiting for Alma as if she brought something more magical · or efficacious than biscuits to eat and schoolbooks to read. It was Johnny who broke the habit of seventy years and sobbed one afternoon — not for the girl, who had never struck him one way or the other, but a little for the horse, which he had broken himself, and profoundly for his boss, who had always been hard and fair. "Hard and fair," Johnny said, "hard and fair," as if the words contained the sorrow.

So Wheeler didn't do much of anything in his parlor, while his son sat, not doing much of anything in his. Alma made cups of coffee and read to Wally, things he wouldn't understand and didn't care for. So much the better. She read him all of *Lear*, with a change of voices, which was a patently melodramatic thing to do, and rather tasteless, only nobody in town knew enough to make this judgment, including Wally. He was lulled and perhaps even a little healed by the good, strong thrum of her iambics. Twice he laughed at her Fool.

Occasionally she convinced him to go call on his son's family (she drove him in her own Ford; things were changing strangely), and then the two generations of Wheeler men would sit in the same room not doing much of anything while Mary Doreen and Alma spoke first in small talk, and then of children, and then, like two instruments sneaking in a theme, of Jessie, her sass, her schooldays, the time she stayed out in the tornado. They never conferred outside these sessions, but each understood and backed the other: If you don't air a memory it will fester.

On the way home Alma would observe that Frank was taking it hard and needed a distraction. If Wally noticed a parallel with his own state, he was too tired to be sarcastic. "He needs to see to his fences."

"I only wish," she said discreetly one day, "he could get back his interest in the quarry," and one day less discreetly, "I don't think Frank will get over it till he's taken up that whole layer of stone." And one day she got exasperated and said, "For heaven's sake, Wally, give him the money to open up the quarry again so he has something to occupy his mind!" Which was, of course, a mistake, because Walter Wheeler didn't take to pushing, and certainly not on a matter of principle.

"Well, Alma," he said stiffly, "I don't know as that's your business."

So she apologized. And back home behind the barber shop she made a fist in both sides of her auburn upsweep, and said to a tintype of the Akron High School Class of '92, "Pigheaded ass!"

About the younger Wheelers, the local wisdom was on target. Frank and Mary Doreen now made up one whole person, in the sense that he could not surface to the concerns of every day, and she could not pause from them. If once she had been subtle, that was done. If once she had suspected before the fact, now her hindsight was all blindness. She did not add two and two at all.

Instead, out of some flat and fallow strength neither she nor anyone she knew would have suspected her to possess, she ran the ranch. She folded Jessie's belongings into a chest to wait for Deborah. She got Li Hum to fetch the eggs and chickens, and Johnny Fousel to keep an eye on the fences. She meted out tasks to Frank. She never needed help, however, with women's work, minding the baby or churning butter, as she had with Jessie. Now she was helpless to mend the damper handle on the stove, she wasn't strong enough to lift the feed sacks, she wasn't up to verifying Li Hum's arithmetic. By such expedients she got Frank off the sofa two or three times every day.

It was she who told the story of Jessie's death on the occasions when it absolutely must be told, interpolating from Frank's first stuttered account, responding with instant invention to any questions, each phrase taking on with repetition a sterling clarity and conviction. Her version of what had happened became so real to her that she might have challenged Frank's witness if he had contradicted her. He woke nearly every night with a start, a cry, a thrash of arm or leg that nearly flung her from the bed, and then would shudder dry-eyed or twist himself away from her. Once he tried to explain, "I see her . . ." and his hand circumscribed a rainbow shape at the level of his eyes.

This did not fit with her understanding. She could not see it. She put it out of mind and, enlarging that motion, she traced the tight arc of his body with the palm of her hand. He allowed this, his back rigidly to her and then, gradually, more loosely bent. She persevered. It was a domestic endeavor, like currying. Little by little over a patience of weeks she made love to him. Though he was finally roused he turned to her grudgingly, as if importuned. She was not hurt by this because she did not have any capacity to be hurt. It was sensible to pull his hips against hers, send her breath along his neck, as it would have been sensible to scrape an apple or make weak tea for a child with flu. When he came, when he clung to her, she thrilled in a practical sort of way, as she would have thrilled to see a fever break.

Beyond that she had no speculation and no ideas. There was, though, a slightly peculiar exchange one day in town, where she ran into Laurel Poindexter on his way to the bank after lunch. Laurel took her hands; he offered his sympathy on her loss and regretted that his own concerns had kept him from calling at the ranch. She asked after the health of his wife and wondered whether Doc Hoskins had been able to prescribe.

Mary Doreen was conscious how rough her index fingers were against the silk surface of Laurel Poindexter's plump palms. He regarded her from pouched amber eyes. He said, "And you? Are you all right?"

She said earnestly, "It isn't easy. I'm bearing up. And you? Are you all right?"

"I'm all right, yes," he said, still holding her by both hands, and held them for a second longer yet, standing on the Main Street boardwalk, while she insisted, "Are you?" and he said, "Yes, thank you. Yes, I'll be all right."

35

IT TURNED MAY, weather for a baking oven. Eleanor lay in the salty sheets. Laurel brought her a May Day bouquet of verbena and hibiscus, and all the bottles disappeared from the sideboard in the dining room. She imagined that he had taken them to the bank, that they were sitting inside the big cube of the Hermann and Company safe, lining its shelves along with banded stacks of dollar bills. Every afternoon the young teller would count the money and the liqueurs.

At first Laurel tried to comfort her. "Does your head hurt? Would you like a cup of tea?"

It felt as if life had stopped, but it had not stopped. It had, merely, so thoroughly changed direction that she could no longer discern direction. If she was to go on, she would go on as someone she could not recognize. In any case, who was she to do the recognizing? She could follow the tail of this thought until it swallowed itself.

The Virgin in her dusty triptych resolutely forgave the floor. Eleanor thought she ought to feel some grief, but all she remembered of the Wheeler girl was a kind of poignant clumsiness. She thought she ought to suffer guilt, but what came to her was dread. Sometimes there flashed into her mind a face she had never seen, but that recurred as if imprinted there, crooked, skull-thin on a stretched neck like a cormorant's, flung about with dark shining hair, the bones of its unfledged wings stretched out to either side.

She knew it was the Angel of Death. Ten Hail Marys or fifty would not erase the imprint of this face.

Over and over again in her mind the chunky, breakable body rose, the feet slipped free, the catapult began. For a time that sight erupted into any shape that approximated such a shape. If she lifted her head from the pillow, if Maria reached to sweep the curtain back, if the curtain billowed, if the sun rose. But eventually the image wore itself out. It emptied of content and became an abstract arc of dread, experienced in her diaphragm while her mind coldly reasoned that in order to make Frank return to his wife, in order to make her find sin sour, it would not have been necessary to smash a girl like a bug.

"Can I get you something?" Laurel asked.

When the girl's image was quite exhausted, when the Angel had burned away, then Digger came, hung his downy lip over her shoulder, hung his mild eye at the level of her eye.

"Do you feel better today?"

Even the crystal glasses had disappeared, as if she were so feeble-minded that she thought escape was a matter of a fluted stem. As if a woman who could build a house could not obtain whatever she chose to put down her throat.

"Shall I call the doctor, Eleanor?"

He smelled of Jeris Tonic and India ink. Sometimes she pitied his awkwardness and would like to have released him. But she did not know how, and the pity would harden to a rind. Then her contempt for him had a life of its own, it came and went. Anger woke her, mornings, and flipped her like a pancake on a griddle. But she could not get up. The cat calmly washed and began its day — this gift of a cat that the girl had flung up toward her before she set foot on desert ground. Laurel woke, and dressed, and went early to the bank. She sent O'Joe to Shaftoe's and sometimes sent him with Maria to the mission, with money, messages, supplies. She could not go herself. Mornings her throat was raw, and it took cognac to cauterize it. It occurred to her that, the arguments of Job to the contrary, her childhood had been a long lie. She took the wine and the brandy from O'Joe, poured them into mason jars, left an inch or two in each bottle for O'Joe, and gave him the bottles to take away. The mason jars she put under the sink curtain with the cleaning fluids. She did these things with an air both imperious and matter-of-fact, and neither O'Joe nor Maria said a word.

She remembered hearing her mother speak of people who "never got over" this or that. She remembered a girl at St. Agnes's whose mother had died just at the beginning of one term, of something with the biblical sound of *gallstones* — and who had become slightly eerie, shunnable, from the vagueness of her focus and her spitting temper. Now, sometimes, Eleanor could see herself from a distance as a person of that vague, bad-tempered sort. Mostly she stuck in self-absorption like wet clay, unable to concentrate for an entire thought. She despised herself and Laurel equally.

"Really, you must make some effort. Shall I have Maria fix you a bite to eat?"

Some nights he tried the only thing he knew for comfort, but it was for his comfort. She endured it stupefied with heat. Afterward he slept while she turned in the smell of bedclothes and her own rosewater turned rancid. *I breathe his air but I am not infected. I take in his sperm but I do not conceive. I consume glass after glass of wine that evaporates in my gullet and leaves me thirsting. I have become a desert where nothing fruits.*

And there was another thing to be gotten through: In the beginning of May a letter from Mama prattled toward real news. The daffs were up and the lilacs hanging in bunches like purple grapes, she wrote, and Weedy the Pekinese missed her so now the weather was fine again that he went to the end of the drive and just sat there whining. Well! This invasion of Veracruz had its repercussions in Baltimore. Admiral Dinsmore said there was bound to be war, but Papa said that was irresponsible damn nonsense. Meanwhile, the navy was on alert, and Vance Jackson had volunteered for duty in the gulf, but he was contrarily ordered to a ship in the Pacific Fleet. He and Amy Whitney were going to be married in a rush, and they would be traveling through Bowie on the seventeenth, on their way to San Diego.

"But did your mama tell you that Vance and I met at your going-away do?" Amy Whitney Jackson put one padded index finger on a fork handle and ran the other up off the tines. It lifted in the air for emphasis. "Oh, yes, it's all your fault. Well, what happened, I broke my chain and he trod on my *gar*-net!" She trilled laughter and wafted the hand down onto Vance's wrist. Vance whipped his arm out and captured her little fingers under his own.

He said, "There's a debt I'll never be done paying, don't you think?"

It was Sunday evening. A couple of dozen passengers were scattered around the Hinman dining room in high-backed chairs, low sun slicing through the shutters and across their starched tablecloths. The train would stop here for only an hour, and the Hinman, having done the after-church crowd and two trains before this, was showing signs of strain. Their waitress was one of the listless Pack sisters — the Hinman employed only white girls to deal directly with the customers. She had a wisp of mole-colored hair escaping from her bun, and she repeated their orders in a native drawl like a plaint: "Flank steak with pearl potatoes. We're out of the peas, it'll have to be succotash or plain limas."

"Don't judge the fare too quickly," Laurel advised with a nervous smile. "The beef is local, and you won't find any finer in the United States. Though I do apologize for the inanity of the potables." He lifted the water pitcher across to Amy's glass. "Presumably in California you won't have to deal with the influence of the Temperance League." It was true that the Hinman served no alcohol, but Eleanor had the sudden irrational notion that Laurel had arranged this deprivation. Amy laughed and rattled her glass, those ice chunks the Hinman was so vain of. Vance Jackson grinned uncertainly and cleared his throat.

Vance Jackson and Amy Whitney! The outrage sat before her denuded of its power. He, rectilinear in every plane, as if his body were an approximation of his righteous principles; she, tending to little globes — of clear brown eye, peach cheeks, full pendant earlobes — all reflections of the wonderful breasts from which her being emanated. She was eighteen. She had a jacket so contrived that the collar stood up in back and plunged in curved lapels to the diaphragm. Her cleavage pouted against a low wedge of lace. She giggled.

"Well, but really. Have you ever known a man heavy-footed enough to smash a *garnet*? I tell him, suppose it had been my foot under there!" She aimed at Vance a theatrics of impish adoration.

Eleanor, too, looked at Vance, trying to remember what it was that had made her fantasize about him across four states. He had pale lashes and a way of angling his head as if to display his sideburns, like strips of yellow animal pelt pasted down his jaw. *Dundrearies,* Mama used to call them. He had freckles and an aquiline nose with an incongruous upturn at the tip. His twill officer's shirt made him look buttoned into himself.

"The shopping was a *nightmare.* Because Sarandon's had put away all the laces for their renovation, and Mama had to call Mr. Router to convince Mr. Frink it was worth dragging them all down; and I never *did* get my *peau de soie,* which would've had to be ordered from New York and there wasn't time — no, Vance, don't, it was important."

Vance had not done anything apparent, but now he raised his hands to heaven, which freed Amy to pick up her fork and stab a pearl potato.

"Naturally we wanted to have the reception at the Emerson, but Maryland Steel had it booked the whole weekend, and I thought for a while we'd end up at the stuffy old Chesapeake!"

All day Eleanor had wandered the house in a peignoir in dread of this moment, holding a wet cloth to her face, lifting her hair off her nape, dabbing witch hazel at her temples. She discarded clothes on the bed, and Maria, offering intense opinions, returned them to the wardrobe. Eleanor had peered in the bubbled mirror, trying to judge the deterioration of her skin. She spent a fretful hour looking for a magazine article she half remembered, which said that a "tan" was quite the rage on the Atlantic Coast. She had dressed at last in the same ivory charmeuse she arrived in eight months ago and that, in spite of her loss of weight, seemed to bind her shoulders and constrict her breath. Once dressed, she drank quickly, just the right amount — a tumbler of wine and an eggcup of cognac — kneeling in front of the curtain that hung from the kitchen sink.

And then, when they met the train and when they settled here to face beef and canned potatoes and cold water, Eleanor had come to understand that neither Amy nor Vance had the slightest interest in her crow's feet. Amy was telling the story of her wedding. It was a story, it had been told many times. It involved misplaced objects and last-minute reprieves, breathless anticipations, betrayals, and heroic feats.

"So I asked Minnie where could it have got to, and she said, 'Doeknow wheah anybody'd put da root beer but in da *rooot* cellar.'" Amy's Negro accent was a parlor trick. She pealed off into laughter, and Vance followed her in a lower key, the rhythm of his breath just slightly studied. He had listened to this before.

"And there it was!" Amy concluded.

But Eleanor, smiling politely, smiled into a memory touched lightly into being by the words *root cellar*. She saw herself crouching on the floor of the apple cellar in the old house on Cathedral Street. Mama was talking to the priest up in the parlor. Eleanor was not supposed to be here. She had come down to get an apple, but she had come, really, because Mama said the priest wanted to talk to her about the catechism, and this word frightened her. The cellar smelled of vinegary fruit going spotty, and the crumbly mix of mouse droppings and old paper. The servants were chatting in low, musical voices above her. She had been hiding for too long and could not now push through the slatted cellar door into the wan light of the pantry and so to the hall, because then her mother would know she had been hiding. But also she could not stop the slow, tickling pain in her piddling button. And then (the lace of her panties brushing the floor where she squatted) she felt the warm release, the relief and the shame, the heat that turned instantly cold as the wet spread on the dark dirt floor. There were bugs down here, and God. She was afraid of the roll-me-ups, the silverfish that seemed to have been called into being by her shameful peeing, and she was afraid of the catechism, which sounded like a dark opening in the earth.

"Well, the navy doesn't wait for you to send out invitations and get your petticoats trimmed!" Amy said. "I'm not saying I had a minute's hesitation. Put away childish things and all. But at the same time, it *is* the end of childhood. I mean, Vance, look the way Sammy carried on about his precious sword!"

It was not clear what she was talking about. Petulant, she scintillated in Vance's direction, and he glanced to her bosom.

"And all the same," Amy said, "it was the prettiest wedding in four states if it *is* me that says so."

Eleanor toyed with the hem of the napkin and inclined herself toward Amy, who was perspiring with the effort of her recitation.

"I'm sure it was."

"I just do regret, Eleanor, that you couldn't have been my matron of honor."

Eleanor nodded carefully. Nothing was less likely than that Amy should have asked her to be matron of honor at her wedding to Vance Jackson, who now cleared his throat again, in preparation for elevating the tone of the conversation.

"Dammit, I hated to make Amy rush like this," he said sententiously, "but when there's a crisis every man has to go where he's sent."

"What crisis?" Laurel asked.

"Why, those brute *hueristas* in Tampico, arresting our sailors and refusing to apologize."

Laurel erupted in a wet noise of dissent and applied his linen napkin to his mouth. "Come along, Vance. It was a mistake. They didn't refuse to apologize, they refused to salute the American flag with twenty-one guns. We were just lucky to have a peccadillo we could invade on."

Laurel's glance was sliding one way and another, never quite lighting on anything. Eleanor realized he was observing her out of the corner of his eye, as if she were going to produce some unseemly display.

Vance flushed. "I wonder myself why Wilson doesn't order us in there to mop up."

Now the two men squared off over the debris of dinner. Laurel said the reason Wilson didn't go in and mop up was that he knew what he meant by democracy. Vance said those people didn't know how to govern themselves. Laurel said that was neither here nor there. Vance said somebody needed to keep order.

"So Huerta says! Whose order do you have in mind?"

As soon as Amy stopped talking she had taken on a shocked and sleepy look, like someone emerging blinking from a train. For a moment Eleanor remembered what it was like to be hurtled west out of Baltimore, shiny as a shelled pea.

She pressed her fingertips against the sharp tines of her dessert fork. She wanted drink. She saw clearly that unhappiness is the natural state. She saw that she had disbelieved in God for quite some time now, probably long before the death of the Wheeler girl. She saw that she had believed in some other salvation up to this very moment that Amy Whitney Jackson pulled a piece of sinew from her teeth with the corner of her linen napkin: that she could go back to Baltimore. She had always supposed she would return to the paved streets and burnished lights, one day when she got her strength back; and that they would save her. Now Baltimore sat puffed in Amy's bosom and sprinkled over Vance's nose. Baltimore was no more than desert tinseled.

"Oh, Eleanor," said Amy, "I don't know what I'm going to do out there on the Coast, surrounded by this talk. How *do* you keep your sanity? What do you do for society?"

36

COMING UP THE WALK, Laurel heard the piano, and he lingered for a moment, gratified to recognize Bach. At quarter past five the day was at its most grilling, the paving stones aquiver, the street deserted except for a Mexican trimming grass a few houses down. But Bach was cool water, like coming on an unexpected falls. There was some little part of his mind disappointed to hear her at the piano again, because Eleanor's illness, even in its most wayward manifestations, made him feel pleasantly protective, competent. Exasperation itself had taken on a familiarity not wholly uncomfortable. But he recognized this was an ungenerous impulse, of the sort all flesh is heir to, and he put it away now as he hesitated on the porch among Eleanor's plants, remembering how Mrs. Newsome backhanded her compliment: "It's so *original* of your wife to put ordinary jojoba and sage in pots!"

The line of music floundered. The piece was of that group — what were they called? nursery pieces? — that Eleanor played as easily as scales, coaxing drama and color out of the lightest leitmotiv. Yet here she was stumbling over a simple phrase. He stood with one hand on the screen door latch, his mind urging, encouraging her. The phrase began again, stumbled on a minor chord, but picked up and carried on at not quite the right tempo. Then she stopped. He heard her talking to herself, and a flush deepened from his tight collar to the crown of his head. She was drunk. Already drunk before suppertime.

The piece began again from the beginning and tinkled forward prettily enough but with a wrong note here and there, uncertainty in the underlying rhythm. He was not a musical man, but he knew when Bach was being mangled.

Anger ballooned in him. He flung open the doors and crossed the narrow vestibule, letting the screen slam behind him and the wooden door bounce against the stop. He stormed into the living room — "Eleanor!" — prepared to have it out once and for all now, where she got it, how much she drank, how far he was prepared to go — disgrace if necessary, divorce if necessary — to see it stopped.

Maria was seated on the swivel stool, her hair elevated into a French knot and her golden nape bent over the keyboard. Eleanor had the cat in her lap and a hand in the air, not beating time but strumming it, as if on a miniature harp; and though Maria stopped instantly and turned with a look of alarm, Eleanor, her eyes closed, completed a single strum of that liquid hand.

He could not check his momentum, but blurted a slightly amended, awkward version of the sentence in his mind: "Please explain what you think you're doing at five o'clock in the afternoon!"

The girl slid sideways from the bench and backed nimbly into the bay window as if, pocketed behind the swag, she might be considered somewhere else entirely. In the midst of his confusion he had room to admire how quickly Maria took stock.

Whereas Eleanor with maddening slowness swiveled her limber neck

"I *think* I'm teaching Maria to play the piano." She gave him a heavy-lidded stare. "And I *think* I may."

He flailed for some substitute anger, anything he might credibly be upset about.

"Why was I not told?"

"Why should you be told?"

"I suppose I might be let in on what happens in my house." He tried to improve his credibility with more force and voice. "I see this is how Maria spends her time at a dollar a day!" What else could he have said? He could scarcely accuse his wife in front of the girl and have Eleanor's drinking become the gossip of shantytown.

Not, all the same, that he was wrong. Eleanor held the cat gently to her neck before, with a sentimental gesture, she bent and spilled it to the floor, and in that minute's martyrdom he could see, knowing her so well, every mincing muscle of her, that she had had too much to drink. She'd have done no better with the Bach if she *had* been playing it.

She rose now in that putting on of dignity she was so good at and that now, dreading the process of his own disillusionment, he saw was part of St. Agnes's training, part of her social skills. Drunk. She stood slowly while the girl in the bay window choked her skirt by handfuls, bouncing with distress.

Eleanor smoothed her own skirt with flat-handed calm. "I am unaware that it has anything to do with you."

"It has a dollar a day to do with me!" he said, was tricked into saying. He despaired.

"Maria," Eleanor said, "come and help me pack."

She turned toward the bedroom, and the girl started after her. Lunacy upon lunacy. How many kinds of injustice are there that a man can blunder into between his pavement and his living room?

"Maria, I would like a cup of tea," he countermanded. Eleanor turned and the girl faltered in her tracks, skirt swinging. He smiled at her. She gave him a despairing look. "I have no objection whatever to your playing the piano, but I do pay your wages, and I would like a cup of tea."

Eleanor stepped toward him, furious. She held herself at full height, hand on her wonderful hair, that willful cascade. "If you have no objection, then what is it you're objecting to?"

"I wish to be informed, that's all."

"Informed of what? Shall I send to the bank for permission if I want to wash my hair?"

"Eleanor, we'll discuss this later."

"Why later? Because Maria can't hear it? Is she neither to play nor to hear? What is it we're supposed to be discussing later?"

She stormed on into the bedroom, where he could hear her dramatically pulling out drawers and slamming cupboard doors, and Maria, after another pleading look, turned and scampered after her.

He was left trapped with his embarrassment on an island of
Bokhara throw rug. His first impulse was to go back to the bank and
give Eleanor a chance to settle down, a chance for Maria to get on
home. But he had tried that once before, and it had ended all in
Eleanor's advantage. If he did it again he'd give the appearance of
someone too weak to stand his ground. And it was *his* ground. He
understood well enough that he had his own clumsiness to blame,
but there was no gainsaying it was his house and he paid Maria's
wages. That was so. Why should he be the one who had to leave?

There was so little room to maneuver in that squalid little house,
no den or library of his own to retire to. The spare room was full of
boxes and trunks, the screen porch was a skillet at this hour. He
couldn't very well make the tea that Maria had failed to make, but
the only other option that presented itself, to fix himself a drink,
would undermine his position in the real quarrel with Eleanor.
That he'd locked the liquor in a trunk in the second bedroom,
would, if he went for it, arbitrarily identify him with her sneakings
and subterfuges. He stood, thwarted. The noises in the bedroom
continued and increased. Eleanor had begun to weep, and her
voice was shrill between the bustling sounds. The sound of her
crying always unsettled him with a mixture of annoyance and
helplessness.

He went to the door of the bedroom. "Eleanor. Please stop this
charade."

She did not reply, but stuffed camisoles and blouses higgledy-
piggledy into a grip. Maria took a stock of folded things from a
cupboard shelf and set them beside her mistress on the bed.
Eleanor swept them up with movement of unnecessary breadth.

"Eleanor. This is not what you want to do."

"How would you know what I want to do? You despise everything I want to do. I want to live out in the air, away from this
stifling town. I want to paint in the dining room. I want to drink a
glass of Madeira out of my old crystal glasses. Where are my mother's crystal glasses?"

"Eleanor. I only want what's best for you."

She stuffed her hands into the grip to make more room. She
looked at him with hysterical despair. "There is no best for me!"

She pushed past him into the hall, to the spare room, charged out again with a giant suitcase, which — he had no other option but brute blockage — made him step back inanely to let her pass.

"Maria, go tell O'Joe to bring the wagon round."

Alarmed, he said, "Stop being stupid."

Now Maria slipped past him, her eyes no higher than his fob and slithering against the doorjamb as if greased. Eleanor was ravaging the armoire, flinging skirts and blouses into the suitcase, letting drop to the floor the evening dresses, the fashionable suits. They fell like so much beaded rubble.

"Eleanor." She knew perfectly well he'd been caught in an awkward situation, but she *would* take advantage of it, she *would* punish him. Surely she wouldn't spite herself to the extent of taking off to that mud ruin? "This isn't about Maria," he said with some exasperation.

"Then what is it about? What did you expect to happen, bursting in on us like that? My God, what a prig you are. I do assure you" — she turned to the little writing desk and wrenched open the drawer, took out the check ledger, and abruptly sat — "that you'll pay no wages for the time Maria spends at her piano lessons."

When she bent to the ledger her hair fell over her forehead, but she brushed the lock back, and when it fell again she brushed it back again, over and over, unaware of the repetition and its pointlessness. The hand with the pen shook. He stood immobilized with anger and uncertainty for the long time it took her to write the check, to fold it down, and to tear it away from the others along the line of perforations. She held it out to him, but he refused it with a shrug, and she let go of it and turned back to her packing. The check floated down and settled on his toe. Even from here he could see the unsteadiness of the handwriting.

"Come now," he tried gently. "You don't mean to go on with this." He thought she wavered. She took a breath and flexed her shoulders forward, as if her back were hurting. "Send Maria home. I'll give her an extra dollar for her trouble, if you like."

"God!"

"Send her home. We'll sit down together and have . . ." At his hesitation her eyes flashed.

"What will we have? Say it, Laurel. What will we have, together?"

". . . a cup of tea."

She turned away from him with a contemptuous laugh and spilled the contents of her jewelry tray into the middle of the case. She closed it. Through the window Laurel saw the wagon pull into place before the house.

"For God's sake, have some sense. You can't live out there. It's nothing but an outsized hovel."

"Can't I?"

"It isn't what you want!"

Her neck and cheeks were damp. Perspiration caught in the down on her upper lip. Even now he would have liked to run his hand over the salt damp of her face.

She said, "I will ask you once more to disabuse yourself" — it was possible she was mocking him; it was a word he used; she pursed her mouth in the way he registered distaste — "of the notion you have the remotest notion what I want."

She lugged the suitcase backward off the bed, stumbling against its weight like some headstrong child running away over an imagined injury, with no thought for how to get itself fed or the fears it would be prey to in the dark. He would not help her. He would not be party to such infantilism. He stepped backward into the living room to let her pass. She dragged the grip and the suitcase toward the vestibule — she'd have painful shoulder sockets tomorrow — and when she got to the front door O'Joe and Maria were there to relieve her of her burdens. She wheeled and picked the cat off the couch, where it had curled into luxurious sleep.

"When you get back," he said, "we'll discuss this rationally."

"Yes, Laurel." Coldly. "By the time I get back, we will have become magically rational."

He half expected her to turn at the bottom of the steps, or at the bottom of the walk, to hear her oxymoron a beat late, her face to light at its felicitous absurdity. Only Maria cast a glance back over her shoulder, bewildered and in stress. O'Joe hoisted the bags in behind the buckboard. Eleanor carried on with her display of righteousness, offering a hand up to O'Joe for help, settling beside him with the cat in her lap while Maria clambered onto the wagonbed to sit on the luggage.

Unwilling to display himself in the figure of the abandoned husband, Laurel shut the door before they had pulled away from the curb. She was stubborn. She might carry on as far as the edge of town, she might even spend the night in the mission.

The piece of music had fallen in Maria's hasty rise, and he picked it up off the carpet and put it back on the piano stand. Nursery pieces, yes. Appropriate. He sat himself on the piano stool and swiveled back and forth. Odd how much quiet a domestic Sturm und Drang left in its wake. Dead quiet. For a moment he was aware of his freedom, the emptiness of the rooms, the expansiveness of solitude. For so many weeks he had lived under constraint, on guard against her moods and their sudden sting. Now relief passed over him like a physical thing. He filled his lungs. The air smelled of molasses bread.

She had been drunk. He was right about that. If there was justice, she couldn't punish him for being right. But exactly on the heels of this thought came the reality of her absence. The rooms were not empty, they were full of this absence, its bulk and power. He would not be allowed to relax, he would have to ward off her absence just as he had had to ward off her threat. There was not justice, had never been justice, only pain. He put his face in his palms. The fact is, she might stay a week to face him down. In which case — it was a question of essential order — he would have to outlast her. He would have to do it the old way, with the tools he had, his patience, his will, the knowledge that he was right. He rubbed the ache above his eyes. He sucked a breath from the heels of his hands.

37

SAN JACINTO PLAZA in El Paso was a wheel of paths through grass plots, down to a rocky fountain at the hub. The trees were in leaf, the lit color of cooking apples. Men in churchgoing bowler hats and ladies hobbled by their skirts were wandering the rim. Lloyd parked the car where he could keep an eye on it and walked down one of the spokes to sit on the steps of the bandstand and think.

Of course, it was a temptation to keep on straight west. Nights curled up in the backseat of the Packard, or under it on his saddle blanket when it rained, he'd daydreamed rolling down Bowie's Main Street past the dry goods store and the school, out the old ranch road and into his father's compound, leaping one-handed over the door in his cream silk suit while Frank's and Wally's mouths dropped open like a couple of Texas sinkholes.

But he couldn't do it. He wasn't brought up for stealing cars. He was brought up to believe in loyalty and property, the sanctity of a handshake on a deal. There was also the fact that if Villa wanted to come after him, there'd be nowhere to hide. But that wasn't the point; the point was that Villa had singled him out in a way his father never had. Lloyd had been a *villista* for more than half a year now, but *villista* meant anybody who rode along with Villa. Once, before he went on home, he wanted Villa to call him a *dorado*, a golden boy, one of the elite.

But there were a couple of problems, one of which was that he wasn't going to try to take a brand-new Packard — well, practically brand-new Packard, two rips in the leather where a gas can or the silver of the saddle caught — through the El Paso-to-Juárez checkpoint. He didn't know what the rules were, but he wasn't going to stop in and find out, nor hand his bill of sale over to his daddy's old friend Zach Cobb. That's the trouble with connections in high places. A friend in Customs is one thing if you're kidnapped on the Mexican side and trying to get out; it's another if you want to get back across on the q.t.

The other problem was money. Crossing Texas had taken longer with the Packard than with Haragana. The car was harder to feed, because although every two-bit drugstore in every one-horse town now sold gasoline, sometimes you ran out of gas before you ran into a one-horse town. It'd be a lot worse in Mexico. Lloyd didn't have the price of a shot of whiskey, let alone a couple dozen cans of gas.

He'd figured out as far back as Waco that he'd have to sell his saddle, not only because his money was going to give out but also because he was nervous for the saddle. In Waco he had gone into the Picture Palace to see a moving picture called *Mexican War Scenes,* and although he used to leave Haragana tied outside without a second thought, somehow leaving a saddle in a backseat was different from leaving it on a horse. He lugged it into the theater with him and kept one hand draped over it in the aisle. He sat in back of a girl with feathers sticking down bothering her neck, while up on the screen Pancho Villa rode into Ojinaga, grinning in the half dark, and out again grinning at half light, and the captions said he rode out triumphant, but there were no pictures of a battle in between. Well, that made sense, because Villa always attacked at night. The girl giggled and flipped at her neck, and then the screen said "Torreón," and this time in broad daylight half a dozen soldiers in *federal* uniform and fixed bayonets came running straight at you down a street, their faces skewered back with strain. One of them toppled off the edge of the picture into you, but the captions didn't bother to say who he was or what happened to him.

There were scenes of supper and campfires with the *campesinas* wrapped in their best flowered shawls, and of *villistas* riding among corpses, shooting at the already dead; but though Lloyd squinted and concentrated, he couldn't identify any face but that of Villa.

Fierro was not in sight, nor Farga, and though on a horse lunging down some narrow street of Torreón he thought he saw one who looked like Cesar Santos, that could not be right, because Santos was dead. The girl twirled at her feather and whispered to her beau. A mule in a braided harness sidestepped over a body on a railroad track. When Lloyd got outside, somebody had screwed off the knob of his gearshift and taken it away.

He had to get back to Villa because his honor was bound up in it. But also he had to get back there because of that moving picture, because seeing the almost-familiar scenes flattened out to black and white and yet somehow more colorful than life — the contrast starker than the washed-out browns and blues of the Chihuahuan desert — made him feel as foggy as smoking weed. The face he'd thought was Santos's stood out from the rest and stayed in his memory, a ghost even to the gray of it. He tried to put together the dates of things: When had the cameras come, and surely Torreón came after Mapimi, and surely they wouldn't take a picture of one battle and call it another? But the more he thought about it the more he thought that had been Santos up there, wisps of white and gray doomed to do nothing but float down a street in Torreón forever. He couldn't be sure. He had to get back to Chihuahua and get things real. He needed a punch on the arm from Farga, he needed Villa to wrap him in that hug, he needed the bite of one of Concepción's ferocious chili sauces.

Across from him, in a beeline over the folded top of his car, behind the big brick box of the Old Mexico Trading Co., sat the long, low, whitewashed face of *Plaza Dining Rooms, Strictly American.* Lloyd was bad hungry. Nearly as hungry as he'd been in the mine that night with Villa and Fierro. He hoisted himself off the bandstand steps and went to see if anybody was looking to buy a saddle.

At first light he was edging off the El Paso-to-Pecos highway just south of Fabens, toward the river. He had twenty-seven full cans of gas, a pound of tenpenny nails in a paper bag, a one-man tree saw, two hundred feet of best cotton rope, diameter five-eighths, and two stout twelve-foot two-by-fours roped lengthwise over the right-hand fenders. What he didn't have was another couple dozen of these two-by-fours, as he would have liked, because the cost of a cut-down tree in El Paso would take your breath away. So he'd have to watch for the lumber on the way, mark it in his memory, and go back for it bit by bit.

In the meantime what he was looking for had to be exactly right. He needed a shallow approach, some tree or rock formation solid enough to anchor a raft, a gentle current; but at the same time a bend in the river such that when he hove off, the drift would take him into the far bank.

It took all morning to find such a place. The trouble was, if it didn't work he could be helplessly awash all the way back to the Gulf of Mexico, or smashed up on a rapids somewhere. But he persevered, and a little before noon, creeping along squinnying the tires among the rocks, he passed a stand of scrub pine that he thought might do for lumber, and about a mile beyond that, a place where the land flattened out like the back of a hand, and the sluggish river spread wide. On this side the bank made a gentle half-moon curve, but on the other it widened and then narrowed, making a hump into which the current swung. It was a good deal wider than he would have liked, but you can't have everything; there was a clump of four mesquite this side to tie to.

He sawed off a chunk of mesquite from another tree, tossed it out, and watched it meander in the current. It was a pretty sight, the dark silt of the shore flecked with mica, the dark-stained water winking in the light, and a chunk of tree trunk like a clumsy canoe drifting and bobbing in the drink. Patting his pocket, Lloyd came across the tooth that Santos had pulled, and tossed it in for luck. He winnowed the end of his rope and whooped when the wood struck the far bank and butted into mud.

He untied the two-by-fours (they'd scratched the fenders with their jostling) and laid them on the ground. Then he drove back to the stand of pine and, one at a time, felled a dozen young trees and cut each into a log just two foot longer than the Packard. That took him till suppertime. He chewed on some jerky and a loaf of bread while he drove the logs back two at a time, six trips in all, to the wide place in the river.

It was dark by then, and his muscles were singing, so he crawled into the backseat of the car. But the gasoline cans kept him awake like a pile of bones — or not so much their hardness as the funny little nasal pings and boings they made when he turned or struck one with a toe. So he made his bed on the ground, and kept getting waked up by anything or nothing much, a kit fox in the undergrowth, an elf owl, a dream that he was sleeping on the gas cans when they caught fire around him.

It was only when he woke he found out he'd been asleep, from his deep grogginess and from the sun, which was higher than he'd intended. His back and shoulders were sore, his fingers raw. But there was nothing for it. He had coffee and bacon and the end of the loaf of bread, indulging himself before he set to it again.

All that day he built the raft. He lay the tree trunks on the ground, hauling them this way and that, turning this one around, that one over, till they nestled into each other. Then he laid his two-by-fours across and nailed at every point of contact. He took the rope and wrapped the raft like a package you're going to send in the mail, once around each end in both directions, with every one of the crossings double-tied. When that was done he sat with a bit of jerky in one hand, thinking bitterly about the way his father had taught him to tie a package up like that, how to secure a load of beef on a flatbed, how to figure-eight a calf's hind legs, how to rope a broken gate. His father had a shaming way of teaching. He always did a thing so fast you could hardly follow, more to impress than to instruct, and so your own efforts afterward were always feeble. You could never do it right. Nobody ever so much as draped a paper chain around a Christmas tree to suit his father.

He sat by his cold campfire nursing a blister and a new burn on an old callus, no worse than branding day. The sky west was in full orange flood, and the only sensible thing to do was quit and start again tomorrow, but thinking of his father had made him edgy. His muscles were twanging like guitar strings. He figured he wasn't going to sleep, and if he didn't he might be in worse shape in the morning. He upended the coffee dregs and packed his gear into the Packard.

With the leftover rope Lloyd lashed the raft to the clump of trees, a loose anchor-lead that he could cast off, and a ninety-foot coil that he could feed from the raft edge. His idea was that if he started going squeejaw before those ninety feet were played out, he could haul himself back to the bank. He waded in, bent over, dragging the raft into water so shallow it hardly cleared his instep, then, once the logs sat in the mud, pushing from the bank side till they floated. The pine sat up perky on the water. He started the car and gingerly drove it on, registering proudly that he'd ridden some roads in Texas corded rougher than this homemade boat.

First try, though, the raft just bogged down in the silt. So he drove onto the bank again, tied the raft on a longer lead, drove the tires into the silt (*please don't let them get stuck*) and onto the platform, which settled again. He'd used all the heft he had in his back before the raft began to show any buoyancy.

But then it was afloat. He scrambled on and shoved off with a spare section of two-by-four — it nudged through mud and hit bedrock, which gave him good leverage — casting off the anchor ropes and feeding out the other.

There wasn't a breath of trouble. The raft waltzed one corner forward and then the other as the muddy current stirred like chocolate batter. Lloyd stood straddle-legged, remembering Haragana with the weight of the river against her sides, holding the rope like reins and playing it out a foot at a time, hand over hand. After a few minutes he hunkered down with his back to the door of the Packard, balancing against the drift. He flipped the coil off the edge, sending a three- or four-foot loop over at a time. When he looked over his shoulder he lost his rhythm, so he had to squat there facing the way he'd come. The sunset caught pink in scoops of water. The pine logs sighed and squeaked against each other, moving lazily in the current.

The last coil lifted off the raft into his loose fist. The knot in the end caught at his palm with a snug sensation, the last second he could change his mind. So he yodeled to give himself courage, flung the rope, and watched it snake back toward the bank. Lloyd stood and edged up to steady himself against the forward fender. The current had a firm bite of that much palm bark, and the raft twisted back and forth, all the time swinging itself across as it wandered downstream.

Until about halfway, a little more. Then Lloyd felt some kind of drag against the bottom, as if it were scraping over the tops of weeds or branches. The way the logs seemed to scud and catch made him imagine bushes growing up tall from the river bottom.

There was a soundless thud and the raft came to a dead stop in something that was hard and soft at once, that both gave and held. Lloyd felt the water pressure build behind him, and the back end of the raft began to lift.

Lloyd scooted backward to put his weight on the aft section, but the water kept gathering so that the raft slowly reared and took him with it. He flailed with one arm, looped it over the back edge, the other hand still clutching at the left rear fender of the car. There was a minute when he hung there watching the color of the light change in the eddies, pink fading out to gray at just that moment, and felt peculiarly interested in the color of the light. The cans shifting in the backseat made a hiccupy, burping sound. The car began to skid forward, tread against the bark. The dried clods on the underside of the fender pulled from his hand, and it was just like he could feel the treads and the bark on the skin of his palm.

He thought: *She's going.*

And as if his opinion was exactly what gravity was asking for, one can somersaulted forward and struck the windshield with a crack; the Packard picked its back tires gracefully off the raft and nose-dived into the water, where for a long minute it seemed miraculously to stand on its grille and float in place.

Lloyd hung where he was, numb, waiting for the car to disappear. But it didn't. It balanced on its grille, a clumsy mammal doing an aquatic trick. The raft began to skew sideways, settling back toward the water, and to his astonishment he felt himself wheeling with the current out to the side and around the car, which held as steady in the water as Haragana with a hundred and fifty thousand dollars on her neck. He reached out, back; she was three feet from the end of his fingers, then five, then seven. He was heading downstream, getting farther away from the Packard all the time. If he left the raft he was without any means of locomotion, but if he stayed he had to go its way and leave his car where it must be — *must* be, evidence of his eyes to the contrary — disappearing to the river bottom. He had to choose; he began to edge off the raft with a dim idea he could lower himself into the water and swim back to catch his car.

Well, it was the dry spring of a dry winter in arid country, and the river widened here where the land was flat. Lloyd eased in to the depth of his boot heels, and the depth of his ankles, and the depth of the second scroll in the stitching on the calf of his Mexican boots. That was it, as far as the water went. He could have forded in second gear. Lloyd could almost hear his father blowing out an exasperated breath; he walked to his car on bedrock under a little sauce of silt not deep enough to get his socks wet.

38

ALMA TIMKIN was at loose ends even more than usual after school let out. There wasn't much use she could be in town. Wally Wheeler wouldn't look under his own nose, and decided to survive by talking global doom. First we were going to war with Mexico, and when that didn't happen we would invade Ulster. When that proved false, why, the whole world was supposed to erupt over the murder of the Archduke Ferdinand.

"Could you find Serbia on a map?" she asked him.

Alma, who thought any revolution was good news, offered him the triumph of the Constitutionalists in Mexico; but Wally said that now they'd beat Huerta, why, they'd just start cutting up each other. She had to admit that was the way revolutions tended. Wally said Villa's Yaqui Indian henchmen were already squaring off with Obregón's bureaucrats in Nogales. Maytorena would goad Calles till he reacted, and when the fight came, Wally wouldn't be surprised if it would spill over our border.

"Well, well," said Alma. She read the papers, too, but she was always more affected by the news of private individuals. The dark design of human events was more real to her on a smaller scale. Near Union, Louisiana, a black man and his son had been lynched for murder and horse theft, although nobody was missing and nobody was missing a horse. The reasoning of the locals was, it was more horse than a pickaninny could come by without foul play.

"Well, well," she said. "In that case you might as well let your son quarry himself a fort."

And she rose to go, but Wally stopped her. He had his blind spots, Wally Wheeler, but he was no numskull. Maybe he heard her to mean she was done nursemaiding him.

"Marry me, Alma," he said. "I'll leave you my money, and then if you want to give it to Frank, that'll be your business."

"Why, Wally Wheeler," she said. "That's surely a convoluted way to get your money where you want it."

"You know that's not the point. Marry me to take care 'of me, then, because you're sorry for a poor, broke-down old workhorse."

And that was a harder argument, even though he said it mockingly, meaning to deal out the truth with one hand and rake it back with the other. Money she knew the use of only up to a certain limit, but nobody had tested the limits of her caretaking. *He needs me.* It was the most potent phrase that had come to her attention yet. It had gotten her into schoolteaching in the first place.

"I can't do it, Wally," she said.

But there didn't seem much *to* do. Now that school was out, Maria wasn't coming around, either. Alma learned at Maybeth's, from fat Estrella, that Maria had moved out to the mission. Estrella said, "To be with her *señora.*" Alma asked her did that mean the *señora* had moved out there, too, and Estrella said "*Sí-sí,*" hardly opening her mouth, as if it was obvious.

Yet when she went to call on Laurel Poindexter he acted like his wife had just stepped out to do some errands. "She'll be so sorry to have missed you," he said, even though the sideboard and half the chairs were gone. "She's a bit stronger," he informed her brightly, though the piano was shut down under a frosting of dust. "This flu *has* taken a toll" — and it was a fact his collar was missing a stud.

So she drove out to the mission, taking Keats and a change of clothes in her satchel just to be prepared for all eventualities. She aimed the Model T gingerly across the flats, weaving among rocks and cactus rumps until she spotted the wheel ruts of a road that cut surprisingly clear and forthright, as if it had had real use. Roadrunners sped in her wake.

It was an amazing sight, O'Joe and a dozen Mexicans stripping bark off a pile of pine trees, women raking out a fire pit, children chasing half dressed around a row of bee boxes. It was *a hive of activity*, Alma thought. The mission wall was built up to a height of twenty feet, and whitewashed, and a whole little village of brush-roofed houses flung up around it. Alma felt more or less as if she had arrived in the middle of the Sahara and found it colonized. The roof of her mouth was dry. While the children crowded around the fenders, she sat pulling her blouse away from her spine, from the tacky heat of the upholstery, her mind still vibrating from the motor and the heat, a fantasy fluting in her head that perhaps villages were springing up secretly in every cranny of the vast. They would spread and sprawl till they touched each other like drops of cochineal dye in a pudding. Eleanor Poindexter and a skinny black dog came rushing out.

"A caller!" Eleanor said. "You don't know what it means to me to have a caller. It's a sacrifice living this far out, I can tell you, not being able to show my Bowie friends what-all we're accomplishing!"

She handed Alma down and plucked her toward the empty arch. What Bowie friends did she have in mind? There was something not right about Eleanor Poindexter: Her eyes and her balance seemed unsteady; her energy had too much edge. "We" were not accomplishing a floor, Alma noticed. What served for a roof was a latticework of logs, and under it they'd constructed a huge sort of raft that held an expensive Persian carpet off the dirt. A cat was eating a lizard on a paisley. Maria Iglesias made a great show of setting out a tapestry chair for her. Eleanor perched herself on another. It was like a stage set of a living room. The audience of children sat cross-legged or hunkered along the carpet fringe, watching the pantomime.

"Paco, Eleana," Eleanor introduced them. "Polo, Felicidad . . . We'll give you a tour of the chickens and the bees. But coffee first."

And Maria — with the stately air that, now that she saw it in this fabulous context, Alma remembered to have been Maria's posture ever since she used to come along with her mother to tidy the schoolroom — Maria served coffee out of a blackened pot into china cups. Afterward she spread a newspaper in the dirt and dumped the grounds. Alma thought: *She's in the wings.*

"Did you see the hives? We're becoming quite self-sufficient here! Gaspar has talked me into a windmill. Don't you think that's a pity when the well is so picturesque? But picturesque goes for nothing with Gaspar. Only water talks with him!"

Her skirt hitched into her waistband on both sides to keep it off her boots, she splayed her hands. She was dark and bright and abrupt.

"But I was saying about the hives. Do you know what a beeline is? Haven't you used that expression all your *life*? Gabrielo took me along — well, what you must do is ride out in the desert at dusk and find one bee. Then there must be three or four of you to watch it, because it tricks you where it goes, in a straight line to here, then there, right angles always. If you lose it you must sit tight and wait for another."

Her hands made beelines, which the children mimicked with outsized eyes, as if this were a story being told for their benefit. "You follow it to its hive — the one we found was in an old hollowed-out saguaro — and then you puff pipe smoke in the hole until the bees fly out, and then you scoop out the queen. Alejandro got two bites, but he says that's a small price. Come! Let me show you where the kitchen goes. You didn't think we were going to live in these primitive conditions forever, did you? Ah! We do have a guest room. You must spend the night!"

Alma demurred, but by rote. Really, she had kept her curiosity honed on trivia and innuendo for the better part of ten years now, and she wasn't in any rush to leave a genuine spectacle. For instance, hardly had she spoken before a Mexican woman with an enormous curly-headed boy riding her hip came rolling across the hall, railing from out of earshot right up to the edge of the raft, about a squall on its way, and the carpet getting rained on. Two men followed with a tarpaulin. Then as the men rolled the carpet — Eleanor excused herself and disappeared into her room — Alma had a chance to walk apart with Maria.

They rounded the wall in front of the fire pit. Out of sight of Eleanor, Maria began flinging herself onto the balls of her feet, an extravagant pent-up motion, a grounded leap. She contorted her bisque features as if effort enough would sculpt the wanted words.

"She has lost God," Maria said, then soughed a breath to register the foolishness of this. She slapped a huarache on the hardpan, shuffled her bones inside her skin. "She has lost her *way*," Maria amended.

"Why is she so unhappy?" Alma asked.

"Oh, why!"

"*Why?*"

"Carmen is unhappy because her baby died. Mama is unhappy because her man went away. But she! She's unhappy because she doesn't know how to make herself *up.*" Now Maria planted her feet as if she would stick by this, and as if she herself was, moreover, an authority on self-invention.

Alma wanted information, not philosophy. "Did she quarrel with her husband?"

More miserable twisting. "She sent us, O'Joe and me, back to get her furniture. It was terrible, like stealing from him. What if he came home? Oh, it was terrible! We couldn't bring the piano because there are no floors."

It wasn't clear which was more terrible, stealing the chairs or not stealing the piano. "Shall I bring your lessons out to you?" suggested Alma. "I could come twice a week or so."

"What for? I'll never get away now." A row of arrowheads had been laid along the pit wall, someone's treasure on display. Maria swept them off with the side of her hand. Then she bent angrily and gathered them up again, dumped them in a pyramid in the same spot on the wall, let a few slide off to the ground, turned her back on them.

Later the squall came up, as Carmen Acosta had predicted. The sky darkened from the west in one gray wipe, an electric murk sliced by a jag of lightning, and moments later, thunder chewed the earth. Alma sat with Eleanor in the palm-thatched portion of the mission that she mockingly referred to as her boudoir. Adobe-walled and dirt-floored, nevertheless it was a handsome space, generously proportioned, with an arched window under a frond overhang, and views onto the wet mountains and the slanting rays of rain. The desert was dark silver. The fringe of water rushed in this direction, slapped over them, and rattled on the fronds. Maria dragged the fancy chairs in and left them alone.

"I daresay you'll think I've come to live among a bunch of fortune-tellers!" Eleanor laughed loudly. "Is it all right to offer you sherry? Laurel said it isn't; he said it would be a major *faux pas.*"

Alma had never had sherry. She said it would be fine. Eleanor rattled among the glassware on the sideboard and poured with an air — what was it exactly? — of thespian precision. She spread one hand on the foot of the glass, tipped the bottle with a flourish, turned, and presented it with an expression that scintillated naughtiness. She was no longer pretty. Her features had sharpened, hawklike. She pushed a bright afghan out of her way with no more attention to it than a scratching bird. Alma held the glass by its stem and sipped at it uncertainly. The sherry itself was a disappointment, like most sin — a sort of sugared kerosene. Eleanor drank hers deep and set the bottle on the nightstand with her glass.

"How *are* your fortunes?" Alma asked, and Eleanor alarmingly flung her face into her hands. As if her head were an unexpected weight she feinted forward, carrying the face down between her knees. Her hair poured over her head.

"Not good, not good," she muttered. "Oh, not good, I'm very . . ." She sat back up on her bed; she scowled out into the metallic light. "I'm so *homesick.*"

"Can't you go home?"

"No, no, I have no home. That's why I'm homesick." She considered this dully and then contradicted herself. "I was building a house there. An altogether *different* house!"

"In Baltimore, you mean."

"In Baltimore . . ."

"Does your husband know it matters to you so much? Perhaps he wouldn't have insisted on coming to Arizona?"

Eleanor downed another glass. "That's another thing you're not supposed to tell. *That* might get you talked about, especially . . . dying!" She put a finger to her lips, glittered, and rolled her eyes over her shoulder. She was like somebody acting somebody acting furtive.

Alma had never seen a drunk person before. Well, she had seen drunk persons, of course, but not in such a way that she was meant to keep up her end of the conversation.

"Are you dying?" she asked conversationally.

"Me! No. Yes. Everybody's *dying.* But some of us quicker than others!" She burst into laughter several ergs beyond what this merited, and Alma felt that incipient unease that an audience always feels when the actors are not quite in control. Something can go terribly wrong. Eleanor reached forward, offered to top up Alma's glass, refilled her own. Her face took on witchy anger. "Don't let anybody know! . . . if you're a Catholic. Or want a glass of something now and again! Shhh. You can give away your old clothes, but keep the *ser*-vants in their *place*." She leaned across her planted feet and whispered, the force of her breath making more noise than before. "And he believes it, here's the joke. Daddy said I shouldn't marry an atheist: *Little by little he won't even mean to he'll change the way you think.* I thought, poor Daddy, what a *nouveau riche.* He didn't understand how fine my husband was, my fine and upright progressive Mr. Fine."

"Have you quarreled with your husband?" Alma asked.

Eleanor gave her a sly look. "Lots of girls settle for a house, you know. They don't admit it, but they do."

"Yes, I know," Alma said. Then Eleanor stood and paced. The afghan sidled to the floor and she caught her boot in it, half tripped, and as if the indignity of a stumble was the final straw, burst into noisy tears.

"My dear . . ."

She sobbed for several beats, subsided, blew her nose. She pitched a gesture at the window, where the rain had slowed to a drip off the overhang. "This wasn't the thing I was afraid of, all this . . waste." She flapped again into the leaden landscape. She sat, boot toes stretched before her. "Somebody told me about bugs in a fire . . . no, I know. Once Daddy threw a log on the fire that he picked up . . . that had laid out in the woodpile too long." She stopped. "It must have come from the bottom, near the grass."

Her eyes looked fiercely into this as if trying to see it right. Alma kept still to let her look for whatever it was she was looking for. She herself brought to her mind's eye a woodpile on the grass — a commonplace of her childhood that she hadn't seen or thought of these ten years. The ends of the logs had attracted her with their perfect concentric circles, like the rings from a stone dropped in a pond. The sawn ends smelled of renewal, some secret freshness sucked out of the earth. Alma was surprised by a clenching in her chest, and she breathed until it passed. She saw how potent that longing was for Eleanor. *Have you smelt the nard in the fire?* Homesick. That was all.

Eleanor leaned to Alma with a show of solemn revelation. Her consonants slurred, although her mouth moved with great care.

"My daddy threw a log on the fire and it went *hisssss!* The bugs came out of it, silverfish, a panic, and potato bugs. A centipede kept coming out and out. That was . . ."

She drank slowly, and slowly filled the glass, which had not been empty.

"Do you see? Always after when the priest said flames-o'-hell, that's what it was."

Alma did see. She saw that the effect of the alcohol was to make Eleanor an appallingly bad actress of her own grief. What Alma was witnessing was pure ham, except that it was also real. She was suddenly reminded of poor Jessie Wheeler, who used to suffer like this, so extravagantly to such little purpose.

Eleanor's face went blank. "You're in the flames yourself, but you can't run, so the spiders run up your legs, the slugs on your feet are hot from being in the fire. *That's* what hell was. Not this . . . starvation." She started up again. "Oh, they will leave me, too!"

She rocked on the bed, back and forth, soundless, her mouth gaping like a yawn that couldn't find its depth. She gulped for air.

"Who will leave you?"

"All of them. Carmen, Alejandro, Gabrielo. As soon as the money's gone. Maria's my only friend, and she can't wait to go. Don't think I can't see it."

"Surely —"

"No, they'll go. Why should they stay? And leave me all alone in this waste, this empty . . . and when my mind is empty, then all there is in it is that girl."

Alma had been following pretty well up to now. "Maria?" But Eleanor ignored this. She bent still closer. Her whisper was a real whisper this time. Her breath was sweet and stinking.

"Here's the secret: Hell is not the fire, it's the falling. Lucifer knew that. Loose, loose, Lucifer." She frowned into her pun, which apparently sat in the bottom of the glass. Then the frown dissolved but she kept staring into the half-inch of unsteady sherry. "See, I fall. Only it's myself I'm falling through. I can keep on falling through myself forever, turning inside out. So. And then sometimes, not all, sometimes she is falling beside me, over the side, up and over the side, sometimes I don't even remember her name, we're falling beside the white stone. She falls beside me, turning inside out. Forever. And I don't care. Don't imagine for a minute that I care! I watch her falling and I think: *Why should this have been done to me?*"

She sat back now with her arms limp, palms up by her sides, and only her chin still searching a little forward, the underflesh faintly blue. Alma carefully with her fingertips balanced the unfamiliar weight of the goblet by its fluted stem. She thought she would go out to the Ford now and fetch in the Keats; she thought she would read aloud, an ode or two, perhaps the lines about Ruth and the alien corn. Meanwhile she set down the glass, bent and retrieved the afghan from the dirt, shook it and folded its brightly colored flowered squares against each other. She smoothed it onto the foot of the bed where Eleanor sat slack as a puppet. When Alma moved only a foot or two toward the door, Eleanor reached after her.

"Don't go tonight. Stay here tonight. . . ."

It doesn't really count for much, whether there's anything you can do. Fold a blanket, bake a pie. Press your hand against a forehead (Alma touched the back of her fingers to Eleanor's hot temple, which Eleanor allowed). All that is an excuse for standing by. Guilt needs a witness, grief an audience. Otherwise how do they know when they have played out their time?

39

CAN YOU FEED VILLA OBREGÓN THREE HUNDRED TROOPS
AUGUST 28 EN ROUTE EL PASO NOGALES STOP LETTER FOLLOWS
STOP COBB.

Wally took the telegram down to the butcher room with him and
sat on a three-legged stool with his boot heels wedged in the grate.
He spent a lot of time here these days, something he hadn't mentioned to Alma Timkin. She'd think it was morbid the way he was
comfitted by the damp, honeyed smell of blood, long years of it
washed into the floor and carved into the butcher block. His house
had been built into the foothill, part of the cellar blasted out of the
igneous root of the mountain. The floor was constructed of cattle
grates that were washed down daily, the water wasting through
them into the thirsty subsoil. Here it was cool all summer long, and
here Wally did his butchering and stored his own meat supply.
Mostly he cut the meat himself, just to feel the competence in his
own hands. The sharpness of a good knife pleased him.

Could he feed Villa, Obregón, and three hundred troops? Well,
yes, he could set that up, supposing he had a wish to, but why he
would want to lay a table for a cutthroat and his cutthroats just to
feed the political ambitions of Zachary Cobb he wasn't clear.

The idea of Zach Cobb was a gob of gristle in his throat just at
the moment, him and his three gussied daughters and his flibberti-
gibbet wife. No doubt when the letter came it would regale him
with the doings of their social successes, because notwithstanding

that Cobb was a good hand and fair insurance to have behind you in the old days, now he was nothing but pomp and family man. When he talked prospects he didn't have ore in mind, he meant husbands for his daughters. Likely as not he'd be into some such thing as a Texas coming-out.

Women are a bad investment, that's what Wally would have advised him. They die that easy. The only thing that lasts is work.

Half a dozen forequarters hung from an iron bar at one end of the room, and Wally stood up, set the telegram on the stool, and patted the carcasses like suits along a rack. He selected one and hoisted it to the butcher block. From the grid on the wall he took a cleaver the size of an encyclopedia, and a butcher knife. He honed the knife a long time, thinking about the frailty of women. He'd had eight years to learn about that with his wife, Phoebe. After Lloyd's birth she had no resilience, she'd flinch at a door slam. There was nothing special about that birth, no complications or particular danger. Just for some reason she never wanted to come out of it, she drew back into herself and made a little space around her and the boy so he grew up soft until she passed. No amount of reasoning could buck her up or make her sensible.

He brought the cleaver down solid to hack away the rib section, the crack of metal on bone oddly brief in the thin acoustics of that stone room. Then he did the simple job, the layering of the sirloin rib, one slice and one cleaver whack per steak.

Afterward they said it was gallstones, and maybe it was gallstones. She never seemed like somebody with any gall in her to speak of.

The meat yielded softly, gave off a faint, sweet scent, and laid open the rich, red flesh shot through with white threads of fine fat. Marbling, they called it. Oh, he saw. It was just like the patterns in the rock when you split it away from the pit. Pity it wasn't as easy with rock as taking a well-honed knife and shearing it off like that. He saw himself slicing the marble into steaks.

It didn't do him good to think of the pit. The thought of the pit put him suddenly in a rage again against Cobb and his superfluous daughters. He would hold a coming-out party for Cobb's daughters in the bottom of that quarry. He would hold a funeral dance for them down there!

That's a crazy way to think. Nothing against Cobb. Cobb was a friend.

But there was this prissy streak in Cobb he couldn't stomach at the moment, this special-agent humbug, making himself such a fine figure of a U.S. gov'ment helping hand. Nothing but pretense; a man forgot the way he'd come up. The very idea of getting citified in El Paso gave a sour taste to your spit. Pretense and baloney, the world is full of it. Not a reason on the earth that Bowie should lay tables for a bunch of raping bandits. But at least you had to admit Villa was straightforward about what he was up to: Kill the owners and take the land. He didn't put on any diplomatic airs; you could bet he didn't waste any time in *dinner arrangements* such as Cobb wanted to haul Wally in on.

Arrangements Wally could beat Cobb at one-handed. Villa, Obregón, and three hundred. Hundred a sitting, two, three servers to a table, in and out in twenty minutes per. Ruffian soldiers roughing up the Hinman chairs, though. Stench of them. Would they use knives and forks or need a bunch of tortillas to scoop up the meat?

Wally had never been in a war. Too young for the Civil and too old for the Spanish-American. He regretted that. Of course, the fight he'd been engaged in all his life was more important than any war. It was what wars were fought for, the right to bring democracy, Christianity, civilization. And he'd done his bit — first on the railway, banding the earth with iron, making geography; and then in the town, order after ordinance, laying down the ties of justice. His was the important fight, for hygiene, duty, piety, to make the desert country safe for women and children (no, not that; he wouldn't think about that).

The West, that was his battleground, his regiment. All the same, some days it was like putting a fist into a dust devil. You wrestle the stingy land, shove crowds of cattle, shout the greasers into working, wheedle a vote out of the very ladies you were trying to protect. It would have been strange and welcome to be a soldier for a time. Just once he would have liked to know who the enemy was. Not gallstones! Just once it would have been good to have had a gun in his hand and a clear duty: *Kill him, shoot them, and it'll all come right.*

He took the point of the stiletto around the filet, trimming fat. This steer had started out at eight hundred pounds, of which three hundred were already on Li's compost heap and down the drain. He'd lose another twenty-five in fat and gristle from this quarter alone (and that's not counting bone; he was counting retail weight), even though all eight hundred of the pounds had to be ranged and looked after. It seemed like the more juice there was to things, the more waste. He liked the desert because it got by on so little of everything. Sometimes the Reverend Newsome referred to the desert as a wasteland, which offended Wally. It seemed to him the desert wasted darned little, compared to people.

If the European troubles blew up now, Frank would be too old, just exactly the age Wally was when the Spanish-American War broke out. Lloyd would be the right age for a soldier, which was sort of a sore joke, Lloyd being the least likely of any Wheeler he remembered to go to war. Little Jessie would have made a better trooper (no, not that). But in any case, where was Lloyd? Gone, disappeared, unreliable as women.

Wally would've done all right in a war himself, he had no doubt. What he didn't have any use for was this piecemeal crumbling away of his life, the dull drag of all this dying and leaving going on around him. It wasn't a question of whether he could arrange to feed some troops, it was did he want to get up off the stool, climb the stairs from the butcher room, get out of bed in the morning. Things didn't have any interest left for him. Why should he bother?

Now he carved a neat semicircle in the cartilage of the shoulder socket, took down a hacksaw, and started on the thicker bone of the shoulder roast. He sweated a little while the blade whined; bone dust and beads of marrow fat gathered in two slow piles on either side. There were some people who couldn't stomach the slaughtering of a steer. He remembered Lloyd as a boy, the first time he'd seen a slit-throated calf hung by the hind heels to drain. A winter it was, steam rising off the trough where the blood ran, and Lloyd's face pinched green around a red-cold button of a nose, just before he keeled dead away on the ground. Even now Wally laughed aloud. He remembered that for a minute there he'd seen it as a kid would, the steam rising as they peeled away the hide, like smoke was already smoldering in the flesh and about to take fire. Whereas that sight had no more pity or horror in it for him than tearing up a lettuce leaf. To the contrary entirely (cleaver to the wedge cut, a fine, flat whack), what he felt toward carving flesh was a kind of integrity. You can trust your hands to remember what they're doing. Work doesn't leave you.

Could he do it? Sure. Get Maybeth Newsome to call a meeting of the Women's Society for Christian Service, impress 'em with the service they'd be doing for the Cause of Peace. Women always go for that.

They'd need everybody in town cooking, they'd have to organize servers and cleaners. The Hinman could set china for a hundred, then they'd need the women to bring a hundred settings and have the first lot ready again for the third serving. There'd be competition among the women who could lay the finest service, all of them pouty-smiling at each other like the Christmas social. He'd ask Mary Doreen to take charge of the generals' table, get her mind off things, get Alma to help her, even ask Poindexter's wife to pull out her back-East tableware. Sure he could do it. They'd have to hire some Mexicans to do the washing up.

He layered the steaks in butcher wrap, bent down for a whiff of them before he rolled them in the *Daily Star*. Once you stopped the cleaver in that room the sound shut down dead. A flat, absorbed silence left nothing but the smell of meat. He supposed that for Villa killing became pretty much the same thing as slaughtering day. If you were a soldier that was your work, and you set about it wanting to get it done in the most efficient manner. A terrible thing, that, for life to be so cheap, to get to thinking of men like cattle, more use to you dead — but all the same that'd be your duty, wouldn't it?

It was no different, if you thought about it, than the doctors that cut Phoebe open. They were very sympathetic, yes, for what that's worth, but they couldn't afford to feel anything for themselves, any more than he could with a steer bleeding under his hands, any more than a soldier taking a bead on an enemy running across the desert like a jack. An execution wouldn't smell that much different from this room right now. He remembered the smell of the hospital in Tucson, a thin, cold, chemical stench that was nothing but a lie, meant to embalm the living. He'd rather the rich reek of the butcher room any day.

Cobb didn't say who'd pay for it, and it might be a challenge getting the other ranchers to cooperate. But he and Johnny could take care of the cutting up. Better wait and see what the letter says.

Probably if you got to know Villa — crude, of course, dirty, uneducated, but — he wasn't so much evil as just plain competent. Wally'd heard he was a teetotaler, which had to count for something; and according to the *Star* (if you could believe that progressive bunch), he didn't want the presidency on the grounds he was too ignorant! Supposedly when the Republic down there was in full swing, Villa wanted to disband the army and send the soldiers to work in colonies. Fields and industries. He'd trained as a leather worker, was what they said.

It *would* be something to find that out for yourself, shake history by the hand, maybe sit across the table from him, ask some questions about how he saw himself. You might even be able to do some good, let the man know that you'd used a weapon or two in your own way, and how an American saw the future of the Mexicans. After that you'd be able to say you'd got it straight from the old bandit himself — maybe that you'd influenced things a bit. You could tell your grandchildren.

Well, grandchild. Not Jasper, he wasn't any use, peaked and whiny, spit image of Lloyd at that age. But little Deborah walking on legs like stripling trunks — she'd fall and stand, and fall and stand, fall and pull herself up again. No stopping her when she got her mind set. And her chubby little flesh that solid!

40

No one knew him, and no one spoke of Lloyd. Sam settled into the shack and took up the same wandering existence he'd had in Mexico, except that now he wandered on the periphery of home. He skirted his old life, watching it through a tough, transparent membrane, wondering if there had always been such a barrier between himself and the town, himself and his self. It no longer surprised him that he wasn't recognized.

He stole eggs regularly from Frank Wheeler's ranch, and jerky from the older Wheeler's when he found it drying on the fence. He ate his father's vegetables but made a staple of mesquite again, and when he found a fallen saguaro he stripped the flesh from the rib to make a hook translucent as cartilage, with which he reached the ripe new season's fruit. The saguaro flesh slit lush, bloodier than any animal.

He slid through town, not taking anything from there, keeping to alleys and side spaces between the buildings. He walked for preference at just past sundown, which had been for months of walking the gentlest part of day, the worst heat past and the promise of sleep ahead. His feet were hard as horn.

Week after week, drawn to his father's store, he watched from across the street the shadows of his parents through the glass. He came to understand a few things about them: how little time they spent outdoors except to walk from home to store, to go to church, to sweep the walk; how the Hum house was placed, drab stucco like the rest of them, on the right side of the tracks but on the wrong side of the station, out of the way, unassertive and unassuming.

Twice more, even after he stole a plain blue work shirt from a clothesline, he heard someone say "Indian" behind his back, but no one spoke to him at all.

Nevertheless, he learned what there was to be learned: that there was a new bank, and a new copper strike at Douglas; that Frank Wheeler's daughter had been killed in an accident and, in the Mexican part of town, Tamayo Peralta crippled by scorpion bite; that the church fund was a little skimp this year, and the woman he had seen on Old Camp Road was doing up the mission into a house. In July and August they spoke of more remote events. The Constitutionalists marched into Mexico City and staged their coup, though Obregón and Carranza led them, and Villa stayed behind, in Torreón. There was war in Europe. Then the president's wife had died. The pope had died. A quarrel between Villa's man, the governor of Sonora, and Obregón's military commander in the same region threatened to split the new Mexican government. Of Lloyd, nothing; and little by little he accepted that Lloyd was dead.

Sometimes he went as far as the mission, although it was placed so it was hard to approach without being seen. Once he got near enough to watch Alma Timkin sitting on the patio with Mexican children cross-legged around her, extending almost to her arm-span the old map he recognized from school, browned and brittle on the folds. But a fat Mexican woman rushed at him, banging a skillet with a spoon.

That day when he got back to the shack he lay on his straw mat, remembering school. His education had been so dominated by the fear of recess time and the walk home that he rarely thought of class itself. Now he remembered Miss Timkin perched in her crackling blouse, stretching her mouth over her teeth to exaggerate a consonant; remembered that in arithmetic you added pecks but subtracted apples, and that when she taught the spelling of *Chiri-cahua* she pronounced it *Cheery*-caw-wa, with the accent on the *cheer*. He remembered Lloyd bent over his sums in the days when he had been Sam's enemy, and those days seemed bright and precious, something stolen from him. He remembered the map *Western States*, the blunt wedge of Mexico in the lower third that showed the distance he had come home.

Twice, too, he saw the woman from the quarry road. Once she was walking her horse in a listless way, from nowhere to nowhere south of the mission and east of town, the reins dragging in the dirt. The other time he watched from a ravine half a mile south where she worked with two Mexicans, her sleeves rolled to her shoulders, plunging her hands halfway to her elbows in a trough of mud, while the men looked ill at ease and made the best of it by laughing.

But not a word of Lloyd. Not one word, not a mention, even though one Sunday he went so far as to conceal himself under the trellised crawl space of the Methodist church, where he saw his mother's button shoes under a heavy calico skirt, and heard Walter Wheeler pronouncing not the name of Lloyd but of Villa, Villa, as if Sam were still in Utres or the flats of Querobabi.

"The two generals are ready to do anything they can to patch it up," Wheeler said, "but if they ride across Sonora they'll more'n likely get attacked by one side or the other."

Sam was cross-legged against a corner support of the church, diamond patterns of sunlight slanting through the trellis onto his knees.

"Pershing is seeing them off at El Paso personally — did you know Jack Pershing is the son of a plate-layer foreman on the railway? — and the president asked me through the Customs officer, who happens to be an old pardner of mine . . ."

The space was high enough to sit almost upright. He had a half ham he had taken from a smokehouse before dawn, and which he had gradually eaten to the bone. He could see the feet ranged around Wheeler while he held court. "Now, *that's* an honor, when the president of the Union, I don't care who he is, turns to the Baby State to maintain the stability and sovereignty of our southern border!" But Sam didn't fully understand until Wheeler said, "I know this isn't the set of folk you'd pick for your Friday night social, but these are troubled times. The SP has turned over the Hinman. Li Hum here will do us vegetables at cost."

Then he shrank back in the crawl space, remembering himself

curled up in the Gringo Chink, waiting, at bay in a cul-de-sac, cloth pressed against his head. The scar around his ear pulsed tenderly with the beat of his heart again.

The crowd gradually dispersed, and the street settled into Sunday silence. On the way back to the shack, Sam understood that his jellied gut had less to do with fear than with smoked ham. He was used to leaner fare. He shit his way from ravine to ravine, and when he got back he rolled himself sweating in his blanket. He shivered in the heat. Villa coming here! Villa pursuing him all the way into America, to Bowie, home, where he and Lloyd had disappeared from everybody's memory, and nobody knew he existed except the *jefe,* pledged to rub him out like a little spot of cooking fat on a boulder. Sam knew better, he knew a coincidence when he heard one, but his mind did little turns away from reason, without his consent.

Sleep came and went, with flash sweats and a turning void in his bowels, and one dream in which Lloyd lay in the mine bound in leather thong while Villa whetted the knife on a luminous stone. Sam felt no great faith in coincidence. He had, after all, traveled with Villa's scouts, he knew how much ground they would cover to find out something they wanted to know, how many ways they had of learning the whereabouts of whoever the enemy was. He checked over the shack. His belongings had not been touched under their careless cover. But he felt both stifled and exposed. He pulled himself up, basketed his compass and his blanket. His card and his ear he still kept in the pocket of his shabby bib with his stone. Climbing, he added a few lettuces to his basket, but he didn't dare eat them now; the fibrous stuff he thrived on was what he could least digest. He climbed to the quarry, where he and Lloyd, just before they left, had gone to collect from Frank Wheeler the seven hundred dollars that would make them rich in Mexico.

The site of the tent encampment was stubbled over, and a droning silence filled the pit. Bald hawks wheeled above the pyramid of marble. The pipe was dry. The sense of abandonment about the place was eerie — a page of an account book blew at him, a woman's hairpin crunched underfoot. He stood panting on the brow of the road in the dazzle of all that stone, and thought of nothing that the view recalled. He remembered his mother's hands through the glass of the storefront, his own face that had the transparency of the dead. Sam wedged himself in a cleft of the marble pile. The quarry was a ghost town, and he was its ghost. His head was light and full of Lloyd. He couldn't get Lloyd off the stool of the commissary where Frank handed over the cash in tired ten-dollar bills. He couldn't remove Lloyd from the mine in Chihuahua where they'd blasted away all that money, heaving pick for nothing, Lloyd's shoulders brown and muscled, hacking under Mexico.

The sun rattled on the pile and into the marble hole. Pain shot through his head, and his vision shifted. Then Sam saw how he and Lloyd had bit into a hillside to chew out the copper that would make pipes and roofs. They had not found enough copper to make anything, but they had gnawed a hole in the hillside all the same. Here at the quarry men had eaten more of a mountain, and left chunks of it spewed on the lip. He saw the mountains jagging down in *Western States,* the nation's spine crushed in the fists of our machines to squeeze the marrow out. And the woman down there with her crew, she was making dough out of earth, she was scooping into the valley floor to make mud pies. He saw we would eat the earth. We would end by eating up the earth, leaving behind the poison breath of our doing, doing.

When the vision passed, his head was clear. No *villistas* were coming after him from Mexico. It was an accident, providential only if he made it so. Twilight was turning the marble blue. He still sweated a little, and if he moved so much as an inch from the rock face he was swiftly chilled. But his head was clear, and he knew what he had to do. It wasn't revenge for his ear he wanted, a little piece of hide no better than cowhide or a sow's ear; it was revenge for Lloyd. Sam could face in the daylight on two feet the man who had kidnapped Lloyd in the hole-in-the-ground, middle-of-the-night darkness of the mine.

He couldn't exactly see it. When he tried, he failed absurdly. He saw Pancho Villa, dressed as Sam had seen him, in a brown tweed suit with yellow flecks, sitting on a wood crate on the Bowie railway tracks. Sam sent the silly image away, but it came back. He couldn't see himself in the picture at all; but no doubt many brave and violent things were done by people who didn't quite believe what they were doing. And he knew where to get a gun.

Tuesday morning he left before dawn and circled west of town to cross the tracks and so come in sight of his father's house from the Mexican side. The stand of tamarack and cottonwood was there by the ditch, the only tall trees in town, the cottonwoods hung with caterpillar cocoons and just finishing their annual seed shower. Sam waited in the thistley drift while across the tracks his father came out and hooked the shutters back, his mother shook a mat and threw a basin of water on the grass, and they walked tidily together around the station toward the store.

The Mexican street faced away from him, and no one was about but a couple of workers at the station, unconcerned with him. Houses in Bowie were left unlocked. He crossed the track and slipped around the back, opened the porch screen door, and was inside.

The house was small and in every way conventional, whitewashed walls, stuffed furniture, braided rugs. His bare feet scraped across the splintery grain of pine boards in the little hall. He brushed a hand across a mop top, upended, still damp, against the wall. He slipped forward into the living room and across to the desk that sat between the windows, edged his fingers under the rolltop, and lifted, fearing it would be locked and startled by the noisy ease with which it gave. He listened for a second. But who would hear? The left drawer underneath the pigeonholes, he remembered — and there it was; it hadn't been moved from here for a dozen years. He bounced the old Colt .44 wheel gun in his hand, the metal blued dull, the rubber grip chunky and rough. It was heavy, but not anything like impossible. He'd never been allowed to touch it, but he'd shot Lloyd's rabbit gun, and there was no reason he couldn't become proficient with a revolver.

The six-round chamber was empty, but he remembered where the bullets were, in a tea chest in the attic space above his parents' bedroom. He went down the hall, Apache-footed on the mulberry runner printed with some kind of back-East leaves. He hesitated — he intended not to be sidetracked by nostalgia — but quickly opened the doors to first his own and then his sister's room. The shutters were still closed here, making thin slats of light on the beds and floors. He was surprised at how small the rooms were, much smaller than the prospector's shack, dark and stuffy. The narrow

beds were made tight, foursquare, and all the evidence of occupation had been removed. The feeling that he didn't exist was on him
again, and for defense he pulled back into the lizard space.

There, a memory came to him, no more than three years old but
confusing, of a strange locking of wills in a house where no one
raised a voice or spoke of trouble, or ever challenged authority. His
sister Sarah, twelve years old then (it was because he hadn't heard
the name for so long that it struck him now what a yoked-together
name it was, Sarah Hum), had run away. She got no farther than
the far end of the rail yard before his father had caught her and
brought her back. Li Hum had untied and spilled a bundle of
clothes from a scarf (a small metal fish green with age and a
lacquered bowl tumbled out). Sarah stood defiant, saying something Sam didn't understand. He was wrapped up in brotherly
superiority at the moment; it made him feel strong and solid to
share his father's outrage. "Maybe you've made me *too* American,"
Sarah said, at which Li Hum had twisted a bar of lathery Lava soap
inside her mouth, even though Sarah was as tall as he, and even
though it was a punishment that had never been Li Hum's way.

Sam pulled the doors closed and turned into his parents' bedroom, where there was more sign of habitation, brushes and bottles, a plumped cushion in the chair, a china cat that his mother
used as a step to mount the four-poster bed. He dragged the chair
under the opening and hoisted the square cover back into the attic
space. The tea chest was there just on the edge, as if waiting for
him. He stopped to listen again, walked the chest forward between
his hands, and lifted it down to the floor. It smelled of ginger and
something more pungent, like sweet fish. There were blankets in it
that he laid aside, and under them a box familiar but not quite
remembered. All its surfaces bowed inward, covered with coarse
brown paper and Chinese characters. He lifted the lid. Inside there
was a bundle of red satin that when he lifted it fell open into a
kimono with a dragon embroidered on the back. The dragon was
bronze and black; it had glass eyes and metal spikes for fangs. An
arc of beaded fire breathed from its nostrils.

He fingered the satin, slightly stiff with the paradox of newness
and age. He remembered it. He remembered his mother, slender
then, thin as a girl, dancing in cloth slippers, moving her hands

with the delicacy of a glass chime in the wind. Meanwhile, she told him, as Sam supposed, the history of the world. How the earth was made, how the people came to it, how they learned to plant, and why they warred. He saw it in the shape of her voice. He was comforted by hearing stories he barely understood, and he was comforted now, because at some time just beyond the reach of memory, he had been comforted in that way.

The packet of bullets was in the bottom of the chest: *CF Cartridge 44-40 caliber No. 6R2409.* He wrapped them with the gun in the kimono. He hesitated, remembering how the old woman who gave him the stone had wanted a gift in return. He rooted in the bib of his overalls and lay flat in the box, in place of the kimono, the identity card that proved he was born a U.S. citizen. He put the box back in the chest and the blankets on top of the box; he put the chest in the attic space and replaced the cover and the chair. He slipped out the back door and carried his bundle west along the tracks until he was out of sight of town.

41

She'd sworn she wouldn't do this. She had sworn today like yesterday and the day before, each time she woke with the sickness swinging in her stomach, steadying herself with the heel of her hand on the corner of the leather trunk. She'd gone through the day saying *not tonight* — a little more pleased with herself hour by hour because she hadn't yet. She worked hard and ordered the men because if she showed herself to be in charge of them she could seem to be in charge of herself.

Then out of nowhere the thirst took hold of her like a fist. Water was no use to it. She longed for the first glass, knowing that by now even the first glass would plunge her into a petty self-obsession; there was no longer a lift of spirits before the sickness, the disgust. She had said *What makes me do this?* and done it. She had said *just one*. She had said *I don't care*.

She was so tired. It had been dark such a long time, and it would be dark such a long time yet before the drink would bring her to that dulled desperation she now knew as sleep. Her throat rasped, and when she stretched it, rubbing a hand against her neck, the skin itched and grated under her fingertips. There were purple bruises on her forearms, acquired in the building work she couldn't remember how, that wouldn't heal. Shadows shifted on the walls, over the furniture gathered hodgepodge in this one-roofed room. Outside the hole in the adobe, the drowned mud of last week's downpour had shriveled into cracks. On the sill sat a desiccated scorpion shell, a translucent, murdering curl.

She went back to bed and lay on the quilt in her clothes. She considered what had brought her here: her marriage vow, misguided duty, the good opinion of her peers. Well, but she had come to save Laurel's life, and look how successful that had been. Look how he had gotten rosier and rounder, his cells plumping in the sunshine. It was she who had consumption, the self-devouring disease, spiritual phthisis; she was a lunger of the soul. Others had felt this, she knew, or there would be no idea of damnation. Was it there, damnation, and this was the feeling of it? Or was this feeling there, and therefore we had made up damnation to account for it?

She raised her head to drink and lay it back down. She chewed a mouthful of dry tortilla and washed it horizontally with acid wine. Inside — throat, esophagus, stomach, bowels — a snake runs through the body; gullet squeezes, the muscles take. There are two truths: There is no God, and all we make is waste. She turned in her heavy body, rough against the sheets. Eaten from the inside. What's left is voluptuous husk.

It was like being twelve again, or as if she had never been anything but twelve, when the nuns made them wear long gabardine smocks to bed, into the bath, to conceal the temptation of their own bodies. The nuns loved *little* girls, stick figures with flat breasts and bendable bones. But under the heavy drag of gabardine she had had expanses of thigh, breasts plump as salted fruit. When she sneaked a glance at her body in Mama's mirror, what she felt was not temptation but irreversible shame. And it was the same now (as if she had never learned to harness those breasts to work for her under the griffin-and-angel lamps), awake in the dark, no longer believing but no less damned.

They could all pretend, the Mexicans grinning without mirth, the women in town giving each other so-proper tea, sanctimonious Maybeth in her tatted ruche, Alma Timkin acting as if poetry is some kind of reason to be alive. Or Amy Whitney Jackson like a candy apple, brittle, slippery sugar-dip of her, and Mama a balloon tied into little sausages of air, never lighting, bouncing over Daddy's temper, buoyant out of ignorance. *Life is just one vale of tears after another*, Mama used to say with a great air of complacency. When she said *It takes all kinds to make a world*, she meant *Isn't everybody odd but me.* When she said *Live and let live*, she meant *I can't deal with it.*

Eleanor clenched her fists to beat her mother off the bed, but it didn't matter who came into her head, if she thought of Laurel or Daddy she could rage the same. She'd prowl her memory or the day's events. She could rage at the doctors who diagnosed the consumption, Frank for seducing her, Maria for incipient desertion. She could blame her horse.

She rose, paced, poured brandy in her glass. The mountain out the arch was a giant rodent with complicated bones. There was a three-quarter moon, and the blackness of the desert shone. She did not want the brandy now, except for punishment. She knew that the moment she threw it down her throat the world would start to circle, the anger would disappear in hurtling fear.

Hawk note. Birds harsh in the dark. *There were four bird notes and then the booming down the mountain and then four more.* She drained the glass and drained the bottle into the glass. *Now more than ever seems it rich to die.* She drained the glass. *Not that I care.*

She leaned into the mirror that Gaspar had hung on the wall with an eightpenny nail, pressed her nose to the glass, and bared her teeth. She stared at the creases around her mouth, the flesh draped grainy on her bones, pores like rain pocks in the dust. She pulled at her hair, and a scant handful came away. She felt her balance going and time stretching itself taffy-thin, she rocked back onto her heels, suspended on the air buzzing and humming in front of her face.

And she was sick again.

She found the door of the hall and waded out unsteadily into the blackness. She knew she could be swallowed up, washed over by the surf of dark. She stepped carefully around the outside of the rebuilt patio wall, her slippered feet tricked by the uneven ground, feeling through their thin soles the plants she stepped on. She went to her knees, retched into a ravine, propped herself on the edge for a time that stretched and contracted and swelled again. She stared down the slope to the wet mess of gristle and slime she had spewed there, shoved herself up by her palms on the hardpan, and turned back in the direction of the patio, taking hold of a handful of powdery tamarack needles to steady herself. The bough bent, her body gave way beneath her, so she awkwardly and gently sat. She had tamarack in her hand and pulled it through her mouth to let the salt take out the bitter taste.

She didn't want to lie down, so she held her head against the bark of the tamarack and sat for a long time with the stars swinging. O'Joe came along the patio wall with his bottle of white mule. He was walking steadily but singing the dirge he always sang after drink and dark, a tuneless lament that came as much through his nose as his mouth. Once started, he would keep on until he collapsed. He collapsed briefly now, crawled for a ways, then pulled himself up against the wall to stand and drink.

She thought, "Hopeless drunk."

She had to close her eyes against an arc of pain that traced over her forehead. *Hope less. Less hope. Less happy, happy, hope.* When she opened them again O'Joe was trying to mount the patio wall. He lifted a boot against the adobe and let the sole scrape back to the ground. Angular, arthritic, he lifted the boot again, and it slid back down. There was a gate ten yards along, but he would mount the wall. He tried it again and again. She mimicked his effort in the muscles of her stomach as he pulled himself up, flung up a leg that grated against the adobe limp to the ground again.

Eventually he succeeded in launching his torso half over the wall, got a foot under his belly, crouched, and balanced for a second, as if he might succeed in standing. One boot wandered into the air, made a wavering circle; then it was almost as if he pitched himself outward to land back where he started.

"Hummun," he hummed despairingly.

The girl appeared, bulk flung into the thin air, then pitching toward the stone; and Eleanor was falling, too, again, beside the girl. Hopeless-falling-drunk. She could not live this over and over for a life of nights. She could not. She wanted to be done with it.

It isn't the girl I don't care about. It is myself.

This was true. She gave herself up to bleak relief. She remembered that she had decided — that night, that ball, that millennium ago in the candlelight — not to come to Arizona. That moment had appeared with the same simplicity, the same force, but she had let herself get muddled with trivia, duty, affections; and look what those had gotten her. When you see deliverance, it's pointless to deny it. *I don't care about myself.*

She started to crawl but got caught in the heavy drag of her skirt, the hardpan clawing at her knees; so she reached between her legs and pulled the hem up to tuck it in her waist. O'Joe was propped now, singing to himself. She hand-over-handed herself away from him along the patio wall to where Quarter was tethered at an olive tree. There was no chance she could lift the saddle, but she could haul herself into the crotch of the tree, and after several false tries, which Quarter endured, she managed to get astride. Face to hide, one fist in the mane and the other arm gripping Quarter's neck, she held the reins in the fist but used her whole body to twist direction into the horse as she kicked her slipper heels into the flanks.

They took off across the plain toward the quarry road in the hot wind and bright dark. The moonlight clicked over the tough little bushes and pointed grass. The light made cobwebbed pools of every depression in the ground, moon craters, miniature mountains seen from height. The earth was rolling on its axis, the wind threaded her sockets and streamed between her brain and skull. She couldn't lift herself from the horse's neck, but Quarter ran as if she knew where she was going, straight across the valley floor. Under Eleanor's eyes the hooves met and parted, met and parted. The blur churned into vertigo. She closed her eyes and gritted her face into the mane, concentrated on the coarse hair in her fist, the flanks rubbing her raw calves and thighs.

And slept, if that was sleep. In it she hung by her fingertips from the bone sockets of her own skull, she pitched out on the humming dark and rode at the apex of imminent fall, conscious of nothing but sickness and a hum.

When they began to lift on the mountain road there came a thin thunderclap that startled her alert; it ricocheted from the mountaintop like a tin echo of that other booming. She waited for the four bird notes, but they didn't come. She became conscious of the massive neck muscles straining under her cheek. She urged Quarter up the trail, rattling over the bridges and past the prospector's shack. There was a layer of panic in her stomach because she was beginning to connect with things again and she hadn't brought anything to drink. She gulped the air and tongued the parched membrane on the inside of her cheeks. Her thirst was fierce.

When they reached the split canyon she slowed to a walk and pushed herself away from the horse's neck, spine stiff, joints aching. She had a hair in her mouth, but the hand in the mane would not unclench to take it out. She was stopped at the beginning of the bend by an unwillingness to take Quarter within sight of the quarry. Mouth open, she sucked the air into her thirst and slid from the horse, supporting her weight on the reins close under its chin. She pulled at her skirt hem and let it fall. She tied the reins to the water pipe and lay her head against Quarter's lathered neck. She couldn't say anything she meant. "Horse," she said. The horse shook its great face. She felt for balance in the thin soles and rounded the bend into the dazzle of moonlit stone.

The Angel of Death was dancing on the rim. He lifted his arms, and his red wings opened into square, shining falls. The sky above him was as black as fur, the pyramid and the pit ghost-blue. A dragon undulated on his back as he drew his hands together and aimed the dull glimmer of the pistol into the pit. The crack of the shot bounced and echoed, thin, like a rock skipped on a pond.

It was like a dream not because it was so strange but because it was so acceptable, not what you had in mind but, yes, there; yes, that. When the ricochet subsided he heard her on the shale. He turned and aimed the pistol at her in both hands. Under the robe he wore a pair of overalls shabby at the knees.

"You see me now!" he said. His voice was belligerent and thin. She agreed that she did. "You didn't see me the other time."

This was also true. The yellow of the girl's blouse above the doughty little horse, the nakedness of her own thigh, the lace catching on the heel of her shoe. Those were the things that had occupied her the other time, though, of course, he had been there. It made the most elemental sort of sense.

He was almost as she had pictured him, but oddly small. He had a face constructed like a drum, parchmenty hide shrunk taut over a framework of bone. His wild hair was bound with a piece of thong, and the thin skin of his face gathered into a hole where his ear should have been. The face had the beauty of a wind-tortured buttetop tree. She didn't know how to greet him, but the dread was gone. He wound the gun in his two fists, as if it were too heavy for him.

She was tired. She wanted to sit down, but she thought it would not be right. He seemed to be expecting her to say something more and she understood that this was a test, only she didn't know what the thing was that she should say.

"You'll have to tell me what to do," she said.

"What?"

"I don't know what to do. You'll have to tell me."

She backed into a chunk of marble higher than her head and let herself slide down against it, feeling the roughness of the stone through her blouse scratching her back deliciously. She held her bent knees together and her slippers together, flat, apologetic for the undignified sitting down.

The angel lowered the gun and stood looking at her. He said nothing for so long that she dropped her eyes nervously among the stones. Over there was where the boy Jasper stood theatening to run down the slope. There were the ashes of the fire. There Frank slit the belly fur and peeled the rabbit skin inside out, like a glove from a hand.

"I know who you are!" the angel said.

She nodded. There was the three-sided shed. The stone where the blanket lay and where she took her hairpins out.

"You're building the house out of the old mission."

And there the rim. Where Digger tried to get his balance, his front hooves fighting backward while his haunches buckled under and her feet slipped free. The girl ascended her arc. Eleanor reached for her, caught her in midair. Jessie. Folded Jessie light as a kitten against her neck.

"Are you all right?"

She didn't know. The unmistakable kindness of his tone unnerved her, and behind her dry mouth the tears began to well. "I'm very thirsty."

He set down the pistol and brought her a waterskin, upended it next to her face until she took hold of it. The horsehair rubbed against her raw cheek oily and animal; she had expected bitterness, but the thin stream flooded her mouth with the clean taste of rock.

"That's it," he said. She didn't understand what he intended, but it seeped into her consciousness, the possibility that she was being forgiven. Was this how forgiveness would taste? The water flushed upward from her throat to her eyes, spilled back onto her hands. The sweat flowed down her back. She shivered.

The angel hunkered in front of her, knees through his frayed overalls. "It's only a little water," he said. "The horse of the sky is sneezing, the monkey-man is making rain." She was still drinking, the water still flushing out of her eyes. "It will be good for the little lettuces, it will make the melons grow."

The nonsense made her choke, but when she laughed, so did he. His laugh was febrile, feral.

"That's what my mother used to tell me when I cried. Shall I keep on talking to you?"

She nodded. She thought he was not well, either. He was feverish and nervous and much too thin.

"What shall I say? What shall Sam say for the lady? It's cold on the mountain in the middle of the night. Why did you come here?"

She didn't know the answer, or not in a way that would make sense in words; or she had expected him to know.

"You come here sometimes," he explained.

She nodded.

"When you want to get away from the valley, get up high."

She nodded. She hadn't quite relinquished the notion that he could turn on her. He seemed solid — thin, but of human substance, human skin. The wings were sleeves. She couldn't say anything she meant. She said, "Do you live here?"

He rocked back from his squat and sat with the robe sagging open, bunched up around his bare feet, the overlong toenails. He considered the question as if it were difficult.

"Is this your home, I mean?"

He deprecated himself in answer. He rolled his shoulders shruggingly inside his sleeves, he ducked his head at an angle, earless side uppermost. She thought he was more tired than she, more ill than she.

"I wouldn't say I have a home. I grew up not far from here, but I went away and I can't go back."

"I know."

"You understand that?"

"Nothing is easier to understand than that." She settled against the rock, and he hunched over his crossed legs. His almond eyes swiveled as if their sockets were some sort of clever setting for polished agate.

"I don't belong anywhere I am. My father said I'm American, but the Americans called me names; there was only one that called me Sam. Pancho Villa won't have me for Mexican."

"Who are you?"

A long silence not quite silent, a motor turning in his throat and failing to catch. She thought of O'Joe's labored speech.

"When I was little and it used to storm, my mother told me old stories, but she was afraid herself because my father didn't want me to hear anything Chinese." He extended a sleeve to show the robe, distended his nostrils, and breathed dragon fire. "She had to take it out carefully because my father didn't want me seeing Chinese things." His voice was rusty with disuse, staccato-paced. He giggled, a thin bray. "My father made the mountains, and he made the mountains fat with melon, but my mother had to hide her dragon in the dark, dark bottom of an old tea chest." His lashes made an extra shadow to his sockets when he lowered his eyes. His belly was wafer thin below the ridge of ribs. He was, she supposed, crazy, but she couldn't fear it, since she had submitted when she thought he meant her harm.

"I traveled a long time, up and down. It was in Mexico, but it could have been anywhere."

She put her hands together fingertip to fingertip. "Limbo," she said.

"Someone harmed me. They killed someone I loved."

She couldn't respond to this, opened her hands, and sat looking at the blue moonlight on her palms. He took her silence as admonition, maybe, took a tear-shaped stone out of his overalls, and scratched a line in the thin crust of dirt over the stone with it — an arc, she thought, a lift and fall.

"In Mexico I thought I was a packmule or a goat, but I couldn't help learning their language. I met a dragon of my own in the desert, though. Instead of fire in its nose it had poison in its tongue. . . ."

He drew mechanically in the dirt; the curve turned into a sagging dragon, snout and tail turned down. *"Caltetepon."* He dragged the stone across it to rub it out. She would have liked to offer him something practical, a meal, a roofed place to sleep, but his body curved in on itself with distress beyond such homely remedies. He looked up at her, a look of serene and hopeless sweetness.

"Maybe I turned into the lizard the first time they brought me to the shack." He rocked sideways on his haunches, the silk sagged, he caught a tired breath, and when he let it go, the skin over his ribs sank between them like a leaf between its veins. The Angel of Death was a skinny boy. "It wasn't what I would have chosen. I wanted something else. I don't know what. But I have to do this now. I don't have any choice."

When the sun came up, he was asleep. Dawn happened behind her back and she watched it overtake them, the stones, the pyramid, the pit. It was an unspectacular morning, a lighter gray behind her head, a milky paling of the marble, a few clumps of grass on the silvering rim. The light poured into the quarry. The quiet was fuller than a sound. There was still a grainy sensation between her skin and skull, but she had a peaceful sense of her insignificance. She carried Jessie folded against her throat, across her heart; not as a millstone or an albatross, but weightless, an accepted ghost. She knew she could sit as she was, spent, doing nothing, flowing forward with the paling of morning over the rim. She understood herself to be no more important than the grass and the stone. She had not learned this, but she knew it: This is what is meant by, and is all that is meant by, *grace*.

42

THE JOISTS WERE LASHED in place and tar-papered over, the tower reconstructed with its arches east and west. Two more men came from Bowie and two from Lordsburg to help with the laying of the tiles. One brought his family. Alejandro had gone to Safford and returned with a curly, coltish wife named Rosaria. On weekends handsome young Maximo de la Luna brought Maria's family out on a mulecart and spent a day clambering over the rafters in feats of acrobatic engineering. The central hall was ridged, but the two restored transepts and all the living quarters — Maria called them *cottages* — were to have flat roofs supported by peeled logs that protruded the pattern of their rings. The little triptych was parked on an adobe dais in the west wing, from which the *nouveau* Virgin cast her gaze on kneelers. Father Vicente had agreed to come from Bowie every two weeks to hear confessions, and Carmen set out a tray to hold his bloody wages.

To what she called *all intents and purposes* Alma lived at the mission now, keeping two changes of clothes in the guest room, using as her excuse that every afternoon she herded the younger children into the patio and taught them reading, history, and sums. She released them at just the hour of the day that was most difficult for Eleanor, when work stopped, and the only thing to do was walk away from the men and their white mule.

Then Alma and Eleanor would prowl the desert from five to suppertime, south toward one mountain or east to another, with some yellow stone for a goal or a wandering ravine as a substitute for a direction. Eleanor talked equally at random.

"I'd fill my glass not quite to the top because then I could tell myself it hadn't ever really been a glassful. I'd top it up so I couldn't count how many I'd had. I never let it get empty, and if I saw it was going to be empty in a few swallows, I'd get a little panicky feeling in the center of my stomach. I used to watch Laurel finish his and set it down, all finished, and I thought, *he's mad.*"

Alma laughed, shook her head ruefully. She pulled out treats from the Hum store, pink wintergreens and pale malted drops, little sour balls or licorice laces. Through the evening after supper she would parcel out the candy, commanding out of St. Augustine: "Become what you eat!"

"The funny thing is that I always thought I was sacrificing myself for other people. I was such a *good* girl. When my father was angry I used to shine his boots. Then I was a martyr when he didn't notice! But how could he notice? He had plenty of people to shine his shoes."

If Eleanor had never considered Alma her equal, now the balance was redressed. For the moment only Alma's matter-of-fact attention, mild eyes under the auburn crown, signaled to Eleanor that she had worth. Away from that prop she was edgy, tentative, and tired. Sleep had been a product of alcohol, and she'd lost the knack of any other sort. After dark she would pace, read, talk, doze for a few minutes, and start up again.

"Well," said Alma, "nobody ever died of lack of sleep," and seemed to be willing to back up this dubious opinion by forgoing her own. Felix had thought of stringing a hammock between two of the new roof supports, and Eleanor would swing there, turning a needle in a pillow cover or a tablecloth, while Alma read by kerosene light. Or Maria sat with them and they took turns at *Nicholas Nickleby* ("...*a melancholy little plot of ground behind them, usually fenced in by four high whitewashed walls and frowned on by stacks of chimneys...*")

After midnight, when Maria had gone to bed, Eleanor would begin again, out of the long-ago-learned impulse to confession, made safe to talk by Alma's unremarking interest.

"I think I've always been a liar. I didn't know it. I remember once we had a young woman in service, very black, with a *proud,* high figure. I used to flounce around her to impress her; she had that effect on me. One day I told her I'd had a dream that I had a magic wand and that I'd gone through the house touching all the servants with it. I told her she had blond curls and a princess's dress. She turned around and gave me a look to strangle me. She said, 'Missy, you don't know *nothing.*' "

Alma's laugh fluted over her needlework.

"I was humiliated. If I'd been able to think up any way to get her in trouble, I surely would."

But Alma had also learned in the schoolroom when encouragement should give way to an agenda. One day she conceived the project of teaching Eleanor Spanish while she improved her own. She sought Maria's aid on the principle of tit for tat, but Maria turned out to be contemptuous toward the idea, and it was little Polo Acosta who became a gracious tutor — patient with Alma's stilted idioms, forbearing with Eleanor's ignorance, joyful when either of them got it right.

"*Tito, Tito, con su capito, subio al cielo y pego un grito,*" he would chant seriously, his moon face intense. "What is this riddle, Miss Alma?" Or, "No, Miss Eleanor, put your tongue like this: *co-rrr-rida.* Okay! *Supremo.*"

Apart from Polo and Maria, the miniature city went about its life without much reference to Eleanor. Carmen scolded; the men shied away or dealt with her in a careful, false good humor. Charging over the roof they were like a little army, their women camp followers dealing with meals and laundry, the mundane necessities of conquest. Eleanor, who had supposed she was their general, realized that in fact she was an irritant — the more irritating because they depended on her for money.

A year ago she had been a girl in a blue dress at a party. Now she was responsible for a bizarre vast space, roofed over a dirt floor. She had blundered into Laurel's life and the Wheelers', and her blundering had left chaos that, if she looked at it too closely, would produce immediate thirst. She had made herself recklessly responsible for the livelihood of twenty people who didn't know that her money was gone, that in fact they were eating this week on credit at Hum's. Her year's allowance due next month would last, with care, till Christmas; with frugality, to the first of February. She had no idea what they, or she, would live on after that.

It was not a question of the distance she had come, but of crucial disjunction. Even the most rudimentary things must be learned over, as a one-armed man must learn to tie his shoes. She must learn how to lie down when she was tired and get up when she was rested. She must learn to eat for fuel, to ask for what she wanted, to walk away from what hurt her, to lean on an unjudging friend.

She tried to apologize to Gabrielo. "I ordered you around because I was afraid you'd think me silly and weak if I didn't. I had no right. I'm sorry."

Gabrielo said "Ough," and made a gesture in front of his neck like fingers on a keyboard, to show that he didn't have any idea what she was talking about and would rather she didn't.

Yet there were rewards in her anachronistic innocence. Her eyes had been opened in a literal way. There had always been some cloud between her and the world, an optic failure or a failure of attention. Now it was gone. Sometimes simple "hunger" — meaning the mere readiness for a meal — in conjunction with the smell of hot onions and cheese would engorge her throat with thanks. Sometimes she was intensely aware of seeing something, as she had not been able to see since childhood — such as the feathers of the cocks, which lay one over the other like scales, tipped in black and bronze, each hair of each feather iridescent on its nether side, much more a miracle than the angel in his unfolding of chinoiserie. She called the chickens to her with cornmeal, watching their pompous dance.

And thought about the angel, Sam. She would like to have gone back up to the quarry and brought him home, but this notion had the quality of the memory itself, a luminous unlikelihood. Although she had done so, she did not believe herself capable of riding all that way, did not see how she had made it to the quarry bareback in the dark, or back the next day in morning sun. Since she left Laurel she hadn't gone as far as Bowie. Alma, who organized the shopping, said "the Indian" was no longer seen in town, and when Eleanor protested that she thought he was Chinese, or part Chinese, Alma said that's as may be, he didn't look it, a mixed breed of some sort, anyway. Sometimes Eleanor fantasized that he would suddenly appear, come to teach them how he lived off the land, while they taught him to let go of his solitude and whatever his grief might be. But she kept this daydream to herself, thinking she had arranged lives enough for this year.

All but one. The morning they tarpapered her bedroom ceiling, she came out into the patio, missing the fronds especially now before the cooling layer of mud was laid. It was dead calm and August-hot. They had no thermometer, but Alma, taking off for town, had guessed a hundred and one. The famous *dry* heat seemed to swell lungs like baking bread. O'Joe sat in the patio with an empty mason jar, and Eleanor asked him if he would walk with her. They wandered in the directionless direction she and Alma had made their habit, and she asked him where he had been born.

"Yuma," he said doubtfully. "Thereabouts."

"And where did your folks come from?"

He nodded over this question, as if to affirm that he recognized its meaning. "My ma, she died, and my Aunt Dor-ty raised me."

"Dorothy?"

"Yeah, Aunt Doro-thy. She dished for the railroad." A hurt passed over his face, an action of the muscles between his mouth and eyes, and then the mouth set in anger. He trudged beside her for a while, chewing over words that did not come out. He squinted at the Chiricahuas. "Aunt Dorty, she whup me 'cause I couldn't talk."

"I'm sorry."

Eleanor remembered that when she was angry as a child, her best revenge was always self-punishment. She would imagine holding her breath until she died, and then see her parents weeping over her poor little limp corpse, she a martyred soul looking down from heaven, Saint Revenge.

It seemed safe to ask, "Was Aunt Dorothy your mother's sister?"

O'Joe carried this question across a gully and over a crest of sand. "I don't remember."

"Where was that?"

"That was in a town, Yuma, Nogales, I don't remember."

"You'll remember more tomorrow."

After that they walked every day together, and twice more O'Joe was drunk when they walked, and then twice he was not. When

Carmen Acosta made sarcastic reference to the lovers' *paseo,* Maria turned on her with amazing vehemence.

"Dimwit gossip! It's not her fault if you have a dirty mind."

"Well, if the *señora* is so pure, is it nice to an old man to make him be in love?"

"He hasn't got anything better to do, has he?" Maria snapped.

Maria herself grew restive in direct proportion to Eleanor's growing stronger. It seemed that she ceased to sleep as soon as Eleanor began to sleep. When Maximo de la Luna was nearby she was shrill with her siblings and disdainful of her mother. Alma diagnosed romance, but Eleanor saw some other misery altogether.

Maria came to them under the box elders one afternoon, where Eleanor was coaxing the dominickers down out of the trees with a scatter of meal, making throaty, clucking sounds.

"We can do honey and chickens," she was saying. "Did you know a rooster will fetch two dollars and fifty cents in Tucson?"

"It's not a lot," Alma pointed out.

"No."

Maria came from the patio. She had that pent mood on her, her hair skinned back from her face and caught tight into a ribbon wrapping like a punishment to her head. There was guitar music coming from the far side of the little houses. She came hot-eyed and fisted, clumps of skirt in her hand and her toes grabbing at the soles of her sandals. "I have to *go.* You're all right but I'm not, I can't stay here and listen to my mother moan, I can't raise Ramón and Azul for her" — looking at the ground in every direction with her bruised-plum eyes — "*I can't. . . .*"

"Your mother can raise them, all right," said Eleanor. Soledad Iglesias had stabilized since Maria came to the mission, had begun doing laundry again both for money and for her own household, and Maria knew perfectly well that they knew this.

"Maximo wants to marry you," Alma guessed.

"Marry! What is marry? My friend Cara Pérez only wanted to marry rich, a man with fences and a cow, and have a lot of *niños.* Now look at her! Her belly swells like a caterpillar sack, and her mouth is full of sap. But there is no husband and no cow. Nobody comes forward to say how she should live. She looks at me from a height as if a swollen woman knows a great secret. I know a great secret! There are fifty women already squabbling for twenty jobs, and babies thinner than they ought to be; too many great *braceros* disappeared into Globe or Douglas, where they only have to pay for a woman one time."

Alma protested. "But Maximo wants to marry you."

"Wants, wants. How does Maximo mean to pay for what he wants?"

"What do you want, Maria?" Eleanor asked.

The girl drew in the dirt with her foot, drew breath. Her energy settled and centered in her; she lifted her face on the sleek stalk of her neck. "In California I will be *criada* to a *hacendado* and save my money. I will live in my own house that no man has paid for. I will wear taffeta and be a famous *doña* with dollars in the bank."

"It's dangerous to go off on your own, a girl like you, and start your life all over," Alma said. They both looked at her. "It was quite different with me!"

Eleanor tore a corner out of Alma's notebook and wrote the address of Amy Whitney Jackson, San Diego, on a scrap of classroom rule. She handed the paper to Maria, who took hold of it carefully and read it aloud. She pronounced "California" as an Anglo-Saxon word: Calla-fornya. She held the scrap flat on her palm, gingerly trapping it with her thumb, as if it were either fragile or toxic — Alma said later she thought Eleanor had called her bluff, all right! — then fell on Eleanor's neck and kissed her, sobbing.

Maria rushed away to tell Maximo, to tell Soledad, Ramón, Azul, to pack; and Eleanor went back to letting the meal sift through her hand, overfeeding the chickens, inventing what she might do next. The long, hot afternoon stretched in every direction from the center of the bowl. Alma stuck to her, chattering.

"School will be starting in less than a month now, isn't that the limit? Where does it fly? Did I tell you what little Joey Eickenberry said last autumn? He said, 'How come the weeks are flying around so fast?' "

Eleanor nodded, picked a feather from her hem.

"Well, I had a thought the other day that doesn't seem to leave my mind," Alma said.

"Yes."

"I don't know what's made me such an old maid, I swear, twelve years in that little hole behind the barber shop. But it does mean I have a bit of money squirreled away, and you have a crew of men all skilled and trained, and Wally Wheeler would surely let me homestead a parcel of his land if he let you. I was thinking of that turn by the sandstone where the clump of palo verde is? Do you know the one I mean? That's about halfway between here and Bowie, if I'm going to keep both classrooms going. I tell you, I saw a place in Tucson with a sort of walled garden back of a grille. Pretty, my! Do you think you could set yourself to drawing something up like that?"

Maria went. Soledad Iglesias and the two children installed themselves in her bungalow. Maximo de la Luna returned to Bowie to tend his heart. Alma went out to inspect the land by the palo verde clump, and Eleanor got her easel out again.

Two days later, when Alma was off in the wagon with O'Joe, Eleanor set about changing the levels in the bee boxes, a task she could now do hatless, with ordinary cotton gloves. She was intent on the hexagons of viscous juice between her hands, the yellow swarms — seeing the bees as so many little units of money (not enough) — so she heard nothing except the flat clack of the tiles against each other, the occasional shouts of the men overhead, until behind her someone asked, "Excuse me, *señora,* do you speak English?"

When she turned, there appeared for a moment a strange, plumpish woman sitting above her on a horse, with her hair haloed in the afternoon sun; but almost immediately this apparition took the form of Mary Doreen Wheeler.

"Oh! I'm so sorry!" Mary Doreen said with a gasp. "Your back was to me, your hair is so dark, I didn't expect to see you here, the light's peculiar" (though it was behind her own head), stuttering so that finally Eleanor shrugged her way into the less awkward of two spaces.

"I didn't recognize you, either. I wouldn't expect you to be on a horse."

"Well, it seemed it was time to learn. It was needed — I've taken over riding fences."

Mary Doreen dismounted and they loosed Sally into the new corral, Eleanor holding the gate and Mary Doreen patting the mare on the rump flat-handed in a display of nonchalance.

The horses had been corralled together from December to April, but hadn't seen each other since the spring (since, precisely, the hour of Digger's death — Eleanor pulled the gate to; that is not the way horses think). Sally had always been the dominant mare and now, still saddled, she lay her ears back and, weaving her head, feinted toward the paler Quarter, who fell away to the side, nodded, and stood with her face pendant. Sally circled, carrying her saddle as an ornament; she lay her ears back, nosed toward Quarter's shoulder but shied short of it, and Quarter made way again. The two women stood while the ritual repeated itself, watching with polite intentness, as if this spectacle had been the purpose of Mary Doreen's visit.

"I've meant to call before . . ."

"I know there's nothing I can . . ."

". . . but there's been so much. I daresay you've heard about . . ."

". . . you feel so . . ."

". . . the banquet for the Mexicans."

". . . completely helpless."

"And Wally wanted to know if — "

"No. What?" They stopped. Eleanor took off her gloves and smoothed them over the top rail, like small laundry laid out to dry.

"I'm so sorry I haven't been before," Mary Doreen began again. "I intended to come and see you ever since I heard you were ill, but what with one thing and another, I've had to keep the ranch pretty much myself, and Deborah's at that stage she's into everything. . . ."

One thing and another continued to fall from her mouth. From the fervor with which she excused herself for not coming sooner, Eleanor saw with what ambivalence she had come at all.

The horses, who had no need either to remember or to avoid, quieted, nodding next to each other without touch. "I'm very sorry about your daughter," Eleanor said, and the blood of an ordinary flush mounted from her neck to the crown of her head. She felt as if she had been deeply concentrating on a stereoscope of some exotic scene, where dimension had otherworldly depth, and had suddenly now been asked to get up and address herself to a real-world task. She was somewhat afraid of it, afraid she had forgotten the counters and turns of ordinary middle-class concourse. She was thirsty, and the thirst reminded her of the hardest lesson there is to learn about the past: It can't be changed. Let go. Let go.

"Come, let me show you the house. I'll ask Soledad to get us something cool to drink."

They entered through the refurbished doors, the great hinges scraped back to iron and fastened into planed trunks of fir, under the balcony that lifted its bent staircase into the new tower, under the tesselation of rafters and the tarred, not yet plastered spaces of the high ceiling. She and the crew had been so intent on details, mixing the bricks with such a leaven of cross-purposes, a Babel of people to have produced anything at all, she had lost sight of the house itself. Seeing it with Mary Doreen, Eleanor felt its beauty as a shock, the cathedral height of a domestic space, light caught in its arched windows, a happy blasphemy. Her spirits lifted. Mary Doreen stood between the tapestry sofas, on the plank construction that still kept the carpet off the dirt. She wound her head, peering at the nave ceiling, saying only, "My!" No doubt she would describe it in town as outlandish, mad. Dwarfed in the middle of the hall, she reached into her basket and pulled out a jar of strawberry jam.

"It's early for jam, but Sacramento had an early spring. . . ." She set it on the coffee table, where the afternoon sun scattered its clear red. Soledad brought sun-brewed tea and they sat with matching postures, knees together and two hands each on their glasses. Mary Doreen held her stout shoes toes together, heels off the floor. She had put on weight these past months; you could see the matron about to bloom in her.

"I've come to ask if you would help serve," she said, and explained Bowie's charge to feed the generals and their troops. "It's a *pacifying mission*," she said with the careful enunciation that signaled she was quoting her father-in-law. "And it offers us a chance to *promote international goodwill*. Mr. Wheeler specially wanted you to be a part of it, because you know so much more than we do about that kind of thing."

"I'm not sure I have any special skills."

"Oh, you think that, but you've set table for military folks before, haven't you? And entertained dignitaries, like they do back East."

Eleanor thought of Admiral Dinsmore one-eyed in his monocle, the buttoned-up, braid-wrapped Annapolis seamen, the ribboned girls.

"Please say yes. Wally will be very disappointed if you and Alma aren't involved. And bring what tableware you think would do us proud."

Eleanor thought that if a lace cloth and a tureen were the price of readmittance to Bowie society, it was cheap enough. "I'm pleased you ask me," she said.

"Well, then." Mary Doreen pulled a laced shoe back under her skirt, heels lifted; she retreated into the details. "There'll be Mexicans to fetch the food in from the kitchen, we'll just do the serving. . . ." There was nothing else to talk about — they would never have a great deal of conversation for each other, these two — but they kept at it because Mary Doreen had come a long way for a glass of cold tea, and because it had to be gotten through, like a first fording or a first battle or a first night sleeping on the ground.

"It will be strange for me to go back into town," Eleanor admitted. "You know I haven't been there for some time."

"Oh, my." Mary Doreen brightened. "You'll hardly recognize the place. We've got three new families for the railroad since the Fourth of July — you know they're expanding the station on account of the new line down from Tucson to Phelps Dodge? And there's a rival dry goods opening up, which has Dan Riggs's nose out of joint! Second Street has four new houses broke ground this month. And there's talk of the Baptists getting their own church. Before we know it they'll be wanting to put streets through the ranch, I said to Frank. . . ."

There was a pause in which the name hung as if inflated by the peak Fahrenheit of afternoon, with more buoyancy than it could possibly maintain. Eleanor sipped at her tea and thought of the splintered ranch house floor, scrubbed to raw, prideful cleanliness, the glass from which she had drunk water sink-pumped by Frank's hand when she had not yet begun to think his hand was a joy and had not yet begun to know what a joy pumped water was.

"How is Frank?" she asked in a tone that was maybe a shade too stern, too disinterested to refer to a man who had undergone a grief.

"He's well. He's better. It's been . . ." Mary Doreen lifted her shoulders and pressed her hands together back to back. The gesture was oddly girlish, shy and secure at the same time. "He's changed, some," she confided. She twisted her hands in her lap, eyes on them and then up, off to the arches, back down. "The way he was raised, he was picked for his papa's boy. I think Wally wanted him hard, a bit. I've been married to him more than a dozen years and, you know, there's some things . . . I'd give all that up. But he's improved, you might say. I guess that's a terrible thing to say. But he softened some. I guess you don't go through that without softening some."

She said this although she herself had palpably toughened.

"Sometimes when people go through a terrible thing together, it makes them stronger in their love." Eleanor offered this convention fervently, as a sacred object, a trinket on the altar.

"Well," said Mary Doreen, "that's so."

The conversation lulled again.

"You haven't got your floor," Mary Doreen observed.

"No. And we're not likely to very soon. Maybe there never was one because the Franciscan fathers were waiting to get marble down out of the Chiricahuas. If it's been waiting three hundred years, we may have to wait a little longer."

"It's a pity, though." Mary Doreen hesitated, plunged. "You know!" She lifted her bosom on a breath, lifted her hand above her lap, the very bright look of someone who has a winning idea if only you have the wit to see it. "*You* could advance the money to get the quarry started, and have your floor, and the marble company could pay you back with interest once it's going. Frank says he could do it for five thousand dollars. . . ."

"I haven't anywhere near that much."

"Oh!" It had clearly never occurred to her that there was a limit to what Eleanor might have. "Oh, well."

Eleanor set down her glass and smoothed her twill skirt over her lap. "Mr. Poindexter thinks that reopening the quarry isn't a good idea," she said gently, noticing that now all the names had been said, all of them but Maria's. "He thinks the cost of transport will always be more than the profit and that Frank will just go broke."

"Oh, yes." Mary Doreen set her heavy heels gently on the floor and shifted forward just far enough to plant her weight on them. "I know." She tucked her chin into her neck with an enigmatic smile, and Eleanor was abashed to understand that "I know" meant "I think so, too."

43

THE EL PASO CUSTOMS shed was long and low and painted a scrofulous color, breeding midges, not a lovely place to sit through dawn in a sticky suit while two U.S. Army regulars slit your upholstery. Lloyd tried to keep upright on the iron-hard bench, but he'd been driving all night and most of yesterday up from Ciudad Camargo, and every time he let his attention wander, his spine wilted like a cut posy.

"You won't find anything but horsehair," he said, not for the first time.

"W-we'll see about that!"

The Customs man was no older than Lloyd, and watery-eyed, and chinless in the bargain. But his notion was that Lloyd had smuggled that Packard into Mexico, and he worried this notion like a puppy with a shoe. He tongued it and he hung on. He wouldn't have any other notion.

"Wh-ere's your clearance stamp is what I'd like to know. You should've had a permit from San Jacinto Plaza."

"Look, I've got this sales receipt and I'm an American citizen. What's it to you if I took my car into Mexico?"

"It's nothing to me, but I'd feel a whole bunch better if you'd gotten a clearance stamp."

"Mister, I didn't come a thousand miles of Mexico to make you feel better."

The eyelashes of the chinless kid whirred. He was important to himself because he'd called out the army. He sat behind a deal table just far enough away that it didn't offer Lloyd anyplace to hide his cream silk baggy knees.

"Well — but understand there's plenty of people'd like to see Villa got rid of. It's our dooty."

The other man, the aide-de-camp who had come down from Fort Bliss with his two flunkies in tow, paced crisply in from the door to the table and back again, a smart turn at each end, and the ghost of a Prussian heel click.

"I have to deliver this car to General Villa." Lloyd told that one dully. He was a little punchy with lack of sleep, and even to his own ears this sounded like a lie. The aide-de-camp, Lieutenant somebody, had the most expressionless face Lloyd had ever seen on a primate. Back like a branding iron for straightness, deep lines around his mouth like double brackets, and if you punched his face into cowhide it'd probably sear it.

"You *have* to squat your flitch of a smoked ass there and tell me what you're running!" screamed the lieutenant.

"I'm not running anything but the car. I told you —"

"Tell me again! How long you claim to have been chasing Villa in this wreck?"

Ten weeks? Twelve? Lloyd wasn't sure. After the fording he'd lost a week dismantling the motor and drying out the parts, and even so, the carburetor had a croupy cough. He couldn't drive at night because the headlights had smashed up on the riverbed. He tried it once and hit a cow. The cow got up and ambled off in the moonglow, but after that for some reason the gas gauge didn't work, and he had to test the fuel level by sticking the jack handle through the filler cap. In the sierras it was sunny and cold, and he would fill the backseat with oranges from deserted groves, which he peeled with the fingernails of the hand on the wheel down hairpin mule trails toward the plains, spitting the seeds over the side, pumping at the brakes, his stomach in his sweet-citrus-tasting throat. At Los Papalotes he stocked up on friction tape and baling wire and got a can of neat's-foot oil to squirt on the clutch when it grabbed. Thirty miles south of that he passed the turnoff to the Gringo Chink Mine, eyes trained over the left front fender till his neck got stiff, concentrating on keeping out of a pothole or a rut, knowing he ought to turn off and take care of whatever was left in that tunnel, thinking of Santos's open mouth and thinking he wasn't up to raising the ground another time; till he got past the familiar sandstone outcrops and all of a sudden it occurred to him: Sam was already buried, in a manner of speaking, handsomely; and that moreover Sam was a casualty of the revolution, one more soldier sacrificed for land reform and the reannexation of the resources of the motherland.

He felt better after that. He didn't have to think about Sam anymore.

But the trouble was, nobody knew where to find Villa. Or rather, everybody knew, which was the same thing. Every mule driver along the way had an opinion, every taco vendor in the towns had heard the latest. Villa was where Lloyd had left him on the tracks above Mapimi; or he was in Nogales settling a squabble between his Yaquis and Obregón; or he'd marched triumphantly into Mexico City, and the hated Huerta was in exile and dead besides. Lloyd listened to the motor losing rhythm, mainly wondering whether, if he couldn't find oil at Playamundo, he could strain the old stuff through a rag and use it over again; and he was halfway to Mexico City before he found out Villa had never gone in with the invaders in the first place, and halfway back again when he'd limped into Camargo hitting on three pistons, hoping to find a livery stable that stocked spark coils; then a *muchacha* with a body like a flexible board thrust the newspaper at his face.

Now the lieutenant barked at his men, "Strip the sumbitch fucker bare!" The lieutenant had a flat swipe of nose and little eyes, no-color hair; and a formal way of moving, together with the foulest mouth Lloyd had ever heard. Lloyd had not heard any cusswords at all until he was about fifteen. His father had not said *darn* on the grounds that *darn* was a substitute for *damn*, which meant *Goddamn*, which was taking the Lord's name in vain. In 1906 he changed his mind when Lloyd's mother died, though at the time Lloyd had the impression that his mother's death somehow transformed the word rather than the piety requirements.

But this young officer had a prodigious vocabulary. He turned to the Customs kid. "What's it say on that sales receipt?"

"New Or-lins twenty April, Lieutenant."

"Right. Puts him here around about middle-a-May. Goddamn May seems to me Villa was in Ciudad Juárez, at which time we had no trade embargo. Is that right?"

"That's right," said Lloyd. "Boy, was I mad when I found that out —"

"Shut up."

"Yes, sir."

"Did you take this car into Mexico?"

"You can see I took it into —"

"Don't smart-mouth me, sunabitch, I'll use your balls to black my boots."

Admiration set Lloyd back silent on his hard bench. The lieutenant cut at his calf with his riding crop, swinging it in a hand with two rings, just like Walter Wheeler wore.

"I would be *vair-ry* interested to know how you explain, if you went into Texas when Villa was in Ciudad Juárez, and if this is, as you say, his car, you've been scumming around the sorry-ass desert where he isn't instead of getting the proper papers to take it across to him."

"Please," said Lloyd, wincing because he didn't want to do this, "send for Mr. Cobb."

"Mr. Cobb sent me. Mr. Cobb is busy with General Pershing and our visitors. Whatfuck would Mr. Cobb want to interrupt himself to come down here for you and your dinged-up sow-dung motorcar?"

Outside, under the ticktacktoe roof of the border between Mexico and home, the two officers pried at the flattened grille, which gave with a groan and a squeal. A little crowd of international curiosity had gathered, and somebody overturned the pile of hubcaps with a toe. The clatter reverberated in the shed. A cloud of midges circled around Lloyd's Adam's apple, and he slapped some into his tie.

"I *told* you. I didn't know he was in El Paso at the time."

"You think I piss purple, you'd better think twice."

Lloyd thought three or four times, but he couldn't figure out what this implied.

"He says he's in Villa's *army!*" squealed the chinless one, chucking his head up and down to the lieutenant, whose trouser creases suggested a man who never bent his knees.

Lloyd wilted in the August air. There were no-see-ums drowning in the sweat behind his ears. There was something brutally unfair about all this, not the car so much as that the dumb puppy and the two clumsies out there carving up his car were on this officer's side, as if Lloyd wasn't the one that knew — because he had been Villa's trust man and had a smoke with men who still had in their hands the bloody stones they had used to knock the gold out of dead men's teeth — what it was to be a soldier.

"Look, I'm telling you, I been chasing Villa for near three months to give him this car."

"What would he want with a pile of dumpshit like this?"

"It wasn't that way when I started out. I'm telling you, I need to get this car to Villa *personally,* and he won't take kindly to you holding it up."

The officer slapped his clavicle, mock-aghast. "Well, isn't that just the monkey's scuzzbum, what you *need.* What *we* just really need, see, is for Villa to get blown to crapping confetti on American soil. You can understand that, can't you, darling face?"

"Look, I drove for Mexico City and I didn't learn till I got to San Luis Potosí that he never left Torreón, so I started back up, only I knocked out two pistons and there wasn't any way to get them, so I been nursing her along on spit and rubber bands. Then when I got to Torreón they told me he was in Camargo, and *then* . . ." This was the whole-truth-nothing-but, but Lloyd didn't expect to be believed. He didn't know how it happened. Sometimes things just happen. He hadn't run into anybody who took the conversation in the right direction. It *was* weird. It's not as if he hadn't been kicking himself half the length of Mexico, the dumb bad luck that he went the wrong way and the craziness thereafter, that when he ran into that Camargo girl like a pine plank hung with a handkerchief, and she shoved a newspaper in his face, it said *el jefe* was headed for Lloyd's own hometown.

The lieutenant set the tip of his riding crop on the knot of his tie.

"Let's go over this again," he said, saccharine. "If you thought Villa was in Mexico City in July, how did you know he was going to be at Fort Bliss this morning?"

"I *read* it in the *newspaper.* Lord, I only found out yesterday. . . ."

The mats came up, the floorboards. Now they were taking one

of the headlamps apart, and the soldier with the nose like a bag of Horlicks drops was rattling it up next to his head.

"Please, send for Mr. Cobb," said Lloyd.

"*Listen, runtshit!*" the lieutenant screamed. "I am the officer in charge here and you will answer my questions and you do not have anything to ask do I make myself clear?"

"Yes, sir."

In spite of the thin voice, Lloyd was impressed with this fellow's power. He saw that he'd maybe made a major mistake, misled by the arbitrary way things had fallen out. He'd stumbled into soldiering but he'd never thought of joining up with the *American* army. Maybe he still could, though, if he could just get home. He could rest up and then look around for what specialty suited him. Maybe a Texas regiment. Your meals cooked on a stove, tubs in the barracks, a vocabulary like this man. Let his father see him then! Then let Frank brag about cracking rocks and Walter Wheeler bring up the shirt on his back!

"Once more: How did you know that Generals Villa and Obregón were being entertained at Fort Bliss this morning?"

"It's not a *secret*. Every *street-corner* kid knows —"

"Do not raise your son-of-a-greased-slut voice to ME!"

"Please call Mr. Cobb," Lloyd said again. He didn't want to say this. He didn't want to do this. He didn't want to rely on his daddy for one lick of help, and especially not under the eye of this ramrod you-ess soldier going places with his shrill bark and his campaign hat that sliced across his forehead so you could set a level on it and watch the bubble ride the center.

But he was saved any more of it, because then there was a slam of metal door and the two soldiers outside stood up, not at attention but in a respectful sort of parade rest, one with a tire iron in his hand and the other with a handful of horsehair and a Bowie knife, and Zachary Cobb bustled through the opening in the shed. Lloyd almost recognized him. He had a flat, gray fringe around his pate; a spry, nervous bobble of a walk. He was half a head shorter than the young lieutenant, but he shrugged off his suit jacket and flung it over the back of the chair like somebody who knows where his own territory is, while the lieutenant's perfect posture suddenly seemed aimed at him.

"Now, what's this?"

"Mr. Cobb," said Lloyd, "I'm Lloyd Wheeler."

"Yes, they told me. What are you up to, chasing after Villa?"

"Mr. Cobb? I'm trying to take him this Packard, sir, which he sent me to New Orleans for."

"Oh, well, too late for that, eh? Lieutenant — what's your name?"

The stiff one knifed a salute into the brim of his campaign hat. "Lieutenant George S. Patton, Jr., sir!"

"Well, Lieutenant Patton, I think you might as well get back to Bliss. Villa and Obregón left El Paso Station about ten minutes ago."

"*NO!*" roared Lloyd, and Zach Cobb gave him a peer over the tops of his half-moon glasses. "Mr. Cobb, I'm *Walter* Wheeler's son, from Bowie."

Cobb peered again, took off his glasses, and agitated them on the front of his vest. "Lloyd Wheeler, Lloyd Wheeler. Good Lord, yes." Chinless giggled nervously. The man with the lumpy nose appeared, brandishing the Bowie knife.

"We didn't find nothing, sir. I think this car is slick as a whistle."

"Why, Lloyd Wheeler, I knew you when you were a little bit of a thing," said Cobb.

44

THAT MORNING ALEJANDRO set the capstone on the tower roof, and they declared the rest of the day a holiday. By noon they had packed the wagon — the nine-foot lace cloth that had come down from Grandma Kenny folded in a laundered sheet, the silverware in its mahogany box, the crystal in a packing crate. Everyone was going except Alejandro and Rosaria, who said she didn't want to look at generals and *dorados,* she had seen enough of all that in Agua Prieta; no, they'd keep here and put the littlest children down for their siesta.

O'Joe set the boxes on the buckboard to make seats. Alma would drive Carmen and the corn relish in her Ford. Eleanor would go ahead on Quarter. Most would have to walk. Carmen kept up a muttering: "Do not sit on the glasses" and "This wagon won't last the year." Polo followed solemnly at Alma's heels, while O'Joe fussed at Eleanor's stirrup length.

She rode on ahead of them, her skirt hem pulled between her legs and tucked into her waistband so that when she arrived in town she wouldn't need a place to change. Her reticule swung from the saddle horn. It was the first time she'd been to town since she left the house on Jefferson Street. She felt precarious, convalescent, but she steadied her eyes on the hills; and she remembered how Alejandro had shinnied the tower to the steep tiles, four ropes tied to his belt and four men on the ground holding them taut so he couldn't fall in any direction. She remembered how, raising the capstone over his head, lowering it like a benediction, he had called out, "*Eleanora!*" — subsuming the "*señora*" into a grace note at the end of her name.

She timed her arrival for just before one o'clock, when Laurel would be heading out from the bank for lunch. When she got to the boardwalk he was turning the heavy key, and he paused, still holding it pointed at the lock.

There was a moment when each of them could have denied that she was there, he to turn left toward the Pierce-Arrow, she to carry on along to Hum's Grocery. Both hesitated, then he raised a hand to mean "just a moment" and she raised a hand to mean nothing but her own ill ease.

"Hello, Laurel."

"Hello, Eleanor. Come in. Just let me . . ." He opened the door again and stood back with a tentative, cold, courteous bend of his body at the hip joints and the neck.

She said, "I hope it isn't awkward of me to come here. I thought it might be more" — she couldn't find a different word — "awkward to come to the house."

"No, it's fine. I'm closing up early because there's a to-do in town. Pancho Villa and Álvaro Obregón are coming through."

"Well, of course . . ." She passed him sweepingly; she always made her gestures larger when she was unsure of herself. "Alma and I are serving with Mary Doreen at the generals' table."

"I didn't know," he said with some bite. "I didn't mean to suggest you were uninformed." He selected the key for the inner office and opened the door.

Each of the wounds had begun to heal, and they went in to chip at the scabs. There was no way to confront each other without abrasion. To her, he seemed at once healthier and harder; he had put on weight, and he carried it formally. He had been ready to gauge her deterioration, a girl fried like a bacon rind; yet when she sat flipping her skirt free of the chair arm, facing him, smiling ruefully, he admitted in her a jaded radiance.

"You're looking well."

She was surprised (why was she surprised?) by a quickness of emotion at the sight of him, and then again, absurdly, by the sight of his diploma on the wall. The room was spare, and all the same —

the gleam of oak, the slender gilt around the lettering — almost elegant, as if Laurel had that effect on objects. Now he placed his hands with cold precision on a linen ledger. She could see he was in shock.

"I hope you've been well," she said.

"I'm well enough" — in a tone that implied *no thanks to you.*

"That's good."

He opened and recapped his fountain pen. "There are half a dozen letters from your mother. I expect she's frantic."

"Yes, I'm sorry. I'll write her."

"How is Maria?"

It surprised her he should ask this; perhaps there was not much that was safe to ask. "Maria has gone to California," she said, severely for some reason. "I've sent her to Amy and Vance."

Laurel cracked a derisive laugh. "Maria will make short shrift of Amy Whitney."

"I was unaware you had such a high opinion of Maria."

"I've always had a high opinion of Maria."

"Ah."

He gave her a sharp look. "Nothing has been bitterer for me to swallow than that you should think I'd begrudge Maria any aspect of an education. It's my belief that education is the key to self-determination in the Southern Hemisphere!"

She reminded herself that it was not part of the plan he should make it easy. She had not come to demand absolution, which she needed chiefly from herself. She took a breath and folded her hands over her reticule.

"I know I've caused you a great deal of pain," she said. "I'm very sorry." This was not adequate. He broke the pen apart, clutching the cap with the hand on which he still wore his wedding ring. She tucked her own hands under the cloth. She didn't think he would be mollified to know that she had shed hers, not in any deliberate repudiation but because it pinched on the bucket handle and slipped off in the chicken feed. "I don't know how to apologize properly. I don't suppose I can. But I wanted to say it all the same."

The ring made her remember one evening when Laurel had twitted Mrs. Ross Hawthorne for wearing four rings on the same hand, and there ensued a discussion of *treasure,* which Laurel said was not anything but a valuation in men's minds. Gold sat for eons in the rock, and was not treasure until man displaced it. "Treasure" referred to something lost or found. Did Laurel remember saying this? Would he care that she remembered? *I will lay up my treasures in heaven,* she thought. But this did not seem directly applicable to her.

Laurel shifted in his chair. "I'm going back to Baltimore," he said abruptly.

She heard him put these words in this order, and it took her breath away. It had not occurred to her recently that one could say: I'm going back to Baltimore.

"I've come around to your opinion about the crudity of this town."

"Oh?"

"You're sitting in Walter Wheeler's chair, as much time as he spends in it. He sits there whittling his boot heel, accomplishing nothing I can see, and tells me how he's changed sides in the Revolution. Not that it's changed his rhetoric, cow-town-crass and Bible-righteous." Eleanor saw that Walter Wheeler was not the real source of this tirade. "I expect to see him running for office any day now — Republican, Democrat, it wouldn't make any difference. I tell you, it discourages me for democracy, to listen to that homespun humbug."

"Are you well enough to go?" she asked.

"Quite well, I'm told. I've had all the tests — skin reaction, sputum, smear. The lesions are apparently all calcified. There are certain precautions I must take, but the doctors assure me I may yet live to make chairman of the board."

"I'm very glad."

"Just what I'm going to do otherwise, with my restored longevity, I couldn't tell you. A *sole véronique* at the Patapsco Club, for a start. Peeled grapes in a cream and curaçao sauce."

She laughed. She hadn't foreseen this, the tug of his wit; his intelligent, angry eyes. Now he was rolling the pen between his thumb and the tips of his fingers. It was a gold pen with herringbone chasing the length of its cap and shaft, which she had watched him roll just so over the course of nearly five years.

"I'm not drinking anymore," she said before she could stop herself.

Laurel gave no acknowledgment of this but the briefest ironic look. "I sat in that bald parlor every evening and read the *Sun* from leader to corset ads. I ordered Burkenhead's *Philosophy of Finance*, but I couldn't get through two pages of it."

"I know."

"I've been thinking about a statue in the Emerson reading room — I don't think you've seen it, a sort of pre-Raphaelized Lady Liberty. Spike headdress and the book and torch, so forth, but her drapery has slipped. I was thinking that's the only obdurate bosom I want to be acquainted with for a while."

She put out her hand to him. "When you go, you take all the wit in this town with you."

He wavered, then took the tips of her fingers. "Eleanor, I do not expect you to come with me. But I hold out that possibility."

An uprush of — something — hope? A woman must follow her husband. Was that what she was meant for after all? To sweep back into that city under its muted light? She saw herself stepping from the train, iron filigree overhead and her spindle heels touching down on home soil. There would be no reason for anyone in Baltimore to suspect any interim reordering of their existence. It would seem natural that she would come home with him if he were well.

"If you wished to have . . . a . . . private portion of your life, we could accommodate each other to privacy," he said stiffly, and let go her hand. This silenced her. She did not want to know what he meant. She would admit no frame of reference for what he might mean. But she would have liked to let him know that she thought it was a mark of character, and great luck, to love a man the way Mrs. Wheeler loved her husband. She'd have chosen it if she could.

"I don't want you to feel that I haven't given you every consideration," he said. He capped the pen with a small final sound, as if he had signed a document representing every consideration. Ending, in any case, her flow of false reasoning. How could she return to Baltimore when she no longer recognized the person who had left it? She saw through Laurel's eyes the alien, unlikely thing she'd made of her life. Let go.

"You have, Laurel. I'm sorry. I've committed myself here now."

"Committed!" He swiveled and faced her. "You know you've fulfilled every expectation the Bowie Methodists have of a Catholic! You've left your husband. You drink to excess. You've gone to live with Mexicans that pierce the ears of little girls!"

She laughed again. And, laughing, smarted to the roots of her hair. If she began to defend herself there would be no end to defending herself. "I don't think I'm responsible for Bowie's expectations."

"There's nothing new in what you're doing out there — communal living, 'tilling' the land. It'll be done again by romantic noodleheads from here on out."

"It may."

"You and Alma are no better than a couple of Methodist missionaries. You were so contemptuous of their Bible schools and their Congo delegations! You'll see how little thanks you get for your charity."

"It's not a charity, it's a business."

"Business!"

"We're going to contract for houses here in the valley. The railroad expects the population of the town to double in the next decade, and the land grants office —"

"Business! You started out a religious romantic, and when you found out marriage involved real responsibility, you just bowed out. And now you've transferred all your romantic notions over to some idea of yourself as an entrepreneur. You've become an eccentric, you know. You'll end up in a hogan eating maize and beans." He was done. He clucked under his breath to register how beyond speech was her innocence.

She had nothing to break the silence, and she thought that perhaps she would have to leave with the raggedness of his contempt still in the air. It was a way of seeing her. Or you could see her as someone who had lost her direction and cut a road of her own, no more than ruts across the hardpan. Or as a ruin renovated out of mud. She slid her hands along the polished oak of the chair arms, slid forward in the seat.

But he leaned suddenly across the desk. "You may send your man for the rest of the furniture. I'm going to drive back to Baltimore."

"All that way!" she exclaimed at random, out of an old impulse to flatter his, any man's, masculinity.

And out of pure generosity, perhaps — because he could be generous — his mouth softened and he shrugged. "You'll want the piano."

"Yes, thank you."

"I hold no grudge, Eleanor. I wish you well. If there's anything I can do for you before I go, I hope you'll let me know."

"Thank you," she said. The thing that peculiarly came to mind was the afternoon she'd smuggled the marmoset onto St. Agnes's sleeping porch. Somebody whose name she couldn't recall had said she couldn't do it. She opened her reticule. "There is one thing."

"You only need to name it."

"I have a house and an annuity for collateral," she said. "I'd like to borrow five thousand dollars."

45

CRAMMED BETWEEN A TANGLE of pick handles and a rack of shelves, standing on an overturned bucket because the window was too high, but hunched a little because it was then too low, Sam peered through the smeary single pane of the shed between Vandercamp's livery stable and the station hotel, turning in his palm the worn, warm stone that was at once blade and haft. The hard spout of a kerosene can pressed into his shin. The shelves gave off a heady mix of saddle soap, must, resin, caustic soda, and a lot of horse. The gun was on its side on a shelf, the barrel stuck between two cans of creosote gum where Sam could reach across at chest height and take ahold of the grip; and every now and again he did that, because the hard, scored rubber sucked to his palm and reminded him he had practiced what to do with it.

This week he'd taken the precaution of stealing new overalls from a ranch porch rail, and a pair of worn huaraches from the back steps of Shaftoe's saloon, ordinary clothes that nobody would remark on. All the same, he'd come here before dawn, afraid that once the traffic started around the station he wouldn't get into the shed without being seen. The heat had built all day, and now it beat through the tin roof like a heart. He'd braided his hair back out of his eyes and tucked it inside his shirt collar, but the window was hung with fly-studded webs, crust and dust both sides, so that his eyes burned with peering, and he had to stop himself from raising an arm to wipe it clear. Through its green fog he saw across six sets of track to the pump house and a couple of scrapped railway cars and, by pressing his cheek against the wall (handy not to have an ear in the way), a section of the station porch and the track where it disappeared across the eastern desert floor. He couldn't see any farther to his right — the station or the hotel. Those were hidden by the plank wall of the shed, though the hotel kitchen was on this side, and every time somebody came through the narrow passage he'd tighten up in his shoulder blades, remembering the way Josef Vandercamp had walked in on him here when he was ten — blacksmith-big, the oily apron around his girth, and the huge voice with its source deep in the layers of his jowls.

The window was fixed, and he didn't dare break a pane, so all day Sam had pared away at a crack between the frame and the wall, enlarging it enough to stick the heavy muzzle out. The old pine was soft, and he'd found a place above a knot where the grain curved away from the frame. With the sharp end of the stone in the slit, he scraped one side and then the other, stopping every third or fourth scrape to listen for movement in the passage and peer through the chink to gauge his progress. He worked deliberately small, making no more noise than a spider, using that as a way to pass the day while he judged just how high the opening would have to be to sight through it and still not call attention to itself.

All day, too, he had watched through the window, six trains west and five east, mail, freight, and passenger, and no one alighting here. The meat wagons had come in the morning, unloaded under the direction of Walter Wheeler; at noon the 4-H Club trooped in to hang the bunting, and the town women with the first load of their tableware, calling to each other and heading home again; then the hotel staff who would chop and stew. Later his father's flatbed drove briefly into view, piled with crates, carrot tops sticking out the slats, potatoes in a heap, the horse (a new one, unknown to him; more evidence business was good) lifting its hooves gingerly over the tracks. His father sat expressionless with the reins high in one hand, expertly turning the horse into the kitchen passage with a single sweep of the reins, so that it looked as if the horse obeyed a gesture of command behind its head. For a few seconds as the wagon turned, Sam faced his father's trouser knee through the dirty pane, and then he hunched on the floor listening to the scrape of crates, Li Hum grunting as he unloaded the vegetables into the hotel kitchen.

For the last couple of hours nothing had happened in the station yard. The smells mixed in his belly, and Sam kept thinking that sleep would overtake him, though the one time he had curled up under the wagon wheel on the far wall, he was suddenly awake again, crawly sensations on his skin. He hunched on the bucket, setting an eye to the slim crack of light between the window and the frame. He had no breadth of vision here, but a clear sight of the crippled boxcar on the far track, whose shadow said it must be after five.

Now women began to cross from Mexican town, dressed for fiesta but carrying their aprons in their hands. The town wives arrived and climbed the porch, bearing casseroles and relish jars; or husbands and children followed them with hampers. His mother didn't come with the ladies and their gear, she came as kitchen staff. He saw her cross the rail yard from the left, from home; she carried nothing, wore a plain bib apron, and like his father she turned down the passage, her eyes on the ground.

As the people gathered, his throat began to tighten. He reached for the revolver, set it snug in the little cradle he'd carved for it, and had a moment to be satisfied that it was as steady as skill and old pine could make it. There was about a forty-five-degree area where he could sight clearly. If Villa crossed from the train on either side beyond that range, he'd have to look out the window, compensate, and hope for luck. What would happen after that he couldn't be sure. He'd withdraw the gun and curl to the floor. As long as no one had seen the barrel itself, there was a good chance that everyone would look toward Villa until Sam had time to judge that the passage was quiet and get out the door. What he couldn't decide was whether to join the crowd or slip toward town. The first was safer, but only if he was calm enough to carry it. The things that could go wrong were: one, that he'd miss; two, that somebody would be quick enough to figure where the bullet came from; three, that he'd call attention to himself getting out in one direction or another. He set the gun back on the shelf and the stone back in the chink, smoothing it now not because it was rough but because the rocking rhythm soothed his nerves.

He had had no food since the last mesquite bread at noon. He could still feel its cheesy texture on his tongue. He had learned in the course of the day to feel, or believe he felt, the humming of the track through the board floor of the shed, and now he thought he heard the train and peered into the empty track off to the east while the noise got louder and louder — only to realize that it was the evening passenger from Tucson, arriving the other way. A big man shuffled down off of it, took out a notepad, and started talking to the men who were wandering in, in twos and threes. From the east came a motorcar driven by Alma Timkin in a proud-brimmed hat, more people on foot and in wagons, familiar women whose names came back to him: Wheeler, Robinson, Newsome, Pack. He spotted the woman from the quarry arriving on the porch. The other women shook her hand and embraced Alma Timkin and each other; and one after another they went out of his sight into the hotel, their men standing tentative and useless, maybe noticing that they were planning to send a foreign army in to be waited on by their wives. Li Hum was talking to Walter Wheeler, and it hurt Sam to see his father with his head hung forward, deferential, pretending or supposing the talk was man-to-man.

The muzzle hole was finished; more carving at it would spoil the shape. He had to wait. He tried to call up the anger that had made him want to wound Eight-Fingers in his half a hand. But Eight-Fingers was dead, and Sam had left his lizard self back somewhere at the quarry with the thirsty woman and the dragon robe. This was something else, not anger so much as a debt he owed Lloyd and also something he owed himself. When the moment came, if he had the courage he would do it. For the moment he was only cramped and tired, smelling kerosene and horse, scared, wanting to lie down.

Then it wasn't the track he felt humming but the people, their attention like storm-heaviness in the air, the voices stopped, the women pouring back out into the yard, all the backs being trussed up by a suck of stomach; and what Sam mainly noticed here inside was a cascade of smells, as if his own breath had stirred up a turbulence; not the livery stable smells that had a right to be here, but the rotten-meat stink of agave bloom and the oily smell of bats, they came from somewhere in him. His tongue stuck to the roof of his mouth, and when somebody ran past in the narrow walkway beside him the hackles rose on his neck.

He could see it in the distance, sketched over the desert, a little gunmetal line that then turned into a fuzzy-topped pull toy as if it had vegetables sticking out of it, and then its metal snout caught the sun and bore down on them like a mechanical and malevolent pig. The train grew, plummeting till you could hear its axles grind. Sam palmed the stone, cramped on his perch and peering, wishing he could wipe the glass. As the train roared in, Sam saw that the carrot greens were men riding on the top, cross-legged and clinging to the metal anywhere they could get a grip. The train screeched to a stop and they pitched themselves off it, cartwheeling from the ladders, shouting, flinging open boxcar doors and laying planks to lead their whinnying horses out.

Sam carefully tucked his stone inside the bib of his new overalls, against his ear, and reached across to palm the crosshatched pattern of the pistol grip. He set the barrel in its cradle in the grain of the wood again, sighted as far left and right as he could, and wiped his right palm on his hip.

The cars opened, and officers, other soldiers began to descend, men in every sort of uniform and mufti — sombrero or cap, *calzones*, cavalry twill. The door of the car just opposite swung open, and two guards jumped down to set a couple of steps. Walter Wheeler detached himself from the Bowie group and crossed the rail yard, followed by the sheriff and the preacher, this last holding by the sash of her dress, for reins, a little girl with a bouquet of zinnias in each hand.

Sam sighted down his barrel — the welcoming committee had stopped short of the car, and he had a clear view of the carriage door in which a stiff, stout general now appeared, brass-buttoned to his chin. Sam fingered the trigger, squinted at the full face under its billed cap, tried to turn the mustache into Villa's but could not. Obregón, then? Sam wondered for the first time if, after all, he would know Villa in the daylight, at twenty yards, after the passing of a year; but he had no sooner wondered this than Villa appeared, unmistakable, bowing a little to the crowd. He was wearing a tweed suit the same as Sam had seen him in the mine, but this one rather grand, long-jacketed like a big-game hunter's, a very small bow tie crooked at his neck. Villa descended behind Obregón in his uniform, Villa with a soft hat in one hand and the other vaguely wafting like royalty too tired to care. Sweat rolled down the inside of Sam's sleeve and slithered between his palm and the pistol grip. He switched to his left hand, stretched and folded the right to limber it, wiped it back and forth on his overalls with a startling sound. Obregón spoke to Walter Wheeler and a round of introductions commenced, polite bending on all sides. There was no sign of the handsome man who had held the knife in the mine. The little girl thrust her bouquets at the generals, who took them with more bows and smiles. Then, abruptly, Villa picked up the girl under her pink armpits and swung her aloft. The crowd gasped. Villa emitted a sentimental crowing from his throat that Sam could hear all the way over here and through the wall. The girl descended again, was released, scampered, and hid behind the preacher, turning a toe in the dirt. The sheriff and the preacher and the father who didn't know his son was dead chatted to the man they didn't know had killed him.

It was time.

Sam sighted through the slit he had made in the wood. The *chink,* he thought cleverly. There was no difficulty in it. Obregón stood to the left and the Bowie men to the right, the little girl behind them. Villa, grinning, was separated in between, the target a button on his belted belly. Sam thought of his practice sessions in the quarry, of taking a bead on a marble chip across the pit. He exhaled and aimed.

The shot sounded half a beat ahead of the time he meant to hear it, a disconcerting lag of mind and muscle, like an earthquake no bigger than the distance from his ear to his trigger finger. A shout went up somewhere down the track, and a general commotion rose. The crowd of soldiers parted. Another shot sounded, then another — no, they were backfires, Sam realized, and realized from the tension in his finger, the trigger still pushing back at it, that he hadn't yet fired the gun — and where the people stumbled aside to make room for it there careened into the yard a rattletrap car blaring its hooter like a flat trombone in a brass band. It squealed its brakes, spun dust, and bucked to a stop; and over the side of it vaulted, in a shiny, scummy yellow suit — Sam raised his free arm and wiped the dirt away — there wasn't any doubt about it: Lloyd.

It was Lloyd. It was Lloyd come back to save him by taking the danger on himself. It was Lloyd after all, and not Sam, who would take his own revenge on Villa. Walter Wheeler turned and saw his son; his face opened up in greeting. But Lloyd raced past the sheriff and the reverend, pushed past his father. He gave a shout and pitched himself with full force on Pancho Villa.

Sam looked for the gun in Lloyd's hand, but there was no gun, no, it must be a knife — a small knife, concealed in his palm? Lloyd would not have gone in there bare-handed, would he? Sam didn't know he pulled the trigger, but he heard the dull clang of the engine bell. For a second this sound wrung in his stomach like a fist, before it registered with him that the bell had rung not because he'd shot Pancho Villa but because he decidedly had not. A metallic vibrato hung on the air. Nobody appeared to notice it. Everyone was riveted on the sight. Of Lloyd Wheeler with his arms flung around the neck of Pancho Villa in a hug. A hug.

46

DOROTEO ARANGO, alias Francisco "Pancho" Villa, represented everything that was anathema to the Bowie Methodists. He was a ruffian, a rapist, a bandit, a murderer, a Mexican. They deplored on principle his ontology and his hygiene.

On the other hand, he was the only famous man ever to come through town.

While the people stood out on the porch, the Hinman dining room lay adorned like a still-unravished bride. The pillars were festooned with oleander, which shed the scent of its bitter milk onto an expanse of bleached, starched, stretched, and ironed white linen. There were twenty-five tables staggered around the perimeter, and in the middle three pushed together made a place of honor for the visiting and local dignitaries. All the tables were laden with china, like a china shop. Fine old serving pieces had been brought down from whatnot shelves or dusted out of storage, more heirlooms than had ever been admitted to in a modest town — a porcelain cake stand on which Britannia ruled waves in bas-relief, a crystal cruet etched with a Confederate flag, a brass dromedary that poured gravy from its snout. Sauce boats burgeoned with homemade Tabasco, pickled peppers, corn relish, chili, spiced tomato, mustard spread, cinnamon pears. In the middle of the middle table Mary Doreen Wheeler's new vintage 1914 strawberry jam sat in a footed silver bowl with the Kenny crest. Here and there a candelabrum reflected from the table an impressive glow of elbow grease.

The Bowie women had taken it pretty well in stride that Eleanor Poindexter was among them. They may have had their ideas about how lean she'd gotten, how stringy and muscular, how brown as a berry or an Indian; and it may be that these theories would be pursued between now and sundown. They may have thought Mary Doreen had gotten her notions of loyalty hindside-fore. But they had taken Eleanor by the hand. They had welcomed her return of health, begged leave to hope that they would see her in church next week, admired her lace and her candlesticks and even the glasses no thicker than a dewdrop, which pinged when you flicked a finger at the bowls on little twisted stems and that *she* called glasses although they made everybody who saw them a little thick at the back of the throat with the word *goblet*.

The Kenny lace draped the center table to a swag of eighteen inches all around; and Eleanor, the first back inside because she had come to honor a request of Mary Doreen's, twitched it straight (it was already straight), admiring the linen rectangles that stretched out to the edges of the hall in the dimensions of the marble quarry. She was surprised by an emotion familiar but disused, which belonged to Baltimore and which she never had expected to feel here: sharp pride at the beauty of things offered up. *We are taught to believe this is a trivial to-do, this fussing among metal and cloth and food. But it is hospitality, the opposite of war.*

She turned to the sideboard that had been set up beside the center table, took out another plate, and began realigning the settings to make an extra place.

She was all right. She had known she would meet Frank, was prepared in small ways, had stopped to look at herself in the window of the grocery store, flushed even under the patina of her work-warmed skin, the loan papers Laurel had given her fanned out in her hand. Her eyes had healed; you could no more see the fracture back of them than you could see a knitted bone under skin. She went toward the station, picking out what words to use; and when Frank had come out of the dining hall door sooner than she expected, crossed the porch in a hurry with some errand, she had nevertheless been able to extend her hand and say, "How nice to see you," and only two or three empty phrases later, "I am so sorry about Jessie's death."

He had not healed so invisibly as she. His face was rigid below the surface, his eyes had lost their sky depth and faded to the blue of creek-washed cloth. She had used a sentence he could understand, if he chose, to mean that she accepted her responsibility. He reached toward her hand but chopped his own in the air short of it, nodding with mechanical solemnity, "It couldn't be helped," as if she had mentioned the loss of money or a calf. "It was God's will," he said, meaning no more, but she understood by the falsity of his tone that he kept his hurt where nobody could handle it. He didn't remember her part in it. He didn't remember her.

Alone now for the moment, she surveyed the dining room again. She had slid the five settings down one side of the table to make room for a sixth, turned for extra tableware, and looked up at the slam of the screen door — but it was only Ben Dargen, pockets full of paper, his amble and his tipped grin under his scudding hair.

"Mrs. Poindexter."

"Mr. Dargen."

"Do you have a minute for me?"

"Really I don't. Mrs. Wheeler has asked me to set an extra place for her brother-in-law. . . ."

"Carry on, I'll just chat while you work — and in any case, what I wanted to speak to you about was, while you're at it, why don't you set a place for me?"

"I'm afraid I couldn't take the responsibility —"

"By no means! Ditch the responsibility, just lay an extra plate. And I could be sitting here when the generals arrive."

"I'm afraid it's not possible."

"I won't involve you, God's truth. If anybody tells me to move, I'll be meek as a lamb."

He looked so much less like a lamb than a buffalo, pawing the floor with a shoe, that she had to laugh. "But you'll write a story from it," she said, "and I don't trust you. You'll write us up as looking foolish, or voracious."

"God's honor. The story is all written, Mrs. Poindexter, all I need is to fill in local color."

"All written!"

"Well, essentially there're only two newspaper stories anyway: *look-how-tough*, and *look-how-good*."

"Really. And which is this one?"

"Which one is it, or which one do I plan to write?"

"Why, either." She worried a napkin into an accordion fan and stuck it in the goblet. It was true she'd spoiled the symmetry now, six places down one side and five down the other. Ben Dargen helpfully stole a chair from the next table over and twirled it on one leg.

"Oh, Villa and Obregón will go down to Nogales and patch up the fight between their underlings. But you could guess within a month or two how long the patch will last — just long enough that it'll be this mama's son instead of that mama's son that gets blown up when the truce explodes."

"But that's not what you'll write?"

"No, ma'am. Because the *Star* is operating with a copper collar. No? That means we're owned by the Phelps-Dodge Mining Company. All the local stories are filtered through the sieve of the mining interest. Interest, as in: *not boring* means *to the advantage of*. And if there's anything the mining interests have an interest in, it's a benign and friendly government sitting over all the tin and copper — maybe oil — underneath that thick Sonoran silt."

"And how will Bowie come out of it?"

"The story, you mean? Bowie'll get the credit for a lot of beef and righteousness."

"Well, I'm putting this plate here, but it has nothing to do with you. I don't know you."

"Absolutely. I'm indebted."

"Yes, you are. You owe me."

"Ma'am, I do. And you drive a bargain like a back-East lady."

Sam cautiously cracked open the door from the stable passage to the kitchen and slipped inside. Along the checkerboard floor a line of Mexican girls wound from the window to the stove, where a hotel cook ladled stew into the tureens they carried. Across the room his mother stood at a table, chopping vegetables. He turned and leaned between the doorjamb and the sink, slack into the corner in the way he knew would make him a piece of the wall. He saw there were Mexican boys in the line as well as girls, in clean, loose shirts, wet hair slicked back. Over their heads through the arch Sam could see the dining room filling now, with soldiers, clatter, and rough voices. He raised his chin to lower the queue inside the back of his collar, lifted one of the pottery tureens off the side sink, and stepped into line.

He held the bowl against his stomach by its handles, watching the neck of the girl in front of him, dark down hairs on her nape like a stack of seabirds. Several minutes passed; the line moved forward ten or twelve paces, four of the waitresses passed back into the dining room, and still no one questioned him. He dared to look around. There were as many as half a dozen youths in line; they must have needed every available hand to feed three hundred troops.

The girl in front of him was having her bowl filled now, and he risked looking across toward his mother, separated from her by about twenty foot-square floor tiles, a heavy deal table, and her concentration on her hands. She had a light touch with a knife — he remembered transparent slices of squash, carrot parings thin as a fingernail. Now, though, she was chopping for stew; her hand whirred, and a potato fell into cubes. The girl ahead of him turned, careful with the weight between her fists, and it was Sam's turn. He held out his tureen; the cook dipped a glossy ladleful, the web of her hairnet inclined over the bowl. A meat-rich steam rose in his nostrils. Su Hum did not look up from her table; she kept her eyes on the deft strokes of her knife, the rapid fall of carrot rounds. The stubbiness of her fingers broke his heart.

He balanced the tureen to the arch and paused, taking in the crowd in the dining room. A hundred or more Mexican soldiers were scraping their chairs, shouting to one another. They draped serapes over the chairbacks, hung their embroidered hats, squeezed in between and jostled each other's elbows. Some of the men were hung with their cartridge belts and some had extravagant mustaches. The local women, including the Mexicans, were so riveted by these curiosities of dress that Sam, his hair pulled back over his ears and tucked in an ordinary shirt, drew not a glance. He saw some of the women he had recognized on the porch, including

Alma Timkin and the quarry woman at the center table. The air
smelled of spiced meat, sweat, and tallow. It was peppered with
boisterous Spanish. Here and there an attempt to translate turned
shrill and escalated into laughter.

Then Walter Wheeler, his two sons, and the two generals were
threading through the crowd toward the center. Sam hung there
in the arch a moment longer, with the weightless sensation that he
was going to pitch himself headlong into that room. He was reminded, too, of the desert full of tarantulas, nowhere safe to put a
foot down. But he had crossed that desert without incident, and he
crossed this one now, the tureen balanced gingerly between his
hands, his eyes on his legs and feet in clothes stolen for their
neutrality, normality. Bright serapes and beaded sombreros, brass
buttons and bullet cases glittered reassuringly on either side.

Sideboards had been set up at intervals of every few tables, and
on these the waitresses were settling their tureens. The first servers
had crossed to the far side, but Sam went toward the center, passing
behind Walter Wheeler, who was saying, "You sit here, General,
sir; and Frank; and Lloyd."

He moved to the sideboard next to this table, set the tureen
down, and stood with his back to the men, looking for an excuse to
stay. He picked up a soup bowl from the stack, turned sideways,
and glanced across the centerpiece. Lloyd had darkened and filled
out, eyes creased into permanent squint. His chin was blue with
stubble and he had a new way of thrusting his jaw against the
tightness of his tie. Alma Timkin and the quarry woman were
pouring ginger ale and sarsaparilla in the glasses of the important
men. Mary Doreen Wheeler was passing out the bread.

This central table had been set up cleverly so that nobody pre-
sided over it. On the far side were two Mexican soldiers, Obregón,
Villa, Lloyd, and Walter Wheeler. This side with their backs to him
were two more officers, Reverend Newsome, Sheriff Robinson,
Frank Wheeler, and the shambles of a man he'd seen get off the
train and who from the slew of pencils in his pockets would be
press.

Over the hubbub Sam could catch only part of what was said, but
he could tell that the introductions lurched forward with much
rephrasing and reiteration. He heard Villa say in Spanish, "This is

a rich man's hotel," which Obregón translated as "General Villa says your fine hotel much pleases," while Lloyd shouted to the Bowie men at the far end, "The general thinks you've put on a swell spread." Then there was a noisy toast at the next table and Sam understood nothing further for a while.

Some of the servers were wandering back to the kitchen, and Sam felt that he would have to go now, too. But he saw that some others were starting to ladle the stew into the soup bowls. No one challenged his having taken this position. For a second Sam set his back to the serving board and stood where Lloyd, if he looked up, would have to see him.

"I said it many a time," Walter Wheeler was blustering, "I said — didn't I? — Lloyd'll surprise us! So if I could've had this in mind, it wouldn't have been a surprise!"

"Nobody was more took aback than me," Lloyd said, then turned to Villa and translated his father's speech. Obregón apparently embellished it for the other officers. The din of laughter and dishware rose, and the men here talked across each other. Sam tried to pick out the signals, who spoke how much of what. None of the Mexicans seemed to have any English except Obregón. Frank and Walter Wheeler had a little Spanish; the big man — reporter? — probably had more. The sheriff and the preacher grinned, hopelessly at sea.

Wheeler stuck a knife in the bread and offered a piece to Villa, pointing the knife then at the filigree bowl. "Try the jam, General!" he yelled, maybe over the clanking around them, maybe at foreign-ness. "That's Mary Do there, my daughter-in-law, and she knows how to make a comfy-ture." Mary Doreen, flushed with pleasure or annoyance or both, flounced an acknowledgment and came toward the sideboard. Sam had a soup plate in his hand, and he picked up the ladle and dipped it full of stew: big chunks of best lean beef in cornstarch broth, diced potatoes, carrots, green peppers cut in eighths; onions not out of a can but picked that morning because this town boasted a citizen who could coax fat life out of stingy soil. Mary Doreen took the plate and glanced at Sam. She hesitated so the stew sloshed on the rim, pursed her mouth in a quizzical look, then thought better of it and nodded thanks. She carried the plate around to serve Villa first. Sam took a second from the stack. He focused his attention on the stewpot and eyed the men on the periphery of his vision. When Alma Timkin came for the plate, he kept his face turned away.

The noise of talk and laughter muted somewhat across the room into the scrape and clank of tableware. At the dignitaries' table attention had settled on Lloyd. The reporter said, "Tell us how you linked up with the Revolution. My readers would be very interested to hear the story." Sam thought wryly that he would be interested to hear Lloyd tell that story, too, but Lloyd only translated to Villa that the reporter wanted to know about recruitment. The reporter, in formal Spanish, added the part about the readers.

Sam saw Villa dollop a mound of strawberry jam on his plate and liberally spread a chunk of bread. "So this is your home city, gringo!" — ignoring the subject, he laughed to Lloyd.

Sam's eyes swept toward the door and picked out his father standing between two tables of boisterous soldiers, the front hem of his jacket lightly in his fists. Sam ladled a plateful of stew and handed it to the quarry woman, whose face lit with recognition. "Sam! Hello." It struck him peculiar, bitter, that he was standing with his back to half a dozen people he'd known all his life — father, lover, teacher, sheriff; the preacher who had bestowed his name with a damp palm on his head — and the only one that faced him and knew him was this newcomer from back East.

"Hello. I'm sorry I don't —" he whispered.

"My name is Eleanor Poindexter." She smiled radiantly at him. She took the plate to Obregón; Mary Doreen came back for another officer's; Sam ladled and they served, and so on around the table.

Villa guffawed and turned to Obregón. "This little asshole held a horse in the Río Bravo for me last year!" The word he used was *tendejitos* — little pubic hairs. The reporter boomed a laugh, but when Walter Wheeler asked, "What did he say?" — Lloyd waved him quiet, and it wasn't clear to Sam whether Lloyd knew he was being laughed at. "It was a cattle deal we did together," Lloyd said.

The smell of the stew was making Sam faint with hunger. He continued to dish and the three women to serve. They had got as far around the table as Frank Wheeler when Sam heard his father's voice. "Please, Mr. Wheeler." Sam froze, then swung with the rhythm of the ladle to glance aside. Li Hum stood behind Lloyd, his fingers still curled and tugging at the bottom of his jacket.

"Please," he said.

Sam handed the plate to Alma. Over his shoulder he could see Walter Wheeler put on a polite, stern face. Lloyd gripped his buttered knife. Villa bestowed barely a glance on the Chinese man and turned back to his food, steam rising to the day's dark stubble on his pouched jaw, the bullets in his cartridge belt gleaming like a row of perfect teeth.

"I'm sorry to disturb your dinner," Li Hum said to Lloyd. "But could you tell me, please, have you seen Sam?" Back to his father over the width of one table, intent and therefore invisible exactly as he had been in Mexico, Sam handed a plate to Eleanor, who carried it to the reporter.

Lloyd's voice was careful, solemn. "Well, no, I'm sorry. Sam, you see . . . we got separated."

In the silence Sam could picture Li Hum's deferential stance, fingering the hem of his jacket, his square face expressionless. "Yes, please?" he said. Someone, Sam thought it was Villa, slurped at his stew.

Lloyd again, enunciating slowly. "We were planning to mine a claim down there, but we got separated."

"Ah. Ah."

There was an awkward pause. When it stretched too long to stand, Sam turned toward the table, but only to see his father retreating in bent dignity. Alma Timkin served Walter Wheeler's stew. Sam thought that tomorrow morning he would go retrieve the Colt from behind the creosote cans and sneak it back into Li Hum's desk. Even though a gun was of no use, he didn't like his father to be without defenses.

"Sam didn't get off with your money, did he?" Frank asked suddenly.

"Of course not. Why would he do that? We got separated," Lloyd said again, as if, having found this useful phrase, he could not let go of it.

Lloyd had not translated the exchange, but now Villa, clapping him on the back, asked, "What does he say?" And without waiting to hear the answer turned to Obregón. "This little gringo, when I met him, he had a China cunt with him. Isn't that right, gringo? A little *chafa* Chink?"

Lloyd was the only one without a stew plate now. He crumbled a piece of bread in a loose fist on the bright tablecloth and looked up, inclining his head toward Villa with a hunching motion like a wince. He sniffed.

"No, gringo?"

Sam waited for Lloyd to speak, and the noises of the room, the metal on porcelain, and the sounds of food and laughter became a kind of dirtied silence. Sam watched Lloyd's mouth and waited for it to say what, in retrospect, he seemed to have understood perfectly in the mine: Don't touch him. He's my best friend.

Lloyd swallowed a lump of bread. And laughed. "That's right, *jefe*. A yellow-belly."

Walter Wheeler said, "I couldn't get that. What's he say?"

For a second longer the babble held itself at bay, and Sam waited for Lloyd to say — waited for him to *have said* — anything else. Then the noise closed down and Sam turned back in the direction of the heat, the hot broth and the carrots bobbing in it like so many lidless eyes.

He raised the last plate and ladled a generous helping, steadied the plate on the edge of the sideboard to free a hand, and felt in his bib for the softer of the two oblongs tucked in the folds. He removed his ear and set it in the stew. The ear sat like a small brown boat, which he capsized with a nudge of the ladle. The lobe sank in the broth. The cornstarch made a silky vortex that carried a sliver of pepper into the whorl. He handed the plate to Eleanor, who carried it to Lloyd. He set his back to the sideboard and rested his weight against his hands.

"He says I was a real tenderfoot when he first knew me," Lloyd was saying to his father. "But then," he addressed Villa again, "I became your trust man, and you sent me for the car."

"Oh, yes," said Villa with diminished interest. "Yes, the famous car."

Lloyd ate a lump of carrot and swirled his fork in the broth. "When you have your way, there'll be a Packard for every man in Mexico, no, *jefe*?" He stabbed his stew with a look of irritation at the toughness of the meat.

His mouth opened slightly. It opened wider on an intended utterance. It closed again. His Adam's apple bobbed and he looked up.

The face of a man learning something really does look as if light is spreading through it. Alma Timkin could have told them that. Sam, watching, saw Lloyd understand somewhere in the skin of his forehead first; and then his eyes locked onto Sam's with the look of splitting stone, the way a man in a certain position at the quarry would see the sun slash through when the marble cracks away.

Sam smiled. Lloyd answered with a look of terror. Sam hadn't expected anything in particular, but he was not surprised by this. It gave him a strangely acid sense of power, that his smiling could make Lloyd afraid — Lloyd the protector, the strong one, the white man's son. Sam couldn't know whether Lloyd remembered that night in the mine when he had made the other choice, and he couldn't know what had happened to Lloyd since. But he could see that whatever had happened, it was already done. Whatever Lloyd had traded, the exchange was made. Whatever he had come home for, it was not for Sam.

Sam stood among the women now, the servers. Lloyd sat with his father and brother, the men of church and war and law. And with the reporter, who now leaned across and said something to Lloyd that Sam didn't catch and that Lloyd didn't respond to, but dropped his eyes and shielded the plate with his hand.

For the first time Sam remembered what he himself had said to Villa in the mine — *Mr. Hum. Mr. Sam Hum* — when all he had meant was to get his right name said. And he understood how far he had come to know what it did mean; he'd had to become a lizard, learn a language, outwit death, and live off dirt; he'd had to hear again inside his head the stories that had been stolen from him before he could learn the tongue that was rightly his.

Lloyd swallowed, although he had not taken a bite of anything. He drummed the fingers on the rim of his soup plate and looked up once, maybe to check that his eyes hadn't played a trick, and dropped them again. Clear as if he had wiped a space on dirty glass, Sam saw that Lloyd would not be able to face him, face to face. Lloyd would have to go with Villa now. He would leave with this army and its appetite.

Nothing happened. Mary Doreen replenished the bowl of jam. The generals ate their sirloin stew. Sam went to the kitchen to fill the tureen again. He got in the line behind a drab girl he recognized only as someone who had been a little less drab a few years ago. His mother stood facing the sink this time, pumping water onto a pile of pots and pans. If she had looked over at him, if she had looked within the shagged outline of his hair, she would have known him. But she did not. A life's sidelong habit, a downcast history — she held her eyes on the sink, the swirl of water over the pans. He accepted this. There would be a time. The cook filled his bowl, and he balanced carefully back into the dining room.

He did not care or question what became of his ear, which had disappeared from Lloyd's dish by the end of dinner, the next shift of men. But when Eleanor Poindexter brought him a bowl for refill, he whispered to her, "Can you use help out at your place?" And she said, "We'll be needing extra hands."

And when Alma Timkin bent to set the pie on the sideboard, he put his fingers light around her forearm and said beneath the clatter, "I am Sam Hum." She looked at him. A quizzical cock of her handsome head, that silent but resonant contralto O of her mouth. She nodded, and he let go her arm.

Jasper Wheeler missed the occasion altogether, having spent the afternoon drowning day-old kittens, in what may have been the most pertinent memorial to his sister. Walter Wheeler drove back to the ranch with Johnny Fousel, feeling bitter that his secondborn couldn't spare a week at home but had to dash right off after his precious general. Mary Dorcen retrieved the baby from Soledad Iglesias, who had been minding her, and went with the baby riding the arm that Frank supported, his fingers under her elbow. Ben Dargen was delighted to have a story after all — *local boy makes bandit's sidekick* — though in fact the most intriguing bit of news he encountered was that Eleanor Poindexter was going into the building trade. He thought he would come back again in a fortnight to write it up.

West toward California, the sun imbued the earth. The army departed into it, having consumed sixteen steers, a hundred and forty pounds of root vegetables, eighty pies, and four hundred seventy-two bottles of Cliquot Club Ginger Ale; taking Lloyd Wheeler with them, leaving behind a lot of gravy stains in linen, a floor in fearsome need of wax, and the hulk of a defunct gray Packard beside the track.

The graves were already filling up at Ypres and Passchendaele. But most of the locals were content. Dinner had gone off well, Mexican stability was about to be secured once for all, and the town fathers had a patriotic, satisfying sense that they could be counted on in a time of crisis.

The Hinman staff was swilling out the last pans. The members of the Women's Society for Christian Service headed severally home with husbands. The 4-H Club was pulling down the bunting.

The group from the mission loaded up their crates and kids and bundles. They went off toward the wagon and the Ford — Alma and Eleanor laughing over something, O'Joe a little ahead, hopping because the wagon was his responsibility and he should be seen to tend to it. Gabrielo and Gaspar had a hand each of the toddler Paco. Polo, always the host, walked with the new worker, Sam. Carmen Acosta was haranguing them. "We should have started earlier. Paco will fuss all day tomorrow."

It made them feel good, her complaining. "We will not be able to sleep late. We have to get the tiles chinked before it rains or we will have mud on the rugs again." It reassured them. It made them feel there were things to be put right in the world.